Goodbye, Saigon

GOODBYE, SAIGON

a novel

Nina Vida

Crown Publishers, Inc.
New York

FOR KATE AND EMILY

Published by Crown Publishers, Inc., 201 East 50th Street, New York,
New York 10022. Member of the Crown Publishing Group.
Random House, Inc. New York, Toronto, London, Sydney, Auckland
CROWN is a trademark of Crown Publishers, Inc.

Grateful acknowledgment is made to Nam Loc for permission to print an
excerpt from the song "Goodbye, Saigon." Reprinted by permission of the
author.

Manufactured in the United States of America
Design by Lauren Dong

Library of Congress Cataloging-in-Publication Data

Vida, Nina.
    Goodbye, Saigon : a novel / by Nina Vida.
        p.   cm.
    1. Vietnamese American families—California—Los Angeles—Fiction.
2. Vietnamese Americans—California—Los Angeles—Fiction.
3. Refugees—California—Los Angeles—Fiction.   4. Family—
California—Los Angeles—Fiction.   5. Women—California—Los
Angeles—Fiction.   6. Los Angeles (Calif.)—Fiction.   I. Title.
PS3572.I29G6   1994
813'.54—dc20
94-8384
CIP

ISBN 0-517-59908-2

10   9   8   7   6   5   4   3   2   1

First Edition

Goodbye, Saigon

SONG BY NAM LOC
ENGLISH TRANSLATION BY PHAM DUY
NOVEMBER 1975

Saigon oi! I have lost you in my life!
Saigon oi! My best time is far away!
What is left is some sad memory,
the dead smile on my lips, bitter tears in my eyes.

On the street is the sun still shining?
On our path, is the rain still falling?
In the park, is my lover still there,
going under the trees, smiling or crying lonely?

CHORUS:
Here I am the bird losing her way.
Day by day my time just passes by...
The life of an exile is painful!
O Saigon...I call you!

Saigon oi! I will be back, I promise...
My lover! I will keep my word always...
Although here passion begins at night,
the city lights are bright,
but you still are in my mind.

1

*I*t wasn't always easy to spot the lucky ones. Not among the Vietnamese, anyway. Oh, no, their faces were blank, and Anh would give them a blank face back, and keep her eyes open for the big-voiced American men, the ones who shouted "Yes!" when they won a hand. Like the American with the gold pinkie ring on his finger, the one she had found three months ago throwing his money away, playing like he couldn't tell one card from the other. She had taken him in hand, showed him how *pai gow* poker should be played. I studied it, she told him, read all the books, know all the odds. I'll be your luck, she told him.

Anh stood now at the glass door inside the casino. The huge football square of playing field lay before her like the misty rice paddies of Vietnam that came again and again in her dreams. Card tables and banners floated without beginning or end on clouds of exhaled smoke beneath mirrored ceilings and crystal chandeliers. Poker, Pan, 7-Card Stud, Omaha, Hold 'em, Asian Poker, Pai Gow Poker, the banners said. Players slouched at jammed-together tables in roped-off sections, eating grayish food from portable carts that crushed up against their legs. They littered the small walk spaces around their feet with wadded-up paper napkins and crumpled cigarette packages.

"*Chào Anh.*" A small Vietnamese man in a wrinkled shirt caught her arm as she started down the steps. "Give me one chip, and I show you *pai gow* winner—pow—none like. I got big luck tonight."

He was a shoeshiner, like Anh. They didn't shine shoes. They shined egos, reassured losers, fawned over winners. They picked a player and stuck to him, whispered advice to him in Vietnamese or Chinese or Cambodian, breathed in all the garlic breath and cigarette smoke that drifted above the tables, waited for a few stray chips, a tip, a commission, a fee for services to come their way so they could finance a game of their own, test their nerve on the cards, fulfill the fortune-teller's prophesies of money pots waiting to be sucked up. They hocked their wedding rings and gold chains with the pawn lady at her station next to the bathrooms and paid more juice than the gold was worth. Anh had been like the other shoeshiners, wandering from player to player, before she found the American who thought he couldn't play without her, who gave her money whether he won or lost. Now the shoeshiners shoeshined her.

"I live in my car," the shoeshiner said. "One chip. Just one and I buy a house."

Anh pressed a ten-dollar bill into the man's outstretched hand. He turned without a sound and raced toward the cashier's booth to buy a chance at his fortune. Anh smiled, feeling good inside to be giving some of her luck to an unlucky man. She smiled all the way through the tight aisles to the table where the American was already sitting and playing.

He was a startling sight, big-boned body next to all those slight ones, large nose and thick brows beside all those narrow dark faces, his thinning hair straggling across his forehead. There weren't many American faces at the *pai gow* tables. It was an Oriental's game, a wild take-it-or-leave-it game, a spit-in-your-eye game, full of twists and hidden meanings. Ah. The quick flush of happiness at the sight of his ugly face, the sweet sensation of relief to see him sitting there.

"Where were you?" He always seemed annoyed when she arrived, as though he had told her to do something and she had refused.

"I go shopping. You like my dress? Nordstrom, one hundred, marked down from three fifty. Big bargain they got over there. I see that dress hang there, and no one even see the price so low, and I say to myself, Anh, you got luck to find this dress. You gonna bring luck to Dennis tonight."

He slipped her a hundred, and she knew he hadn't heard a word she said. The dealer, her hair the same black straight sheet as Anh's, looked bored, but she had seen Anh and already given her silent okay. A middle-aged Vietnamese man in white shirt and work pants was shaking the little metal hat so the dice sounded like sizzling rice. The American had a stack of chips in front of him and was bobbing his head up and down in time to the rattle of the dice. "Yes, yes, come on, yes."

"Red is luck," Anh said. "See, I bring you red tie." She opened her purse and pulled out a striped tie and looped it around the American's big neck. "We gonna eat duck tonight, and tomorrow it bring you more good luck."

"I don't eat Vietnamese," he said.

The Vietnamese man banged the hat with the sizzling dice smack on the felt, and then plopped into his chair and, smug-faced, waited for the dealer.

"Not Vietnamese," Anh said. "Chinese. Duck is good, bring good luck, duck." She giggled. "Luck, duck. See, it go together. Not steak. How you eat steak all the time, that big, fat, heavy meat in your stomach. It make your stomach turn over too many time. You eat Vietnamese and Chinese, you gonna win and feel good at same time."

He wouldn't eat with her. He never even looked at her when the game was over.

It was a crowded table, six people seated around it and two standing. There were no other good luck charms at this table, no men shoeshiners whispering into the players' ears, pockets open for tips. No women shoeshiners, young and pretty, like Anh. No Cambodian players speaking loudly to one another to take away their opponents' concentration. Just a clutch of round-faced Chinese men with dark freckles and black moles, dress shirts open at the neck beneath their light jackets. And two Vietnamese, a middle-aged man, who seemed excited to be playing, and a younger one, in pegged pants and slicked-back hair, who slid his cards and tossed his money the way the Chinese players did, as if none of it was connected to him. And the American.

The American's cards were open in his hand now. He had a pair of kings and three twos, a jack and a trey.

"Put your pair of king up first," Anh said, "and then the three two behind it." When she first found him, he would play his cards rashly, holding the bad ones for his five-card hand and always losing on the two-card. He was blinking rapidly now, the tie like a red tongue down his chest. He didn't shove Anh away when she leaned over him, her cheek brushing his. It always surprised her, the texture of American skin, the prickliness of the stubble of beard. Vietnamese men's faces were smooth, the hair skimpy and soft.

He smashed the kings facedown in front of his chips and the remaining five behind that. He would be going to the bathroom soon to make his nose red again, then he'd get too sleepy to play, and then he'd be gone.

The dealer fanned her cards out and began examining the players' hands. The young Vietnamese man was standing now, a girl leaning against his shoulder. He won high and low. The girl, Anh could tell, had had her eyes done. The surgeon had made a mistake in the corner of one lid. A stitch he forgot to take. Or maybe it had been an infected area. But a bit of skin had grown inward. The girl picked at it with her fingers.

"Good cards," the dealer said to the American, and shoved three piles of chips toward him.

The American stood up. It was time.

"See, I bring you good luck," Anh said, and held out her hand.

~

THE VILLAGE OF NGA TU BAY HIEN, NEAR SAIGON, 1968

Anh always knew when it was time for her mother to go to Cambodia to buy silks and Cuban cigars and tortoiseshell combs. Those were the times she left her jade in the lacquerware box in the upstairs room and put on a plain white ao dai.

"Loan steals when you're away, Me," Anh told her mother. Loan was the nurse, the one who looked after ten-year-old Anh; her nine-year-old brother, Manh; and Vy, her baby sister. The three older boys were away fighting the Communists. Ba, their father, sometimes went to fight, too, but mostly he stayed in the Rex Hotel and gambled with the American officers.

"What does Loan steal?" Me asked. "My jewelry is always here when I come back." She talked to Anh in a rough way, her voice

sounding like the sharp branches of the trees that the wind sometimes pushed against the house.

"She steals the money you leave for Yony to feed us," Anh said. Yony was the cook, the one who watched the house when Me went on her trips to the west.

"You always lie," Me said.

"But I'm not lying. It's true. I told Ba, and he believed me."

"Your stars and his are the same. That's why he believes you. I don't have to believe you."

Me was a good smuggler. The best. Ba sometimes brought money into the house, but it was Me, buying goods in Cambodia and smuggling them into Saigon, bribing people along the way, risking death at the border, who had bought the biggest house in the village and furnished it with French furniture. It was Me who hired the maids and counted out the money and ran everyone's life.

Anh watched while Me strapped her money belt beneath her ao dai. And she followed her downstairs to where Loan was sitting at the table, Vy on her lap. Loan was putting the hot food into her own mouth to cool it, and then taking it out and feeding it to the baby. Manh was swinging in a hammock on the porch. Anh could see him through the window, writing a poem in the unlined book that the sisters at the Catholic school had given him. The sisters said he was smart. More than smart. He wrote poems in French and drew pictures to go with them.

Anh went to the Catholic school, too, but she was always too busy to write or draw anything in a book. She liked to spend her afternoons in the marketplace watching the merchants weigh out their goods, waiting to see if she could tell when they cheated someone, watching their thumbs like Ba told her to do. Every merchant has a thief in his thumb, he said. Anh liked the idea of selling things. People won't always want to listen to poetry, she told Ba, but they'll always buy good things to eat and pretty things to wear.

"I'll be back in two weeks," Me said. She bent down and kissed the top of Vy's head and then squeezed the nape of the baby's neck with her fingers. It was almost like Vy was a kitten and Me was going to pick her up by the neck. But she stopped before the baby could cry. In fact, she did it so softly, pinched the skin so gently that Vy didn't even lift her head or stop eating the food that Loan was stuffing into her mouth.

Anh wished that Me would touch her, too, sometimes. It didn't have to be a kiss or a squeeze on the neck. A touch on the arm would be enough. Once Anh tried to kiss Me's fingers, but Me snatched them away and made a face. Ba said that was just Me's way, that she believed in the fortune-tellers, who said that Anh was born under a star that didn't match her mother's. Ba didn't go to fortune-tellers. He did believe in luck, though. He said he could feel when his luck came and feel when it went. It was like a cold river running from his toes to his knees when his luck was bad. When it was good, the river ran hot, he said, and made his yellow skin turn pink.

2

The Dennis Morgan law office was on the first floor of a building that had portholes instead of windows overlooking Newport Harbor. Jana usually parked in the first stall next to the seafood restaurant downstairs, but Dennis had gotten there first. His red Jag was parked sideways, and the door was ajar. She pulled her Toyota in behind the Dumpster, then undid the belt on Andy's car seat.

"My Ninja," he said.

Jana lifted him out of the car and stood him up beside it, then put the stuffed Ninja in his arms.

"Remember what I told you now, Andy. Dennis doesn't like noise. So what are you going to do?"

The three-year-old put his hand in hers. "Play quiet," he said.

As they passed Dennis's car, Jana looked in the window. Chunks of wadded Kleenex were scattered across the floor. An open bottle of eye drops was on the dashboard.

He was in the bathroom when she came in. He hadn't even bothered to turn on the lights or switch the sign from Closed to Open. He spent most of his days in the bathroom lately. It had started two years ago, when he won the four-million-dollar products liability case on the defective lawn mower. His client's chewed-off toes had given him so much money so suddenly that it had taken him a while to figure out what to do with it. He bought a house in Emerald Bay with his own private tram going up and down the cliff to the beach. He bought a Jag for himself and a Mercedes for his wife. He put some of the money up his nose. Jana had no idea what he did with the rest.

"Dennis? You in there?" She stood at the bathroom door, listening. He was usually out by now and making frantic phone calls to adjusters trying to settle cases. Looking for money. He was always looking for money.

"I'm here, I'm here." The door opened and he stepped out. He was tall and pale, almost sick-looking, with long arms that had once given him a basketball scholarship to a college in the Midwest.

"You're not going to bring that kid in here."

"My sitter quit." She sat Andy on a chair and turned the sign around in the window.

"Did Lieb call with an offer on the Dooley case?" he asked.

"I told him no."

"You told him what?"

She opened a file drawer and rummaged through the files till she found the box of crayons and a coloring book. She usually kept them in a "C" folder for crayons. But here they were under "R."

"I told him that Mrs. Dooley couldn't work, couldn't have sex with her husband anymore, could hardly remember her own name," she said.

"I had him set, goddamn it."

"I unset it."

She rolled Andy toward the side of her desk and gave him the crayons and the coloring book. "Look what I found, Andy. Your crayons. Color a picture for Mommy."

"I'm not going to court, Jana. I don't go to court. I don't do that kind of stuff."

"She can't work, Dennis."

"That's not my problem."

She looked up at him as the phone rang. "What is your problem?"

"Answer the phone."

"What about the money you promised me from the toes case?"

"Now? You want to talk about that now? The phone's ringing."

"Law offices," she said into the phone.

"I'm not here," Dennis said. He turned and went into his private office and slammed the door.

It was Chavez from State Farm.

"I got you ten thousand for that broken hip, Jana."

"You're just like a vulture, Steve. A goddamn vulture." She dragged the phone cord over to the file cabinet and began flipping through the case files. She'd always meant to do something about the files. Give them a number or a date or something she could go right to, instead of remembering their positions in the drawer.

"Here it is," she said. "Clester, Marion." She could hardly read her own handwriting. She preferred to type her letters on the old manual that sat in front of the unused computer. And she wrote comments in the files in longhand. With a pencil. That faded in the damp marine air.

"I've got it right here in front of me. Ten thousand for Clester? Did you see those doctor reports? Those X rays? My God, Steven, you gotta be kidding."

"It's all it's worth."

"Dennis'll never go for it, and you know it."

"Come on, Jana."

"He won't. We need at least thirty."

"You've got no teeth to bite me with. I didn't see your name on the bar roster. What are you going to do? File a complaint? Go to court? Dennis hasn't filed a complaint or gone to court in two years. He's busy sniffing his way into disbarment."

"That's how much you know. He's got a man out right this minute filing complaints. Three damn cases. Big ones, too. A rotator cuff, a wrongful death, a products—"

"You're good. I'd give you the Oscar if it was up to me, but you're not a lawyer."

"Thirty thousand, or no deal."

"Sue us."

"I will."

"You can't."

She hung up the phone and had started dialing again when Dennis's door opened and he stuck his head out.

"Did we settle that Bergman case?" he said.

"Yesterday."

"Then where the hell's the check?"

"In Riverside."

"The fuckin' money doesn't do me any good in Riverside."

"I'll send a messenger to get it." He was about to shut the door again when she said, "The toes case, Dennis. What about the toes case?"

"What about it?"

"You promised me a bonus when you won. I'm still waiting."

"I know, I know. And you'll get it. Didn't I tell you you'll get it? Christ, you drive me crazy."

"You promised me. I've been waiting patiently. Oh, Lord, I am patient, but I've got obligations. You know damn well and good the obligations I've got."

"You think I don't have obligations? Christ, you think you're the only one in the world? I've got things holding me up moneywise just like you do."

"A million dollars' worth, Dennis? What kind of things have you got moneywise that a million dollars can't cure?"

He slammed the door between them. The phone rang again, and when she picked it up, she heard her mother's voice, slightly breathy, more than a little frantic.

"Daddy's lost again," her mother said. "I can't find him any- where."

Jana drove slowly down the street. It had begun to rain, a soft rain that wet the streets just enough to make them steam.

"I just turned around and he wasn't there," her mother said from the backseat.

"You've got to keep the door locked."

"He opens it."

Andy had caught his grandmother's nervousness and was leaning forward in his car seat, straining to see through the spotted wind- shield.

"You're scaring him," Jana murmured. She turned and grinned at Andy. "You look out that side for Grandpa, and I'll look out this side."

"There he is," her mother said.

"You stay in the car with Andy," Jana said. "I'll get him."

Her father was peeing against a tree, his hot stream breaking into rivulets when it struck the exposed roots.

"Rain always makes me want to pee," her father said.

"It does the same thing to me," Jana said. The fences in this part of Inglewood were glazed with graffiti, and despite the rain, the vendors were out selling sliced fruit and tacos.

"He thinks it makes things grow," she said to a boy at the edge of the crowd that had gathered to watch. "Could you just help me give him a little push toward the car. Once he's aimed in that direction, he'll get in by himself."

Jana and the boy half pushed, half dragged the old man toward the car.

"Oh, you're all wet, Jack," her mother said as he got in the backseat beside her.

"Am I?" Her father looked satisfied, as though he'd done something special. "I did a little gardening," he said. "That's enough for me."

"I can't keep coming over here and looking for him," Jana said.

"I just didn't know what to do," her mother said. She was a tiny woman with hands that shook when she held anything. She had a cup of coffee in her hands now, and it was bouncing around, slopping dashes of brown liquid onto her housedress as she lifted it to her lips. Everyone always said how much Jana resembled her. You look like sisters, they always said. But now the mother's round brown eyes lay deep in their wrinkled sockets, and her hair, once the same rich brown as her daughter's, was thin and nearly white.

"I do a little gardening," her father said. "That's enough for me."

He had been a furniture maker, custom furniture, with a work-room in a bower of grapevines. He had let Jana sand the teakwood, showed her how the grain of the wood emerged like magic beneath your hand.

"You could sell this place and move to a retirement home," Jana said. "It'd sure as hell relieve me."

"It would kill your father," her mother said.

"You could get shot one of these days. I just read the other day where a kid playing Monopoly on 134th Street—in his bedroom—"

"I don't read the newspapers," her mother said.

"The shot came through the window," Jana said.

"It's too terrible to read the newspapers."

"You like living in a war zone?"

"It's a war zone everywhere."

Jana had grown up in this house, with its painted cupboards and tiny rooms and overstuffed furniture. She had gone to school in the neighborhood. She had rolled along the cracked sidewalks in well-oiled skates. Where lush grapevines had once covered half an acre behind their house there now were apartments, and the streets looked like Tijuana, and the nights were broken by the rat-tat-tat of gunfire from cruising cars.

Her father looked impatient now. Restless. His thumbs drumming the table alongside his napkin, which he had used and then refolded into the shape of an airplane. He looked too young for her mother, with his straight back and trim build. His auburn hair, parted in the middle and plastered toupeelike to the sides of his head, was all there, with hardly a white strand in it. Only the brains inside, as twisted as noodle pudding, gave him away.

"Don't upset him," her mother said. "He hears you."

The coffee cup rattled as she put it down on the table next to a stack of envelopes. A crocheted doily was curled beneath a potted plant. There were potted plants everywhere in the house. They twined their way down the sides of the television set, leaned toward the sun in the living room bay window, lined the walls. Earth and damp grew out of the seams of the wallpaper, clung to the upholstery.

"These bills came," her mother said. "What should I do—"

Jana stuffed the white envelopes into her purse, along with last month's.

"Can you pay them?"

"I always do."

Andy crawled out from under the table where he had been playing.

"Look how serious he looks," her mother said.

"He's a worrier," Jana said.

"Not like you."

"No. I'm a tiger."

~

When Jana got back, Dennis was bobbing around in the doorway to his private office, looking sicker than usual.

"We found him," she said. "The traffic was terrible on the 405. Sorry it took so long. The rain makes everyone pile up and head for the exits. Saw at least three fender benders. I don't know what gets into people when it rains. I guess the notion that they might slide a little puts them into a panic."

There were about ten messages on the answering machine. Dennis hadn't even bothered to pick up the phone.

"I don't know what it is about rain," she said. Dennis was trembling wildly. She took his arm and eased him into the chair at her desk. "Get Mommy some water," she told Andy.

Andy filled a plastic cup with water and brought it to her.

"My mother made us stay for lunch," she said, holding the cup to Dennis's mouth. "My dad's really falling apart lately." Dennis's lips looked swollen. His whole face looked bigger than it had when she left. "I'm the one they look to. I don't know how it happened. I feel like I've got three kids, not one."

Dennis was slipping out of the chair, feet straight out in front of him, rigid, as though someone had slipped steel rods into his pants. He was looking at her strangely, his cheeks distended, overflowing his jaw.

"Maybe even four," she said.

He wobbled his lips, tried to speak, and then slipped all the way out of the chair. As his head bopped the floor, it made a sound like a ripe coconut falling out of a tree.

3

The house Anh lived in with her brother Thinh, her sister Vy, Vy's four kids, and Me was an old one, thin-walled and small-roomed. A Japanese truck farmer built it when Orange County contained the most fertile growing fields in California, when every piece of dirt was abloom with something to eat, when lush fields of strawberries, cabbages, and corn hugged Highway 39 as it wandered through gray, underpopulated, nondescript towns with plucked-out-of-the-air names like Garden Grove, Stanton, Westminster, Midway City.

The Japanese farmers were interned in Arizona during World War II, and tracts of houses sprouted on their abandoned fields. For two hundred dollars down, a worker in the nearby shipyards could buy a white box of a house with a patch of grass in front, a chain-link fence in back, along with an incinerator for burning trash. No trees, no shrubs, no sidewalks. Highway 39 was renamed Beach Boulevard, and kids from Los Angeles drove their jalopies down it, past the small towns that had houses, bare yards, and incinerators, all the way to the sea.

After the war the Japanese came back to reclaim what land was left. They imported Mexican labor to stoop in the fields at harvest time. The Japanese prospered, sold their land bit by bit to speculators, while the Mexican laborers clung to the shrinking fields and waited patiently for better days. The war workers who hadn't gone back to Oklahoma or Arkansas or Nebraska found work in tin-roofed machine shops relining brakes, straightening dented fenders, spraying cheap paint on prewar cars. The gray, underpopulated, nondescript towns stayed that way until the end of another war, when the Vietnamese arrived and settled themselves right smack along the strip of highway leading to the sea.

Suddenly everything changed. Unpronounceable signs with strange combinations of letters embellished with squiggles, quarter moons, and slashes appeared in store windows. Women in *ao dais* walked along Bolsa Avenue, their heads shaded by colorful parasols, their slim hips swinging to rhythms remembered from another time and place. The gray towns sparked to life. Vietnamese generals opened liquor stores. Lawyers ran noodle shops. Teachers worked in manicure parlors. Doctors sold herbs. The Vietnamese didn't seem to need to sleep. They could work two jobs, three jobs, even four, without sleeping. Everything they did was speeded up, in a rush, in a hurry, a video in fast-forward with everyone scrambling to make money any way they could.

The Mexicans complained that they were being pushed out of the way by these newcomers, run over, outnumbered. The workers in the tin-roofed shops said watch out for those Vietnamese, they know more scams than you can ever figure. And don't turn your back on them if you don't want a knife in your neck. Why, they've got gangs of kids that will kill you for a dollar. Or for nothing.

Vietnamese children grew like exotic crops on the region's furrowed fields. Most went to school and studied hard, and their teachers said they were the smartest, the best behaved, the quickest students they had ever seen. But there were others, some of them orphaned and left on their own, who dropped out of school and idled away the days from early morning to late at night in coffee bars. Lean boys with lank black hair, girls in tight skirts with ribbons in their hair and sweet smiles on their lips, they held their secrets close. They joined gangs, robbed people in their homes, and shot at one another in the street.

Anh kicked off her shoes at the door and stepped into the house in her stocking feet. Vy was in the kitchen, the latest baby in her arms.

Her three other kids, none over five years old, were sitting on the living room floor in front of the television. They were called Boy, Little Boy, and Little Little Boy. The baby was Baby Boy. Anh let the packages slip out of her hands onto the table.

"Why do you let them watch so much TV?" Anh said. "Their brains are going to turn sour with all that crap they watch."

"What did you buy me?" Vy asked. "Open it up. Open it up." She was little more than a child herself, barely twenty-five.

"A dress," Anh said. "Do you ever take them outside, get them air? Kids need to be outside to grow, you know."

"Oh, it's blue. My favorite. Blue."

There was a pot of noodles on the stove, and Anh ladled some into a bowl and sat down at the table. An altar with offerings of fruit and wilted flowers stood against one wall of the kitchen, a picture of Buddha and one of Jesus side by side above it.

"Oh, I was so hungry," Anh said. She banged one stockinged foot nervously against the table leg as she ate. "I eat and eat, and still I'm so hungry. Every hour I need something in my mouth, and still my skirt is so loose, it's falling off my hips."

"You work too hard."

"If I don't work, who's going to buy food for all your kids, pay the rent, buy gas? And what about tires for the car? The damn car needs tires again. And if I don't have a car, how am I going to take you and the kids to the doctor, and—"

"I don't ask you to buy me dresses," Vy said. She hooked one finger under the chain around her neck above the baby's head. A carved jade Buddha. "Ba is here. He brought me this. Good luck for the baby."

Their father came sometimes once, sometimes twice a month. He always brought a little gift for Vy, never anything for anyone else. He would go into the bedroom with Me and stay there until it was time to leave.

"I decided I like the name Kelly," Vy said. "The lady-who-never-smiles told me Tammy is an old name, I shouldn't use it anymore."

The lady-who-never-smiles was an American who lived next door with her Vietnamese husband. She gave Vy names, like castoff clothes, to try on. Cute American names. Short and peppy. Oh, it made Anh so mad that that lady kept giving Vy all those stupid

American names; Anh wouldn't even look at her when she saw her outside.

"You change your name every day," Anh said. "You've had so many names this past year, I can't remember them all."

"It's Kelly now," Vy said. "Call me Kelly, or I won't answer."

"You're not going to get to be an American by changing your name."

"You keep harping on the same thing. Names. You're just jealous because I came early enough to speak English well, and you're still stuck somewhere in Vietnam, thinking in Vietnamese all the time, butchering English. Do you know how you sound in English?"

"How do I sound?"

"Like you're ignorant. You should hear yourself sometimes. You really should."

"I hear myself."

"Then why do you talk the way you do? Why don't you try to fix your English? My God, Anh, you're in America now."

Oh, look at that little sister pulling the tiger's whiskers and thinking it has no teeth, thinking she knew how to get Anh, knew how to put her in a corner, let her know she wasn't so smart. She was the one who wasn't smart.

Anh got up and put her dish in the sink. She covered the noodles and put them in the refrigerator, then took the sponge and began to wipe at the grease stains above the stove.

She wouldn't argue with Vy, wouldn't let her see how mad she could really get. Oh, Vy had no idea what Anh could do if she really got mad.

"The lady-who-never-smiles told me about a doctor," Vy said.

So now she was being nice. She always did that. Jabbed at Anh as hard as she could, and then got scared and drew back. Anh felt sorry for her, sorry that she didn't know how to jab all the way to the bone.

"A good doctor. And cheap, too. I can find a rich American if I fix my nose and eyes. For three thousand dollars I can buy a nose with a bone on the top, and eyes that look at everything at once. Then I'll move out, and you won't have so much to worry about."

Anh filled the sink with soap powder, ran the hot water, and began scrubbing a pot with a piece of steel wool. "I saw a girl at the casino last night," she said. "You should have seen the funny eyes that girl had. Oh, they were funny-looking all right."

"I'll get a big American doctor, not one who learned to sew in a rice paddy."

"American doctors want a lot of money, and then they ruin you. That girl last night, the doctor probably told her, you ugly Vietnamese girl, I'm going to make you look like a beautiful American, and all the time he was laughing at her."

"It's an investment. There's a lot of competition out there, Anh."

Rice had baked onto a glass dish, and Anh pried at it with one fingernail.

"Or maybe you want to go see that lady who has a shop on Asian Way," Anh said. "She's got a doctor's name on the window, but she's a beautician. She can put a curl in your hair and give you American eyes all at the same time. Noses, too. Tits, too. Maybe you ought to go over there and let that lady beautician operate on you. Maybe she'll do it in the backseat of her Mercedes. I hear she's really rich from all the Vietnamese women wanting American faces and tits."

"Come on, Anh, I'm serious."

A door opened down the hall, and Anh heard the sound of her father's voice. She could barely hear her mother's answering him. He was buttoning his pants as he came into the kitchen. He bent and kissed the baby's head, then sat down at the table and began to sip the tea that Anh poured for him. He was a skinny man. Skinny as a blade of grass, with gray-flecked hair that he kept cropped close to his small head.

"This is bad tea," he said.

"American tea is garbage," Vy said.

"This is Vietnam tea," Anh said. "Imported. I bought it from Mr. Hoang's store. I told him it was for my father. I told him I didn't care what it cost. I wouldn't give you American tea, Ba."

"It tastes bad," her father said. "How much did you win tonight?"

"Not much."

"Didn't you count it?"

"I never count. My luck'll turn bad tomorrow if I count today."

"I'll die before you get me enough to buy a restaurant."

"You won't die, Ba. You're going to be cooking soon, I promise."

She turned and took the noodles out of the refrigerator and stood in front of it, eating the cold noodles with her fingers. "I'm always so hungry," she said.

"Why don't you give me what you have," Ba said. "I can take it to the Western Club and make the restaurant grow right there on the table."

"I'll keep it in the bank, making interest."

"You're a selfish daughter," her father said.

"I brought you some noodles," Anh said.

The room smelled of her father. Tobacco smoke and semen. The bed was rumpled, and her mother, wrapped in a silk kimono and sitting in a small straight chair in front of the television, didn't look up when Anh entered. A Chinese video dubbed in Vietnamese was on.

"I need eight hundred dollars," Me said. She was slender and had a straight back and a long neck and in the dark room looked young at fifty-two.

"Eight hundred dollars? Why do you want eight hundred dollars?"

Me turned and gave her daughter a sharp look.

"Vy needs diamond earrings. She has a bad life."

"She makes her life bad herself. Diamond earrings won't help."

Me turned toward the television again. She spent most of the day watching Chinese soap operas, waiting for the times her husband came to see her. Sometimes she watched ten at a sitting, coming out of her room only to prepare meals and stare out the open front door into the street.

"Your brother Thinh is gone," Me said. "Four days and he hasn't been here. Find him."

"He doesn't like school. I talk to him and talk to him. He tells me to go away, he won't listen to a girl."

"Find him."

"I can't make him come home if he doesn't want to. I can't make him do anything. He doesn't listen to me. He doesn't listen to anyone."

"This is your thirty-fifth year, a dangerous year for you. You'd better be very careful not to disobey me. If you do, you'll bring misfortune on your head."

"My thirty-fifth year is the same as the last one. And Thinh will still do what he wants to do."

"The day you were born the sun nearly fell out of the sky with misery."

Anh lay down on the bed and watched the serial as though she cared what was happening on the flickery set. She came in here every night hoping that her mother would speak to her about that last day in Saigon. Vy didn't remember Saigon, didn't know what happened that last day, didn't know what really happened. Oh, Vy was lucky, lucky, lucky not to know.

∼

NGA TU BAY HIEN, 1969

Me didn't bring the girl home all at once. She brought her a little bit at a time. First she took her to the fortune-teller to see if this was the right kind of girl. She left her there for a month while the fortune-teller looked the girl over.

"She looks strong and healthy," the fortune-teller said at the end of the month. "She can probably have lots of boys, and that will be good. She is a little mean and talks when she shouldn't, but you can train her. Even dogs can be trained."

Then Me took the girl to Uncle Kou's house. He was Ba's brother. A rich man, some people said, but there was no sign of gold anywhere. Uncle Kou and his wife, Auntie Chi, lived in a hut with all of Auntie Chi's relatives, everyone sleeping on mats on the earthen floor. There were so many people sleeping on the floor, the dirt beneath the mats had turned hard and glossy.

"I don't want her here," Auntie Chi said.

"I have to do this," Me said, "or Ba will die."

"Some people will talk. Think what you are doing. Don't be a crazy woman."

"She can stay," Uncle Kou said.

While Me was moving the girl step by step from place to place, waiting for the right moment to bring her home, the war was getting worse. The nights, still and full of heat, would shriek awake when the rockets came. The noise they made when they hit the ground would bring everyone, even Loan and baby Vy, out onto the porch to see where the fires were. The rockets were like birds shot out of the sky, their feathers a graceful arc of orange and yellow light.

When the rockets fell, the next morning there would be charred bodies floating in the silty water of the rice paddies. Manh could squat beside a dead body for hours, swatting away the flies, sketching, sketching, sketching. He had one whole book full of little dainty pictures of rotting noses and splattered brains. Anh sometimes went with him. The bodies were of no interest to her. It was Manh, his lack of fear, his absorption in what he was doing, that fascinated her.

That was the bigger war. Then there were the little wars. In the rice paddies. In the fields. At the side of the road. Wharumphs and rat-tat-tats. Shouts and screams. It would be quiet between the big war and the little ones. That was when the villagers would come out to work in the paddies, and Me would let Manh and Anh go to school. That was when the American soldiers rode through the village in their jeeps, and Anh and Manh would ride their bicycles to meet them. The soldiers always had big smiles. Sometimes they tossed candies, and Anh would race her brother to see who could catch the most.

It was on the morning that an American rocket scooped out a giant pit in the road and the soldiers had to drive their jeeps across the field that Me finally brought the girl home.

"This is your second wife," Me said to Ba. He was in his undershirt, smoking a cigarette, his uniform hanging over the back of one of Me's French chairs.

"Her name is Khanh, and she's fifteen years old," Me said. "The fortune-teller told me you would die young unless I found you a second wife. This is a good one. She'll be a good sister to me and a good second wife to you, and the fortune-teller said she is sure to have boys."

The girl was barefoot and had road dust clinging to her straight black hair.

"I don't like her," Anh said.

"You call her Auntie Khanh," Me snapped.

"She smells bad," Anh said.

"You give me nothing but trouble," Me said.

Manh went up close to the girl and stared at her a long time before she pushed him away.

"I'll draw your picture," he said.

"Is she a Buddhist or a Catholic?" was the only thing Ba wanted to know.

4

*m*y brother Thinh is good boy," Anh said. "It all those bum he hang around with. I tell him and tell him, Thinh, I say to him all the time, Thinh, you run with those gang boy, you gonna end up screwed."

The principal kept his eyes on the blue folder he had open on his desk. Anh could see out his office door into the hall of the high school. Girls the age she had been when she arrived in the United States. Boys the age Thinh was now. Some Mexicans, but mostly Vietnamese.

"Vietnamese boy smart," Anh said, staring at a serious-looking boy, books hanging from his thin fingers, neck bobbing on his skinny frame. "Thinh just like all the Vietnamese boy. You ever see Thinh adding number—pfft—he do it like machine. Bam, bam, bam. And every number in right place. In his head, too. Don't use those Jap calculator. Right from his brain. He just know that stuff like hell. He just like to play around sometime, get into little bit trouble. Don't mean nothing. You ever see him divide? Now, that something to see, watch Thinh divide those number, get the answer before I even think which way to start."

"He hasn't been to school for a month."

The school was on the edge of Little Saigon, on a boulevard of apartment houses and industrial buildings. The railroad tracks cut in behind it, and the towering red pagoda of a Chinese restaurant provided shade on the rear lawn, where students were eating their lunch.

He flipped a page. "F in English, D in science, D in shop—" He looked up at her. "What's wrong with him?"

"He sick this week. All week. Bad cold in the chest. I make him special tea last night, and still this morning, cough, cough, cough." She put one hand against her chest and smiled at the man. He didn't like her, she could tell.

"Does he live with you?"

"And my mother and sister. We rent house. Nice house. Thinh mow the lawn and water the grass. He make bookcase and put on new roof. It was leaking. Water coming in, coming in. I sleep at night and dreaming I taking a shower, that how bad that roof leak. And I tell the man who own the house, and he tell me pay more rent or learn to swim. So I tell Thinh, I say, 'Thinh, we need new roof.' Pfft, just like that, he put it on. No trouble with it. He can learn to do whatever he want. Smart. Oh, that kid so smart, he gonna think hisself right into trouble one of these day. You want him to learn something in school, you just show him the book, and he do it in one minute. Just watch him."

He was studying the file again. "He transferred from a high school in South Dakota. Is that where you used to live?"

"When we come from Vietnam. Oh, Jesus, that South Dakota is cold. I never feel cold till I got to that place." She grabbed her arms with her hands and scrunched up her eyebrows to show how cold it was. "Vietnamese people don't like it so cold. I have relative still there, but my mother and me and Vy, we left there and come to California. We got relative here. Some up in Santa Maria, too. We got relative everywhere. Do you know how come they send Vietnamese to South Dakota?"

"Can't say I do. And your father?"

"He came, too."

"Where does he live?"

"In some apartment. I never been inside it, but everybody say it pretty nice. He told me the roof don't leak." She smiled warmly at him and bounced her foot up and down. He was looking at her foot now, at its nervous bouncing, at the soft leather.

"Ferragamo," she said. "Italian. Pretty shoe, ain't they? I bought them on sale. I don't pay full price. Looking for the bargain is what I like. Make me sick to pay real price. Your wife shop? I tell her where to go for the bargain stuff. You been to Little Saigon yet—you know, Brookhurst, Bolsa, that place called Asian Way, all those shop over there—she like jade? Best bargain in jade. Oh, you won't believe the bargain. I know the lady that got the best spot in the jewelry mall, next to the Last Emperor Restaurant. She give you a deal if I send you over there. The other one, people I don't know, sell all that crap, and who know whether it the real stuff or not."

She giggled. A little short, practiced giggle. "You got to watch out for the Vietnamese. They learn how to cheat you when they still a baby. Sell you colored stone they put in the oven, not real jade."

She opened her purse and took out a card and laid it on the gleaming desk in front of him. "My name Truong Anh. I take you and your wife to Little Saigon for jade. Maybe pearl, too, big long string of pearl. And knockoff—Gucci knockoff, Fendi knockoff, I get you all that stuff." She tapped the toe of one shoe against the heel of the other. "Not these shoe, though, these real one." She held her purse up for his inspection, practically put it in his lap. "See this purse, everyone ask me where did I get it. A knockoff. Made in Hong Kong. You can't even tell."

"You don't want to tell me where your father lives?"

"I never go there."

He sighed and closed the folder.

"If you find your brother, tell him he's expelled."

"Have any of you guys seen my brother Thinh?" Anh stood at the side of the table and shouted to be heard over the rock music that was blasting from the overhead speakers. There were three boys at the table, all with small cups of strong coffee in front of them. Anh never came here. This was where the girls stood out in front, bending over so you could see their bottoms. Inside, the gang boys, the ones who couldn't stay out of jail for longer than thirty days at a time, who could kill you and jump in a car and disappear before you even started to bleed, sat at stainless steel tables and made their deals. Like this one, Hong, his specialty was petty theft. He had a long good-luck whisker sprouting from his otherwise smooth cheek. It looked like someone had begun to sew his face, then stopped after one stitch and left a piece of black thread dangling there. The boy next to him, the one turned sideways playing a video game, the one who never spoke, sold dope and stolen jewelry. And the one next to him, his back to the dirty window, extorted money from shopkeepers.

"He hasn't been going to school," Anh said. "I'm looking for him."

"He's in jail," the extortionist said. He had infected pimples on his forehead and a patch of soft beard hanging from his chin.

Anh sat down in the fourth chair. "Jail?"

"He beat one of them police guys in the jaw, and they took him to jail," Hong said. He was picking at his teeth with a toothpick, his left hand hiding his right as he dug at his gums. "I called you, but you weren't home. It was my car. The police guys stopped me because my license was falling off the back."

"Jail because your license was falling off your car?" Anh said. "What were you doing, robbing people in the Brookhurst mall, grabbing people's purses? Maybe pushing old ladies down and ripping off their jade bracelets?"

Hong put the toothpick down. Anh could see little drops of blood on his gums where he had poked the toothpick in too far. "We had a stick in the car, in the back. The police guys said what am I going to do with it? Thinh told them guys we need it for protection from the guys in the Bolsa Gang. He's crazy, that brother of yours. The police guys got him on a deadly weapon, and me, too, because it was my car. But I got the bail right away. Your brother's got assault, too. The police guy's jaw broke. I tried to call you, but you weren't home."

"You've got a felony charge now," Anh said. "How are you going to go to college? How are you going to be a doctor?" She slapped the side of Thinh's head with the flat of her hand. "You don't think. You don't know what you're doing." Her brother had been brought into the visiting room of the Orange County Jail along with a bunch of Americans. He looked small and frail next to them, hardly strong enough to break a police guy's jaw. He sat with his head down now as Anh berated him.

"I told you I'm saving money for you for college. Me doesn't know how bad you are. And if I told Ba how bad you really are, he'd come over here and kill you. Tell you what a bad son you are first, and then kill you. He doesn't know you never go to school. He doesn't know you're always in trouble." She hit him again. "Are you listening to me?"

"I'm listening." His voice was so low, she could hardly hear the words.

"I don't see the police sitting here in jail. You're the one who's got a felony charge on him. You, not the police. Did you have to hit him, lose your temper for nothing? Are you stupid, or what?"

"The police hassle me, Anh. All the time. They see me in a car, they stop the car. They see me on the sidewalk, they ask me where I'm going. We had a broken taillight, Anh, that's all. And a stick in the backseat. A stick. A lousy stick."

There was a large bruise on his cheek. She touched it with her fingers. "Where did you get that?"

"One of them police socked me when they brought me in. Threw me against the wall and banged my head a few times. Gave me a bad headache. I think he broke my ribs. Hurts when I breathe. Scratched my arm here and here, too. Look." He pulled the sleeve of his T-shirt up to show her the marks. "This place is worse than anywhere else, you know. I gotta watch out for gang guys even when I'm sleeping. Those Mexican gangs are as bad as the Bolsa guys, and there's no room, we're all jammed in here, you know, like a buncha pigs. A Mexican guy pulled a knife on me last night 'cause I asked if he had any cigarettes—pulled a knife right out of his hair or somewheres. I just asked about a cigarette. I didn't even touch him."

He was like a little boy, like one of Vy's kids. She could remember when he was born. The hospital in Sioux Falls was so small, there wasn't enough room for all the relatives' cars in the parking lot. Ba had been so happy that day, sitting next to Me's bed and talking about how one day they'd go back to Vietnam and take this child with them. Not the girls. Just this boy child.

"If I was thinking straight, I'd leave you here," Anh said. She leaned forward and gently grazed Thinh's head with her own. "But I'm not thinking straight."

Anh kept her money in a cloth bag in her bedroom closet. The closet door had a special lock that no one knew the combination to. She told everyone the lock was for her clothes. Expensive clothes. Designer labels. I don't want anyone stealing them, she said.

Now she stood in front of the closet and stared at the hole. The hinges were there, but the middle of the door was gone. It was like someone wanted to put a window in her closet, that's how even and square and neat the sides of the hole were. There weren't even any splinters on the floor.

Vy was warming a bottle of formula under the running water in the sink. She glanced at Anh, then closed the tap and wiped the bottle with a towel.

"My closet," Anh said. "Someone stole my closet."

"I was home all day. I didn't see anyone. They're just clothes. Who cares?"

Anh ran down the hall to Me's room. The television was on, and Me was asleep in a chair. Anh shook her mother's shoulder, and Me woke with a little scream.

"I was dreaming," she said.

"My closet, my money, who took it?"

"You told me you keep your money in a bank."

"It's those gang boys, the Bolsa Gang, I know it. They stole everything. They cut a big hole in my closet with an electric saw. They came in the house with a saw. Who let them in? Who showed them where my closet was? How come you didn't hear them? What were you doing? What do you sit here for, in the dark? What do you see in that awful box that makes you love it so much that you don't hear that saw taking away all the money I've worked so hard to save, the college for Thinh, the restaurant for Ba?"

"All your money?"

"Everything."

5

*M*r. Bui's office was on the second floor of a square white building in a crowded mall off Bolsa Avenue. He had one desk and a battered file cabinet and a dead palm tree with a red ribbon around it. The certificate on the wall behind his chair said Bui Thi Income Tax, Insurance, Mortgages, Bail Bonds, Personal Loans. But there was a different man sitting at Mr. Bui's desk, someone Anh had never seen before.

"Where's Mr. Bui?" Anh said.

"He went back to Vietnam."

"He's crazy to do a thing like that. I know Mr. Bui a long time. He was never that crazy before."

Anh emptied the paper sack on his desk.

"How much for two jade bracelets?" she said.

"Ah, apple green," the man said. He held them up close to his eyes, twisting the green hoops in his fingers. "Nice." He put them down and smiled at Anh. "How much do you need?"

"Five thousand."

"Mmmm."

"I know everyone in Little Saigon. How come I don't know you?"

"I don't know."

Anh pulled a card out of her purse and gave it to him. "My name's Truong Anh. Ask anyone in Little Saigon who I am, they'll tell you. We came in 1975. How about you?"

"Nineteen eighty." He was pleasant-looking in his white shirt and tie.

"How about this diamond?" Anh pulled a diamond out of her change purse. "Three carats. Big stone, very fine, white. No flaws. The jeweler's a friend of mine. She gave me a deal. I'll give it to you for three thousand."

The man looked at the stone with a loupe squeezed beneath his eye and cheek. "I see a flaw."

Anh grabbed the diamond out of his hand. "Where? If there's a spot in this diamond, I'll give it to you for nothing." He handed her the loupe, and she stared at the spot of carbon in the center of the stone.

"I was cheated," she said, and put the diamond on the table between them. "Are you married?"

"I have a wife in Vietnam."

"I'm not married. I'm thirty-five. My mother tried to find me a husband from our village in Saigon when we got to South Dakota. He was an old man. Awful. Awful. I told her, 'Me, what am I going to do with an old man like that? Maybe he's sick. Maybe I'll have to feed him his medicine. Maybe he won't leave me alone. Maybe he'll want me to take him everywhere I go.' How come your wife didn't come to the States with you? Don't you like her?"

"We had four children to get out of Vietnam before she could leave. One by one over the past twelve years, she's been sending them out. One was in Cambodia for a year. We thought he was killed, then he showed up. Then our daughter. Then two more boys got out by way of Malaysia. They're all in college now."

"We were in a camp in Malaysia. My brother Thinh is going to go to medical school. Be a doctor. He's a smart Vietnamese kid. Born here. All American. He's so smart, it could make your hair turn white thinking about how smart he is."

"We need Vietnamese doctors."

"Do you speak English?"

"And French. I studied law in France."

"Rich, huh?"

"I had a good education. Napoleonic law." He picked the jade bracelets up again. "They don't have Napoleonic law here."

"Too bad. So when's your wife coming over?"

"Maybe next year."

"While you're waiting, you can come over and eat at our house. I'm a good cook. You sure I don't know you? I know everyone in Little Saigon."

"I've been here a while."

"Well, we can do business, anyway." She settled her elbows on the edge of his desk. "See, this is the way I work. I get a commission if I sell something. I do a little gambling. I used to be a courier, but that's another story, too long a story to tell you now. Anyway, I've got an American in the Western Club who won't put down a bet without asking me first."

"You must do well."

"Good enough for now. But I'm always figuring. You don't get anywhere unless you do. So if you want to come over and have dinner and meet my sister Vy, maybe she can keep you company till your wife gets here. Vy doesn't pick good boyfriends. Sometimes I tell her, 'Vy, let me pick them,' but she won't listen. Gang boys is what she likes. And gamblers. One stupid guy tried to sell her, you know what I mean? I threw him right out of the house the minute I heard what he was doing. None of her boyfriends have any money. They tell her they do, and then they come and eat our food and don't pay for anything, don't even bring Vy's kids a piece of candy. I always have to pay for every little thing. It drives me bananas how every time Vy gets a new boyfriend, I end up paying for it. She's got no shame. And every single one leaves her with a baby. One stupid boyfriend leaves, she gets another stupid one, and he leaves her with a baby, too. It's expensive, you know, feeding all those kids, worrying about the bills. You got a girlfriend?"

"No." He picked the diamond up again and looked at it a moment before handing it to Anh. "The diamond's no good. The jade bracelets—" He reached into his pocket. "Five hundred for the bracelets."

"Five hundred? Mr. Bui, are you crazy? You know what I think? I think you're as crazy as a baboon. Five hundred? Are you trying to cheat me, or what?"

"Mr. Le. Paul Le."

"Who's he?"

"You called me Mr. Bui."

"You think you're a big shot because you went to France

and learned about Napoleon and can speak English like you were born here."

"It has a flaw. I'm sorry."

"My brother's in a gang. Did I tell you that?"

"No, you didn't."

"Well, he is. I don't know if you know it, Mr. Bui—"

"My name's Le."

"I like the name Bui better. I don't know if you know it, Mr. Bui, but there are bad gangs and good gangs. My brother Thinh's in a bad gang. Very bad gang. I need five thousand to get him out of jail."

"What about the American gambler, the one who won't put down a bet unless he asks you first?"

"Are you trying to be smart, or what?"

"You told me that yourself."

"So what? You think I'm going to shame myself and my family by asking an American for money for bail? You think I'm going to go around telling people I know that Thinh's a no-good rotten kid and I need five thousand to put him on the street again so he can get in some more trouble? You think I'm going to do that?"

"I'm sorry. I didn't mean to insult you."

"So keep your mouth shut, then." She yanked the bracelets away. "Give me those."

"I can let you have a little more, but really—"

"How much more?"

"Three hundred."

"Hah!"

"Four."

"Hah!"

"I'm sorry."

It was the wrong place. How else could she explain it? She had come into the casino, walked past the shoeshiners and down the steps, nodded to the security guard, turned toward the *pai gow* tables, walked straight, straight—it couldn't have been any straighter—toward the table. And he wasn't there. The table was still there. And the dealer, the one who always nodded when she came up behind the American, was looking at her funny.

She went back out to the parking lot and stood between a row of cars looking at the rusted door to her black Mustang. People get sick. She had a cold herself just a few weeks before. Maybe she breathed too close to his face and gave him a cold. Maybe she made a mistake, and she didn't go to the right table. Maybe they changed the dealer to the table, and he was sitting right where he should be sitting, and she didn't see him. Maybe she had walked right past him. He was always there. He hadn't missed a night in six months. She would go back in and find him and tell him she had a problem, tell him Thinh was in jail and she needed to bail him out. Tell him she'd pay him back. Tell him she'd make him rich. Tell him she'd bring him more luck than any man in the world had ever had.

She put her hand out and touched the cold door of her car, then slid down and sat against it, hearing her hose rip, feeling the puddle of oil slide up her legs, feeling her luck, like a satin sheet, slip away. First Ba stole her money, and now Dennis was gone.

~

NGA TU BAY HIEN, 1970

Me's belly and Khanh's grew big at the same time. But Me acted like her swelling was nothing and Khanh's was everything. She told Ba to leave Khanh alone now, not to sleep with her anymore if he wanted the baby to be a boy. Sleep with her, and it will be a no-good girl, she told him.

Me treated Khanh better than a daughter. Better than a sister. She saved the best parts of every meal for her, and wouldn't let her walk too much or help Yony with the cooking. Me was happier about Khanh's swelling belly than her own.

But the war was beginning to ruin everything. There was always a noise in the air now. Helicopters, sirens, gunfire. And more bodies. So many that Manh got tired of drawing them and talked about going to join his brothers in the army, although he was only eleven and was so skinny he could hardly lift Ba's rifle to his shoulder.

The month before Tet began, Me went on a smuggling trip to

Cambodia. When she came back her belly was flat again, and the baskets on the back of her motorcycle were empty. All she would say was that the Communists were everywhere, even in Phnom Penh, but when Anh and Yony brought the buckets of hot water for her bath, Anh saw big black stripe marks on her back and ugly round sores on her stomach like someone had tried to cook dumplings there.

"It was a boy child," Me said when she saw the frightened look on Anh's face. "The ones who beat and raped me weren't even Communists. They wore uniforms just like the one Ba and your brothers wear."

Yony smeared Me's wounds with an herbal paste and wrapped her breasts with strips of white cloth so they would forget the empty womb, but would not lose their youthful fullness.

Anh didn't sleep well after that, but would awake several times during the night to go and stand by Me's bed. Ba slept curled like a bent wire beside her. Oh, Me was stronger than anyone in the whole world. North or south. East or west. No one could conquer Me.

Tet came, and the fighting stopped for a while. Ba wasn't winning much in his games at the Rex Hotel in Saigon. "The more the Americans lose at war, the more they win at cards," he said.

Then Loc, one of Anh's older brothers, came home from the army with one leg and one arm missing.

"It's your fault," Me told Anh. "You've been nothing but bad luck since the day you were born."

Oh, Anh had felt Me's anger before. When Anh dropped the porcelain Buddha Me was going to sell to the antiques dealer in Saigon and broke it into a thousand pieces, Me beat her with a broom. And when Anh didn't wrap the bolts of silk well enough and some of the string untied and the bolts fell off the back of the motorcycle, Me threw her shoes at Anh's head and beat her with her fists. But this was anger without reason. Without logic. A mean anger. Anger that tried to heap all the bad things that had ever happened to the family onto Anh's head. And the closer the time came for Khanh to have her baby, and the scarcer food got in the house, the meaner and angrier Me got. She screeched at Anh, threw shoes and stones at her, talked to her like she didn't even belong to the family.

Then one day when Ba was gone, Me put Anh on the back of the motorcycle and took her to Saigon, to a little house near the bird market.

"I want you to take this girl off my hands," Me told the woman who lived in the house. The woman was not young, but Anh could tell that even though she wore her hair pulled back tight against her skull like an eighty-year-old, she was not much older than Me. The house was clean, with pillows on the floor to sit on and a table with a vase of flowers on it.

"She can clean and do whatever you want," Me said. "I heard you had no children and were looking for one."

"I had a son," the woman replied, and Anh could hear a sad sound in her voice when she said that. "My brother was taking him to our home village in the north, and the truck turned over and my son was killed."

"Aaah," Me said. "You probably want a boy, but I don't have any extra. Loc is thirteen, and a mine exploded and took off his left arm and leg. Vuong is sixteen and Trung is fourteen. They're both in the army, but you won't blame me if I say I wouldn't give them away even if they were here. Boys are valuable. Too bad you lost yours."

"My brother has two sons, and I told him to give me one since he killed mine, but he refused. Can she cook?"

"A little bit."

"I won't pay for school or clothes."

"She doesn't need to go to school. And your old clothes will fit her, I'm sure."

"Why do you want to give her away?"

"Her horoscope is wrong. The fortune-teller told me to give her away when she was born, in 1958. That was when the war started. But my husband wouldn't let me do it."

"Ah, she started the war."

"I wouldn't be surprised."

"What will your husband say when he finds out she's gone?"

"I'll tell him she ran away."

Anh sat on her haunches and stared at the floor the whole time Me was talking to the woman. The woman said her name was Trang, and her husband drove a car for an American general.

"I could use a daughter," Trang said. She came over to where Anh was squatting and stroked the top of Anh's head. "I can feed her. She looks like she doesn't eat much."

"Oh, she doesn't," Me said.

"I would like some money if you're going to leave her here. Food is expensive, no matter how little she eats."

Me gave Trang five thousand dong from the small purse she carried on her belt.

"That isn't much money," Trang said.

"She isn't worth much," Me replied.

Me spoke to Anh once more before she left.

"Obey your elders," she said.

Anh wanted to cry, but she didn't. To cry would have been to show disrespect.

6

*T*he money, Dennis, I need it," Jana said into the hairy ear. "Where is it? What bank? Andy needs it. I need it. My God, Dennis, my folks need it."

Jana was as close to his ear as she could get without entangling herself in the tubes and lines that crisscrossed his body. They ran from left to right, armpit to groin, nose to mouth, navel to chest, everything ending in a bottle or a tube or a hanging bag.

"He can't hear you," the nurse said. It was a male nurse. He looked to Jana like a ballet dancer, sliding gracefully alongside the bed on the balls of his feet, yanking a line here, lifting a bottle there. Or a magician, fluids zooming up one line and down another at the mere touch of his fingers.

"Don't die on me. I've got to know the bank. I'll take care of everything. Just tell me where it is."

"You're talking to the wall," the nurse said.

Sheree, Dennis's wife, a tall blond woman in a square-shouldered gray suit, was at the bedside now. She owned an art gallery in Laguna Beach. Big cotton-awning, dripping-yarn, fuzzy-wool-balls kinds of things meant to hang on corporate walls. Weavings that looked like knitted socks gone wild. Rainbow-glass sculptures of unrecognizable objects rotating beneath spotlights on acrylic stands. Dennis said she never sold enough to pay the rent.

"Is he awake yet?" Sheree said.

Jana bent even closer to Dennis's ear. "I'll keep the office going as long as I can. Clean up some cases. Goddamn it, Dennis, I was depending on you."

"You saw him doing stuff all day," Sheree said. "It's your fault if he dies."

"I've got a kid and no money," Jana said, straightening up. "Don't tell me about whose fault this is."

"You watched him go under and didn't do anything about it."

"Fight outside," the nurse said. "I can't concentrate."

"Is he going to die?" Dennis's mother asked from the doorway. She was wearing the same loose rayon jersey dress she probably wore to church bingo games, a lost look on her face. She had come all the way from New Jersey the day before to stand helplessly in a hospital doorway. She never stepped more than a foot into the room. It was as though she were at the zoo, gazing into the lion's cage.

"Ask the doctor," the nurse replied. "I'm just in charge of tubes and fluids."

"I want what's in the trust account," Sheree said to Jana.

Jana leaned over the bed again. "Did you hear that, Dennis? Where's the trust account? Are you the only one on it? The bills are coming in, I've been piling them on your desk. I didn't know what else to do. You've been sleeping for a week now, and I'm telling you that if you don't wake up soon, I'll kill you myself."

"Are you telling me you don't even know what bank Dennis uses?" Sheree asked. "Didn't you deposit checks, for Chrissakes?"

"If you girls don't stop it," the nurse said.

"He didn't trust me with checks," Jana said. "The bastard didn't even trust me enough to tell me where the bank was."

"Will he die?" his mother asked again.

"My God, how'll I pay the rent on the gallery?" Sheree said.

"If you need me for mornings between nine and eleven, I have a class," the girl said.

She had Andy by the hand and was sitting on the porch watching him play in the sand. Her name was Arleta. Her father had a bait shop on the Balboa pier, and there was the faint odor of fish in the house the first time she baby-sat Andy. She had been his relief baby-sitter before the regular one went back to Mexico.

"Well, how's my big boy?" Jana said.

"*Aquí*, Mama," Andy said, inviting her to sit down on the patch of sand beside him. He sometimes mixed Spanish words with English ones.

"You taste like sand," Jana said, and kissed him. "Mmmm, I love the taste of sand." She looked up at Arleta. "Did he eat lunch?"

"We walked down to the pier and got a taco. You owe me seventy-five cents extra."

"There was cheese in the refrigerator. I distinctly remember telling you that."

"He wanted a taco. If you need me tomorrow, catch me at my dad's before I go to school. I can sit from noon to five, and most evenings, unless I have a date. It's pretty slow in the bait shop this time of year. Evenings I can take Andy with me if it's just a movie, if you don't mind. My boyfriend's a careful driver. Got a few speeding tickets, but he's really a good driver."

Jana and Andy ate Campbell's soup and toast in the darkening kitchen. It was cozy here, looking out the window, with Andy beside her, the old refrigerator humming comfortingly behind her, the waves loud and steady on the other side of the glass. An old Schwinn bike leaned against one wall, stacks of newspapers surrounding it. The papers were, she knew, a fire hazard, being so close to the stove and all, and she had been meaning to move them somewhere else, but had never gotten around to it. She had also thought about throwing them away, and had even started undoing the twine one rainy afternoon, but then started reading them, and changed her mind. She didn't even really need them to remember what they said. She knew exactly the pages where everything written about that time almost four years ago was, every article, what section of which newspaper, what size type the headline was, if it had a byline or not. She had that kind of memory. Telephone numbers, some from as far back as grammar school. License numbers. The numbers on the television screen that said call this number.

"I didn't know you liked tacos," Jana said.

"I like it," Andy said. He had a rim of red tomato soup above his lip and was holding the spoon like a shovel.

"And I like you," Jana said. She reached over and wiped his mouth with a napkin. His eyes were green tonight, not blue. Tim's had been blue.

"I like Teresa," he said.

"Teresa wanted to be with her own children."

"Why?"

"Because they miss her, being so far away in Mexico, without a mommy. I told you that."

"Why?"

Jana felt chilled. A bank of cold fog came up from the ocean when the sun went down. A layer of skimmed sea vapor that swept into the cracks of the old house and didn't leave till morning.

"Her little girl missed her, I told you that. I couldn't leave you. I'd die if I left you."

"Why?"

Sometimes he understood concepts, but not when he was tired. When he was tired, he was just three years old.

They watched *The Little Mermaid* together on the VCR, and then she put him to bed with his stuffed animals and trucks and books. Then she called her mother. She called every night. A good call was one in which her father hadn't done something scary. A good call was her mother complaining about the heat or the cold or the humidity or the dryness.

"So turn down the thermostat," Jana said. "That's what it's for."

"It doesn't work." Her mother's voice was shaky tonight. Sometimes it was smooth. Sometimes it matched her hands.

"It worked when I was there," Jana said.

"I think it's too dry for your father's sinuses. He keeps blowing his nose."

"He always blows his nose. I'll be by tomorrow night with the groceries."

"Tomato sauce, I forgot to tell you. And bar soap. Is everything all right?"

"Everything's fine."

After the phone call, Jana went out on the front porch and sat in the night chill and watched the waves. The cottage couldn't have gotten any closer to the water without washing away at high tide. It was right behind the bicycle path, in a row of wood frame houses the movie people in the 1920s had used for weekend getaways. Floors in the cottage creaked, and the empty clay flowerpots on the front steps were cracked and turning back to sand. The original glass doorknobs had all been stolen by past summer renters, replaced one by one with cheap metal knobs that had quickly turned to rust in the damp air and left brown stains on your hands. Jana could have rented an apartment with a dishwasher and good doorknobs in Balboa, where the surfers hung their towels and wet suits on the balconies. But she liked it here with her back to the ocean. She didn't check doors here to make sure they were locked.

"Oh, shit, what do I do now?" she said aloud.

Dennis might die, the doctor said. Cocaine stopped his heart. He might need dialysis the rest of his life, if he lives. Heart damaged, kidneys damaged. Who knows what it did to his brain? Can he practice law? she asked the doctor. Can he tell me where the bank is? This is a sick man, he replied. Let's just worry about whether he survives.

There were lights from an oil-drilling platform out at sea. Behind that the moonlight picked out faint outlines of Catalina Island. Harebrained ideas had been swirling through her head for days now. Was she willing to take the chance? She could win big or lose everything. Who said that, every action had a reaction? Oh, did she ever know that. Just looking at Andy told her everything she needed to know about that.

7

Law and motion, which courtroom?" Jana had Dennis's brief-case in one hand, her purse over her shoulder, and Andy riding sidesaddle on her hip.

"Over there, the second door on the left," the man said.

She could have asked anyone. The custodian scooping cigarettes out of the sand at the side of the elevator. The woman hurrying past the drinking fountain, arms piled high with files. But she'd asked him. Maybe because he was just handy. Maybe because he was in a suit and had a briefcase in his hand and was walking with such deliberate sureness along the courthouse corridor. And maybe also because he looked like someone who wouldn't take a simple request for directions the wrong way.

"Thanks." He was heading there, too, and stood beside her as the courtroom door opened and everyone who had been waiting outside went in.

"Your first court appearance?" he asked.

"Does it show?"

"A little."

He followed her to a seat and sat down next to her.

"Let the clerk know you're here," he said. "She'll tell you where you are on the list, unless you've already called in."

"It's okay. It'll be a surprise."

He bent his head close to Andy's. "What's your name, tiger?"

"Andy."

"You going to be a lawyer, too?"

The clerk, glasses hanging on a chain beneath her chin, was seated at a desk in front of the courtroom. She stood up as the judge swept in from a side door.

"Rules of my courtroom," the judge began. He looked like a crow with a long neck and arms jutting out of his winged black robes. "There'll be no smoking or spitting or talking out of turn. Wait to be called, and come up to the bench promptly. Be prepared. I have no patience with anyone who's not prepared. And don't waste this court's valuable time in digressions, but get to the point, say what you need to, and make room for the next case."

"Dooley versus Garcia," the clerk said.

Jana felt the pressure of the man's shoulder beside her as he stood up.

"I'm coming, too," she said.

He looked confused. "Isn't this Dennis Morgan's case?"

"Yes."

"Hmm," he said, and held the gate open for her. She still had Andy in her arms.

"Are you in the right place with that child?" the judge asked.

"He's liable to walk away if I put him down," Jana replied.

"Sam Knowlton for the defendant, Your Honor."

"Are you representing the plaintiff, young lady?" the judge asked.

"I am, Your Honor. Jana Galvan from Dennis Morgan's office."

"And where is Mr. Morgan?"

"He had another matter to attend to, Your Honor."

"Highly unusual. The child, I mean."

"My baby-sitter has a class in the mornings."

"I'll make it brief, Your Honor," Sam Knowlton said. "I move for dismissal for failure to answer interrogatories in this case. I spoke to Dennis's—to Mr. Morgan's secretary last week, and she said they were being prepared. I never received them."

"And I'll make it brief, too," Jana said. "I'd like a continuance."

Sam Knowlton turned his head sharply toward Jana. "You can't do that."

"I'm doing it. I want a continuance. It's as simple as that."

"Let me explain something to you," Knowlton said.

"Counsel," the judge said. "That's enough."

"But, Your Honor, I've had no letter requesting a continuance. It's obvious this young lady is unprepared and is stalling for time. On what grounds does she want a continuance?"

"On what grounds?" the judge asked, looking at Jana.

"Poverty."

"Oh, come on," Knowlton said.

"Poverty?" the judge said.

"Your Honor, I'd like to—" Knowlton began.

"Poverty, Your Honor," Jana said. "The plaintiff's too poor to travel to our office, and we couldn't file the necessary papers without her."

"What kind of chickenshit plea is this, Your Honor?" Knowlton said.

"You want a contempt citation, Counsel?" the judge said.

"Sorry."

"All right, then, let's hear Miss Galvan out."

"Miss Dooley's poverty is due to the fact that the defendant ran her off the road on the night of December thirty-first, 1990, forcing her into a ditch and causing her to break both legs," Jana said.

"Goddamn it, I object."

"Counsel, one more time, and that's it," the judge said.

"But she isn't pleading correctly, Your Honor."

"Furthermore," continued Jana, "her poverty is a direct result of the defendant's negligence, Your Honor. Mr. Garcia not only ran Miss Dooley off the road, but he fled the scene, didn't get help for her, when she might have still salvaged those blood vessels that—"

"You just said you had no facts," Knowlton said.

"—were feeding blood to vital nerves and muscles," Jana continued. "Your Honor, Miss Dooley lost her job because of Mr. Garcia's negligence. She can't drive to work because you have to have use of your legs to press down on the gas pedal and brake."

"Very creative," Knowlton said. "I move for dismissal in the case."

Andy was reaching for Sam Knowlton's hand, pulling on his coat sleeve.

"Not now, Andy," Jana said.

"This isn't a nursery," Sam said, and yanked his arm away.

"You were talking baby talk to him a minute ago. Now that you're losing the motion, you hate him."

"I don't hate him."

"Well, my baby-sitter quit. The new one had a class. Sue me."

"Miss Galvan—" the judge said.

"I'm not hard to get along with, Your Honor," Knowlton said.

"You could fool me," Jana said.

"Are you going for a tie, Miss Galvan?" the judge said.

"It was just a comment."

"Keep them to yourself."

"Miss Galvan had the opportunity to call me before this appearance, Your Honor," Knowlton said, "introduce herself, ask me for a continuance. Where was she? Why didn't she? I have to be in Van Nuys in an hour, and I could have spent the time more profitably than writing up a motion to compel and doing all the paperwork and driving over here and—"

"We have witnesses who saw the fleeing car, Your Honor," Jana said. "Witnesses who will testify to the erratic driving of the defendant, witnesses—"

"This isn't the time to argue your case, Counsel," the judge said. "Why didn't Mr. Morgan ask for a continuance before this?"

"A family crisis, Your Honor. Illness. His mother. He had to fly to Boston. I was holding down the fort the best I could, but there are only the two of us, and I admit Mr. Morgan has been a little late in answering pleadings and returning telephone calls, but he's doing the best he can, and so am I. Illness is illness, Your Honor. You know how desperate someone can become when faced with the illness of someone close to them. It makes everything pale in significance. It makes you do things you would never think of doing."

"There's no reason why we couldn't have taken care of this before, Your Honor," Knowlton said, "illness or no illness, crisis or no crisis. A telephone call would have sufficed."

"It was a question of priorities," Jana said.

"I thought you said it was illness," Knowlton said.

"It was. But in order of importance, your telephone calls got by me."

"Well, so—"

"Oh, come on, be nice," Jana said. "Give me a break."

Knowlton was from a good law firm. She knew the firm. She had purposely not called him in advance. What would she have said? Dennis is in the bathroom putting cocaine up his nostrils? I had two years of law school at San Francisco State and then something happened which I can't go into and which changed my life forever, and I didn't finish and I'm not a lawyer and I don't want to go to jail for impersonating one?

"This is really embarrassing, Your Honor," Sam Knowlton was saying. "My client is expecting me to win this thing today. I told him I thought the other side was going to cave, I gave them plenty of time, they didn't have a case, didn't answer pleadings."

Jana shrugged. "I've done my best," she said.

"How long a continuance do you need, Miss Galvan?" the judge asked.

"I don't really think, Your Honor—" Knowlton said.

"Whatever you think's fair, Your Honor," Jana replied.

"That was some pretty bizarre pleading you did in there," Sam Knowlton said. He and Jana were standing in front of the elevator, waiting for the down button to light up.

"I won the continuance, didn't I?" Jana said. "And if you want to continue the fight, I can match ferocious tempers with you any day of the week."

"Your temper doesn't interest me." He kept pressing at the button and looking up at the floor indicator.

"I'm hungry," Andy said, and he squirmed in Jana's arms.

"Look, just don't talk to me, all right?" Knowlton said.

"He's talking to me," Jana said.

"I don't mean the kid, and you know it." He stared at the elevator button for a moment, and then turned and looked straight at her.

"And you're not a lawyer, either."

"Oh, yeah?"

"Dennis Morgan doesn't have any associates. Just a secretary with a kid."

"So I'm not a lawyer. Call the bar. Bring the police. Get out the handcuffs. Why didn't you tell the judge?"

"Tell him what? 'Hey, Judge, this old army buddy of mine, we used to smoke dope together in Vietnam, I dumped the habit and he didn't, and now he's using his secretary to plead his cases'?"

"It would have gotten you on the freeway to Van Nuys in three seconds max."

"Well, I'm not the one who's going to get Dennis Morgan disbarred. I'll let you and him do that all by yourselves."

"Dennis may never do anything again. He's in the hospital with a cocaine overdose. On a ventilator. In a coma."

He stopped pressing the button and looked at her.

"So you bring your kid to court and plead his case on some crazy poverty grounds?"

"He doesn't know what I'm doing. He's in a coma, I told you. And even when he isn't, he's a lousy lawyer. He couldn't have done any better than I did."

"That's it? Your boss is sick so you decide to come down to the courthouse and play lawyer?"

"He owes me money."

"Great. He owes you money. I like that theory, too. I suppose you know that impersonating a lawyer is a felony."

"I'm going to keep his office going till I find out where he's put the money he owes me. I've got an ancient mother and a senile father sitting in a house that the State of California says is in the path of the new Century Freeway. I've got a kid to feed and rent to pay. What have you got?"

"Nothing. Not a thing. But if you're looking in Dennis's direction for money, forget it. He hasn't got any. He borrowed money from me two months ago to pay his office rent."

He knew he was saying something stunning, and as he said it, he looked exultant, the way he might have in the courtroom if he had won the motion.

"I don't believe it," she said.

~

"I found Dad on Hawthorne Boulevard around six-thirty this evening," Jana said, "no clothes on, strolling along sweet as you please."

"It was cold today, too," her brother, Bart, said. He had driven down from Hollywood when he got her call.

"He had a shovel with him," Jana said. "He said he was going to do some gardening. Last week he went for a walk and peed against a tree."

"Probably tried to soften the dirt up so the digging would be easier," Bart said.

"He wouldn't eat his supper. Cried through his bath. It took a Valium, a Xanax, and three aspirins to get him to sleep."

"He's just old," their mother said. She was in her easy chair across the room, facing the dark television, staring at the screen, her hands twitching in her lap. The airplanes were flying low tonight into LAX, the ripply whine of engines periodically vibrating the walls of the old house, rattling the dishes in the cupboards, and making the glass in the windows jingle off-key. "Like you two will be someday."

"We need some help here, Bart," Jana said.

"You mean money?"

"For a start."

"I don't have any. I don't have a job. Ron gives me enough to keep myself up, but other than that—"

Bart had been a fashion model in his twenties and gave it up to keep house for his lover. He was in his forties now, her adored older brother, gloriously handsome and forever young in faded jeans and black leather jacket.

"Mom, what do you want us to do?" he said.

"Nothing. I don't want you to do anything."

"She says that," Jana said, "but I'm the one she calls."

"Next time don't come," her mother said.

"A retirement home," Bart said.

"They won't go," Jana said.

"You go live in one," her mother said.

"Dennis is in a coma," Jana said.

"Jesus," Bart said.

"Drugs. I don't know what's going to happen to him. No one does."

"This is really a bad time for me financially, Jana. I'm not trying to make excuses."

"I pretended to be a lawyer today, went to court. It's a felony. If I get caught, I could go to jail."

"You won't get caught."

"Opposing counsel is a friend of Dennis's. He knew, but he didn't tell the judge."

"They say the first felony is always the hardest."

She pulled her bare feet up onto the edge of the worn easy chair and hugged her knees to her chest. "You should have seen me, Bart, smacking that lawyer back every time he opened his mouth."

"You always did like to fight. Me, I like the easy way."

"How *are* you doing? Is everything all right?"

"Fine, fine."

"Have you—" She glanced over at her mother. "Have you—you know what I'm asking?"

"Ron and I are monogamous."

"Are you sure?"

"I know *I* am. Is anyone ever sure about anyone else?"

"You hear such crazy things."

"What does she need with a husband," their mother said. "First you let them take you out to dinner, then they want to come in the house and the next thing they want to take their shoes off, and before you know it you're in the kitchen with the pots and pans."

"We're not talking about husbands, Ma," Jana said.

He was standing up, jiggling his keys in his pocket, anxious to leave.

They walked out on the porch together, and he put his arm around her.

"I don't know what she's thinking," Jana said. "Sometimes I think she's ashamed because of him. It pulls her down."

"Well, don't let it get you."

"Dennis may have spent all the settlement money he got on his big products liability case."

"You're kidding. How do you know?"

"I don't for sure, but he's been borrowing money to pay the office rent."

"What are you going to do?"

"Weave and dodge and try to keep the train going, and hope he didn't spend all of it."

"Maybe he's just hiding it from the IRS."

"Maybe."

He kissed her cheek, letting his lips stay on her skin a few seconds longer than he usually did.

"I'm sure sorry, Jana."

"I know you are."

"I'd give my right arm."

"I know you would."

"You'll keep the train going. There's no one deserves a break more than you do. With all the bad that's happened to you, there's nothing but good left."

"Do you really think so?"

"I wouldn't say it if I didn't."

8

*I*t was a little street off the driveway. Not an alley exactly. More like the little lanes they had in Saigon. Garages were next door to the apartment houses, so there was a door, a door, then a garage, then a door, a door, a garage. Pickup trucks and fast-looking cars were abandoned at the cul-de-sac at the end of the drive, and every garage door was open. In one of them Anh saw three Vietnamese men watching her. One of them was talking on a cellular phone.

"Keep your guns in your pockets, boys," she said in a joking way, and they grinned at her like they knew her, although she had never been here before.

A man answered Anh's knock.

"I want to see Hon," she told him.

"You from welfare?" The door was barely open, but Anh could see over the man's shoulder to the little girl with the chicken pox sores on her face and the littler girl on the tricycle, and the boy pulling a wagon filled with wood blocks. And she could smell the smell of the new arrivals, the ones who kept their shoes on a shelf by the door and padded barefoot on linoleum floors, the ones who couldn't speak a word of English yet and carried the scent of Vietnam in their pores.

"I'm not from welfare," she said in Vietnamese, and pushed the door inward. "Someone told me, a good friend, that Hon knows her business. I don't believe that stuff, you know? Where is she? Go get her. Tell her Truong Anh is here, maybe she's heard of me."

Anh walked in and didn't take off her shoes, just to show the man she'd been in America a while and was no peasant. He turned and left her sitting on a plastic couch.

"You ought to be outside in the sun," she said to the little boy, and he smiled shyly and pulled the wagon through a beaded curtain into another room. As the beads swung free, Anh saw stacks of material and sewing machines and boxes of hangers. Probably a dining room, but there was no sign of table or chairs. None of the rooms looked American. Except for the plastic couch she was sitting on and the square low table in front of it, she could have been in Vietnam, with the Vietnamese calendar and huge map of Vietnam on the wall. She counted eight Buddhas on the shrine against the opposite wall. Each with its own offering of a bowl of fruit, its own stick of bird-of-paradise in a vase, its own flickering red lightbulb. She had no use for fanatics, and didn't even know why she had come. One Buddha was enough for anyone.

The woman came into the room bowing, her head forward, hands pressed palm to palm.

"Are you called Hon?" Anh asked.

The woman raised her head. "I'm Hon."

"Pham Bao said you were good."

"Ah, Pham Bao," the woman said, and smiled. Pham Bao published a Vietnamese newspaper, a good one, with the best news in it of any paper in Little Saigon. His own story was better than any story he ever wrote. How he left Vietnam on a leaky raft and everyone on it but him died.

"My name's Anh."

The woman went out of the room again, and when she came back, she was carrying paper and pencil and a little book and a deck of cards. She put everything down on the low table, then turned her legs inward and, as though they were scissors, sank cross-legged onto the floor in front of the low table.

"What do you want? I can do signature, palm, cards, horoscope."

"I lost my luck."

"That's a bad thing."

"No one reads palms right. I don't believe in signature reading. I can fool you and turn the loops any way I want. I know how to do it so you'll never know. And my horoscope is always the same. No one can change your horoscope."

The woman's face was round and open, not so much Vietnamese-looking as maybe Mongolian. And she was plump, her body lumpy beneath her loose-fitting rayon dress. Hardly any Vietnamese were plump. Anh herself could eat and eat and eat and lose weight. Sometimes she got up in the middle of the night to eat, she was so hungry, and she never got plump.

There was a ridged scar like a broken zipper beneath Hon's collarbone.

"You get shot?" Anh asked.

"Shrapnel."

"I got one on my leg. See." Anh raised her skirt and pulled her hose tight against the long, straight scar.

Despite the smell in the house, the woman looked clean. Her brown hair was shiny, and her fingernails looked white at the edges. Her teeth were clean, too, with no food sticking in the cracks. Anh was feeling happy to be here, like maybe something good was going to happen.

"Your kids go to school?" Anh said.

"I keep them home with me," Hon replied.

"You send them to school, or they'll never be any good in America." Anh leaned over and talked right into the chicken pox–marked face of the little girl. "You need to go to school, learn how to speak English, learn to get along."

"What day were you born?" Hon said.

"I don't believe in this stuff," Anh said. She looked in her purse and found a package of rice cookies. "For you," she told the little girl, "but you've got to share with the other kids. Don't be selfish. If you're selfish, no one will trust you."

"I can't do your horoscope without your birth date," Hon said.

"Pham Bao said you were the best, and I lost my luck, and what's the difference if I believe in it or not?" Anh said. "May first, 1958."

Hon picked up the book and flipped through it, her eyes close to the pages. "The year of the pig," she said, and began writing on the paper, drawing lines and connecting them to each other with arrows.

"You do that real fast," Anh said, "like you know what you're doing."

"The year of the pig," Hon repeated, looking up at Anh. "It goes fine with the year of the monkey, so you don't have to worry about that."

She laid out the cards faceup and began telling Anh all the things fortune-tellers had always told her. You'll have a good year this year. Bad times are over. You have to be patient, wait for your luck to come back. Anh's happy feeling started to leave her. This woman was the same as all the others. Nothing new to say.

"Shuffle the cards," Hon said, and she handed them to Anh. "Thirteen times."

Anh stared at the eight Buddhas on the shrine, closed her eyes, and shuffled.

Hon took them back and laid them in little piles in a rectangle on the table.

"Ask me questions, and I'll give you the answers," she said.

Anh opened her eyes. The woman was staring at her like she was studying her insides, checking the way her brain sat in her skull, examining how her skeleton fit inside her skin.

"I went back to find my luck in the casino, and he wasn't there," Anh said. "I went back every day for a week, and he never came. My brother's in jail and my money was stolen, and it's up to me to get him out and I don't have a way, and I'd give your little girl twenty-five dollars right this minute, and the other girl over there a hundred, and the boy maybe two hundred, that's how I don't care about money—because what do I care about it, it's nothing but trouble. I only care about it because I need it."

Hon flicked her eyes away for a moment and turned up two cards, a jack of hearts and nine of clubs.

"You're very independent. You take care of things," Hon said.

"How do I get my luck back?"

Hon turned up another pair, the ten of clubs and ten of spades. "You'll have a big business deal this year. Very big. Lots of money."

"With what?"

Hon turned up two more cards, the queen of hearts and seven of diamonds.

"You worry about a woman."

"What are you talking about? Sure I worry about a woman. Me sits watching television all day, and Vy looks at all the magazines with the American faces and high noses and big round eyes." She motioned to the other cards. "Find the American in there, and I'll believe you."

Hon turned up two more cards, two aces.

"Success," she said.

"How?"

"The American."

"I don't see any American in those cards. Where?"

"I charge ten dollars without signature or palm." Hon picked up the cards and the book and paper and rose gracefully to her feet.

"Ten dollars, and you'll have three good years. Everything will go okay. Once in a while you'll get tired, but you'll keep going. All past unhappiness is gone. People will have great respect for you. The jealousy will stop."

~

SAIGON, 1971

The only one Anh missed was her brother Manh. She wondered what he was writing about now, whether his poems were about bombs or birds, or if he was still going out to the paddies, still drawing pictures of corpses. And Ba. She missed Ba, too. Maybe Vy was the baby and everyone thought she was his favorite, but Anh knew he loved her best, and that if he knew Me had given her away, he would have stolen a truck or a jeep or a car, or even a bus, and driven all up and down the rain-soaked roads looking for her. He wouldn't have stopped looking, even if it was a year or two that he had to look. He wouldn't care how long it took him to find her, he loved her that much.

But Anh didn't miss her mother. She had a new mother, a better one. Trang was Anh's mother. She was what Anh dreamed a mother should be. She spoke to Anh in a sweet voice and didn't beat her or scream at her. She showed Anh off to the neighbors, and said how lucky she was to find a girl so pretty and bright, a girl who would stay with her and Duy until they were both old. A girl who, when they couldn't walk or see or hear anymore, would put them in a cart and wheel them around and buy them the tastiest fruits. A girl who, when they died, would put their pictures with the rest of her ancestors.

Me came for her four months after she'd left her.

"A rocket hit the house," she said. "Manh was inside. They killed him. Blew him up. I couldn't even find the pieces."

Trang cried when Anh got on the back of Me's motorcycle.

"You gave her to me," she shouted as Me started up the engine.

Couldn't find the pieces?

"I'm taking her back," Me said. "We have no house now, and we're going to go live with my husband's brother."

"But you promised me. She's going to take care of me and Duy in our old age."

"Well, you've got bad luck then. I changed my mind."

The motorcycle was trembling beneath them, vibrating as though it were alive.

Couldn't find the pieces?

"They bombed the flower market," Me said as they sped through the streets.

"Trang was my mother," Anh said, and Me took one hand off the handlebars and hit her in the face.

"I'm your mother," she said.

"Why didn't Ba find me?"

"He wasn't looking."

They passed the bombed flower market. The awnings were on the ground, and there were flowers everywhere, filling the air with the sweetest smell Anh had ever smelled.

Couldn't find the pieces?

"Anyway," Me said, "Trang's husband Duy is a Vietcong. He works for an American general, but he's Vietcong just the same."

Uncle Kou's house was on the waterfront in Huntington Harbor. A sailboat was moored at his private dock, and Auntie Chi brought tea and kiwifruit tarts and put them on the table beneath a big umbrella. It was a bright day for January, with the sun sparkling like bits of crystal on the quiet water. Out beyond the island, Anh could see the roofs of the stores on Pacific Coast Highway, and then the big swatch of blue ocean, and beyond that, like the smudged outline of a big rock, Catalina Island.

"I won't give you anything that will go to your father," her uncle said. He was thin like Ba, and had the same small features and tiny hands. But he didn't talk like him. He said what he had to real fast, spit his words out as though they were hot and if he let them stay in his mouth too long, they might scald him.

"It's for me," Anh said. "A business deal."

"Look what he did to your mother," Auntie Chi said.

"What kind of business deal?" Uncle Kou asked.

"A fish store," Anh said. "Fresh fish. Some guy owes me three thousand dollars. I could go in partners with him if I bring another ten thousand with me."

"I won't give you any money if it goes to your father," Uncle Kou said.

He owned liquor stores in Westminster and Huntington Beach and had three cars in his garage. Inside his big harbor house the rooms were filled with American furniture and heavy rugs. But he and Auntie Chi slept in a room at the back of the house on a mattress on the floor.

"Look what he did to your mother," Auntie Chi said again.

"If the money is for your father, I won't give it to you," Uncle Kou said. "If it's for your brother to get him out of trouble, I won't give it to you. If it's for your sister and another baby, she can go in the street, I won't give it to you."

"You should see the business the guy does in fish, Uncle. Live fish, lobster, anything you want he's got it. He even sells fish to a big restaurant in Little Saigon, the Last Emperor. You know the one I mean?"

"Maybe he's trying to cheat you, tell you he sells fish there," Auntie Chi said.

"You can go talk to the emperor yourself," Anh said. "I don't lie. How long have you known me? You ever hear me lie to anyone? Go ask the guy at that restaurant, see if I'm telling the truth."

"What do you know about fish?" Uncle Kou said.

"Oh, I hang around there. I know everything about fish."

"Ten thousand?"

"You want to know about fish, just ask me."

Uncle Kou was glaring at her, trying to break her down, but she could feel herself strong inside, harder than he was, needing more than he did. He had to pretend hardness now. He was out of practice. Soft. Soft as a woman. Not like he was when he ran the brothel. Oh, no, he wasn't the same man at all.

"How long you need it for?" Uncle Kou said, and Auntie Chi turned and went in the house, her bare feet soundless on the American floors.

"One year is good," Anh said.

~

"He's gone," the bondsman said. He was looking for Thinh's name in the applications for bail.

"He not gone," Anh said. "I didn't have money to bail him. Look, I got five thousand cash. I'm not trying to trick you. No way. I got the money all right."

"Nope." He was looking at his documents and the cash alternately, like he was sorry her brother really was already gone. She knew he'd have taken her money if Thinh was still in jail. She put it back in her purse and stood up.

"He shoot his way out?" she asked.

"They only do that in the movies," the bondsman said. "But come to think of it, there was a guy went down the waterpipe on a sheet last year."

"Who bail Thinh out, then?"

"You want me to go through the papers again?"

"Don't make me mad."

"Nep Lai's the guy's name."

"The Nep family?"

"Nep Lai is what he said."

"Those guy are big gangster, not little gangster like they got in the Bolsa Gang. You sure?"

"That's what it says. Look for yourself."

Sure enough, there it was, Nep Lai, the leader of the family.

"You saved yourself five thousand dollars," the bondsman said. "You can buy a lot of jade bracelets with that, honey."

9

a wooden sign on the front of the building said Dennis Morgan, Attorney at Law. There was no one in the office, just a piece of paper stuck on the window with Scotch tape. Sorry we missed you. Anh cupped her hands against the glass and tried to see past her reflection into the interior. A bunch of magazines lying haphazardly on a coffee table. Metal filing cabinets. A couple of desks. Papers on the floor. All that money he threw on the table in the casino, and his office looked like he didn't have a dollar.

She walked around to the front of the building, where the seafood restaurant was. It had an open-air patio, with blue canvas chairs and white plastic tables. A great big anchor hung on the wall next to a long-nosed, flat, shiny fish. A man and woman were drinking coffee beneath the flapping umbrellas, and Anh wished she had some hot tea right now; she could feel the bumps on her skin, she was so cold.

There was a Ferris wheel in front of the building on the bay side. Anh stopped and looked through the wire fence at the padded seats. There was no one in them, and the enclosure gate had a big lock on it. Maybe people came here on the weekends. Or in the summertime. She'd find out. Then she'd bring Boy and Little Boy here and let them go up in the sky and hear them scream with happiness. She wouldn't be afraid to put them on a Ferris wheel that was as small as this one. It looked like a toy, not like those big things that made you think if you went up in them, you were going to die.

She went into the cookie store on the corner, next to the carousel.

"You know the lawyer next door?" Anh asked the girl behind the counter.

"What lawyer?"

"You got more than one lawyer on this street? Boy, you must know lot of important people, you don't know you got lawyer in the building over there." She grinned at the girl, who looked like she sampled lots of the big round cookies on the trays in front of her. "A big American guy, skinny like he going to die with something any time you look at him. Maybe heart. Did you hear if he sick maybe?"

"I just sell cookies."

"How much for one of those spotted cookie, the one on that back dish there?"

"Chocolate chip?"

"Are they good?"

"You never had a chocolate chip cookie?"

"Oh, sure, in Malaysia they sell them there in the PX with the apple turndown."

The girl was laughing at her, and it was making Anh angry, so angry she could hardly pull the dollar bill out of her wallet.

"Have a nice day," the girl said.

"Maybe it gonna rain," Anh said, and smiled her way out of the place.

She sat on a bench in front of the carousel for a while and fed the cookie, piece by piece, to the pigeons. It was cold and a weekday, and there were no kids on the painted horses, but they were galloping round and round like they had somewhere to go, with the music turned up so loud, it flew like a dart through the damp air, past the bench where Anh was sitting, over the railing and out into the bay. A ferryboat was coming over from Balboa. It reminded Anh of Vietnam, the flat way it lay in the water. They ran fast for that boat in Saigon that last day, jumping off the truck and running and slipping in the mud to get on board.

She shivered now. She hated the cold. Even the warm cold, like it was in California. And rain. Oh, rain made her so depressed, she wanted to go to bed and forget everything. She hoped she wasn't right when she said it might rain. But there were some clouds in the sky, heavy, dark ones, puffy ones. Rain didn't surprise you in California. It let you know it was coming sometimes days ahead of time, plenty of time to get real depressed and sad.

When the cookie was all gone, she walked along the bay side, looking at the houses across the black water. Balboa. She'd buy one of those houses on Balboa one of these days and put Me in it with her television and videocassettes. She'd put a little playground right in the front lawn for Vy's four boys. She'd go shopping. Oh, she'd bring things from the stores that would make everyone open their eyes and say how successful Anh was, how good she was to her family, how smart for a girl.

She got up and strolled past the cookie place again, and waved at the girl inside, and the girl waved back. Then she went and looked one more time at the building with the wooden sign in front. It had taken almost a month to find him, and she wasn't even sure if this was the one. The cashier at the casino said he thought a lawyer named Morgan was the one she was looking for.

There were two cars parked outside the house. Not right in front, but down a little way, like maybe the drivers didn't exactly know where they were going. Or they didn't want anyone else to know where they were going. Anh didn't recognize either of the cars. She stared at them for a while, and then looked up the walk at the house. It was dark. And quiet. Awful quiet.

And the door was unlocked. She always told Vy, at night keep the door locked, keep the kids inside. You don't know what's going on out in the street—could be bad stuff, could be dangerous. If they try to pry the door open, you've got time to get the gun in my bedroom and shoot their heads off.

The moment she opened the door, she knew that her advice had been good.

"Get her!"

"Jesus!"

"Don't fight!"

"Jesus! My arm. What you doing to my arm?"

"Where is he?"

They had her on the floor now, and there were all kinds of noises.

Kids crying. Vy screaming in Vietnamese. It was too dark to know where anyone was.

"Thinh Truong, where is he?"

"You breaking my arm."

Lights went on, and Anh could see the trouser leg of the man who had her arm pinned behind her. He pulled her head back, and she could see the heavy twill sleeve of his parka. Me was flat on her face on the floor with her arms around Boy, Little Boy, Little Little Boy, and Baby Boy. Vy, in her ratty cotton bathrobe, her hair all soapy—like maybe they caught her in the shower—was next to Me, facedown on the floor, too. Then in the corner was a man. Looked as though he had been knocked out. She couldn't see his face.

"What the hell you doing?" Anh said.

"Police," the man said. "We're looking for Thinh Truong."

There were three other guys with parkas moving through the rooms. Husky ones who filled the house up with just their shoulders.

"They send four big one like you to catch one skinny Vietnamese boy?" Anh said.

"Where is he?" the policeman said.

Another policeman came into the room, and she felt the pressure on her arm ease and then the pulling on her neck stopped, and she fell forward onto the floor. It felt so good to be free of the pain that she wanted to cry. It was like a sweetness, to just hug the dirty floor and feel her breath coming into her mouth without thinking that her neck was going to snap and let all the air out.

The other policeman had a cardboard box in his hands. From the corner of her eye Anh could see all of Me's jewelry in there, and the jade Buddha that Ba had just given to Vy. And the diamond with the big black spot in the middle of it. Even her cheap, fake pearl necklace with the rhodium-that-looked-like-platinum clasp. And the jade bangle that wasn't very good—just nephrite dyed a pretty shade of green.

"I went to the jail and he was gone," she said, and began to cough. The strings in her neck vibrated and burned, and she checked her hand to see if there was blood coming up with her coughs.

"Where to?"

"I don't know where he go." The floor smelled terrible, like old wax and Baby Boy's urine. She could hear doors banging as the policemen went from room to room, and lots of kicking noises, as if they were too lazy to open the closets with their hands. Soon there was a pile of goods next to the front door. A camera. Vy's stereo. Me's Sony TV. Anh's leather jacket with the suede lining.

"Those earrings you're wearing, take 'em off."

"Those earring are mine."

"Might be stolen. Got to check it on the list. In twenty days, if no one claims them, come down to the station and I'll give 'em back."

"I got to sit. I can't do it breathing the floor at the same time. Let me sit and I take 'em off."

"Go on."

"You know you got the wrong place," she said, and dropped the earrings into the cardboard box. "I think you broke something in my neck."

"I don't think so."

He pushed her back onto her face.

"Where'd you get five thousand dollars?" one of the other policemen said. He had her purse open now, and she could see the green edges of her money.

"My uncle."

"I'll bet."

He put her money on the table next to the cardboard box, and when the other three guys weren't looking, he put it in his pocket. Real fast like he was used to doing it. It made her so sick in her stomach watching that money disappear that she almost forgot the pains in her chest and neck. Baby Boy was howling now, a steady howl that she'd never heard out of him before. The other kids were crying, but Baby Boy was screaming so loud, she could hardly think.

"Look what you doing to these kid, making them so afraid," she said. "What the hell you think you doing?"

They had the unconscious man on his feet, slapping his face to get him awake. One of them put him in a chair near the window and came by every few minutes to look into his eyes with a flashlight and ask him if he was okay.

"Whoa, what's this?" One of the policeman had found the gun. She turned her head so she could see him standing in the doorway to the hall. He was holding the butt of the gun with his fingertips, swinging it slightly back and forth in front of his face.

"That gun belong to me," Anh said. "I buy it in the store. You can check."

"A .38? What do you need a .38 for?"

"To shoot any guy come breaking in here, making mess like he at some party or something, pushing us around like we don't matter."

"We'll be back with arrest warrants if it turns out to be stolen."

"You go fuck yourself." She thought maybe that would bring a bullet to her brain. She hoped it would, she felt so ashamed, so full of unhappiness, so angry, so helpless.

The policemen just laughed over that one, as though a Vietnamese girl shouldn't even know American words like that.

"You tell Thinh Truong we're looking for him," the policeman who took her money said. And then they were gone.

But they had left the big vase that stood in the corner next to the door. It was painted to look like an antique, with pictures of Chinese girls in a garden and a Chinese man looking out at them through a window. Talking. Or laughing maybe. Looking happy, anyway. Anh had bought it in a shop in Little Saigon where the jades were serpentine and the diamonds had big black spots in their centers. Anh stared at it from where she was sitting on the floor listening to Baby Boy howl. Then she crawled on all fours over to it and pulled herself up alongside the cold porcelain and stuck her hand down, way down, past where the big, muscled hand of an American policeman could reach, and pulled out the rest of the ten thousand dollars Uncle Kou had given her. Five thousand dollars, it was all there.

Me sat in the middle of the floor of the kitchen, and the little grandkids crawled over her, crying and hanging on to her neck and pulling at her ears.

"You should have got my gun like I told you," Anh told her sister. She had soaked a towel in hot water and wrapped it around her neck.

"I couldn't find it," Vy said. She had her head under the kitchen faucet and was washing the soap out of her hair.

"It has no bullets," Me said.

"Who said it has no bullets?" Anh said. "I bought bullets. Next to my bed in that little green box with all the dots on it, there's bullets in there."

"Bullets in a box don't kill anyone," Vy said.

Anh went into the living room and looked at the man sitting in the chair. It was Mr. Bui—or whatever his name was. Sleeping nicely and, except for the round bump on his forehead, looking as though nothing was wrong with him.

When she went back into the kitchen, Vy was rubbing her wet hair with a towel. She was making bold, angry swipes at her head like she was trying to hurt herself or knock what had just happened out of her mind.

"You know that guy?" Vy said.

"I saw him once," Anh said.

"Bad luck is who he is," Me said.

"He said he wanted to buy that big old diamond you got cheated on," Vy said. "When the police came in, he was sitting on the couch waiting for you. They looked at him, and he said, 'Do you have a paper to come in here? You need a paper,' or something like that. And one of them just, pow, hit him in the face, and he fell off the couch and didn't move. You get me those bullets, I'll go shoot those guys."

"It's too late now," Anh said.

Me rose from the floor slowly. She resembled a trim little tree with kids hanging like leaves from her arms.

"I told you to fix your brother," she said. "You don't listen."

"I went to the jail, and he was already out of there," Anh said. She took Baby Boy and Little Boy in her arms. The weight of them made her eyes burn with pain. "And the police would have come anyway."

"Not if you pay the money," Me said. "It only takes money, and they leave you alone."

"That isn't the way it is here, Me. Here they have their own way."

"Then learn how their way is."

They left Mr. Bui sitting in the chair, just as if he belonged there, just as if he had come over to visit and had fallen asleep in front of the television. Me went into her bedroom and shut the door. Vy went into the bathroom and put her hair up in hot rollers. Anh put the four boys all in the same bed in her room, they were so scared. Then she sat by the window and waited for them to go to sleep. Vy was talking to Baby Boy's father on the telephone. Anh could hear her sister's voice through the walls, speaking Vietnamese, rattling it off like that was all she ever spoke. Anh envied her. It was a mystery how Vy sounded as though she had been born in the States, could speak two languages as if they were both her own, and Anh could speak only one and a half.

Vy was through talking now, and the house was quiet again. Not even the sound of a Chinese video. The police had taken Me's VCR, too. Anh got up and looked at the kids on the bed. They were making little grimaces in their sleep and whimpering. She covered them with the quilt and then went back into the kitchen. Mr. Bui was standing at the sink dousing his head with water from the tap.

"You picked a bad time to come visit me, Mr. Bui. If you told me you were coming, I would have made you good Vietnamese food. Fried shrimp and yam, noodles and pork. This way, I have no time to do it."

He dropped down into a chair, the water running in rivulets from his hair, down his cheeks, and onto the floor.

"You need a doctor?" Anh asked.

"No."

"All those police guys coming in here made me hungry," Anh said. She stood at the open refrigerator, holding the door with one hand and lifting the lids of the pots inside with the other. "We've got noodles and rice, pork bun. We've even got a McDonald's cheese-burger." She reached in and pulled it out. "The kids like Mc-Donald's. They won't eat noodles. French fries and cheeseburgers. Junkie stuff. That's what they like."

She poked her finger into the bun. It was hard and had begun to grow mold around the edges. "It's probably been in there a week," she said, and tossed it in the sink. "Vy doesn't care. Me doesn't care. If I didn't look into the refrigerator, we'd have grass growing in there. How about tea? You want some tea? Cold rice, how about that?"

"No."

She filled the table with food and started ladling gray, congealed, glumpy masses onto a plate.

"It looks bad, but you'll like it. The flavor is better when it's cold like this. The spices get hotter. I'm a very good cook. Ask anyone."

She wiped a pair of chopsticks carefully with a paper napkin and set them down in front of him.

"People have to talk and they have to eat around me, or I don't trust them," she said. "You know what I mean?"

"What did the police want with you? Are you in a gang, too?"

"Me? Are you crazy? There's nothing in this house that I didn't pay for. And if Thinh brings it in, he has to show me a receipt. I don't allow stolen goods in this house, where my sister's kids are living. I don't want them figuring that all you have to do is take what you want and say it belongs to you."

She opened the refrigerator again and looked into a bowl. It was congealed soup. She ran two fingers across the greasy top layer, then put them in her mouth.

"Not bad," she said.

"You said your brother was in jail, that's why you needed money, was to get him out."

"Oh, he got out all right. You want some soup? I can heat it in a minute."

"I came over here to help you."

"You've got a wife. Help her. I don't need it."

When the soup was steaming hot, she ladled some into a bowl and put it in front of him. "Eat it while it's hot. Everything else tastes good cold, but soup tastes like soap if you don't eat it when it's hot."

He lifted the bowl to his mouth, and it made Anh feel good to see him do it. He knew about Napoleon and had gone to school in France, but he was Vietnamese and didn't need a spoon to eat his soup.

"It isn't my fault you got hit," she said. "What are you doing here, anyway?"

"I was going to buy that diamond from you."

"You said it wasn't worth much." She shrugged. "Good thing, too. The police have it now."

"Do you think he'll show up here—your brother?"

"Not if I stop him first."

She sat down and watched him eat.

"I thought maybe those police guys were going to kill me," she said. "They pulled my neck so hard, it almost broke off."

He put his chopsticks down and stared at her.

"I could kill somebody," he said. "I could kill somebody."

"Oh, you don't have to do that. I'm all right now. Maybe tomorrow I won't be able to turn my head around, but I'm okay now. I still have a head on top of my neck, and that's the important thing."

"They shouldn't have done it. You aren't to blame for what your brother does. You aren't to blame for anything." His face was all hot now, as if some of the steam inside him was leaking out. "You didn't know he was stealing, did you?"

"Not right away. Oh, he fooled me all right. He'd bring things home and say, 'I got it from my friend.' Maybe it was a toaster or something. So I said okay, he's got a friend who gave him a toaster. Then he brings a computer in the house and says, 'I know this guy who works in a plant making computers.' What am I going to do when he tells me that? You ever seen a Vietnamese boy, how mad he gets when his sister tries to tell him something?

"So one day he brings in a TV with the carton and everything and says, 'I bought it at the swap meet.' I'm not stupid. I know every trick. Every single trick.

"I decide to follow him, see where he goes. I follow him to a coffee shop and wait outside for him to come out. When he comes out, he's got a bunch of guys from the Bolsa Gang with him. They get in a big green van with windows that curve all around. I once took a ride in a van like that. It made me sick the way that window curved around and fooled my eyes into thinking I was going around in a circle.

"It was a crazy night that night, raining so hard I almost couldn't see to follow where they were going. They went all the way to Santa Ana, to a house on some big street—something like Bolsa Boulevard—you know where that is, up near Harbor Boulevard—there aren't any stores over there or anything, no fields, and the trees aren't too big, like maybe they planted them not too long ago. Even in the rain I could tell it was a nice house.

"The gang boys got out and went into the house. In a little bit they came out again—running out—their arms all full of stuff. Televisions and VCRs. One of them was even carrying a kitchen table, holding it up over his head like he was trying to keep the rain off him. Then Thinh came out, too, and he helped shove that big table into the back of the van.

"I let them drive away. I figured to myself, I don't have to get killed here. They're liable to shoot me and shove me into the van with the table.

"I went home, and the next day I went into Thinh's room. Little Boy and Little Little Boy sleep in the room with Thinh. The other two sleep with me. Vy doesn't like kids too much. She has them, but she doesn't like them.

" 'Thinh,' I said to him, 'did you hurt someone?'

" 'No,' he said, and he smiled at me. That smile made me so mad, I hit him. I never hit him before. That was the first time. And he let me do it, didn't try to hit me back, or anything like that. So then I knew he was going to listen to me.

"I took him by the arms, and I squeezed him so tight I left marks on his skin, and I told him, 'If you bring anything—computers, TVs, kitchen tables—anything in this house and tell me you got it at the swap meet, I'll take you to the police myself.' How do you like the soup, Mr. Bui?"

She dipped some fish sauce into his soup without waiting for an answer and stirred it around with a chopstick.

"It's very good," he said, and lifted the bowl to his mouth again.

"I told you I'm a good cook. I could have been a chef in Vietnam if I'd wanted to. Everyone says I learn things faster than anyone. But tonight wasn't a good night for you to come here."

"You should make a complaint. You have rights."

"You're so funny," she said, and got up from the table to put some water and rice in the electric steamer.

"I get so hungry at night," she said. She twisted the knob, and nothing happened. "The damn thing's broken."

"Maybe it's just loose. Here, let me take a look at it."

She stepped back to let Mr. Bui look at the pot.

"Thinh usually fixes electric things for me," she said. "I'm good at everything but electricity."

Anh watched while Mr. Bui twirled the knob around, and then the light went on, and the steamer made a gurgling sound.

"You know," she said, "sometimes when I'm sleeping, I dream about eating, and I feel so bad because I'm thinking about all those people who died on that boat the last day because they were hungry. Do you ever feel that way? Ashamed because you're hungry?"

"No."

"When we first got to the U.S., I wouldn't eat anything. I said to Me, 'I'm going to give all my money away to other people, let them eat.' It was a terrible feeling. I had it for a long time. I stopped thinking that way when I saw my bones starting to stick out of my skin. Oh, look how good you eat. Your head must be okay now."

She sat down again.

"You know, I'm telling you about Thinh because you don't care, but in case you do, I want you to know he's really a good boy. There's nothing wrong with Thinh. All those other boys come to the U.S. with no one to help them or show them the right way to act. No one tells them what the Americans want, how to go to school, how to get a job, all that stuff. But Thinh has me. He knows he has me. I won't let him down. I tell him all the time, forget you're Vietnamese, pretend you're an American. But it's hard. You know in Vietnam Ba and Me told me what to do, and I listened. I always listened. If you don't respect your elders, no one's going to respect and take care of you when you're old. It's different here. It's not Thinh's fault."

"If he thought about you, he wouldn't do what he does. I have three sons. All of them good boys. None of them are in a gang. None of them are in trouble. It doesn't have to be the way you say."

"You have three good sons, huh?"

"And a good daughter. No trouble at all from any of them."

She sat at the table and swung her leg up and down. It felt good just sitting there doing nothing, swinging, swinging, swinging her leg, and thinking about Mr. Bui's good kids.

Finally she said, "I had a snake in Vietnam. You know, one of those big long ones. They don't eat you or squeeze you when they're little. They're so pretty and smooth. I kept him wrapped around my neck, even when I was sleeping. And then one day, I don't even remember when, he bit me." She put her hand out on the table next to the plate of noodles. "Right there, that mark there. See it, that red spot on the thumb?"

"I see it."

She took her hand away, he was staring at it so funny. "That snake killed me," she said. "I died. Me said I did. She said my skin turned the color of a dead girl's skin. She took me to a lady who said she had seen the Virgin Mary in a grain of rice. She brought me back to life."

He shook his head. "I like to listen to you. It makes me forget everything just to listen to you."

"Uh-huh." Anh bounced her leg a few more times and stared at the empty soup bowl. "I don't believe in fortune-tellers or superstitions, you know, stuff like that. Oh, sometimes I go to the fortune-teller and ask her a few questions, but I don't believe in it, I don't really listen to what she says. But Me said my skin turned back to the right color right while I was there in the room with the lady."

"Maybe you'll let me come back again."

"They said she cured a woman with cancer."

"Maybe I can help you."

There were globules of fat left in the soup bowl, and a few grains of rice. "For a long time—months and months—I kept looking, looking, looking for the Virgin Mary's face every time I ate a bowl of rice."

"I don't think you were dead."

"Well, if I was, I don't remember any of it."

10

*O*oh, so cold down here by the water. I been sitting in that old car and eating all those spotted cookie and freezing waiting for you." Anh was in the door before Jana knew it, pulling a paper cup from the Sparkletts dispenser and pouring water into it and grinning, all at the same time.

"Who are you?"

"Truong Anh. Call me Anh."

She was wandering around the office looking at magazines, sipping water, picking up scraps of paper, glancing at them, then tossing them on the floor next to stacks of files and toys that Andy had played with over the weekend. She stepped behind Jana's desk and looked over her shoulder at the open tort book. She even glanced at the papers on the desk.

"I'm looking for some guy Dennis Morgan." She was at the wall now, looking at Dennis's certificates. She turned toward Jana again.

"You got kid, I could tell. Kid like to leave crap lay around, all this Tinker Toy and junk. I got four nephew, and I tell them, you want to play Tinker Toy, you pick 'em up when you through. You take your kid on that Ferris wheel out there?"

"We don't have a client named Truong. What do you want Mr. Morgan for?"

"This place such mess, I could bury you here one week, you wouldn't know."

Jana was on her feet now. In control. Sort of. The girl—maybe she was a woman—it was hard to tell with Orientals—had surprised her, the way she came in, like a wind off the bay, pushing the door open and talking fast.

"We don't need any magazines. I don't want any insurance. Mr. Morgan isn't here. If he was here, he'd say no to anything you're selling." Jana tried to maneuver her back toward the door, but the girl kept slipping away. She knew how to move. Jana had sold cemetery plots for a short time when she was in law school, and this girl knew the tricks. Keep moving. Keep talking.

"I seen you once or twice when I come here looking for him. You got toothpick? I got something in my teeth. Those nut they put in the cookie, my teeth close together, catch all kind of crap in there. I don't like popcorn, either. I eat just little bit American food. You ever eat Vietnamese?"

"I don't have any toothpicks. There's a drugstore on the corner."

"You messier than my sister and her four kid. They got stuff everywhere. I tell them and tell them, keep the place clean, it give me headache to see crap all over."

She had dropped to her knees and was picking up papers off the floor and stacking them on Jana's desk.

"Don't do that," Jana said, suddenly, unreasonably angry. "Leave everything just where it is. I know where every single thing is."

She was straightening files out on the floor now, smoothing loose papers into place.

Jana pulled at her arm. "I said *leave things alone.*"

"I guess you like crap around you." Anh stood up and faced Jana. "See, I do business with people. Everyone in Little Saigon know me." She tapped her right forefinger to her temple. "Thinking. That my job, thinking. I like to clean stuff, too. Like this place, it terrible how dirty it is. How come you let it get so dirty?" She made a face. "You can't have client come in and see this shit, it make them sick. And look at how you dress."

She was in Jana's line of sight, right in front of her desk, a skinny Vietnamese girl whose skirt waistband was loose around her middle.

"You selling cemetery plots?"

"Me?"

"You."

"No way. I don't sell stuff like that." Anh pulled out a card and handed it to Jana. "See that. My name. Truong Anh."

Jana glanced at the card and then flipped it onto the desk. "So?"

"Little Saigon—it really Westminster. Garden Grove there some Vietnamese, but not too much like Westminster. Shoe, purse, dress, jewelry—I got connection everywhere in Little Saigon—you need it, I get it for you. I don't charge much. Sometime nothing. Depend. You look all stressed up. You got headache? When I'm hungry I get headache. Some people, their stomach hurt, but my head is the one. Vietnamese food is good, you ought to try it once or twice. Not like Chinese—Vietnamese you got all those vegetable and fish sauce—"

"Please. Please." Jana could feel her teeth tightening in her jaw, feel the little pulse in her forehead vibrating.

"See, I used to go to the casino, and I doing all right, betting little bit, bringing little bit luck to some of those guy for a few dollar. Then this American come in, and I shoeshine him, tell him how good he play, how smart he is, tell him what card he got to play, how to do it, when, all that stuff. I never seen anyone throw money away before like he done it.

"He look sick to me all those week he was playing so big, putting so much money on the table, tipping me so much I thought I could get rich. He use cocaine whole lot. Big gambler. Bigger than those Vietnamese guy, or those Cambodian guy. They like to gamble, but he, seem like he like to lose."

Jana's legs suddenly felt weak. She sat back down in the chair. The money Dennis got on the toes case. He hadn't hidden it away from the IRS. It wasn't in some Swiss bank account. He had gambled it all away. Every bit of it. Everything.

"You don't dress like lawyer. You always wear pant like that? That T-shirt make you look like little girl. Who listen to little girl in T-shirt? You don't look too busy to me. I been looking in your window little bit. I hardly see people in here. You want client believe what you tell him, you got to make him think you got money. Everybody know that. You ever been to Nordstrom?"

Jana shook her head.

"You oughtta go. They got good clothe on sale all the time. See this skirt. Oscar la Renta. On sale. Forty buck. Smell this perfume. Giorgio. The real stuff. No fake. I don't buy fake perfume. Smell like old fish after one hour. Little Saigon, I take you there, you won't believe it. Really, that the true story."

Jana got up and crossed to the door. She held it open, breathing in the cool air. "I thought there was money left."

"Sick. He look real sick to me. He eat all that meat and doughnut. All those big potato with lumpy butter. I don't know why he like it so much, it taste like paper smear with oil to me. No flavor. I tell him I bring him some good food. One time I cook up a soup of dry radish and lotus seed. I put some ginseng in there, and I tell him, you drink this, you won't need coke no more. He wouldn't do it. You take your kid on that Ferris wheel outside?"

Jana nodded her head.

"I don't like to go up too high, but Boy and Little Boy, they like to get scary, so I always looking for thing to make them scary. But not kill them. You know what I mean?"

"I know what you mean."

"One time I bring Dennis tea—special tea—cost one hundred sixty buck a pound. From a tree that got only a few leave on it, and it make you strong and healthy. I told him, you drink this in the morning, not at night, or you be up, wide eye. It better than coke, I told him. He never did drink it. He didn't like me much. I could tell."

She was wandering again, prowling catlike in front of the window, her gaze directed at the island across the bay. "All those pretty house over there. I'm going to buy one of those when I get my luck back." She turned and looked at Jana, a straight-ahead look. Fearless.

"Where is he?" she said.

The cafe was next door to the Balboa Theater, just across the street from Dennis's office, on the ocean side of the highway, where the T-shirt store was and the surf shop and the bicycle rentals. It wasn't noon yet, but a few of the locals were already at the tables, reading newspapers and waiting for the chickens to be done. The guy cooking the chickens had a tall, stained white hat on, and was turning chickens and slapping mayonnaise on slices of white bread.

"I've been looking for a trust account," Jana said, "hoping he had money somewhere."

"He spend it at the casino," Anh said. "Quit looking."

"How do you know it's Dennis?"

"I know. He take my luck. If I don't get it back, my life is shit."

They were drinking thick black coffee that moved like syrup in the brown mugs. Anh had poured six teaspoons of sugar into hers and then stirred and stirred it without even taking a sip.

"So Dennis take my luck and take your money," Anh said. "You pretty mad at him, huh?"

"I didn't think of gambling. He never gambled before. I thought there was an account somewhere with money in it. The only thing I could never figure out was why he was always looking for money when he had a million dollars in his pocket."

"He gamble every night. Six month he was there gambling. He give me some good money, too."

"Oh, shit."

They sat and stared at each other now. Jana opened her mouth a few times to say something, then didn't. Anh just swung her leg back and forth against the table.

"Do you have to shake your leg like that?" Jana said. "It makes me nervous."

"I think you nervous anyway. So you got some client left in that office make you some money?"

Jana could barely make out the block letters on the old marquee through the cafe windows, the glass was so smoked and greased by the cut-up chickens sizzling on the grill next to the front door. Rocky Horror Show Friday Night, the marquee said. There was a Rocky Horror Show every Friday night. Everyone knew that. Why did they have to put it on the marquee when everyone knew that? Why did she feel so irritated by this girl? Or woman. She was a woman, after all, no question about it. Why didn't she shut up? Why did she keep offering herself up like some goddamned dog? Why didn't she stop her incessant talking? About nothing. About everything. Why didn't she stop? Just stop.

"It's none of your business how many clients there are," Jana said.

"You crack me up with that mean look you got. You always so mean?"

"I'm not mean."

"I seen mean people before. Your brother been in Vietnam?"

"What?"

"Sometime when American act funny with me, their brother was in Vietnam. Or maybe their father."

"Dennis is the only one I know who was ever in Vietnam."

"So you just the same as Dennis. You don't like Vietnamese people."

"No, there aren't many clients. There never have been many clients. Dennis is a lousy lawyer."

"What about you? You lousy, too?"

"This is about Dennis, not me."

"You keep the money that come in the office?"

"Dennis has a wife. Sheree. She gives me a salary for keeping the office open and running the cases."

"Tall lady with big feet and hair up high on her head?"

"Yes."

"I seen her. I told you, I been—"

"Looking in the window."

"You give her the money?"

"I said I did."

"Ah."

Anh's leg was shaking against the table again. Jana glanced at it, and Anh clapped her hands against her knees. "You ever been in South Dakota?"

"Once."

"South Dakota, Sioux Fall?"

"Once. The guy I was with was in a hurry. I didn't see much of Sioux Falls. We weren't sightseeing."

"Lutheran people in Sioux Fall bring us over from Malaysia camp. Sponsor us. That the way we get here. Pretty lucky, huh?"

"It was snowing the time I was in Sioux Falls, and we didn't have chains."

"The way Dennis eat make me crazy. He gamble and eat at the same time, right there at the table with the card and the money. Push the food into his mouth, don't take time even to taste it. We have PX in Malaysia, and they got all that kind of food, but the GI the only one eat the stuff they got there."

"We were there in the middle of a blizzard. The guy I was with didn't have time to put chains on the tires even if he'd had time to buy them. He was heading for someplace he knew about. He didn't tell me where it was. I had no say in the matter, anyhow."

"We eat candy bar. Babe Ruth. I like Babe Ruth. Snicker bar. Peanut butter. Stuff like that. Who was this guy you was in Sioux Fall with?"

"My husband's murderer. He was running away. He took me with him."

"I like California better than Sioux Fall, anyhow."

Jana went up to the counter and got the coffeepot and came back and refilled their cups.

"This coffee taste like car oil to me," Anh said. "If you give the money to Dennis wife, what you get out of it?"

"I thought I'd run the office while he was sick and then when he recovered he'd pay me back."

"Hah! Dennis don't give fuck for you—not for me, either."

The cafe was filling up now. The cook kept looking over at the table where Anh and Jana were sitting.

"Let's go. We're taking up space."

"Maybe the cook has brother was in Vietnam," Anh said, and picked up the check.

"Give that to me."

"I ask you to have coffee. In my country, if you ask, you pay."

They walked outside and stood on the sidewalk.

"The sun's trying to come out," Jana said.

"I hate cold," Anh said.

"Sure."

"I hate it."

"Sure."

"Your husband was murdered, huh?"

"Yes."

They started back toward the office. Pedestrians and bicyclists had come out with the sun. Skateboarders, wheels clacking down the boardwalk, zipped in and out among them.

When they reached the office, Jana unlocked the door.

"You want to come in?"

"No, no. I got lotta thing to do."

"I'm not prejudiced. I'm Jewish. I don't have any opinion or feeling one way or the other about Vietnamese people. You came in talking so fast, I wasn't expecting it. I don't like strangers much. I like to know all about the people I'm dealing with. I like to know where I stand. I like to be comfortable, figure out things in advance. And then telling me about Dennis when I wasn't expecting anything like that. I knew about the drugs. I knew he was a spender, liked expensive things. But I had it figured out from what he was spending that he should still have at least half a million left out of the settlement. And all those cases he sold out, like he was so hungry for money, I just didn't think about him losing it gambling—I just didn't think of it. Okay. Okay. So now I know there's no account. I won't drive Sheree crazy looking for it. No money left. All gone. I'll get used to the idea."

Anh was looking at her strangely, her head tilted sideways, as though she could see her better on an angle.

"I can tell right away when I look at someone what they are inside," Anh said. "Maybe we can do business."

"You want to sell dresses out of the office here?"

"You ever eat rat?"

"God, no."

"Taste like dog. I'm serious."

"I'm sure you are."

"Dennis a rat. Maybe we cook him. Not eat him. Just cook him little bit. Use his name, start law business. I know everybody in Little Saigon. You need something, anything, I get it for you. Cheap, too. Everybody know me. I can bring client in, you won't believe how many client I bring in." She pulled at the collar of her silk blouse to show Jana the two large brown circles on her neck. "The police guy did that to me. Came in my house and beat me and my family up and took five thousand of Uncle Kou money. Some jade and TV and other stuff, too. Make me mad. I want that stuff back. I want that police guy."

"I'm not a lawyer."

Anh straightened her collar across her neck and smiled. "So?"

11

They had brought the crane in from a construction site and rolled it right down the main street of the cemetery and up the hill where the meditation garden was, then parked it so the BMW hung from boom and cable over the open grave. The car was slung upright, a winged chariot swinging as gently as a minnow above the maw of a shark. Anh left her car in the lot where the gilded Buddha sat and walked up the small hill toward the crane. There were at least two hundred mourners there, most of them in white, and Anh knew just about every one of them.

"Hey, I haven't seen you in a long time," she said to the lady who sold knockoff designer purses in the Bolsa Mall.

"I've been busy," the woman said.

"I'm never too busy for a friend," Anh said, and handed the woman some business cards. "Put them on the counter where people can see them."

Someone with a video camera was taking pictures of the car. Anh could see the corpse sitting in the driver's seat with his hands on the steering wheel.

"*Chào Anh.*" An old lady in sandals and trousers peered at Anh from beneath a black umbrella. Her son owned the Viet Gardens Trailer Park on Brookhurst.

"*Chào bà,*" Anh answered back. "Hey, you need a ride to the doctor, give me a call."

"Where is your mother?"

"Watching television. She doesn't do anything but eat and watch television. You give me a call if you need a ride, don't forget."

She was close enough to see the red carnation in the lapel of the corpse's gray tuxedo. He looked so natural sitting there that she expected him to start the engine up and drive away.

"Hey, if you've got a problem finding someone to watch your kids, bring them over to my house, my sister will watch them for you," Anh said to the woman who ran the herb shop on Newland. "I don't know how you work in there with all those kids running around you. It's not too good little kids smelling that stink all day, anyway. How do you like this funeral? Pretty good, huh? Bury a whole car for one gang boy?"

There were flowers everywhere. On the grass, on the hood of the BMW. There were standing flowers at each corner of the grave.

"Promise you'll call me when you're ready for customers," Anh said to the round-faced girl whose family had just opened a bakery on Asian Way. "I know people who eat doughnuts for breakfast, lunch, and dinner. They wake up at night and go in the kitchen looking for doughnuts, they love them so much." She gave the girl a handful of business cards. "Don't forget."

The corpse's eyes were partly open, as though he were dozing, or maybe bored by the whole thing. Mrs. Nep, the corpse's mother, was standing beside the car. She had her arm stuck through the open window and was combing her dead son's hair.

"Did you take care of that guy I sent to you?" Anh said to the man from the cleaning store on Magnolia and Bolsa. "He needed cleaning bad. I never saw a suit have so many spots as that guy's did. I told him you'd give him a good deal."

She had reached the car now.

"*Chào bà Nep*," Anh said. She bowed and then put her hand in next to Mrs. Nep's and fingered the satin collar of the corpse's gray suit.

"Bad suit," Anh said. "You need another funeral suit, you call me, I'll get it for you cheap. And a good job, too, nothing like this shit. See these stitches. Lousy. Bad work. The place I'm going to take you, you won't believe how good a job they do."

The mother took her arm out of the car to blow her nose into the handkerchief she had wadded in her hand.

"Well, don't cry," Anh said. "He looks pretty good, anyway, even in that lousy suit."

Mrs. Nep let out a loud wail, and four of her other sons rushed toward the car and pushed Anh away.

"Hey, this is a free cemetery," she said. She pointed to the BMW. "Nice car."

"It was his favorite," Nep Lai said. He was tall for a Vietnamese, and his white tuxedo hung on his thin frame as though it had been made for someone else. He was the oldest brother and, everyone said, the most vicious.

"It's a big waste you putting that car in the ground," Anh said. "I could use that car. Mine is all banged up, and something's wrong inside, knock, knock, knock, so I can't hear when the radio's playing. Thinh used to fix it, and now I've got to take it to some tricky Vietnamese guy and pay an arm and leg, and it still won't run right." She looked around her. "I heard my brother was going to be here. I heard you got him out of jail. So where is he, anyway?"

"You going to make trouble here?" Nep Lai said.

"He's my brother. What trouble is that? Hey, you need anything, you call me. You know, I know people. You heard that before, didn't you?"

"I heard you're no good."

"My brother said that?"

Anh could see Thinh through the crowd now. He was standing with some boys on the other side of the crane, where the overnight rain had turned the mounded dirt as shiny as beaten eggs.

"Well, you call me," she said. "Maybe we'll do business." She was backing away as she spoke, smiling, inclining her shoulders, trying to show him she was submissive, not trouble like he thought.

"What are you doing here?" Thinh said when she reached him. He was wearing a white tuxedo and a frilly shirt, the same kind of suit the Nep brothers were wearing. And he had let his hair grow long and wore a jade stud in one ear.

"I'm at this gang boy's funeral," Anh said. "The guy died, didn't he? Bang! Shot in the head. They did a good job fixing the hole. What did they put in there? Cement? Maybe bread dough, and then they baked it in the oven. Looks like a pretty good job to me. But the suit. I don't like the suit."

"You better not hit me here in front of everyone. You better not."

"Oh, I won't do that. These guys have all kinds of guns, and now that you're a big gang boy yourself you can hold me down so they can aim better."

"She's gonna beat you up, Thinh," one of the other boys said.

"She likes to talk. I let her. I don't care."

"Don't let them mess my head up when they shoot me, Thinh," Anh said. "I don't want bread dough fixing the holes in my head." She put a finger on her left breast. "Here's where it ought to go. I've got a dress that will cover any hole you make up to my neck, so don't worry."

"You're crazy." He was looking around him, kicking the wet dirt with his shiny patent leather shoes, as if embarrassed at the way she was talking. "I don't have to listen to you anymore. I can do what I want. You go boss Vy's kids around. I'm out of it."

"She looks like a gang girl to me," one of the boys said. "She can go in my car anytime. I've got good dope, we'll have a party."

"I went looking for you in jail," Anh said. She had hold of the frilly bib of Thinh's shirt and was examining the material.

"Watch it," he said. "You tear it, you'll eat it. I paid a hundred bucks for this shirt."

Anh kept her hand on the material, even gave it an extra tug.

"You're so stupid. You paid a hundred bucks for this piece of crap when I can get you a shirt from Rodeo Drive, Beverly Hills, a two-hundred-dollar shirt marked down to forty bucks."

"They're not the same."

The boys were laughing real loud now. Anh let go of Thinh's shirtfront, but she moved her face closer to his, so close it looked as though she were going to bite his cheek.

"I had the money from Uncle Kou, five thousand to waste bailing you out, and you weren't even there," she said.

"I'm with the Nep family now."

"They going to feed you and buy you clothes and all that stuff?"

"What do you think?"

"I think you're rotten, that's what I think. Why didn't you join the Cheap Boys or the Bolsa Gang or the Santa Ana Boys? Why pick a gang worse than the Mafia?"

"Lai says I'm smart. He likes me."

"Oh, that cracks me up. He likes you." She gave him a punch in the side of his chest with her elbow. "The police came looking for you and took everything in our house, including Me's TV and her VCR. I bought her a new one. You owe me eight hundred bucks."

Thinh took his wallet out of his pocket and peeled off four one-hundred-dollar bills.

"And they took some of my dresses and a skirt that still had the price tag on it."

"I need the rest," he said, and put his wallet back in his pocket. "I've got expenses."

A Buddhist monk, in yellow cotton linen robes and shaved head, had arrived and was chanting at the edge of the grave, a nice, sing-songy sound, while the crane lowered the BMW bit by bit into the pit. The car was nearly entirely in the grave now, only the roof and the corpse's head showing.

"Look how that dead guy's trying to see over the door," Anh said. "Could be you, you know."

"Tell Me I'll be coming to see her maybe next week. I'll bring her a new video."

"That's why I came looking for you, to tell you I don't want you coming around anymore."

He looked startled.

"That's what I said. I've got little kids in that house, so I don't want you coming around anymore. Never. Never, never, never."

He cleared his throat, but his voice was still wavery when he spoke. "I can see my family. It's my family. You can't keep me away."

"You've got the Nep family now. You told me that. Didn't you just tell me that?"

A white Honda was coming up the path now, its top covered in a wreath of white roses.

"When you're ready to go back to school and you're ready to promise me you'll be a good boy, do what I say, then you can come home. Everything's waiting for you when you come. But if you stay in the Nep gang, you're dead, don't call me, don't come running if you're in trouble. Don't try to see Vy's kids or talk to them on the telephone or tell them anything about what you're doing, because I've got a gun and I can shoot you myself."

The white Honda was slowing as it rounded the hill.

"Hmm, all of Little Saigon is here today," Anh said. "Everyone likes a good funeral."

"Me wants me home. You can't tell me I can't come home and see her."

"I tell you what to do, not Me." Anh's voice was hard so he'd know she meant it.

The monk stopped singing. Mrs. Nep stopped wailing. Only the sound of the crane cranking its load could be heard. And then the door to the Honda opened. For a moment, Anh thought she was in a dream. Or a movie.

"Are those your crazy bastard friends?" Anh said as machine gun fire skittered across the wet grass. But Thinh was gone, running, running, running. Everyone was running, or crawling along the ground, trying to hide behind pots of flowers and slabs of marble. People were jumping right into the grave. Splat! Right into the rainwater from the night before. They jumped and fell and dived right onto the roof of the shiny BMW. They lay flat in the flowers and hugged tight to the BMW's chrome trim and tried to conceal themselves under each other. They tumbled through the car's windows and piled onto the seat beside the corpse. The corpse looked like it was dancing, so many people were lifting it, shoving it, pushing it. Anh just stood and watched and listened to the mechanical sound of the machine gun. There was no use running. She was in a graveyard and her luck was bad. If they shot her, she'd just crawl over to the hole and drop herself in with the rest of the people. Save Me all that money putting her into the ground.

"Hey, you guys, you gonna kill me, or what?" she shouted at the open door of the Honda as bullets beat the grass up around her feet.

Then she heard the police sirens, and the Honda's door slammed shut, and the car squealed away, and the grass turned quiet, and she was still standing. It hadn't taken more than two minutes.

"Who started this?" Big American policemen were climbing out of their cars, helping people out of the grave, tending to the wounded. It looked like a battlefield, all trampled grass and bloody shoes.

"Hey, you, where you going?"

The policeman was calling after her, but she didn't stop. The time to run was now. Not before, when her luck was bad. It didn't matter what you did when your luck was bad.

She ran out the cemetery gate, past her car, and kept running along the sidewalk, full of happiness. She had looked into the nose of a machine gun and lived. She had stood there and seen people fall around her. Oh, what a day. There was no mistake. Her good luck was back.

∽

"I can smell Ba in here," Anh said. Her mother was in her chair watching her new TV.

"He was here," Me said. "Then he went. Where have you been all day?"

"I went to a funeral. Where's Vy?"

"She went dancing. I put all the kids to sleep in your bed. They talk too much, like you. They ask questions, questions, questions. I've got no patience for all those questions."

"Who'd she go dancing with?"

"I don't know. She wouldn't tell me."

"Another one who'll give her a baby, and she won't even tell you who it is? Did you ever see him before?"

"Boy saw him. He came here in the afternoon sometime. I didn't pay attention to it. Whose funeral did you go to?"

Anh sat down on the edge of the bed. "That Nep boy the cops killed outside that house on Newland."

"Did they give a good funeral?"

"It wasn't bad. There was some shooting. Last week one of the Nep family killed one of the Cheap Boys, so today one of the Cheap Boys killed one of the Neps. A young one, about Thinh's age. A lot of people got hurt."

"Families are split to pieces here, ruined," Me said.

"They put the body in a BMW. Maybe they'll put the other dead brother in the car with him."

"America has ruined everything."

"Thinh was there."

Me's head snapped up.

"He's okay. He got a bloody foot, but he's okay. I saw him in the coffee shop after with a bandage on him."

"Families were better in Vietnam."

"Not our family."

Me turned the sound off, but didn't turn her head in Anh's direction.

"I told Thinh not to come here anymore," Anh said. "We've got four kids in this house, and now he's hanging around with gang boys. Maybe one day we'll go to Thinh's funeral, and they'll bury him in a Lexus or something."

"It's your fault," Me said, her voice as sharp as a knife. "The fortune-teller told me when you were born that I should shun you because our dates were wrong. I didn't listen. I pretended she was wrong, and I treated you like a good daughter, gave you everything."

She stopped talking when she saw the rage in Anh's face.

Anh waited for her to say she was the one to tell Anh and that Thinh and Vy and everyone else in this house what to do. She could see Me's eyes from the side. They were staring straight ahead of her, the light from the television darting in and out of her dark pupils. Anh felt her heart beating, beating, like a little trembly bug in her chest while she waited for Me to use her power. She waited and waited. Finally Me just shook her head and slid slowly down into the chair again.

"I had to do it, Me, I had to tell Thinh to stay away. Vy's kids—I don't want Vy's kids turning out like him. I tried to tell him, look, anything you want I can get it for you, you don't have to steal, you're too smart to be a gang boy, you could do anything, you were born here, you could be president, you could be anything. But he doesn't listen, and I can't take chances with Vy's kids, Me, I just can't take chances. If Thinh's the way American boys turn out, I don't want Vy's kids turning into Americans."

"Leave me alone," Me said.

∼

NGA TU BAY HIEN, 1971

There were thirty-three people, not counting babies, living in Uncle Kou's house, everyone so jammed up together they looked like chickens in a coop. There was a lot of fighting to the west of the village. You could hardly talk sometimes, the noise of the guns was so loud. It was like firecrackers were exploding in a metal pipe, pounding your ears till all you could hear was a long, high-pitched whine. No one was sleeping anymore, just kind of dozing, lying on the mats, drinking tea, and praying for silence.

Anh was in charge of Vy now that Loan and Yony had gone back to their families. Vy wouldn't walk anyplace, just clasped her arms around Anh's neck and wrapped her legs around Anh's waist, and cried if anyone tried to pry her away.

Me had turned sullen, hardly spoke. She squatted on her haunches in a corner of the hut and cooked over a wood stove like a peasant woman, barefoot, in cotton pajamas, her silk ao dais and jade bracelets and French furniture still in the smashed-in house where the pieces of Manh that no one could find were buried. Khanh's stomach was ready, and every day she dragged herself from her mat and sat outside the hut and shrieked and wept and begged the baby to come out. Anh could hear her except when the rockets were exploding, and then no one could hear anything. Auntie Chi told her relatives that Khanh was Me's sister and that her husband had joined the Vietcong. They were all Catholics and wouldn't have allowed Ba to have two wives sleeping in the same hut they were sleeping in.

Uncle Kou didn't look like a peasant. He had clean hands, and his fingernails were smooth, as though he cut them instead of letting them wear off digging at the earth. He would disappear for a week at a time, riding his bicycle down the road as if to an appointment, pedaling fast, bobbing his head, as though to keep bullets away. Even when the rain was the worst, and the fields had turned to swamp, he would get on his bicycle and go down the road, the thick tires splashing the mud up onto his trousers until they were black. When he returned, hair pomaded to his head and smelling of perfume, he would always bring presents for Auntie Chi.

Ba moved through the hut like a sleepwalker, like someone who had gotten lost in a mangrove forest and was trying to find his way out. Sometimes he squatted next to Me and told her how to cook, or he sat beside Khanh, his arms crossed over his knees, or he played cards with some of Auntie Chi's relatives. He wouldn't look at Loc, at the way he dragged himself over the ground with his one leg and one arm.

One night Ba said to Uncle Kou, "Your brother-in-law Cong cheated me at cards today."

Uncle Kou said he never knew Cong to be a cheater.

Ba told him he was.

The next day Ba and Cong played cards again, and when Cong put his cards down, Ba pulled a gun out and shot him in the head. The sound of the shot was so quiet with all the war noise outside the hut that hardly anyone noticed that Cong was dead. Auntie Chi noticed, and she screamed once and ran to find a doctor. Me went outside with Uncle Kou and Ba, and they all yelled at one another while shells exploded in the paddies to the west and the air smelled of smoke and burning flesh. Anh could hear them yelling, even with the war making all the noise it could.

The next morning Ba put on his uniform and said, "This place is worse than war, worse than death, worse than starvation. I'm going back to the fighting. I'm going to go see if I can find a card game and maybe kill a few Communists at the same time."

Uncle Kou didn't even wait a day after Ba left before he put Me and Anh in a bicycle-drawn cart and took them to Saigon.

12

*I*t was a test. If Anh was going to go into business with Jana, she had to find out if Jana was smart enough. Sometimes Americans weren't too smart. They were always doing things the way someone told them to. Couldn't figure out the simplest things. Couldn't have lasted a day in Vietnam.

Oh, Anh didn't want her stuff back from the police. She didn't care about that. That junky stuff. Some of it she didn't pay for, anyway, maybe got it for a favor she did someone. Like the suede jacket, she didn't pay for that. It was in the window of Tam's Leather Shop and the collar got faded, and Anh had signed her name so Tam could buy a car when he first got to the States, so he gave her the faded-collar leather jacket. And they could keep Me's VCR and the jade bracelets and the black-spotted ring. She could get better stuff than that. New stuff. Pretty stuff. The important thing was to see how smart Jana was. Test her on Uncle Kou's five thousand. See if she could get it back. See if she was clever enough to invent answers to problems that no one had ever given her before.

She let Jana have a few days to think about it. Everyone needed time, even smart people needed time to figure things out. Even Anh needed time to get the right answers hooked up to the right questions. So she stayed home and gave Vy a permanent wave and took Boy and Little Boy to the movies and waited for Jana to figure it out.

Jana called her on the telephone at the end of the week. It had taken a little longer than Anh thought it would. She had thought three days. It was four.

"Small claims court," Jana said. "It only goes up to five thousand dollars, but the police can't bring an attorney in against you to fight it like they'd be able to if we filed in superior. Just one of their own men is all they can have in small claims. You and one of their men. How's that?"

"It don't matter to me," Anh replied.

The judge in Westminster Small Claims Court was a woman, Judge Noreen Land. She had pink hair and blue-framed eyeglasses. A Pekingese dog lay snoring on the bench next to the water pitcher. She was petting the dog, smoothing its ears upward, running her fingers over the white ribbon around its top knot, and looking through the folders the bailiff had put in front of her.

"If anyone is here with an attorney, forget it," Judge Land said. "No attorneys in this court. You sue, you plead. You don't plead, get out. You have stage fright, take a pill. No attorneys allowed to talk, give advice, hand you gum or notes or anything else while you're up here stating your case."

"We eat dog in Vietnam," Anh whispered to Jana.

"The clerk said she loves that dog," Jana whispered back.

"She looks like a nasty bitch to me," Burton said to Jana.

"The dog or the judge?" Jana said.

"Both." Burton was a short-haired, middle-aged man, with a watermelon stomach that pooched out the buttons of his double-breasted suit. Jana said he was a retired cop. The one who saved her life in South Dakota.

They were number three on the calendar, and when their turn came, Judge Land said, "Anh Truong versus the Police Department of the City of Westminster," and asked the bailiff who the man in the fifth row was who was doing all the whispering.

"I don't know, Your Honor."

"Do I give her my name now?" Burton whispered. "What's the skinny in California?"

"Wait till she asks," Jana murmured.

"Let's play a game," Judge Land said. "You in the fifth row in the gray suit and crew-cut hair, are you an attorney?"

"No, ma'am."

"Don't call me ma'am. Don't ever call me ma'am. Do you hear me?"

"Yes, ma'am—yes, Judge."

"Your name?"

"Burt Steele. Burton Steele."

"Are you an expert witness?"

"Yes, Judge."

"Weren't you supposed to be here at eight-thirty to check in, put your name on the roster?"

"I don't—" He turned to Jana and said in a low voice, "What's the deal?"

"It's all right, we're doing fine," Jana murmured back to him. "Just tell her you were held up in a case in Judge Tannenbaum's court. It had priority." She slid the words out of the side of her mouth and then pretended to look back toward the door like she was waiting for someone. Anh watched her, watched the fast way she could think, the slippery way she could maneuver. Oh, smooth, smooth, smooth.

"I was held up in a case in Judge Tannenbaum's court," Burton said. "It had priority."

"So you think municipal court is more important than small claims?"

"Noooo."

"You just said so."

"I'd never say that, Judge."

"Well, Judge Tannenbaum isn't going to give you six months in county jail, but I am." Judge Land turned toward the bailiff. "I see a gun inside his jacket. Take it."

"Trouble," Anh said. The bailiff was walking down the aisle toward Burton.

"First thing you learn in police academy," Burton said to the bailiff, getting to his feet, "is never give up your gun. It's a no-no, Sonny Boy." He had his wallet out with his identification.

The bailiff winced. "Oh, shit."

"Take his gun," Judge Land said.

"I can't do it, Your Honor," the bailiff said. "He's a policeman."

The judge's face turned as pink as her hair. "Fine, fine. Go out in the corridor and find someone who will."

While the bailiff was gone, Judge Land picked up her Pekingese, tucked it under her arm, and disappeared into a side door.

"Trouble, trouble," Anh said.

"We're all right," Jana said. "No one'll do it."

The bailiff came back into the courtroom shaking his head.

Then the side door opened and Judge Land was back with the dog. The judge looked as if she had put on fresh makeup, and the dog now had a blue bow instead of a white one.

"I can't find anyone who'll arrest him, Your Honor," the bailiff said.

Judge Land ignored him. As though nothing had happened. As though she hadn't even left. "How do you pronounce this name?"

"Truong," Anh said.

"Come up here if you're going to speak. I presume Mr. Steele is your expert?"

"Yeah." It felt funny standing up in a courtroom and speaking in English to a lady with pink hair who was petting a dog instead of eating it.

"You're asking for five thousand dollars in stolen goods, is that right?"

"Yeah."

"State your case."

It was easy enough for Anh to say what happened to her in the house the night the police broke in. She just said it. Told about the way they pushed everyone around, grabbed her by the neck and choked her, how they took all the jewelry and Me's VCR and the leather jacket and the diamond ring, how they scared the little kids and knocked Mr. Bui out. I've got receipts, she said, can prove every single thing they stole.

"Miss Truong, what do you do for a living?"

"This and this. That and that."

Anh turned, looked at Jana for help. Jana was whispering something into Burton's ear.

"I smell an attorney in the courtroom," Judge Land said.

Jana looked up.

"Are you an attorney, young lady?"

"No." Jana was holding her face with both hands, like she was thinking about something serious, but Anh knew she was doing it to keep from grinning. Oh, it made Anh want to laugh the way the judge just fell into the trap. Just walked along, sweet as an onion, petting that ugly little dog that probably wouldn't even taste good no matter how much ginger sauce or lotus seed you put on it, and fell right into Jana's trap.

"Then what are you jabbering about back there?"

"We're old friends," Jana said. "This man once saved my life. That's all we're talking about."

"Come up here, Mr. Steele."

Burton walked up to where Anh was. Slowly. He was a slow walker. Anh counted his footsteps. Thirteen, fourteen.

"Qualify yourself."

"B.A. in criminology, University of Wyoming; B.S. in ballistics from Fordham; instructor in methods of search and seizure at University of Southern California."

"Fine, fine. Tell us why the policemen acted inappropriately in this case. Isn't it true that the police have a right to search a residence with a search warrant?"

"It's true about search warrants, what you said."

"If what I said is true about search warrants, on what basis can she make a claim?"

"Easy. The warrant was wrong. It should have called for the seizure of Thinh Truong's property, no one else's. The officer in charge should have known better than to let his men do what they did. That's the basis."

Judge Land looked like she was drowning.

"Is there anyone here from the City of Westminster Police Department to answer this woman's complaint?" The judge's eyes scanned the courtroom. Zip, zip, zip. No answer. Nothing. "I can't believe the police department is going to let this go to default. Mr. Bailiff, do you know anything about why the police aren't answering on this?"

"No, I don't, Your Honor." The bailiff had a book open on the desk in front of him and was writing in a notebook. Copying answers or doing homework. Maybe drawing pictures.

"Would you call, please, and find out, then?"

Tap, tap, tap on the table with her pencil. Oh, she looked nervous now, not so sure she could arrest anyone just because she wanted to. Not so sure she could throw a little Vietnamese woman out of her courtroom without giving her what she wanted.

The bailiff made the call. "They lost the paperwork, Your Honor. They thought the suit was frivolous. That's all I could find out. I could call again later, if you want, maybe get someone else's opinion."

"Frivolous?"

"Frivolous, Your Honor."

"You're telling me that I pay taxes in this city, and they think the awarding of five thousand of my tax dollars on a default judgment is frivolous?"

"I could call back, Your Honor, and ask them that."

"They stole all that stuff and won't give it back," Anh said. "I go down there and I tell them give me my stuff back, and they say they don't know nothing about it. I got kid to feed and all those bill, and I got police coming in my house stealing my stuff, what do you think I can do? A poor Vietnamese girl like me, no husband, a sister who got a kid every year with a different guy, and I don't speak English, don't know how thing go in this country, don't know a person can help me, I ask you, what in hell I suppose to do?"

Judge Land looked as if someone had put her on top of a roof and taken away the ladder.

"You say you have receipts?"

"Sure." Oh, Anh had friends. You want receipts, they told her, we'll give you all the receipts you want. What was a receipt, anyway, except a piece of paper? She piled the stack of receipts in front of the judge. Five thousand dollars' worth of receipts.

"Lost the paperwork," Judge Land said. "Lost the paperwork." Tap, tap, tap with the pencil. "For the plaintiff, five thousand."

"What?" Anh said. She had heard it. She just didn't like the way the judge spit it out, like it hurt her mouth to say it. She wanted to hear her say it again.

"I said five thousand for the plaintiff."

"I'll take it," Anh said.

~

"This computer used, only worth three hundred," Linh said. He owned a computer store on McFadden and had volunteered to come down to the police department with Anh and Jana and the marshal. Anh had already put little white tags on a water cooler, a magazine rack, a ficus plant, and a palm in the lobby. Now they were in the inside offices, checking out the computers and printers, asking Linh how much this one was worth, how much that one was worth. No one seemed to care what they were doing, putting all those little tags on things. One of the secretaries even smiled at Anh. It was like they were just walking around, picking out underwear at Penney's.

"And I want computer for the kid to learn on, too," Anh said.

"That's six computers you've attached at three hundred each, is eighteen hundred dollars," the marshal said. He was a heavy-hipped man with hairy arms sticking out of the sleeves of his uniform. He had the writ of attachment stapled to a sheet of blue paper. "With the other items, that comes to forty-three hundred. You've got another seven hundred to go."

"Pretty bored job you got, huh?" Anh said.

"It can be," the marshal replied.

"Are you sure you want that many computers?" Jana said.

"What the hell do you think you're doing?" A policeman was blocking their way, standing in front of a desk, his right hand resting on his gun holster.

"We're not fixing the air condition," Anh told him.

"Yeah, what the hell are you doing?" Another one came up behind the first one. Policemen were coming out of the inner offices.

"This making me nervous," Anh told Jana.

"Don't worry. The marshal will take care of it."

"We're attaching goods," the marshal said. He didn't say it like he meant it, though. He said it like he was ashamed to be hanging around with two Vietnamese, even if there was an American girl with them. "I checked in at the desk. Here's the writ."

There were three policemen in front of them blocking the way to the printers.

"You heard him," Jana said. "A writ. You know what a writ is?"

"Wait a minute, wait a minute."

"Do you see the guy who stole the five thousand anywhere around?" Jana said to Anh.

"No. All police look alike to me."

"Jesus." The policeman hollered over his shoulder at someone. "Anyone know anything about a judgment?"

"You got laser printer?" Anh said. "I like laser. Make letter look like it come right out of a book. You know what I mean?"

"If you've got one with Vietnamese lettering, by any chance, we'll take it," Jana said. "And in case you're interested—and I don't suppose you are—this woman was victimized by a creep who works for you. You guys just ought to be glad I didn't take this thing up to the superior court. Maybe if I had, I could have attached your whole goddamn building."

Oh, Anh wanted to jump up and down, up and down. It was so sweet the way Jana did it, the way she got even. Who cared if the marshal didn't like it and the judge didn't like it and the police didn't like it. Jana passed the test all right. She was perfect. Mean and perfect, and she knew what she wanted, knew how to get it and wasn't afraid of anyone. Oh, she wanted to hug her. She was her sister now. That's it. No question. Anh would put her on her back and carry her wherever she wanted to go.

~

SAIGON, 1971

Uncle Kou brought Anh and Me to a white building on a tree-lined street near the presidential palace. There were American cars in front and a bar downstairs where the girls sat drinking at tables or stood near the bar or just leaned against the wall waiting.

Upstairs were the rooms, each one with a bead curtain that crackled in the breeze. From somewhere on the open-air balcony came the sound of a woman's sweetly hoarse voice singing an American song.

"I own this place," Uncle Kou said. "It's mine. I'm a rich man." That's why he smelled the way he did. That's where he went on his bicycle. That's why he brought Auntie Chi presents when he came home.

"Pretty, pretty, pretty," the other girls said when they saw Anh.

"What kind of house is this, Me?" Anh said.

"It's our house now," Me replied. "We have nothing, and Ba is gone. Uncle Kou will take care of our family."

"But why are we here?"

"You stupid girl. You know why we're here." She pinched Anh's cheek with the same two fingers she always placed so gently on the nape of Vy's neck. It was a deep pinch, as though Me wanted to take part of her daughter's flesh.

Two women in jeweled ao dais, their faces powdered white and their cheeks painted red, took Me and Anh upstairs. Anh in one room. Me in the next. Oh, it was hot that day. Anh could feel their hands hot on her body as they washed her and put the lotions on, and rubbed them into her skin. Then they brought out the little boxes of paint and smeared some on her cheeks and on her lips, and oiled her hair and twisted it around her head and put little jade combs to hold the twists. She smelled like Uncle Kou now, and it made her cry.

There was a bed, one window, and a dresser with a round mirror. When the women left, Anh sat on the edge of the bed and admired herself in the mirror. Turned her head first to one side and then the other. Smiled. Made silly faces. Drew her lips together. Opened her mouth to show her teeth. She looked much older than thirteen with her face painted like this.

When she got tired of staring at herself in the mirror, she went to the window and looked down at the street. People riding bicycles. Women with parasols. Soldiers. Lots of soldiers. A woman selling soup from a cauldron on the sidewalk. Oh, Anh wanted one of those cups of soup. Her mouth was so dry. She could almost feel what it would be like if she could get some of that soup to drink.

"You look pretty." Uncle Kou was at the door. "Come and sit down on the bed."

Uncle Kou was kind. He was always so kind.

He took her hand and put it on his lap. "Feel that," he said.

Anh started to cry.

"Now, now, now, if you cry, it will hurt."

"Me, Me, Me." Her pretty silk trousers were off, and all of Uncle Kou's weight was on top of her.

"Me, Me, Me."

One of the women was back, a jar in her hand.

"Give me that," Me said. Oh, she had come. There she was,

standing in the doorway looking so pretty, so young, so beautiful, breathing fast, the beads slapping against her face.

"Oh, Me. Take me home, Me. Take me home."

"Be a good girl," Me said.

"It's always this way at first," Uncle Kou said. He stood up, and it was as though the weight of the bed had been taken away. Anh felt so happy that Me was here. Me would protect her.

"You scared her," Me said.

"Take me home, Me. Take me home."

"First we'll do this, and if you don't like it, we'll take you home," Uncle Kou said.

"Do you want to wait outside?" Me said.

"I want to watch," Uncle Kou replied.

One of the other girls came in and held Anh's arms down while the other girl held her feet. Then Me put something between Anh's legs. It felt sticky and warm inside, and like warm tea as it trickled down the insides of her thighs.

"Try it now," Me said.

Uncle Kou lay down on top of Anh again and pushed. Anh could hear him groaning, pushing, grunting.

"Eeeeeeh," Anh shrieked.

13

You can't bring food in here." The nurse, a heavyset woman in a starched uniform, came out of the dark corner of the room, head shaking from side to side, eyelids going up and down for emphasis. "He's on a special diet."

"It's *bánh chửng*," Anh said. "Make him healthy."

"Vietnamese cake," Jana said.

"I don't care what country it comes from," the nurse said, pulling the twine away from the banana leaves and poking her fingers into the sticky rice cake.

"Has his wife been in today?" Jana asked.

"She hasn't been in since last Friday," the nurse said. She licked her fingers. "He can't eat it. It's loaded with fat."

"You take it," Anh said. "It bring you luck and good health. Got bean and chopped pork in the middle of it. Go ahead, take it, go on. It make you healthy, then you be able to do your work better."

"I'll go get a knife," the nurse said. "Watch him till I get back."

"You go ahead," Jana said.

Dennis's eyes were flickering, as though he had heard them and was trying to rouse himself.

"Sometimes he talks to me," Jana said. "But he doesn't say much. Just asks me how much money came in." Jana leaned closer to Dennis's face. "Settle, settle, settle, Dennis," she said, and his eyes opened.

"That mean money, huh?" Anh said.

"It's a little joke between us." Jana tapped his shoulder. "You in there, Dennis?"

"Don't touch him," the nurse said behind them. It sounded like she had her mouth full of sticky rice cake.

"Break that cake in two, you find chop pork like I told you," Anh said. "I make it myself. I alway make it for Tet, but Vy kid like it so much, I make it maybe one, two, three time a month."

Dennis's eyes were fully open now, and he looked first at Jana and then at Anh.

"Jesus Christ," he said.

"What'd you say, Dennis?" Jana said.

"We play some *pai gow*," Anh said. "Come on, get dressed, I take you there now, I got my luck back. You don't believe me, come on. You win big this time."

"I think Dennis needs some medication or something," Jana said. The nurse was at the bedside, her greasy fingers on Dennis's white wrist.

"I'll be right back," the nurse said.

"We got business with you, Dennis," Anh said.

"Go away," he said.

"I know you lost all your money gambling, Dennis," Jana said. "And I won't even ask for all the back pay you owe me. Do you hear me?"

"I hear you."

"I want you to know that I'm taking care of things and you don't have to worry."

"Aaaah."

"And when you're better, you won't have to do anything but sit on that balcony down in Emerald Bay and watch the seagulls land. I'll bring you money in buckets."

"Aaaah."

"Anh's going to bring us clients."

"You're a thief, Jana," Dennis said.

"Come again." She put her ear to his mouth.

"He look pretty bad to me," Anh said to the nurse, who was back with a hypodermic needle.

"You girls are going to have to leave," the nurse said.

"You're a thief," Dennis said as the nurse rolled him onto his side and pulled up his gown.

"I'm just stealing your heart, honey," the nurse said, and stabbed his rear end with the needle.

"You're cheating me," he said.

"Whoa, Dennis," Jana said. "Are you talking to me?"

"You."

"Cheating you? You bastard, I'm working my ass off for you."

"Stealing my money."

"What's going on here? Did Sheree tell you I took some money?"

"You hide checks."

"I hide nothing. I write briefs. I go to court. I answer interrogatories. I file complaints. I prepare answers. I turn over all the checks that come in to Sheree. And you've the gall to tell me I'm cheating you, stealing from you?"

"Sheree told me." His voice was getting weak, and his head was shaking.

"Seem like he don't trust you," Anh said.

"This isn't going to work, ladies," the nurse said. "You're upsetting him."

"He just accused me of stealing," Jana said.

"Well, did you?" the nurse said.

"You want to butt out of this?" Jana said. She put her face close to Dennis's mouth this time. "Listen to me, Dennis. I've never stolen from anyone in my life. I live one step away from homelessness. I've got a father who irrigates trees by peeing on them. I've got a mother who won't sell her house in the barrio and lives with bullets flying around every night. I pinch every goddamn dime before I spend it. I only use one light in the office to save on electricity. I file papers myself rather than use a process server. I take Andy to court with me sometimes so I don't have to pay a babysitter. Cheating you?"

"You better go," the nurse said.

"I've been coming to see you every day for three months. I thought you cared about me, Dennis, appreciated what I was doing. I was going to make something for all of us, and give it to you on a silver platter, so if you ever got well you'd never have to worry again."

"He ain't listening," Anh said.

"Get out, get out, get out," the nurse said, "before you kill him."

∽

"That's it," Jana said. "The gloves are off. I thought the bastard was my friend. God, I really thought he was."

"I don't know about American people, what you mean when you say someone your friend," Anh said. They had left the hospital in her car, driving south down Pacific Coast Highway. The sun was peeking in and out, trying to blot the rain clouds dry. "It don't mean nothing to me. Friend. What that mean, anyway?"

"You don't have any friends, for Chrissakes?"

"Vietnamese people got family, they got people they know, people they do business with, people they owe something to, people owe them something, people they like to sit and talk to, people they like to gamble with—"

"It doesn't matter. Look at that rain. The sun's shining and it's raining. Drives me crazy what Dennis said, just crazy."

Anh turned right on Beach Boulevard, past the trailer parks and the oil pumps.

"That's what I need, an oil well in my backyard," Jana said. "A goddamned, painted-green, spouting-money oil well, and then my worries'd be over."

"First you got to dig hole, then you got to know about how to sell the oil that come out the hole, how to get rid of it. It stink, too. I heard all those million-dollar house up in Huntington Harbor, they got oil stink coming up out of the floor and don't know how to stop it. You got to do business with thing that don't stink and don't mess your clothe."

Vacant lots gave way to town houses, their roofs the same soft pinks and greens as summer vegetables. At about Ellis the road widened, a center divider appeared, and traffic became heavier. The land sloped upward here, away from the beach. Imperceptibly, like the sun going down, the blue of the ocean dipped out of sight, and there were no more houses, no more ocean views, just gas stations and car dealers and body shops and car washes.

When they hit Midway City, the area turned honky-tonk. Steak houses and Western bars and boot barns. At Bolsa, where the Peek Mortuary and the Catholic Seminary ate up a couple acres, a small sign at the side of the road said Little Saigon.

"I've never been this far east," Jana said.

Anh turned right on Bolsa, and suddenly the signs were all in Vietnamese. The shoppers in the strip malls were all Vietnamese. Umbrellas against sun as well as rain appeared like mushrooms on the sidewalks. There wasn't a sign to show that this was an American city.

～

"*Chào Anh.*" The proprietor of the restaurant, in a sport shirt and dirty apron, came out of the kitchen and escorted Anh and Jana to a table near the lobster tank.

"I guess they've never seen an American before," Jana said as people turned to stare at her.

"So how's business, Mr. Pham?" Anh asked in Vietnamese.

"Good, good. Very good."

The place was crowded and noisy, with no special decor except for a shrine with a porcelain Buddha on the floor next to the pastry counter. Little lights blinked off and on around it. Jana kept trying not to stare at the other diners, who were staring at her. She looked down at her legs. They weren't heavy. She didn't exercise, but they weren't heavy. And her arms inside the sleeves of her jeans jacket weren't overly round. She was a size eight in the summer, when she and Andy went bike riding along the beach, maybe a size ten in the winter, when all she did was walk to and from the car. And yet, sitting here in this restaurant surrounded by nothing but thin, short Vietnamese, all of them so thin they looked starved, all of them so short they seemed childlike, she felt like a monster. A fat, ungainly monster.

"What do you want to eat?" Mr. Pham said. "*Nướng vĩ? Bánh bèo?*"

"My friend's never eaten Vietnamese food before. I think the best thing is to bring us the seven courses of beef." Anh turned toward Jana. "You like spicy?"

"Sure. I like everything. But I'm paying."

"No. I bring you here. I pay."

"How did that work, what you said—you know, how if you ask someone out to eat, you pay?"

"Next time," Anh said. "Bring my friend a fork, Mr. Pham."

Mr. Pham bowed and smiled. "How is your mother?"

"Good. Watching television and eating. She's very good."

"I'll bring your friend a fork."

"I loan him the money for this place," Anh said when he left the table. "Eight thousand. He pay me back two year ago, and now you can't touch this place, it cost you arm and leg you want to buy it. Everyone in Little Saigon come here."

"Too bad you didn't take a share instead of just loaning him the money."

"With Vietnamese people, if I got money and you need it, I give it to you. If I need it, I ask for it back. No paper. We don't believe in that stuff, paper and all that. Just you and me, we make deal."

"No one pays interest?"

"Sure, but interest less than credit card. Nobody pay tax. That the way Vietnamese people do it."

The restaurant was full of smoke. Jana looked around her. Thin, short Vietnamese, eating and looking starved, and everyone smoking. As if they had never heard of lung cancer. Or didn't care. Mr. Pham was back with a plate of glistening lettuce and sliced carrots and pickled vegetables and a fork.

"The seven courses of beef is coming," Mr. Pham said. "Does your friend want hot sauce, too?"

"Bring us everything you've got in the kitchen," Anh said. "Just bring it. Don't ask me so many questions."

"I don't understand how Dennis can turn on me like this. Even if Sheree lied about me, he knows better than that. He knows *me*, for Chrissakes."

"You know, Vietnamese people think it bad luck being around sick people. They know you sick, they think your bad luck going to happen to them, so unless you dying, you don't tell people you sick. They think you weak, or why you get sick like that in the first place."

"Dennis used too much cocaine, and it stopped his heart and ruined his kidneys. It had nothing to do with weakness or bad luck. The bastard."

"I don't believe that superstition, either. Lot of Vietnamese people believe in superstition, but not me."

Jana stabbed at a lettuce leaf with the fork. Anh was using chopsticks, her slender fingers hooked around the bone sticks in a way Jana thought they should slip right through. A casual, offhanded way, fingers merely grazing the smooth surface of the sticks. Not clutching them. Not even paying any attention to them. Using them as though they were two extra fingers.

"I can't believe he thinks I stole from him. I just can't believe it."

"See, one time Mr. Pham wife, she was going to have baby, and the doctor said they had to cut her stomach up, you know, to get it out. Mr. Pham too scare to go in there with her and watch them do it—oh, you never saw no one so scare in you life. Mrs. Pham scare, too. Both of them scare to death. So I told Mr. Pham, I said—" Mr. Pham was back, a platter in each hand. "Put it right down there, Mr. Pham." Anh pushed the vegetable tray away to make room for the platter of meats and the dishes of rice crepes.

"What do I do with all this?" Jana asked.

"I show you." Anh stood up at the table and began putting things on Jana's plate, rolling bits of meat onto the crepes and adding pickles and fish sauce and slices of carrots, and then rolling them into sheer envelopes. She waited while Jana picked one of them up and bit into it.

"Hmm," Jana said. There was a strange taste in the sauce. Like fish about to go bad. It looked muddy in the little glass dish and tasted like rotting fish.

"You want some hot sauce?"

"Maybe just a drop."

The hot sauce cured it. Now the flavor was sharp, with only an aromatic reminder of the sea.

Anh sat back down again and began rolling a crepe for herself.

"So I said to Mr. Pham, 'You want me to go in there with you wife?' He told me, 'Ask the doctor.' I said, 'I don't have to ask no doctor. You tell him she my sister.'

"So I go in, and I sit where they put her head, you know, and I hold her hand and talk to her the whole time. I was more scare than Mr. Pham. I was more scare than Mrs. Pham. But how you gonna leave some woman alone like that? So I keep my eye away from that place where they slicing, I don't want to look."

She interrupted herself to pour more tea into Jana's cup and to make her another rolled crepe. "You can eat two thousand of these and not get fill up."

"I ought to go back to the hospital and put a pillow over Dennis's head," Jana said.

"Then I hear the doctor say, 'Look at this big baby boy,' and Mrs. Pham crying, and I laughing and screaming like she really my sister. So when Mr. Pham need eight thousand for restaurant, I tell him right the minute he ask me for it, 'You got it.' "

"What if he hadn't paid back the eight thousand?"

"But he did."

"But he might not have."

"But he did."

"What if it was a hundred thousand and he didn't pay it back?"

"I loan a guy eighteen thousand for a shoe factory in eighty-six and he never pay me back."

"What? Are you kidding?"

"I'm serious. The truth."

"Did you try to get it back?"

"How?"

"Jesus."

"He in Texas now somewhere. I don't care."

Jana was looking at her real steady now. "So how'd you get eighteen thousand dollars? Don't tell me it was by hanging around the gambling casino waiting for tips. I won't buy it."

"No, no, no. It was before. It was when I was courier, taking money for people back to their family in Vietnam. You get caught by Communist giving American money to people in Vietnam, the Communist kill you. Take you money first, and then kill you. I did it one time. That was enough."

Mr. Pham was back with a big noodle dish. Anh waved it away. "Too much food."

"You told me to bring everything in the kitchen."

"I didn't mean *everything*."

At the look of disappointment on Mr. Pham's face, Anh said, "All right, put it down. If we can't eat it, we'll take it home."

When he had walked away again, Anh said, "How come you know so much about law if you ain't a lawyer?"

"I was in my third year of law school when my husband was murdered. I never finished. But I got enough out of it to know my way around. And then working with Dennis—well, he didn't teach me anything, but I saw how it all went together. I saw what he was doing wrong and did the opposite. Why don't you find a Vietnamese lawyer and set up an office? What do you need me for?"

"There ain't too many Vietnamese lawyer. All those kid born here still too young to go to law school. You not born here, you don't speak English good, so they want to be engineer or work on the moon. There law office on every corner in Little Saigon, but no lawyer in there. Smart people find some lawyer and use his name, and they settle case. They never go to court, just take what insurance offer. Rip off client. Rip off everybody."

Jana leaned forward over the table. "Look, I don't know how to say this."

"Say what you want. You don't scare me."

"I've heard stories, you know, about the Vietnamese, how they conduct business, especially with outsiders."

"You mean cheat you?"

"Yeah, cheat you. Turn on you. I have to know that you're not going to do that to me."

"You think I gonna cheat you?"

"I don't want to go to jail. That's all. If we do this thing, it'll have to be on the up-and-up. A real law office, with real cases, real accidents. I've got Andy to think about, and my folks."

"And I got Vy and Me and all those kid in the house, too. You think you the only one? In Vietnam every day the people have to figure out how to live. Every day they get up in the morning, look outside, decide what work they going to do, what deal they going to make, what business they going to have. Every day. We learn to do it. We got to do it. Maybe some people cheat you. I don't cheat no one. No way."

"I want it clear, that's all. This is not a real law practice, and I'm not a real lawyer, but we won't hurt anyone if we keep it as straight as if it were."

"Everything going to be straight, hundred percent, like you said.

I don't cheat. I don't lie. Oh, maybe sometimes. But not with this. No cheating on this."

"You're sure?"

"Sure I'm sure."

Anh was staring at her, not shifting her gaze, not wavering.

Jana took a breath. "I'll need a bar number."

"Dennis got a number. He never going to come out of that hospital. I seen it today. He going to die in that hospital. We use his number."

"Risky, but I suppose it'll work."

"So then we in business. You got another question, something more you like to say to me, so we settle it now, know how we stand?"

Jana rolled the crepe around and around on her plate, kind of played with it with her fork till the envelope broke and vegetables and beef spilled out. What more was there to say? You talk too much? Nonstop talking that wears me out, makes me tired, gives me a headache?

"I just want an honest operation," Jana said. "I can bend the rules, I know how, but I won't stand for any sharp practices. You know what I mean by sharp practices?"

"Sure. And I know business. Business is sharp practice. When you in business, you watch out for yourself, the other guy watch out for himself. If he cut himself on the sharp practice, that his problem. If you cut yourself, you stupid. That what business is."

14

*a*nh drove carefully down the shaded main street in Laguna Beach. A few out-of-season tourists were crisscrossing the block, licking ice-cream cones and walking in front of cars. Above the roofs of the buildings, the hills rolled and curled with the weight of million-dollar houses.

"I never been to Laguna Beach," Anh said. "Vy kid was asking me all the time how the ocean look like, so I took them to Huntington Beach one time. We stood in the water—big water—high like a house. We got knock over. Vy kid like it, but I don't. I been as far up to Long Beach and as far down to Huntington Beach. I never been here, though."

Across Pacific Coast Highway young men in sneakers and T-shirts were jumping at a basketball hoop, chasing each other around the cement strip in the middle of the beach, blue water sparkling at their backs.

"Park there." Jana pointed to a diagonal space in front of the ice-cream parlor. "Someone's backing out. Here's a quarter for the meter."

"I got one," Anh said, and shoved the quarter away. "I never been to San Diego either."

"You better teach your nephews to swim," Jana said as they got out of the car. "If you live in California, everyone's got to know how to swim. Kids are always falling into backyard pools and drowning, or turning into vegetables on life support. Neighbors' pools. Drainage ditches. The San Gabriel River flows right through Little Saigon. It flows right through everywhere. There's no escaping the San Gabriel River. The minute it rains, the thing starts overflowing. It only takes a slip of the foot, and there's another dead kid. I don't know how you walk in those high heels."

Anh looked over at Jana, walking fast along the sidewalk in her clunky shoes and blue jeans. "You got a dress?"

"One. A green one. I bought it in law school. It's almost brand new. I only wore it once or twice."

It was a short walk up the street to Sheree's gallery. Large panes of tinted glass fronted the building, and above the door It's a Trip was spelled out in twisted acrylic and brass tubing. Inside, a young couple in shorts and sandals were staring at the installation of green wool hangings that lay as tangled and slimy as ocean kelp against the white walls.

"Sheree's a little hard to talk to," Jana said. "Let me handle it."

"I talk to hard people before, don't worry," Anh said. She stared at the walls, then walked over to the closest field of green and touched it with her fingers.

"Sheree'll kill you if you leave fingerprints," Jana said.

"You like this ugly stuff?" Anh asked the young couple. The man shrugged. The woman merely made a stuttering sound, something like a giggle, deep in her throat. Anh opened her purse and handed the man a card. "Little Saigon. My name Truong Anh. I can get stuff from Taiwan, Thailand, Singapore. You ever seen Vietnamese painting? Flower, bird, pretty girl. Good stuff. You want art, I can get you art. The Philippine, I got connection there, too."

"She's watching us from the office," Jana said. Sheree's face was framed in a small tinted window to the rear. A big chunk of gold on the lapel of her black suit glinted in the gallery lights.

"Call me," Anh told the couple. "I get you bargain you won't believe."

Sheree's office was a tiny cubicle with a desk, a few hard chairs, a refrigerator, and a hot plate.

"I had to fire my assistant," she said. "Where's my check?"

"You put some purse and shoe in this place, maybe you make some money," Anh said.

"Who are you?"

"My name Truong Anh."

"Did you tell Dennis I was stealing from him?" Jana said.

"Who's she?" Sheree asked, pointing to Anh.

"Did you?" Jana said.

"Aren't you?" Sheree replied.

"This a big place," Anh said. "You could put a lot of purse in it. I know a lady got connection to Thailand, they make the best Gucci purse you ever seen. You don't got too many customer here. What is that crap you got on the wall, anyway?"

"He was making ten thousand a month before he got sick," Sheree said.

Anh reached over the desk and let her fingers slide over Sheree's gold pin.

"How much? I buy it right now. Give me price."

"He was taking people out to dinner, going to Bar Association meetings," Jana said. "He brought clients in. There hasn't been a new case in the office since he got sick. What's there to steal? What's left to take? I work my ass off, I even go to see Dennis and bring him things, do his errands, and you tell him I'm stealing."

"You saw an opportunity, and you took it. I've been there, so I know the temptations."

"You're saying it takes a thief to know a thief?"

"I got jeweler in Little Saigon can make stuff like this real cheap," Anh said. "I show it to him, and he make it, pfft, just like that. He make diamond setting you can't tell from Tiffany."

"Dennis is lying sick as a dog in that hospital, and you're stealing money we need to pay bills," Sheree said.

"You say that one more time, just one more time—"

"Dennis gamble the money away," Anh said. "I watch him do it. I help him do it. Dennis big gambler."

Sheree's head snapped in Anh's direction.

"Dennis never gambled in his life. Not even a lottery ticket."

"Oh, he gamble all right."

A half-eaten sandwich lay on top of the copy machine in the corner. Anh picked it up and began to munch on it.

"This bread sure taste stale to me, but all of sudden I feel hungry. I eat anything when I get hungry. I once eat doughnut so hard, it break my tooth. I don't know, I just get nutty when I got to eat. See, that the way I am. I can't help it."

"I'm going to call the police, tell them you're an embezzler," Sheree said.

"You do that, and I'll tell them I was playing lawyer in your husband's office with your knowledge and permission," Jana said.

"Listen to me," Anh said. "I know people in Little Saigon. I can make real big law business."

"Who *is* she?" Sheree said in exasperation.

"Put down the sandwich and let's go," Jana said. "There's no use talking to her about anything."

Anh didn't move. "No one come in here too much, I bet. How you make money?"

"I don't steal it," Sheree said. She stood up and walked to the doorway, then motioned in the direction of the front door of the gallery. "Get out."

"You know what," Jana said. "I don't like you, Sheree. I really don't. I never have. All those times we went to lunch. Politeness. I couldn't wait to finish eating to get away from you."

"Like I care."

"Your name Sheree, right?" Anh said.

Sheree's face tightened. "Get out," she said again.

"I could tell Dennis going to die, Sheree," Anh said. "He not going to get out of that hospital, with that kidney machine, and his heart flipping around his chest."

"Are you a doctor?"

"Me? No."

"Then shut up."

"I've wanted to tell you what I think of you for a long time now," Jana said. "Well, this is the time. You're an arrogant snob with no taste. You're a bloodsucker, a liar, a—"

"Wait," Anh said. "Take it easy. She ain't going to throw money away. I can see she ain't that dumb to go throwing money away."

The young couple had wandered out the front door, and a tinkly security bell rang as they passed the electric eye. Anh poured herself a cup of coffee from the pot on the hot plate. Then she sat down on the copy machine and swung her leg.

"This coffee cold. I don't like coffee hot. I hate coffee cold. But that bread so bad, I need something to push it down in my stomach. You ever try chocolate coffee? They got it at Price Club, six buck for two pound. Cheap. Sometime I drink coffee. Me don't like it, and Vy drink Coca-Cola. Sometime the kid drink my coffee when I pour my cup, but it got to have four tablespoon sugar in it, then they like it. Or they eat doughnut with it. Got to be sweet, or they won't drink it."

Sheree was staring hard at her now.

"We need Dennis lawyer number," Anh said.

"What?"

"Jana want to use Dennis number. I told her I can buy number in Little Saigon. People buy doctor number, lawyer number. Anything you want. But Jana figure out Dennis going to die, she can use his."

Sheree walked slowly toward her desk and sat down in the chair behind it.

"You want to use Dennis's name and bar number to run your own law office?"

"Ten percent to you for every case we make money," Anh said. "You don't do nothing. My agent and me bring in all the case, Jana do the law work, you get ten percent. I send you the check. I bring it here to you, if you want. You got no expense, no worry. Just put the money in your purse, and that it."

Sheree looked from Anh to Jana. "Is this a joke?"

"I thought twenty-five for you," Jana said, "but when I ran out the figures, I knew we couldn't make it on twenty-five. Anh pointed out the expenses that we'd have for entertainment et cetera. Then there's the agents who'll bring cases in, they'll want a percentage, so that'll eat up some more, and Anh has obligations, so do I—we don't necessarily want to get rich on this, but we don't want you to rob us, either. You did a pretty shitty thing telling Dennis I was stealing."

"The doctor didn't say he'd die," Sheree said.

"Fifteen," Anh said.

"Twenty," Sheree said.

"Oh, no," Anh said. "You trying to take advantage. You see this poor Vietnamese girl, she got no education. You know what? I went to high school in Sioux Fall one whole year."

"Clever," Sheree said to Jana. "She'll rob you blind, you know. Vietnamese are like that."

The electric eye rang, and Sheree looked out into the gallery through the small window.

"A customer," Sheree said.

"Come on, Anh, let's go," Jana said. "She's not listening to us. The whole thing's making me sick."

Anh stood up. "You ain't making money here. Fifteen. Cash money. No check. No way for income tax to get you. That my offer. That what I give you, and not anything more. You want it, take it. You don't, we going right now. You won't see us, you won't see money, and how you gonna know we don't use Dennis name anyway? We just trying to be honest and fair with you, give you a chance. You ain't going to last long here, and Dennis, he going to be dead before you know it, and then what you going to have? Nothing. Yes or no?"

"I told Dennis a thousand times he was too trusting," Sheree said, "he didn't know what he was doing, letting Jana run the office like it was hers. 'How do you know what she's doing behind your back?' I told him. But he's so generous, so sweet, always saying how bad a life Jana had, how devoted Jana was, how honest, how—"

"Bullshit," Jana said.

The whole thing was making Anh mad. She could have gone into business without doing any of this, without coming here and looking at all this ugly stuff and talking to this stupid woman, but Jana wouldn't do it any other way.

"Are you dumb or smart?" Anh said to Sheree.

"Seventeen percent," Sheree said.

"I told you fifteen. So are you dumb or smart?"

"Who the hell do you think you are?"

"That's it, I'm through with this stuff. I try to give you something, you don't want it." Anh turned and started out the door.

"All right," Sheree said. "Fifteen."

"Fourteen," Anh called over her shoulder. "I give smart people fifteen. Dumb one only get fourteen."

~

SAIGON, 1972

Uncle Kou made it a game. Every man you fuck, you get two points. He put the numbers on a board in the bar so all the girls could see their points adding up. You could use the points any way you wanted. So many points to go to the movies. So many for the Vietnamese opera. So many for a day off. So many to go outside and take a walk. You could exchange the points for money, too. Week in and week out Anh fucked more men than anyone else, and always had a big package of food and clothes for Uncle Kou to take to Vy and Loc when he went back to the village.

Me didn't have many customers. Sometimes Me played pai gow *in the bar and didn't go upstairs at all. But Anh fucked so much, she hardly got out of bed to use the douche bag or go to the doctor. Sometimes she just had to go to the doctor or it hurt too much, but Uncle Kou wouldn't let her tell anyone she was taking medicine. Sometimes she would tell anyway. If she liked the man, she would tell him.*

There were bad things and good things about fucking men. Anh made a list. Good was that she had her own room, that she could take a bath in a bathtub, that she wore pretty clothes and ate good food, and could pretend she was an actress in the Vietnamese opera. Bad was the men who hurt her, called her names, made her suck their cocks.

The war was still on, and sometimes a bomb would explode outside in the street while someone was pumping in and out of her, making faces, making noises. Faces and noises were different for everyone. She liked the American soldiers better than the Vietnamese. The Vietnamese wouldn't even say anything to her when they fucked her, just did it quick, hardly came in through the beaded curtain before they had their pants off and had her down on the bed. American men liked to talk first, and some of them, especially the ones who came to fuck her regularly, brought her candy and flowers. Of course, if they saw her out on the street, they pretended not to know her.

Customers could come into Anh's room any time they wanted, but no one else could. Not any of the other girls. Not even Uncle Kou.

They had to call out to her first. Uncle Kou said he liked that. Standing in the doorway in his own house and waiting for Anh to say come in.

And she no longer clasped her arms and bowed when Me spoke to her.

"You have no respect," Me told her. But Anh didn't answer. What was respect, anyway? Me was the same as she was now. Just a whore in Uncle Kou's brothel.

15

*B*oy and Little Boy got into the limousine first, and then Anh. Vy stood out on the sidewalk in front of the house with the neighbor kids, watching, and it made Anh feel that she had done something special, just letting everyone see her climb into that long, shiny black car in her new yellow dress with the matching satin shoes.

"I feel like I forgot something," Anh said.

"You called the priest for the blessing?" Vy asked.

"Yes."

Vy was in a new dress, too, blue with sequins across the shoulders, and looked as if she were going to climb in and come see the law office open up and drink a couple glasses of champagne, and maybe dance to the band music. But Anh had heard her talking on the telephone early that morning and knew that she was dressed up for something else, something Anh would probably have to fight with her about later.

"How come there isn't a telephone in that limousine?"

"Binh, how come you haven't got a telephone, Vy wants to know."

"Costs too much," Binh said.

Anh was the one who gave Binh the down payment for the limousine, an old hearse with a hundred seventy-five thousand miles on it. He had painted it a cream color, installed plush seats with purple velour upholstery, and stuck a bar and color television in the spot where the casket would have gone.

"Keep those kids' feet off the seat," Binh said.

Vy put one foot onto the padded carpet and pulled Little Boy out and placed him on the sidewalk. Boy was still inside sipping a soda, and opening and closing the little latch to the portable bar.

"Auntie Anh's got to go," Anh said. "Give me a kiss and get out now."

Boy's lips were cold from the ice in the soda, and Anh could feel the impression of the kiss clinging to her cheek even after he had gotten out and was standing on the grass watching.

"You coming later, or not?" Anh said to her sister.

"You need me?"

"No, I don't need you. I've got Me cooking and all those people from the Brookhurst Market in there, and the lady from the cleaner, she's helping, too. And Mr. Bui is picking up the champagne. I don't need you."

"Then I'm not coming."

Binh closed the door and got into the driver's seat.

"You feed those kids what I cooked last night," Anh said to her sister through the open car window. "Little Boy looks like he's starving to death, he's so skinny. I mean it."

"It's ten-thirty," Binh said from the front seat. "If we're going to pick up the lady in Balboa, we've got to go now."

"Ten-thirty," Anh said to her sister. "Jana's waiting for me to come get her. Have you got some good luck for me before I go?"

Vy handed Binh a foil-wrapped package. "Dried duck," she said. Binh handed it over his shoulder to Anh.

"You keep that off my seats," he said.

Anh had never been in an American house before. It had a different smell. It looked different. Full of magazines and newspapers and books. And it was messy, with things on tables and hanging out of drawers. She could see through the living room to the small kitchen. Plates and dirty paper napkins lay scattered across the tile counter.

"Dad disappeared for two days last week," Jana said. "He and Mom are going to stay with me till I figure out what to do."

Jana's father smiled at Anh. "I like gardening," he said.

Jana's mother didn't look anything like Me, but she reminded Anh of Me, the way she was sitting in front of the television, her feet in worn slippers, her hair held down by combs. She was holding Jana's little boy on her lap.

"I think this dress is too big," Jana said.

"Where the belt, anyway?"

"There is no belt."

"It wasn't too big when you try it on," Anh said.

They had found the dress in a shop in the Asian Garden Mall, a beige two-piece, with a jacket to match. It said Albert Nipon on the label, but it cost only sixty dollars, and there was no hand-stitching on it that Anh could see, which meant it was probably made in a sweatshop in Santa Ana with labels imported from Hong Kong.

"The shoulder leaning one way," Anh said. "Lift up as high as you can go, maybe it straighten itself up."

"It's a little loose around the hips," Jana said. Anh could see what was wrong now. The right sleeve had been sewn in higher than the left one.

"All the women in my family have small hips," Jana's mother said.

"Just pull the right side down every time you think about it," Anh said, "and it gonna be fine."

Anh took the brush out of Jana's hand and tried to coax her hair into a curly bang. Jana was looking impatient. It was the same look she had had when Anh took her to the beauty school in Midway City and the girl there said she should put highlights in her hair, and Jana said are highlights the same as high beams, and the girl, who spoke only enough English to order a meal in a Bob's Big Boy, had asked Anh for a translation, and the words got so messed up that Jana just turned and walked out. Now her hair was going every which way. Looked as if she liked to slide around on the pillow when she slept.

"You got some jewelry, a ring, something?" Anh asked.

"What did you do with that gold locket I had, Jana?" Jana's mother said.

"I never saw a gold locket," Jana answered.

Anh took off her new jade bracelet and put it on Jana's wrist.

"Where's he going?" Jana said. Her father had the front door open and was unzipping his fly.

"In the bathroom, John," Jana's mother said.

"Do you want me to drive?" Jana said. She had caught her father by the arm, was holding him still. He looked like a mummy to Anh, all pale and dried up, like something that died a long time ago.

"I got limousine," Anh said. "Vietnamese people like to see you spending money. It mean you rich. They like to be with you, maybe they get rich, too. All kind of people I know in Little Saigon for long time coming to our party, going to check you out, see if you look smart enough to make success, smart enough to give law case to. They don't want to see you in no broken-down car. What kind shoe you got to wear with that dress?"

"I only have one pair of heels. Black."

"Let me see."

Jana went off down the hall. Her father was standing in the middle of the room now, looking confused.

"Come on, I take you to the bathroom," Anh said, and took his arm. "Where the bathroom, anyway?"

"Down the hall on the right," Jana's mother said.

"I'm here," said a voice from the open front door. A young girl, her arms full of schoolbooks, was standing on the small porch. Binh was on the stairs behind her, pointing to his watch and shaking his head.

"I'm coming, I'm coming," Anh told him.

"I'm the baby-sitter," the girl said.

"My name Anh," Anh said. "I got to take Jana father to the bathroom. You get some milk for the little kid, and pick up some of these paper, the place look like shit."

"Well, I only get paid for—"

"And if you eat, you clean up the dish. Don't leave no mess around. Wash the kitchen up, too, I bet it smell in there."

Jana's father was standing with his hand on his zipper, a pained expression on his face.

"I ain't forgetting you," Anh said, turning toward him.

"She only pays me three dollars an hour," the baby-sitter said.

"Don't tell me your trouble," Anh said. "Just do what I said."

She walked Jana's father to the bathroom and stood at the closed door and listened to his stream. It sounded like it was going into the basin or the bathtub instead of the toilet. And he was singing in a loud, unmusical voice. Anh listened to him and waited for the door to open. Oh, this was a crazy house, all right. And a crazy family. Like her own. Only different.

~

Saigon, 1973

Uncle Kou said, "You can't have any babies in here. You get rid of it."

Me said, "You're stupid, you didn't fix yourself, and now look what happened. I told you what to do, you didn't listen."

Anh loved the baby. She called him Manh, after her brother. Manh had round gray eyes and soft brown hair. Anh had no idea who his father was, she had fucked so many American soldiers with round gray eyes and soft brown hair.

"You take that baby out of here," Uncle Kou said. Anh was keeping it in a cradle behind the dresser. Sometimes it cried right when one of her customers was about to shriek with pleasure.

"Uncle Kou will put us both out on the street," Me said. "Send it back to the village. Khanh will take care of it."

"I won't see it, then," Anh said. She was spending her points now on time to be with the baby. Every afternoon she carried Manh to the bird market and sat on a bench and cooed to him while birdsong circled their heads.

Uncle Kou complained again about the baby. And again.

Me was always mean when she spoke to Anh about anything, but now she tried to be sweet, talk to her nicely.

"You can take the baby to Trang's house," Me told her. "You remember how much you liked it there, how you called her your mother. She'll take care of him for you. You can see him every day for a little while. But if he's there, he won't cry and scare the customers away. Think of the family. Uncle Kou will throw us out, and Khanh and her baby and Loc will have no place to live. What will Ba say if he comes back and finds out you let us starve?"

Uncle Kou was very happy when the baby was gone. He came up and told Anh that because she was such a good girl, for every man she fucked from now on he would give her an extra four points.

16

*T*he parking lot was roped off, and there were food tables set up next to the noodle shop, their paper tablecloths fastened with clothespins. The whole minimall was draped in banners, and the shopkeepers were standing in their doorways watching the band set up chairs.

"I don't want you to do nothing," Anh told Jana before they stepped out of the limousine. "I take care of everything."

"If someone asks where Dennis is," Jana said, "where's he supposed to be?"

"In court."

"It's Saturday."

"Nobody here know there no court on Saturday."

Binh had a paper banner with Good Luck written on it in Vietnamese, and he held it up over the car as Jana and Anh got out.

"*Chào bà,*" said a young man in peg pants and an oversize shirt.

"This Dung Do," Anh said to Jana. "He a big singer in Vietnam—got video and everything. Sing French, English, Spanish—you name it, he sing it."

"You better watch those electric cords," Jana said, eyeing the thick black lines that lay like garden hoses across the lot. "I read where someone was electrocuted playing a guitar at an outdoor concert. It began to rain, and before you knew it—"

"This is Miss Galvan," Anh said in Vietnamese. "She's a big lawyer from Newport Beach. She's going to make this corner famous, you wait and see. We've got to go now. The priest is waiting upstairs with Mr. Bui to bless the office."

"I sing you pretty song later, miss," the singer said to Jana.

"Something French," Jana said, as Anh pulled her toward the stairs.

"I find out there another lawyer upstair next door," Anh said.

"There's nothing we can do about that," Jana said. "It's Mr. Bui's lease, and we're not on it."

"It really, really bug me. Damn lawyer, he know we going to move in here, we been up here painting for two week, and yesterday—look at that window, he trying to make the letter on his window bigger than our window. He not even a lawyer. His brother a lawyer, and he sign the paper, but he live in Florida. There no lawyer in there."

The whole second-floor balcony of the building was buried in plants with red ribbons tied around them. A boy in a paint-spattered T-shirt and a baseball cap was standing in front of the freshly painted window. Income Tax, Insurance, Mortgages was on one pane; the other read Dennis Morgan Law Office. We Sue for You.

"The stencil cost a hundred dollars," the boy said.

"I pay you later," Anh said.

The big square room that had seemed empty with only Mr. Bui in it was now full of desks and chairs and so many partitions, it looked like a rat's maze. There was a partitioned area for Mr. Bui, with his own file cabinet and desk and chair. And one for Jana, with a big desk and a soft plaid couch and a wooden sign that said Attorney Miss Jana Galvan. And one for Anh, the same size as Jana's, with her own desk and telephone and a plaque that said Anh Truong, Administrator. The palm and the ficus from the police department lobby were standing in front of the window. Also a *phát tài*, a leafy green plant with a single white flower on it. The minute Anh saw that little white blossom unfold, she knew good fortune and money were going to flow in from all directions.

Dennis's partitioned cubicle was the biggest space of all, right against the corner of the building where the two windows came together at an angle and overlooked the parking lot. He had a huge desk and a black reclining chair, and Anh had put a stack of file folders next to his telephone, along with a few notepads that had his name imprinted at the top with little embossed scales of justice in all four corners.

"Anh, *chào em.*"

"How're you doing, Mr. Bui?" Anh said. "You look nice." He had a fresh haircut and was wearing a new brown suit with a striped tie. "Did you see those good used computers the police gave me for beating me up and knocking you out? You can use them anytime you want. Got a laser printer, too, that writes in Vietnamese, so if you want to write your wife a letter sometime, you go ahead."

"Someone's going to get electrocuted in the parking lot," Jana said. "You ought to notify the owner of the building. He may be liable."

"They come up here, and we sue for them if they get electrocute," Anh said to her, and then to Mr. Bui, "How do you like my dress, Mr. Bui?" She twirled around in front of him.

"You look beautiful, Anh. Beautiful."

"Well, don't kiss me. You save that for when your wife comes over from Vietnam."

There were about thirty people wandering around the office sipping white wine from a jug on Dennis's desk and admiring the good-luck plaques that had been arriving all week. Mr. Bui had hung them up on the wall to the right of the door, little wood-framed rectangles of ribbed velvet with twenty-four-carat gold good wishes gleaming under glass.

"Is my father here?" Anh asked, looking around. She hadn't spotted him in the parking lot or in the coffee shop at the foot of the stairs. Maybe he had come after all and was standing in the corner behind the last partition near the storage room where the cooking was going on, looking over Me's shoulder, telling her what to put in the food, how long to cook it, the way he used to in Vietnam.

"People have been coming all morning," Mr. Bui said, "but no one said he was your father."

"Where's the priest? He promised to come bless the place at eleven-thirty. It's eleven forty-five now."

"He's in the bathroom."

"That suit sure fits you good, Mr. Bui. Did you get it where I told you to go?"

"They treated me well when I gave them your name."

"You see. I told you. Everybody knows me in Little Saigon."

Me was cooking over hot plates in a corner of the office, squatting barefoot, like a peasant woman, near the police department water cooler. She glanced up at Anh.

"Is Ba here?" Anh said.

"He won't come here. You know that. Why are you waiting for him to come?"

"To bless me."

"You've got the priest for that."

"I want Ba's blessing, too."

"Thinh is coming. He told me he's coming."

"Thinh called you and told you that?"

"Last night. He said he wants to see this big business you're in. I told him come and see it for himself."

"I told him I don't want him around. Why did you say he could come?"

A toilet flushed in the small bathroom near the storage room, and the priest came out, smoothing his hair with his hands.

"You ready, Father?" Anh asked. He was the priest in the small Vietnamese church in Long Beach. He had baptized all of Vy's boys and heard Anh's last confession, the year she turned twenty.

"I'll stand here near the cooking pots out of the way so we can get as many people as we can in," the priest said.

"You don't have to bend your head or close your eye when the priest praying," Anh whispered to Jana.

"It doesn't bother me," Jana said.

The priest said his prayers in Vietnamese, and some more people came upstairs and crowded in around the thirty that were already there. Those that couldn't fit into the office stood in the doorway or pressed their noses against the fresh stenciling on the window. Anh looked up once when the priest began spraying the holy water. Some struck her lips, and she stuck out her tongue to catch the drops. They tasted like honey. Like sweet, sweet honey. They tasted like success.

When the prayers were over, someone came upstairs and told Anh that Thinh and Nep Lai were waiting in front of the video store and wanted to talk to her.

~

"Did I tell you to stay away, or not?" Anh said.

"Me told me you were having a party," Thinh said.

"And I don't want you bringing any of your gang boys around here, either."

"We like a good party, too," Nep Lai said.

The parking lot was so packed that an extra unit of policemen had been dispatched from the Westminster Station to keep the noise down and direct traffic. They finally had put a cordon around the entrances to the lot and wouldn't let anyone in or out. The owner of the noodle shop said he'd let people use his bathroom if they bought a dish of noodles, and so there was a line of people eating noodles and waiting to go.

"I wanted to come after I heard about your good fortune," Nep Lai said. "It's not Thinh's fault. You want to fight with someone, fight with me."

"I don't want to fight with you," Anh said.

"Big party," Thinh said. "Where'd you get the money for such a big party?"

"I had some left from Uncle Kou that the police didn't steal, and I picked up a few things here and there."

"My bail money."

"It wasn't your bail money. Uncle Kou gave it to me. I could do anything I wanted with it."

"So what kind of lawyer you got here?" Lai asked.

"American. Dennis Morgan. Have you heard of him? Big, important lawyer from Newport Beach. You ever been to Newport Beach?"

"Sure, I've been to Newport Beach."

"Lai's been everywhere," Thinh said.

"They've got a Ferris wheel there," Anh said. "I'm going to take Boy and Little Boy on it one of these days. You can go get some food as long as you're here. Me's cooking upstairs, and some of the girls from the minimarket on Brookhurst are helping serve. They're bringing food down the stairs as fast as Me can cook it."

"We ate at the Last Emperor," Lai said.

"Lai doesn't pay at the Last Emperor," Thinh said.

"They like you there, huh?" Anh said.

"I protect them from the gangs," Lai said, "so no one comes in and shoots up the place and robs their customers while they're eating."

"That sounds like a pretty good service," Anh said.

"You've got a different business here, though," Lai said. "You don't need that kind of protection."

"I've got a gun, anyway," Anh said.

Thinh laughed. "She has no bullets."

"I have bullets," Anh said. "You know what? When the Nep family has legal problems, you come here, and we'll give you service free, no charge."

"I've got a lawyer in Los Angeles," Lai said. "American lawyer. The best kind."

"What do you think we've got here? We've got a real office here, with real law work going on. None of this shit where some guy in an office is calling himself an attorney and he doesn't even know where the court is. Dennis Morgan, does that sound like a Vietnamese name to you?"

"He doesn't come around here, I bet."

"We've got two lawyers. Two big ones."

"One's a girl," Thinh said, and Nep Lai snickered. "An American."

"Americans don't like Vietnamese," Nep Lai said. "She'll use you and trick you. What do you think, she likes you or something? You better trick her first."

"Listen to Lai," Thinh said. "He figures everything out in advance. I've never seen anyone so smart before."

"I'll bring you business," Lai said. "I heard you've been going around in Little Saigon asking people to send you cases for a commission. I've got business I can bring you, too. We'll work something out so the American girl doesn't get too much. We can work some bank accounts. I've got friends in Midway City Bank, they'll switch funds from one account to the other anytime I ask them, the American girl will never know."

"We're legitimate here."

"Who said I'm not legitimate?"

She got up so close to Nep Lai that she could smell his shaving lotion and see the tiny hairs of his sparse mustache. She was smiling sweetly, still tasting the priest's holy water on her lips.

"Well, then, we'll do business. I'm not afraid to do business with you. But I've changed my mind about you staying and eating Me's food. And I don't want you drinking any champagne Mr. Bui went and got from the wholesale place in East L.A. If you want to bring me legitimate business, you do it. But I don't want you hanging around here, because it just makes me sick to look at your face."

It was during a break in the music, when the band was eating, and Dung Do was signing autographs, that Sam Knowlton appeared. He came up from somewhere near the line at the noodle shop and edged his way around the plywood bandstand, and Jana kept watching him and thinking what in the hell was an American doing here with all these Vietnamese, and she thought he looked familiar, and kept trying to think where she had seen him, and couldn't until he was right in front of her, saying, "I called Dennis's office. The phone was disconnected."

"The interrogatories," Jana said. "It's you."

He looked more relaxed in slacks and a T-shirt. And younger, as if he had put his age and worries in his suit and left them somewhere.

"I went to the hospital," Sam said.

"I'll give you a medal."

"He didn't look like he was ever going to practice law again."

"Cocaine can do that to you."

"Then I saw the notice in the *Journal* about the opening of his new office. I said to myself, 'Little Saigon—isn't that where they machine gun people in restaurants?' "

"That's Chinatown," Jana said. "They do home robberies here mainly. It's a specialty."

"How's your boy?"

"Fine. Andy's fine." They stood and smiled at one another.

"I don't think you got out of your suit and came all the way down to Little Saigon just to watch a law office open."

"I've been on a murder trial in Modesto," he said, "or I'd have looked you up sooner."

"I suppose you're going to tell the bar I'm not a lawyer."

"I don't give a shit whether you're a lawyer or not."

Jana looked across the parking lot at Anh, at the way she was standing, toe to toe with two Vietnamese men. Knowlton was talking about his murder case, about how the defendant packed the corpse into a Samsonite overnighter.

"You know how they fit shoes in a box," he was saying, "how you never can get them in that way again, well, that's how that body was packed in there. Like a jigsaw puzzle."

Then he switched. "You can't trust the Vietnamese, you know."

It jolted Jana the way he said it. One second he was talking about suitcases, and then he puts in a little firecracker. Not a cherry bomb. Just one of those nickel poppers the kids play with after school.

She turned her head and looked at him. "That's a disgusting thing to say."

"They're like rodents," he continued, "all scurrying around, climbing up each other's backs, scheming. They've got centuries of scheming on you and me."

"I don't want to hear this."

"It's the way they live, what they've had to do to survive. They know more scams than you can imagine. Intrigue and deception is mother's milk to them."

"You keep it up and I'll lose my temper. You don't want to see that. I guarantee you, you don't."

"Fine. Do what you want to, then. I just came down to tell you to watch your pretty ass, or they'll bite it off."

"Vy, are you sleeping?"

"Huh?"

Anh could make out two figures in the bed, two lumpy forms plastered together beneath the covers.

"You don't come in my bedroom in the middle of the night and ask me if I'm sleeping, Anh," Vy said. She turned on the bedside light, and Anh could see the dark hair of the man beside her.

"Oh, now, this is the limit," Anh said. "You're going to make another baby, and I'll have to pay the bills." She went over to the bed and pulled the covers back. "Get up, get dressed, and get out of here before you make my sister pregnant."

"Anh!" Vy screamed at her.

The man was sitting on the edge of the bed now. His head was slightly forward, and Anh could see he was no Vietnamese.

"You Mexican?" Anh said.

"Indian," the man answered.

"You mean like in the cowboy movie or like those guy with the white skirt?"

"Anh!" Vy shrilled again.

"What your name, anyway?"

"Ruben."

"What business you in, Ruben?"

"Stereos. Car stereos."

"You put 'em in or take 'em out?"

"You mean steal 'em?"

"You know electricity?"

"Sure. Why?"

"I need someone put alarm here in the house, you know, for burglar, people who want to come in. You do it?"

"Why not."

"You do it right, and show me it work right, you can come see my sister again."

"How'd the party go?" Vy asked. She leaned back against the pillows.

"Good. Did you feed the kids?"

"We dropped them at Ruben's sister's house. We went dancing."

"I asked if you fed them. I don't care where you went."

"Ruben's sister fed them."

"Good," Anh said. She arranged the quilt neatly around Ruben's bare buttocks, and then patted his shoulder. "Good. So, Ruben, you fuck up and don't put the alarm right, then I don't want to see your dirty face in my sister bed, not one time more, not any time more."

"Come back to sleep," Vy said, and turned the light out again. "She's just crazy."

~

SAIGON, 1974

"Come here and sit on Mommy's lap," Anh said.

Trang let go of the baby's fingers, and he walked unsteadily toward Anh. Smiling. He was always smiling.

"Oh, look at you," Anh said. She couldn't wait, but grabbed him up, held him in her arms. They swayed together in the garden of Trang's house while Trang watched them, the jealousy seeping out of her eyes.

"I brought you a bean cake," Anh said, and she sat down in the deep grass near the clear tank of water where Trang kept the eels she sold in the market. The grass bent beneath her, and let its grassy scent escape. There was the sound of gunfire out in the street, but here the grass was sweet and the eels swam mindlessly through the tank's murky water.

There were bean cake crumbs now on Manh's lips, and Anh kissed them off. She could taste him in the bean cake crumbs. Oh, she could squeeze him tight and taste his lips.

"He likes to play with my jade necklace," Anh said.

"He has legs like American legs," Trang said. She was lying in a hammock now near the eel tank, fanning herself with a palm leaf. It always took her a few minutes to let go of him when Anh came, a few minutes to recognize who his mother was.

"We'll walk in the park tomorrow," Anh told the baby. He was intent on the piece of jade, his face beneath her chin, his soft fingers turning the lucky frog over and over. Then he looked up at her and said, "Me."

Oh, he had never called her that before. She had wondered if he would ever call her that. "I love you, I love you," she said, and she squeezed him again, felt the fat arms around her neck, felt him melting into her body. Just so, his cheek against her cheek, his heart against her heart. Held tight. Like this. There was no war.

"You are so beautiful," she said. "I love you more than life."

"He doesn't miss you when you leave," Trang said.

17

The courtroom was full. Attorneys walking in and out. Bail-bonds people bringing release forms up to the bailiff for the judge's signature. Prisoners in the holding section peeking out when the guards weren't watching. Anh was standing to Jana's left side, but there was so much commotion in the courtroom, so much going on, that she could hardly hear what Jana and Deputy D.A. Maloney were telling the judge. The judge had let Anh stand up there next to Mai Lam. Anh was kind of holding the girl up, trying to keep her from falling over.

"What exactly is your case against Miss Lam, Mr. Maloney?" Judge Nokura said. "I'm having difficulty following your line of reasoning."

A woman judge. Japanese. Spoke perfect English. The worst kind. Anh knew it the minute the judge looked at Mai Lam before the hearing started. She could tell what she was thinking. I'm not part of that bad gang of Oriental thieves out there. I'm not one of you. Anh understood that all right. Hating yourself. Wanting to pluck out your almond eyes and put round ones in.

"Well, Your Honor," Deputy D.A. Maloney said, "Miss Lam is part of the larger fraud ring we're trying to break. There are fake accidents being staged and phony injuries and bogus claims being made to insurance companies, and we've got to stop it. We've got to get tough with these offenders before insurance rates go through the roof."

"Deputy District Attorney Maloney means to solve the whole auto-accident fraud problem by putting poor Miss Lam in jail," Jana said. "Poor, unfortunate, non-English-speaking, recent immigrant Miss Lam. And pregnant, too, Your Honor."

"You'll have your turn, Miss Galvan," the judge said.

"I think Miss Lam knew all about what was going to happen," the deputy D.A. said, "that a phony accident was being prepared. She wasn't an innocent person yanked off the street and put in that car. She was being paid. She knew what it was for."

"I object," Jana said.

The deputy D.A. was a slight man with glasses and flyaway hair that looked as though it had been combed down against his head with water. It had dried into little shafts that stuck out above his temples like horns.

"Are you going to want to go to the bathroom and vomit again?" Anh whispered to the girl. Mai had her head down almost to her chest. She was only twenty, with a long black braid hanging down her back. The braid cut right into the middle of the words Orange County Jail stenciled on the back of the gray sweat suit that hung like oversize pajamas on her thin frame. This was just a preliminary hearing, Jana said. They never release anyone at the preliminary. They always give the D.A. the benefit of the doubt, treat the accused like they're already convicted, hold them for trial, make them sweat. But maybe, just maybe, Jana said, we can change that. Maybe Miss Lam will be one of the lucky ones.

The girl didn't answer. She hardly talked. It was like she was in shock, like she had been in the war, like a bomb had exploded right next to her head and she couldn't hear or see or say anything. The court interpreter was on the girl's other side, translating everything that was being said in English into Vietnamese, and the girl didn't look as though she could hear that, either. She must have been able to see and hear and speak a few weeks ago when she got in that car. Oh, her hearing and eyes must have been okay when she took the two hundred dollars, watched the car get carefully bashed in, and then climbed into the backseat.

"The accident was staged, Your Honor," Maloney said. "Two Vietnamese guys—"

"I object again, Your Honor," Jana interrupted. "What relevance does their being Vietnamese have to this case?"

"Overruled."

"Two Vietnamese, Your Honor," Maloney continued. "They parked their car at the intersection of Magnolia and Bolsa, and got out and waited while a second car driven by a Vietnamese male rammed the first car. When that was accomplished, Miss Mai Lam was put in the backseat. The police were then called, and an accident report was made. It's called stuffing, Your Honor. Stuffing a person into a car after a staged accident and claiming injuries."

The girl was three months pregnant. Anh's arm was going numb where she was hanging on to it. She didn't want to move, though. If she moved, the girl would fall down. Faint, maybe. Vomit right here on the floor in the courtroom without waiting, the way she did before, to get to the bathroom.

Deputy D.A. Maloney was now telling the judge all about how the fake accidents are done, how the district attorney's office was trying to break up the ring and Mai Lam was the only one who'd been caught. The others had disappeared into the Vietnamese community, changed their names, he said. Some had even probably gone back to Vietnam.

"It's all gang-driven, Your Honor," Maloney was saying. "We just don't know which gang."

Anh looked up and caught the judge watching her holding Mai Lam up, trying to keep her from falling down.

"She's pregnant," Anh said out loud.

"Objection," Maloney said.

"You can stand here, but don't speak," the judge told Anh.

Oh, it was all so cold in here. No one wanting to hear about this poor girl and that she was pregnant and that she was only here three months and probably thought two hundred dollars could buy her a house.

"Insurance rates are going sky-high because of this, Your Honor," Maloney said. He turned and looked at Jana. "You might ask Miss Galvan why she's here defending this woman."

"Are you accusing me of something?" Jana said.

"Well, I don't know. You tell me. You practice in Little Saigon. Your office administrator has gang connections."

"Wait, wait, wait," Jana said. "Just a goddamn minute. You're accusing me of—"

"Not yet. But I will be."

Jana started toward him, had her arm up like she was going to sock him in the face, and stopped only when the judge's gavel gave one loud, sharp rap on the broad plank of polished wood in front of her.

"If you have some claim to make against Miss Galvan, make it in the proper manner," the judge said, "not in open court."

"Take it back," Jana said. She was still facing the deputy D.A., her eyes so bright Anh could feel their heat from where she was standing.

"I'm not taking anything back," Maloney said.

"Do you have reason to believe that Miss Galvan is involved in this insurance-fraud ring?" the judge asked.

"Well—"

"You bet he doesn't," Jana said.

"I might if I look hard enough."

"That's hardly the basis for making such a statement as you've just made, Mr. Maloney," the judge said. "You *might* if you *look hard enough*?"

"I mean I could if I could see Miss Galvan's files."

"This isn't a police state," the judge said. She was looking a little feverish herself now, biting her lip and running her hand up and down the carved handle of her wooden gavel. "Get your evidence, Counsel. Present it to a grand jury. Get an indictment. Don't come in here and make wild accusations against a fellow member of the bar."

Jana was looking in her jacket pocket for something. Anh reached over and handed her a Kleenex. Oh, this was too close for comfort now. Jana was wiping her face with the Kleenex. Slowly. Taking her time. Getting herself together. Waiting to see whether the D.A. knew something about fake lawyers or not. But Maloney was looking through his file now, not saying anything.

"Your Honor, my honesty and integrity can stand any test Mr. Maloney wants to give," Jana said finally, her voice so steady it made Anh blink in admiration, "but I'm not going to stand here while he characterizes the bloated, greedy, overprofited insurance industry as some impoverished body in need of rescuing when this poor girl is being railroaded."

"Railroaded?" Maloney said, looking up from his papers. "Railroaded? Was she or was she not in that car?"

"All right, all right," the judge said. "If you're going to fight, we'll recess."

"And she hasn't had medical care, either, while she's been in jail," Jana said. "Your Honor, I've asked for a doctor's exam and haven't gotten one yet. She's always nauseated, can't eat, can't speak English to the guards. If you ask me, Your Honor, this falls into the category of cruel and unusual punishment. I don't intend to let it go on. I don't intend to stand here and let this—this man—this—"

"No one asked for a doctor for her," Maloney said.

"I certainly did," Jana said. "You know damn well I did."

"She won't die of pregnancy."

"How do you know?"

"All right, all right," the judge said.

Oh, Jana could get hot about things. Real hot. Real fast. She wasn't even getting any money for this. This one was for free. And she was putting herself in danger just being here. She was swimming with sharks, could get her legs bitten off any minute now, and she didn't even care. How did she get this way, let herself show all the anger in her and not care what anyone did with it?

"Mai Lam is a recent immigrant," Jana said, "unaware of our laws. She needs protection. I'm here to give her that protection."

"Objection," Maloney said. "Ignorance of the law, Your Honor, is no defense."

"Sustained."

"She's been victimized all the way along," Jana said. "She was brought here by family members already here and then put to work in a plastics factory working twelve-hour shifts. She was attacked at work, and a pregnancy resulted. She was hospitalized, and upon release her family refused to take her back, thinking that the pregnancy was something she invited. The night of the so-called stuffing, she was picked up at a shelter by several men she didn't know and told she could make two hundred dollars if she just went and sat in a car and did nothing. She has a right to some understanding from this court. To some compassion from this court. Your Honor, you have to look past Mr. Maloney's prejudiced posturing, past his poisonous, unfounded statements. You have to look into your own heart and see this girl's innocence."

"Get the violins," Maloney said.

"Does Miss Lam have a job now?" the judge asked.

"She's been in jail since the incident, Your Honor," Jana said. "But her family is now willing to take her back. Your Honor, it's clear Mr. Maloney doesn't have anyone to pin anything on and he's hoping to dump everything he can onto poor Mai Lam's shoulders. I say his is the crime, not hers. I say if you let this injustice go on, then there is no compassion, no understanding, no—"

Oh, Jana was getting going again, her eyes sparking, her cheeks red.

"Please," the judge said.

"What does compassion have to do with this?" Maloney said.

The judge looked him over good on that one. She even closed her eyes for a moment. And her lip quivered.

"It's almost over now, Mai," Anh whispered to the girl.

"Dismissed," the judge said.

"You're just going to have to train them to make appointments," Jana said. It was only ten-thirty, and there were already fifteen Vietnamese sitting in the chairs underneath the red-and-gold good-luck plaques.

"Don't have appointment in Vietnam," Anh said. "No such thing. They wait. They like to wait. They used to waiting. Here that guy file I told you about."

"Great," Jana said. "I knew I'd flush him out."

"I told him we was going to call the bar on him," Anh said. "I know there no American lawyer in there, just a bunch of Vietnamese guy settling everything for no money."

Jana was already reading the file. It was as though Mai Lam was just a dream. Her family waiting out in the corridor at the courthouse all pumping Jana's hand up and down and Jana looking ashamed almost, like she wasn't worth it. And then not even talking about the case in the car on the way back to the office. Ignoring it. Acting like nothing ever happened. Acting like she hadn't almost had a stroke defending that dumb girl.

"They didn't do much, no depositions, no investigation," Jana said, "and it's a good case." She had her suit jacket off. She still wasn't comfortable looking like a lawyer. She liked to look like a college kid in her white blouses and skirts. Put a jacket on her, and it made her all stiff and unhappy-looking.

"I bet she's got a rotator cuff injury," Jana said. "God, look at this, they had her going to an acupuncturist—with a rotator cuff. Jesus." She looked up. "How much do they want for substituting out?"

Anh shrugged. "He say whatever I send okay with him." She didn't move away from the desk. "I call Pioneer Insurance. They gonna fix that Deung guy car."

"Did you set up an appointment with a doctor for him?"

"He won't go to American doctor."

"He's got to go to an American doctor. Did you explain to him how important it is, that the insurance company won't take his claim seriously, won't believe he's hurt if he doesn't go to an American doctor?"

"He go to Vietnamese guy on Magnolia. His uncle brother. Same village. That the way it is, so don't sweat it."

"Jesus."

"And we got three new case this week. One from girl in the nail shop—that new one just open on Ward—one from car wash on Newland—guy pick up his clean car and bang it into the guy run the car wash. That make two. Third one from real estate guy office on Bushard—his wife got rear end by Mexican guy in Santa Ana on her way to buy some balloon at K mart for her kid party. Those Mexican guy drive car like Vietnamese, like they in a race."

"Did you arrange for rental cars?"

"All fixed. And I'm yelling, screaming all the time with the insurance, give me this, give me that. Those guy bug me, you know, how they act, like I'm making these case up, like no one hurt at all. They really drive me banana."

"Give the tough ones to me. I'll talk to them. Did you settle the Diem case?"

"All settle. No check yet, but all settle. We keep it up, this time next year we living on hill next to Dennis house looking down on Emerald Bay."

"Do you think Mai Lam's going to be all right?"

That was the first time she had mentioned the girl since they left the courthouse. "Sure," Anh said. "Don't worry. I talk to her mom, explain the whole thing, how it wasn't Mai fault."

"Good."

Mr. Bui was at the opening to Jana's cubicle now, staring at Anh's back.

"Good morning, Mr. Bui," Jana said, and Anh turned around.

"Hey, Mr. Bui, I brought doughnut from the new shop down the street for you. Those people want income tax, so I told them Mr. Bui make the best form in Little Saigon and don't even get you screwed with the IRS. He get you money back and pay you refund before he even mail the thing, so you don't wait one minute for your money. The girl name Mary. Vietnamese, though. You look a little sick, Mr. Bui."

"I've got some Anacin in my drawer," Jana said.

"I got a letter today," Mr. Bui said.

"Letter make you look that color green, don't read them," Anh said.

"My wife's coming from Vietnam."

"Oh," Anh said. Mr. Bui went back to his cubicle, and Anh followed. Mr. Bui sat on the plaid couch. Anh sat down next to him.

"I haven't seen her in twelve years," he said. "I don't even remember her. All I've got is a picture of her. It was taken on our wedding day. A pretty girl with shiny hair, and I don't remember her."

"You've got four kids," Anh said, "you better remember." She spoke to him in Vietnamese now, her voice low and sweet. "I'll show her around when she gets here, help her pick out some new clothes. You'll fall in love with her all over again. No knockoff clothes, either. The real thing. Show her you love her if you spend some money. I'll get her some real designer labels, you won't believe how she's going to look."

"Oh, Anh."

"You think you love me, Mr. Bui. I think you just need a woman. You ever had a woman, Mr. Bui, in twelve years?"

"When I lived in Fresno."

"Did she sleep with you?"

"Yes."

"That was a good thing, then. But now your wife is coming here, and you'll have to change. Everyone has to change when they come here. Look at me. I'm a different person than I was in Vietnam. I'm not the same."

When Anh came out of Mr. Bui's office, there were more people waiting near the door. Some of them were in slacks and white shirts, as if the weather were tropical, even though the air had a coldness to it that felt like rain. A few of the women were in sandals and cotton trousers and shirts, faces patient, eyes dark and dreamy.

Thinh was there, too, standing near the police department palm tree, looking around.

"What do you want?" Anh said.

"Nep Lai wants to talk to you at the Rio Club tonight."

"I don't want to talk to him."

Jana was looking at them from her partitioned office, was getting up out of her chair and coming toward them.

"My brother Thinh," Anh said. "The bad one."

"Hi, Thinh."

"Hi."

Jana always looked as though she were waiting for you to ask her for help. She was looking at Thinh like that now, her mouth slightly open, as if she were trying to mouth the words Thinh should be saying. He let his eyes drop, the way he did when he spoke to Ba, then mumbled something about meeting Nep Lai at the Rio Club and turned and walked out of the office.

"Who's Nep Lai?" Jana asked.

"A gang guy," Anh replied.

"Dangerous?"

"Like a snake."

There were bean fields on both sides of the Rio Club, and a few warehouses and self-storage places and a wide highway that went from the edge of Little Saigon all the way out to Buena Park. Anh had read in the Vietnamese paper the week before that the bodies of two Cheap Boys had been found right out on Katella, sitting in their cars, not far from Knott's Berry Farm. The gangs usually didn't go that far, were careful to keep their dead bodies inside the boundaries of

Little Saigon, but sometimes they slipped and dropped them off where the Americans lived.

Inside the club twinkly balls of colored light darted beneath the mirrored ceilings, then doubled and tripled in the mirrored walls. All those colors flashing by played tricks with Anh's eyes, made her dizzy, made her feel drunk. The band was playing a tango, and there were dancers on the floor, the men in dark, tight-fitting suits, and the women in spangles and satin, their stiletto-heeled feet darting tightly in and out against their partners' legs.

Security guards funneled everyone through a small anteroom, checking purses and jacket pockets for weapons, and patting down anyone who looked like he was there to make trouble.

"She got a machine gun in there," Anh told the guard, who was poking his fingers into the corners of Jana's purse.

Thinh and Nep Lai, who had a black ribbon for his dead brothers clipped to his jacket lapel, were waiting at a table near the stage.

"Why did you bring her?" Nep Lai said.

"I don't want any trouble with anybody," Jana said. "That's all I want to tell you. No trouble." She smiled at Thinh. "Anh says you don't go to school anymore. How come?"

"I don't know. Just don't like it."

"What don't you like?"

"What is this?" Lai said. "What are you talking about?"

"You buy us a drink?" Anh said.

Lai waved two fingers in the air, and a waiter came to the table.

"Rum and coke," Jana said.

"White wine," Anh said. "Not too sweet. Not too dry. Dry wine make me sneeze."

Lai lit a cigarette and blew the smoke out of the side of his mouth. "I heard you're doing good."

"Cases is coming in," Anh said, "but not too much money yet."

"We're working them, not settling out for whatever the insurance offers," Jana said. "We've got a good office going. People trust us."

"You pay commissions?"

"How you think we get cases?" Anh said. "Standing out on the street with a flag, stopping the car?"

The waiter brought their drinks and set them down.

"I got people arranging accidents," Lai said. "That's how I want to do it. You want to share it with this American, that's up to you."

"Let's go," Jana said.

"So what you want is the whole thing, then?" Anh said.

"What are you trying to do, negotiate with this slime?" Jana said.

"You got other cases to make money on," Lai said. "This is for your protection. I told you your business was different than the rest of them, I had to figure out something special for you."

"I'm leaving," Jana said.

"You shouldn't have brought her," Thinh said.

"You shut up," Anh said.

"I've got four done already," Lai said. "I didn't want to bring them to you till we figure out the percentage. I want forty for myself. The people will get something from me. Then I want expenses. We got to bust up the cars a little, make it look good. Maybe a few scratches on the people inside, so they got to go to the hospital, that costs money. And we got to pay off people to say they work there and didn't come in and how much wage they lost, so that costs money, too."

"This so funny," Anh said. "I mean it, you crack me up."

"Careful, Anh," Thinh said. "Lai's got a temper."

"Oh, that scare me." Anh leaned across the table and put her hand on Lai's. It felt like a snake's skin to her, all damp and cool and sticky. "Listen," she said, "this year at Tet, I try to get home before Thinh, because I know the first person who come in the door at Tet is the one going to bring you bad luck or good luck. Midnight I go out of bed and go out the back door and come in the front door, so I'm the first in the house when Tet start. And there is Thinh sitting in the chair. He got there first. Oh, it bug me so bad, I can't tell you. You know why? Because I know right then and there that he going to bring me bad luck. Sure enough. First Dennis get sick, and now you trying to rob me."

"You can't blame a family member for bad luck," Lai said. "Only strangers."

"Thinh is stranger to me now," Anh said, and she pulled her hand away from Lai's and wiped it on her skirt. Back and forth, back and forth. Wiping it hard so he could see.

"I don't know about good luck or bad luck," Jana said, "but I'm going home."

"You gotta do it, or we make you do it," Lai said.

Jana stood up. "Come on, Anh. Let's go."

"So what's your answer?" Lai said.

"My answer is this whole thing happen during Tet," Anh said.

"I can't believe you're talking to this guy," Jana said.

"On Tet you not suppose to sweep the floor the first day," Anh said. "I didn't sweep it. I didn't want to sweep out any money gonna come to me during the year. I sweep on the second day, but I don't throw the dirt out, I pile it in one corner. And I don't let pregnant people in the house during Tet, because that bring bad luck, too. And I don't go on a trip on the seventh day of the month or come back on the third day of the month. And I don't let Vy hit any of the kid during Tet because that bring bad luck, too. And I don't steal during Tet, because if you steal, you steal the whole year. I don't borrow money, because if you borrow money, you borrow all year. I did everything right. Only Thinh come into the house first."

"She believes all that stuff," Thinh said.

"You know what I heard," Anh said. "I heard Vietnamese people getting gun so all you gang guy can't rob their house so easy. And I got an alarm now. You try to come in my house, that thing ring like a son of bitch and the police there in five minute."

"You'd be dead in five minutes," Thinh said.

"I'll shut the office before I do fake accidents," Jana said.

SAIGON, APRIL 1975

The end of the war was coming. There was no question about it. The Vietcong were bombing Tan Son Nhut Airport, shelling the city, knocking down buildings. There were a lot of South Vietnamese soldiers deserting the fighting in the north, running through the streets of Saigon, looking for refuge, trying to escape.

Me kept going to the post where Ba was supposed to be stationed, but no one there knew anything about him. Anh just waited, trying to figure what to do, worrying, worrying, worrying every day that Trang's house would be bombed and Manh would be killed. She told herself she'd kill herself if that happened. She even had a pistol that one of the Americans had given her. It had bullets in it, and she knew how to shoot it. And she knew the right spot in her head to do it so that she would die in a minute and not suffer.

Every day, even when the shelling was the worst, she would go to see Manh. It was like food to her just to see him, just to kiss his fat face. He could take a few steps now and say chào ông and xin chào ông. He liked to dip his hands into the tank where Trang kept the eels. He would churn the water and then shriek with joy when the eels bumped against his little fingers.

"He's so beautiful," Trang said. "I love him the way I loved you."

Business was still good, but some of the Americans looked at Anh as though it were her fault the Vietcong were winning. They came in without candy or flowers now, not talking much, just getting it over with, listening to the explosions and pumping away like it was their last fuck.

18

This car sure run smooth," Anh said.

"There's something wrong with the transmission," Jana said.

"You jamming that gearshift, that's why," Tri said. It was his used-car lot, next to a taco stand on Beach and Bolsa. A line of multicolor plastic triangles slapped against the windows of the trailer he used as his office, and on top of one of the used cars was a hinged sign that said on one side, in English, Good Wheels, Honest Deals, Van Tri Never Steals. On the other side, in Vietnamese, it said I'm a War Hero. Buy a Car from Me. Tri was Anh's cousin, the son of Me's sister, who was still back in South Dakota putting wires on circuit boards in a computer assembly plant.

"I'm doing it as easy as I can," Jana said. She jerked the gear lever into reverse again, and the car shot backward down the lot.

"I don't like Volvo, anyway," Anh said. "It look like car someone with kid wanta drive."

"So, that's me," Jana said. "I got a kid. Volvo has a terrific safety record, too. *Consumer Reports* says if you've got kids, buy a Volvo. The frame is the sturdiest on the market. If you get hit, you've got a chance to survive. All the statistics show that Volvo is—"

"Maybe we need BMW, Tri," Anh said, "like the one they bury that Nep gang boy in. You got one like that?"

"I got a blue one, got fifty thousand mile on it," Tri said.

"I don't know what's wrong with my old Toyota," Jana said. "It's gotten me where I want to go."

"Stop the car," Anh said. "Tri and me, we going to look around little bit. Maybe we find better car for you."

Jana slammed on the brakes, and the car jolted forward, then back. Tri got out of the front seat and opened the back door for Anh.

"She ever drive before?" Tri asked. They spoke in Vietnamese now. Jana was still in the car, playing with the gearshift.

"Sure. She needs a good car, that's the problem," Anh said. "She drives an old wreck. I don't let her drive to the office. I go all the way out to Balboa every day and pick her up, so nobody sees that shitty car she's got. Something like what you gave me, maybe, the Porsche, a good-looking car like that. Or if you've got a BMW like that Nep kid was buried in, that'll suit her okay."

"They're expensive, Anh," Tri said. "You already owe me for the Porsche, you didn't even give me a down payment. You promised to pay cash in thirty days. Where is it? I haven't seen the money."

"Did Me go and get you and your mom and sister in Saigon and bring you to the boat? Did I give all my money to the family when we lived in South Dakota together? Did I get you that car, and then you sold it and bought two more with the money, and now you're a big shot car dealer in Garden Grove? Did I do that for you or what?"

"I don't know what you're doing with that American, anyway."

"I'll pay you in another thirty days. The cases are coming in the office, but it takes time to get the money. You've got to settle them, or you've got to file and go to court. It's not as easy as it looks."

"You could use my kid. He works for a lawyer, he knows all about it, how to file cases, how to do insurance papers, the whole thing."

"We don't have that kind of office. We do real law in that office."

"She do law like she drives?"

"She's better than she looks. Smart. Real smart."

"Well, I've got one BMW with a hundred thousand, it's got a little dent on the side. You can hardly see it."

"It's got to look good."

"It looks good."

Jana was driving the Volvo around the lot now, accelerating, stopping, testing the gears. The car lurched up and down every few seconds, like someone wearing big heavy boots was stomping on it.

"She'll ruin that car before she's through," Tri said.

"She has to get used to it," Anh said.

"You've got trouble with the Nep family, I heard."

"No, no. No trouble. He wanted to make a deal with me, and it was no good, so I told him no."

Tri shook his head as though she had just told him she had cancer and had only a few months to live.

"Remember, no shitty cars you want to get rid of on me," Anh said. "The car she drives has to look good."

"It looks good okay."

"Then give me that BMW with the dent, and we'll get out of here."

"I think I'm getting the hang of it now," Jana said. "It's that old Toyota, you've got to baby it just so, or it won't go. I'm not used to this. Jesus, this is smooth, isn't it?"

They were on Newland now, heading into the Santa Ana barrio. It had been hot all day, unseasonably hot for April, and the Mexicans in the run-down apartment houses along the street were outside barbecuing meats. White smoke from rusted cookers curled against the night sky.

"We didn't even sign any papers," Jana said. "I could steal this car, and he wouldn't have a leg to stand on."

"Tri is my cousin."

"He's not *my* cousin."

"I told him you honest. Why, you want to steal the car?"

"I had a new car once."

"Keep to the right, we gonna turn pretty soon."

"My husband's murderer wrecked it."

"See that signal down there, that where you gonna turn."

"I don't think he used the brakes once. He'd just bang into things to stop."

"Why you let him have your car, for Chrissakes?"

"Let him? He murdered my husband and stole our car and kidnapped me. And he had a gun."

"Look where you driving. There some cop car behind us gonna give you ticket if you keep driving like you driving."

Jana clutched the wheel and stared straight ahead. "He raped me every day for a month."

Men in white undershirts, glowing cigarettes clinging to their lips, stood talking in the dark, while the women, a baby or two on their hips, leaned against apartment steps, sat on the grass, watched the traffic go by, waited for the meat to cook.

"Tri give me good deal on this car," Anh said.

"I'll pay you back," Jana said.

"You always talking about that murderer. It wasn't that good in Vietnam, either. I can tell you some things."

"I don't want to hear them."

"I told you that cop gonna give you ticket." The red light was steady behind them, glowing like a hot coal in the BMW's rear window.

"Am I supposed to pull over?" Jana said. "What the hell did I do, anyhow?"

The police car angled the BMW in toward the curb, where the Mexican families were barbecuing their dinners. One of the policemen got out and stood in the road, his hand on his holster, while his partner talked into the car radio.

"What are they doing?" Jana said. She was rummaging in her purse, fingering her license, checking her social security card.

"I don't like it," Anh said.

"I'll bet there's no taillights on this car," Jana said. "I should have turned left on Magnolia. I shouldn't have listened to you."

"There something wrong," Anh said. "I don't like it."

Jana had the glove compartment open and was flipping through the registration papers. "I'll bet it's stolen," she said.

"He want to talk to you."

The cop was tapping on Jana's window, motioning for her to roll it down.

"Both of you out, with your hands over your heads."

Jana stepped out first, and Anh slid across after her. The other cop got out of the police car and came over to the BMW. He bent down to look into the front seat, then played his flashlight on the underside of the dashboard, ran his fingers under the fancy cover plate.

"Hey, what you doing?" Anh said when he began pulling at the seams of the cushions, looking under the carpets, lifting the floor-boards.

"We just bought this car," Jana said.

"Registration papers?" the first cop said. He was writing information on a big white form stuck to a clipboard.

"I buy it from my cousin," Anh said, knowing that it didn't matter what she said. "This lady nere, she got to use that car. Careful what you doing with it."

"You been on Westminster Boulevard near Fourth tonight?"

"We been at my cousin's car lot. We look at some Volvo, but Jana can't drive it, and I don't like it anyhow."

"Lean against the car."

"Jesus, what did we do?" Jana said.

"Lean against the car."

"You look like nice guy," Anh said.

"Lean against the car." The cop ran his hands up both sides of Anh's skirt and across her breasts, then banged her head against the hood of the car.

"Ow, what you doing?"

He had his flashlight in her eyes now.

"Raise your hands and walk."

Anh teetered a moment, dizzy from the blow of her head against the sheet metal of the car.

"You drunk?"

"I ain't drunk. We been in the office all day, then went to my cousin Tri to look at some of his car, and then—"

"Tri what?"

"Van Tri. He the son of the sister of my mother. There three boy, all good, not a bad one. All work hard, take care their family. Tri sister kill in Vietnam. You married?"

"What?"

"If you married, I can get stuff for you wife wholesale. Jewelry, clothe, shoe, perfume."

"Are you trying to bribe me?"

"No, no, no, no, no."

He had the handcuffs out and was twisting them around her wrists. He was looking like he could hurt her, like he wanted to hurt her.

Just waiting for her to move wrong or say the wrong thing. Oh, he could do what he wanted all right. Punch her, knock her down, say she gave him trouble, say she tried to run. It looked to Anh like the other cop was being so careful and nice with Jana, touching her skirt oh so gently with his fingers, talking to her in a soft voice, looking as if he were sorry the whole time.

"I know all about Little Saigon," Anh's cop said. "Crap they sell there. Pure crap."

"You got to know where to go," Anh said.

Jana's cop stepped away from her and wrote some more stuff down on his paper. It looked like he was all through, like he had nothing else to say. But then he said it anyway. "What's a nice girl like you doing with this gook?"

Jana screamed.

"Give me a hand over here."

"What the hell—"

Jana had climbed onto the cop's chest, was hanging on to his neck, clawing his face with her fingers, butting her head against his. And screaming. The Mexicans came down from the barbecues and stood on the sidewalk, their faces round and glowing in the beam of the police car's light.

"She got a temper since she was little kid," Anh said.

"Hold her down. I got her now. Hold her, damn it, hold her."

"You watch her," Anh said. "She get you in the neck with one of those chops, you dead man."

Anh felt so happy watching those two big cops trying to get Jana down on the ground. She was slippery all right, weaving in and out of their arms like she had trained for it all her life. Kicking those feet like a wild woman. Deep, hard, wide whip kicks. Cars were stopped in both directions now, and the Mexican men were coming down to the curb so they could see better, drinking their bottles of beer and watching.

Oh, this was a different Jana. Anh really liked her now. All this time she was just someone to use to make money. A messy girl who looked at you cold-eyed and told you what she knew. A steady girl who took care of her crazy family because no one else would. Now she was someone you could like, kicking the shit out of those cops and screaming as if to call the world to attention.

"Get them, Jana," Anh shouted. She had never seen such anger in anyone before. Nowhere. Never before. Oh, Anh wished she could kick those cop legs the way Jana was doing, feel their shins bend, hear the bones crack. Oh, she wished her eyes were round and her nose high and her tits big. Oh, she wished she could show the whole world how angry she was.

~

SAIGON, APRIL 30, 1975

The Vietcong were coming now all right. The Americans were taking the last of their soldiers and embassy people to the airport in buses, and all the girls in the house had left. Everyone trying to find their family, trying to figure out how to get away before the Communists got them. Oh, there were stories about the Communists all right, about what they'd do to you if they caught you, how they'd torture the men and rape the women. And freedom. Everyone was talking about that, how there wouldn't be any. Anh didn't know what that meant, but she knew she didn't want to stay if the Communists were coming.

Uncle Kou went back to the village to get the family, and Me and Anh went out in the street looking for Ba. Everything was quiet now, no more fighting. It was like after a hurricane, with the trees ripped bare and houses falling down. And the bodies. They were all over the place. A city full of bodies, just lying where they fell, some of them looking as though they were asleep, others without arms or legs or even heads. One of them was lying next to a motorcycle. Anh could see through the hole in his stomach straight through to his backbone. Right straight through.

Me pulled the motorcycle upright. "Get on," she said.

Anh hopped on the back, and they went riding through the streets looking for Ba. Every block Me would stop, and she and Anh would get off the motorcycle and check the bodies. Me was the fastest. She could tell whether a corpse was Ba or not in just one pull of the head up by the hair. Anh was a little slower. She knew they were dead, but she still felt as though they could tell when they were touched, that they knew she was turning them over and looking into their faces.

They rode the streets all day and into the night, looking at dead bodies until their hands were caked with blood and they smelled like the rotting corpses.

At dawn Me gave up.

"I want my baby now," Anh said. "Let's go to Trang's house and get my baby."

Trang tried to hide in the alley behind the house when she saw Anh and Me coming on the motorcycle.

"Trang, give me my baby," Anh shouted at her.

Trang started to run, but Anh was young and fast, and it was her baby.

"Oh, sweet, sweet baby," Anh said, and grabbed him away from the woman.

"You promised to leave him here. Please, please, don't take him."

"Don't you know the Vietcong are coming, old lady," Me said. "Come with us. Uncle Kou has arranged for us all to go on a boat. Come with us."

"Duy will look for me when he comes home."

"Your husband is probably in a ditch right now."

Trang pulled at Manh's foot, tried to get him away from Anh, and Anh began to scream at her and slap her fingers.

"He's my baby," Anh screamed. "My baby."

"Just leave her," Me said. "If she doesn't want to save herself, leave her."

Me got the motorcycle going again, and Anh got on behind her, Manh in her arms.

"A baby will die on a boat," Me said.

19

They were in Police Lieutenant Chaffey's private office, waiting for him to come back in with the police report. Sam Knowlton was sitting in a chair halfway between Anh and Jana. Wearing white shorts and a T-shirt that said Lakers on it. Going to shoot baskets after a hard day in court, he said when he showed up. You caught me halfway out the door.

"The officer who arrested me was badge number 8496371," Jana told him. Her blouse was ripped all down the inseam and hung like a curtain against her arm. "The other was 9943820. I have a thing about numbers."

"If you want me to, I'll call in someone else," Sam said.

"I called you, didn't I?" Jana said. "If I wanted someone else, I'd have called someone else. You do criminal, don't you? You told me you were on a criminal case in Modesto, didn't you?"

"I lost the case in Modesto," Sam said. "It was an insanity plea. I've never won on an insanity plea yet. Were you insane when you tried to beat the cop to death? If you were, I'm not your guy."

"Oh, stop it. I think I'm in trouble. I really lost it."

"She kick the hell out of them," Anh said, and Sam looked at her. He had looked at her a lot since he walked in the door. Oh, she didn't trust this guy. She could read his mind. I know everything about you, his mind said, who you are, what you do, what you think, so don't try to fool me.

"I don't even remember much of it, except my feet hurt," Jana said. "The toes especially. They're numb."

Chaffey, a patient-looking man with tired eyes and nicotine-stained fingers, was back with the papers. He sat down in his chair and sighed. "Let's see what we've got. Okay. This thing says there was a home invasion and robbery at 335 Fourth Avenue in Midway City. People were tied up and goods were stolen, among them a Sony stereo, two RCA televisions, fifty *luong* of gold, and four jade bracelets. The perpetrators got away in a 1990 BMW, blue in color, with a small dent on the side. One of the parties resisted arrest, split one officer's lip, and broke a bone in the other one's knee."

"Do these two girls look like Vietnamese gangsters to you?" Sam said.

"What the hell's going on?" Jana said. "What are you talking about, home invasion? Are you crazy?"

"I'll handle it," Sam said. "Did you ask me to handle it, or not?"

"I know the reason they're doing this," Jana said. "It's perfectly clear to me. I beat them in small claims court and attached their lousy equipment. That's what it's all about." She leaned over the desk and glared at Chaffey. "You want to see a lawsuit? I'll give you a lawsuit will make your toes curl."

"Come on, Jana," Sam said.

"The car not paid for yet, either," Anh said. "Those guy rip the whole thing apart, boom, boom, boom, take the pillow out, throw paper around, make the whole car look like shit."

Oh, Anh was sorry she said that. She had made the police lieutenant turn her way, notice she was there. She'd better keep her mouth closed, or he would let Jana go and keep her.

Chaffey sighed and read some more. "The car was a perfect make. And the officers had information that the occupants were an American female driver and a Vietnamese female passenger."

"Did you find any stolen goods in the car?" Jana said.

"Yeah," Anh said. "If we steal stuff, where is it? It ain't in that car. No way. They rip that car apart. So where is it?"

"You could have dumped the goods somewhere along the way," Chaffey said.

"That's bull, and you know it," Sam said.

"She beat the cop up pretty bad."

"Self-defense. We'll claim police brutality."

It was all too much for Anh, too weird. No one was getting it right. No one was saying the stuff that would let them go home.

"I got to tell you something," she said.

"Forget it," Jana said. "You'll just make it worse."

"Let her talk," Sam said.

"My brother was good boy when he was little kid. Eat his food. Don't cry too much. When he fourteen, he start going out night late, and we don't know who he with or what he doing. He start bringing marijuana home, and it make me so mad him smoking that shit with all the little kid around the house."

"Does this have anything to do with anything?" Chaffey asked.

"My brother is big gang boy now in the Nep family."

"All right."

"See, this is how it go. Nep Lai want Jana and me to fake accident case for him in our law office. We tell him no. Nep Lai shoot his own mother if he feel like it, he that mean. He come to the U.S. and live in the house with his best friend from Saigon, and then he start fucking his best friend wife, and then he think why do I got to have best friend anyway? So he shoot him. He say the best friend commit suicide. Uh-uh. No way. Crack me up when I heard that word. Suicide.

"So Nep Lai probably pretty mad when Jana and me say no to his business deal. Probably go to Tri used lot, and Tri scare of everything, and I owe money for the Porsche, and now the BMW, too. So Tri think maybe he won't get the money, and Lai maybe say he gonna put Tri out of business, or something like that. So Tri do what Lai say and call the cop and tell them some fucking lie that we stealing stuff. Then you guy ruin the inside of the BMW, it gonna cost money to fix it so it look like something good again."

There wasn't a sound in the room now. Anh could hear typewriters somewhere. Sam was staring at the ceiling. Jana was looking at her with her mouth a little bit open at the edges. Chaffey looked more tired than before. Oh, it was all right now, Anh could tell.

She pulled out a card and put it on Chaffey's desk, right next to the paper with all the lies on it.

"You ever need me to take your wife shopping, if I got the time from my law business, I help you," she said.

There were a couple policewomen in the ladies' room when Anh went into the stall and sat down. Talking about lottery tickets, about what a bad bet they were, about how they never heard of anyone winning more than ten dollars, twenty-five at the most, and what was the state doing with all that money, and why was everyone still complaining there was no money for education when everyone said the lottery was going to cure all that. Anh flushed the toilet and came out and washed her face and hands at the sink. The policewomen, stern-looking in their heavy black shoes and green twill uniforms, stopped talking when they saw her, and just kind of sat against the sink while she combed her hair.

"I got arrested," Anh said finally. "It make mess out of your face and hair, you know that?"

"Prostitution?" one of the policewomen asked.

"Robbery," Anh replied.

Sam Knowlton and Jana were in the corridor when she came out.

"How's your head?" Jana said.

"Just a little headache left," Anh said.

"They dropped the charges," Jana told her. "You want to sue 'em for battery?"

"Your word against theirs," Sam said.

"Turns out there wasn't even a robbery at a house on Fourth Avenue," Jana said. "And the car isn't a stolen car, either. The whole thing was just a setup. Harassment, plain and simple."

"You take the beat-up car home," Anh said. "I call Vy to come get me."

"I'll put in a claim for the damage and see what happens," Sam said.

"I'll take care of it," Jana said.

Why was he still standing there, looking like he didn't want to leave yet? It was making Anh itchy, wishing he'd go. Why was he still hanging around? Why was he looking at her that way? She knew all the looks in the world and this was one of the looks that made the most trouble for her. Oh, she didn't like it. She didn't like it at all.

"Well, I guess I call Vy to come get me," Anh said.

"I'll take you home," Sam said.

"What's he doing here?" Vy kept peeking into the living room, where Sam was sitting. Little Boy had left his trucks on the floor, and Sam was fixing one of the wheels that had fallen off.

"He got me out of jail," Anh said. "He brought me home, and now he's sitting in the living room fixing Little Boy's truck. How am I supposed to know why he's here?"

"He's pretty handsome. I like his butt in those shorts."

"He's a lawyer, a friend of Jana's. She called him. Not me."

The tea was boiling now, and Anh steeped some of the special blend she saved for when Ba came.

"You giving him Ba's tea, that expensive tea you bought?" Vy said.

"You said it was no good."

"I just said that to make you mad."

Anh brought the tea into the living room and put it down on the low table beside the couch. She had changed into trousers and was barefoot. She sat down on the floor on her haunches so he would know for sure she was Vietnamese and that he had made a mistake coming here.

"Me watch television all the time," Anh said. "If she come out here during commercial and see some American guy talking to me, maybe she kill you."

Sam looked up from the toy truck. "Did he put this thing in the street and let the cars run over it?"

"Me don't like American guy too much. American rocket knock our house down. Just the cellar left. We lose one brother that way. Another brother step on something in the street and blow up his arm and leg."

"What village are you from?"

"Nga Tu Bay Hien. Pretty small place near Saigon."

"I was probably the one who fired off the rocket."

He sipped his tea and stared at her. He had put the toy truck back down on the floor with the other toys. It was awful the way he was looking at her. She was thinking now that maybe he had a reason. A real reason.

She lifted her trouser leg. "I got shot right here. I got lot of stuff happen I don't have to tell you about." He was looking at the scar on her leg, letting his eyes stay on it until she pulled the trouser down.

"I'm sorry," he said.

"Long time ago," she said.

They sat without talking now. Not looking at each other and not talking. And then he said, "You and Jana are playing with fire. You've got no friend in the police department, and if something happens, one of those gangsters really decides to move in on you, they're not going to come to your rescue."

"They do what they want. It no skin off my face."

"Jana doesn't know the risk you're taking with these hoodlums."

"I told her."

"That's not the same as knowing. You and I know. She doesn't."

"You tell her. Don't come here and bother me. You want a cookie with that tea?"

He shook his head.

"Vietnam fuck you up pretty good, I guess," she said.

He looked like all the other Americans she had ever seen. Tall and fair and straightforward. What was there about him? There were too many to remember. It couldn't be that.

"Were you in a brothel in Saigon in 1972?"

Oh, why do Americans always say what they think? Why do they always do what they want? Why are they all so sorry afterward?

"You go home, and don't come back," she said.

SAIGON, APRIL 30, 1975

Everyone was to meet at Vung Tau Harbor. Me left Anh and the baby there waiting while she went to get her sister Vo and Vo's husband, Phu, and three children from the tennis club where Phu was an instructor.

People were jamming the beach, trying to get to where the two fishing boats were, but they were kept back by men with rifles. Anh was shoved away when she tried to push through with the baby. Everyone was screaming at the men with rifles. Just screaming and crying like they'd kill themselves if they couldn't get on board.

Uncle Kou showed up at midday with Auntie Chi and a truck full of relatives. He had found Ba and Anh's two older brothers, Trung and Vuong. He even had Ba's second wife, Khanh, and her little girl, Cuc, in the truck. He had Auntie Chi's sisters and brothers, nephews and nieces. Everyone had some of Uncle Kou's gold bars strapped to their bodies under their clothes.

There was a priest who was going on the other boat, and he came through the screaming crowd to talk to Uncle Kou. "If something happens to your boat, we'll take you on board. Will you promise the same?"

"I promise," Uncle Kou said.

When Me got there with her sister and her family, she threw herself at Ba and held him tight for a long time. "I looked everywhere for you," she said. Then she hugged the two boys. She hadn't seen them for six years.

"Where's Loc?" Me asked.

"He can't walk," Uncle Kou said. "We can't take him if he can't walk. We left him in the village."

Me started crying. Anh had never seen her cry before. It was a strange sight, seeing the way her face squeezed up and the tears came out the sides of her eyes instead of the middle. Ba just looked away. Anh waited for him to do something, grab Uncle Kou's arm and make him drive that truck back to the village and get Loc, but he was looking at Anh's baby instead. Looking, looking, looking.

"What's this?" Ba said.

"We have to get on board," Uncle Kou said. "I've paid a lot of money to save this family." And he started forcing his way through the people, dragging their arms away from his clothes, pushing the relatives with the gold bars strapped to their skin beneath their clothes toward the boat they were going to board.

"Where are you taking that baby?" Ba said to Anh.

"It's mine. It's my baby," Anh said.

"It looks like an American," Auntie Chi said. "Where did you get an American baby?"

"Who will take care of Loc?" Me shrieked. "Who will get him food?"

"No American babies in this family," Ba said, and he pulled the baby out of Anh's arms.

"Nooooooo." Anh's scream was lost in all the other screams. "My baby. Give me my baby. Oh, Ba, please give me my baby."

But Ba had it, was holding it up over his head, and the space that the baby had taken in Anh's arms closed up. She felt herself being squeezed by arms and elbows, kicked by knees, lifted up, carried forward. Pushed. Pushed. Pushed.

"Ba, don't, Ba, don't."

Ba was being shoved, too, and Anh could see him coming closer, and she tried to touch the baby's leg, tried to get it away from Ba. She had her fingers on the smooth skin, was trying to hold tight, not to lose her grip. And then the baby slipped away, and there was nothing to hold on to.

Ba held the baby for a few more seconds and then tossed it away. A small package, with so little weight it seemed to float in the air. Like a sack full of feathers. Like a bag filled with trash.

20

Our client was just standing in line at Build and Brick," Jana said. "How'd she know the guy in front of her was going to swing his basket so his two-by-four caught her behind the ear?"

"She should have been looking," Sam said. "Build and Brick can't be responsible for what one of their customers does."

"I don't buy that. I don't buy that at all."

"You want some tea?" Anh smiled at them through the doorless opening of Jana's office. He had that big office on Wilshire. Why was he always coming here? Doing cases I don't know how to do, Jana told her. Handling the ones I'm afraid I'll get caught on.

"Doughnuts," Jana said. "Send Cookie for a box of lemon-filleds. No strawberry. I break into a rash with strawberry."

"I don't want any," Sam said. Why was he always looking at her? Looking at her through the door and over the partition. Looking at her like he was remembering things about the two of them.

"Hey, Cookie, go down and get a box of doughnuts," Anh said.

Cookie was the daughter of one of Me's brothers, a tomato grower in Santa Maria. She was a slender girl who could type faster than anyone Anh had ever seen, little fingers like mosquitoes buzzing over the keys. Sometimes the clients just stood and looked over Cookie's shoulder, clucking their tongues and pointing at her fingers.

"The ones with the yellow stuff in the center. No red ones. Jana got bumps on her face from those red ones you bought last time."

"What do you think, Sam, should I take twelve thousand for the Gallagher case?" Jana said.

"I'd hold off. Let them sweat. Don't answer the offer too quickly. They'll think you're hungry, think you're afraid to go to court. They don't know you're a litigating maniac."

"I think I'm starting to get that reputation. I heard through the grapevine that the adjusters are telling each other not to fuck with me."

It was ten-thirty in the morning, and already there were ten new clients waiting to see Jana, waiting to tell her how they broke their foot, how they slipped their disk, how the other guy was at fault, how they couldn't sleep, couldn't eat. How much my case worth?

Cases came fast now. Like rain falling down. Like bundles of money dropping from the skies. Everyone driving quick and bumping into things with their cars. Everyone slipping on holes in market parking lots. Everyone going to the hospital with scrapes and cuts and broken bones. Then coming here. Wanting to sue. Wanting money. Wanting everything that was coming to them. Oh, they sat on the floor with their umbrellas and babies slung over their shoulders, and they smelled of the earth of Vietnam, but they knew their rights in America.

There was a row of plastic chairs along the front window for them to sit on, but most of them were squatting in little clusters near the flimsy wallboard partitions. Anh was taking names now, writing them down on a yellow pad, walking among them in her stocking feet, so that if she stepped on a few fingers or toes or kicked someone in the head, it wouldn't hurt them too much.

"And you, you go deliver this paper to Santa Ana Courthouse," Anh said to the boy standing guard at the door. His name was Nam. He was one of the five boys from the coffee shop downstairs that she had hired to watch out for trouble, make sure people coming into the office were really looking for a lawyer. For a whole month she had been hearing things about Nep Lai, how the business with the BMW and the cops was just a little warning, how he was planning to do something really bad to her.

Oh, those guys from the coffee shop could scare anyone, with their oily hair and too-big white shirts and their hands never far from the guns they had stuck halfway down their baggy pants. They slouched around, always smirking and joking, their language full of Vietnamese slang, shooting the dirty words out in little grunts like their chests were being squeezed.

"Do I need a filing fee?" Nam said.

"The check is in there," Anh said. "Just look. If you look, you won't have to ask so many questions."

Anh had to be tough with these boys. Even Nam. Oh, he looked so shy, so tender, not like the others. But he was the same as they were. Always in and out of jail. Always in trouble. "You want to keep out of jail, make something of yourself," she had said when she hired him, "then behave, listen to me, come and go when I tell you, and maybe I'll send you to school. Don't tell the other ones, because I don't think they're smart enough to go to school. But I'll send you if you're good. I'll pay for you to go to college, maybe make you a lawyer. But you better keep doing what I tell you. You fuck up, I'll kick you out, and that's that. You'll be gone in a minute, pfft, just like that. I'm serious."

When Nam wasn't guarding the door, he was sitting on the edge of Cookie's desk looking at her with lovesick eyes.

Mr. Bui came out of his office holding a tie up against his starched white shirt. His wife was coming from Vietnam today, due at Los Angeles Airport in two hours, and all he could think of was what tie to wear.

"Maybe this one is better," he said.

"I like the blue one, with all the dots," Anh said. "Go get that one again, and I'll tie it for you. You don't know how to do it. Your ties always look lumpy around your neck, like you've got a tumor."

Cookie was back with a big white box. Anh followed her into Jana's office.

"I don't know, Sam," Jana said. "You keep trying to blame this accident on an innocent, injured, unaware plaintiff. I still say Build and Brick shouldn't let their customers carry goods in a dangerous manner."

"What's a dangerous manner?" Sam said.

"Any manner that risks injury to their other customers. Are you just arguing for argument's sake, or do you believe what you're saying?"

"I'm giving you opposing argument. People carry wood around in a place that sells wood. You have to expect there'll be some sticks and slabs and steel rods being carried in a store like that. Right?"

"Maybe." Jana motioned for Cookie to set the box of doughnuts down on her desk. "Their attorneys think she's faking her injuries, that she doesn't have headaches, that she just doesn't like sex anymore and is using the accident as an excuse."

"Okay, so maybe they're right on that one, too. You can't go off half-cocked. You know what it takes to prove lack of consortium?"

"You want one of these junky things, too?" Anh asked Sam. "Make your teeth rot and all your bone ache, but you go ahead and pick one out."

"I'd bet you'd like for my teeth to rot and my bones to ache, wouldn't you?"

"I never say that. Did I say something mean like that? I never say that." Anh turned to Cookie. "Go give the rest of this junk to the people out there. They don't get too much junk like this. Maybe they'll like it."

"I get it all the time," Jana said. "I'd never have believed it, the prejudice against the Vietnamese. I mean, these people are hurt. We don't run a mill here." She put her hand in the box and squeezed one of the round, sugared blobs till the lemon filling oozed out, then put the oozing doughnut on her desk. "Oh, my God, what time is it?"

"Eleven," Sam answered.

"Gotta go," Jana said, and stood up.

"What about the airport?" Anh said. "Mrs. Bui coming from Vietnam. I promise Mr. Bui we go to the airport with him. He so scare, he almost wear out his neck putting on all those different tie. And all those client sitting waiting for you."

"They'll wait. They're used to waiting. Bye, Sam."

"Take your beeper," Anh said.

"I don't want the beeper. I feel like a dog on a leash carrying that thing around."

"What if someone want to settle some case?" Anh called out after her. "Maybe someone smash his car and want to get sign up?"

"She's gone," Sam said.

Anh turned around and looked at him. "Every Thursday, pfft, like that, no matter what she doing, eleven o'clock and she take off. She won't tell me why, where, how, or nothing else. You know where she go on Thursday?"

"No idea."

"You gonna hang around while I go with Mr. Bui to the airport?"

"Why do you call him Mr. Bui? His name's Le."

"When I first see him, he in Mr. Bui office, at Mr. Bui desk, so I call him Mr. Bui. All these month I call him Mr. Bui, wait for him to tell me don't call me Mr. Bui, my name Mr. Le. But he too polite. I think he like the name Bui better, anyway. You going to hang around, or what?"

"No. I've got to be in Van Nuys Court after lunch."

"Jana give you that case with the lady got hit in the head with a board?"

"She says the other attorney knows she's not a lawyer."

"She give you the case?"

"She gave me the case."

"I already give the client two thousand dollar. I told her it was good case. She expecting lotta money. You gonna give me that money back?"

"You give everyone money in advance?"

"Only the good case. You gonna give me two thousand?"

"It puts pressure on the case."

"So you ain't gonna give me two thousand?"

"If I win, I'll give it to you."

She began cleaning Jana's desk, brushing up doughnut crumbs and dumping them into the wastebasket.

"All these kids with guns," he said. "You run this office like your own private army. You're not a bad general, but your soldiers are too skittish. One of them's going to accidentally kill a client. I can see the headlines now. 'Mother and three children escaped Vietnam only to be shot to death in a law office in Westminster, California.' What do you need so many guns for?"

She pulled a tissue out of the square box on Jana's desk and wiped away the smears of yellow custard.

"You been getting threats from those gangsters, haven't you?"

She kept cleaning, stacking dirty cardboard coffee cups, moving papers into piles.

"You haven't told Jana what a gang threat means, have you?"

She wadded the greasy tissue into a ball and tossed it into the wastebasket next to Jana's desk.

"If I tell her, maybe Jana get so scare, she leave. Maybe you and her thinking of starting business over on Wilshire without me. Maybe you and her already got the furniture pick out."

"That's what you think? That's really what you think?"

"Sure, that what I think."

"Well, you can stop thinking. I've got a job. I don't need another one. And if you haven't figured it out by now, Jana's loyal to the bone. She's not going to run out on you. You're the one who's going to run. One call from the bar association, one tip that someone's going to come in here and investigate, one hint of trouble, and you'll be gone. You'll be out of this office so fast, Jana won't know you were ever here."

"So why you care? What you doing hanging around here all the time, anyway?"

"Watching you."

She stopped cleaning and looked up at him. "I knew it. I knew it." Oh, this was too much. He was trying to shame her, trying to bring back that filthy war, that awful time, bring it back and put it on her, make her wear it, make her choke on it. "You bug me so much. You know that? Who care what you know about Saigon, about me? You think I remember you? You think I know one American from the other American over there? You think you so special, so handsome, you screw so good, I going to remember you? The curtain open up, the guy come in, I lay myself down, I shut my eye. I was thirteen, for Chrissake. They come in, I do it, they go out." She took a breath. "I don't remember you."

"I remember you."

"Tough."

Oh, he made her mad. How come he could make her so mad? She swiped at the desk again with a fresh tissue. "I don't know how Jana mind so neat and her desk so shitty."

"Why were you in a brothel? Did I do that, too?"

Her breath stopped somewhere beneath her ribs. He was on his feet, moving toward her, a giant in a gray suit. She could feel the heat of him so strong, her eyes burned. She remembered a village full of smoke and flaming trees. And then she swung her arm. Oh, it felt good to swing that arm. Oh, it felt good to see that red spot bloom on his cheek.

"You don't understand," he said.

"Oh, I understand," she said. "I understand everything."

She was about to do it again. Had her arm up. In position. Sam was staring at her, waiting for the blow to fall. He didn't even back away. Then Mr. Bui's voice came, sharp and quick, through the door.

"We're going to be late," he said.

Mr. Bui's kids were good ones all right, standing in the waiting room waiting for their mother. Anh had never seen them all together before, and they looked so clean and nice. One of the boys was married, and his wife's stomach was sticking out full and round in her dark blue dress. Mr. Bui's daughter, Jun, had her mother's picture in her hands.

"Let me see that," Anh said. She looked at the picture and then at Jun's face. "You look the same. I've never seen anything like it, how you look like her. Do you remember her?"

"A little."

The girl was shy. Anh remembered how she was at seventeen, running through the streets of Saigon. Looking, looking, looking.

"Let's get you a glass of water, Mr. Bui," Anh said. "You look like you're going to faint."

"I'm all right."

The lounge was crowded with families waiting. But there was hardly any noise. Not even the babies were crying. It was as though they were all at a funeral, peering into the coffin and waiting for the corpse to show signs of life.

There was a surge forward as the doors opened. People pressed in on one another. They pushed at each other's shoulders, flattened themselves to get closer, and still there was no sound. When the first person came through the door, the wailing started. Anh had never stood and waited for corpses to come alive. She had never heard this sound before. The sound of agony mixed with joy. Jun was swaying back and forth, the picture clutched to her chest. Her brothers had formed a ring around Mr. Bui, as though they were trying to protect him from disaster.

"Where is she?" Jun cried.

The people coming through the door looked bewildered. Strange arms tugged at them. People screamed.

"I don't see her," Mr. Bui said. Jun kept glancing at the picture. Back and forth from the door to the picture.

"Twelve years," Anh wondered. "What will we all look like in twelve years?"

A woman came out of the crowd. "Paul Le," she kept saying, "Paul Le." A tiny woman in a silk gown, jade ornaments in her hair. She stood right in front of Mr. Bui, and he didn't know her. Jun stared at her a moment and then looked at the picture and began to cry.

Anh had seen faces like Mrs. Bui's before, on women who had heard that their husbands in America wouldn't want them if they showed up with narrow Vietnamese eyes. Mrs. Bui had probably had hers done just before she left Saigon. They were black and blue and swollen, and one was rounder than the other one.

Anh put her arm around the woman and felt her trembling deep inside, little shivers that came from the bones and wiggled their way up through the skin.

"I'm Jun," Jun said, and took a few steps closer. The boys had formed a new circle apart from Mr. Bui. They were trying not to look at their mother's face. Mr. Bui was tugging at his tie as though it were choking him.

"What did you do to yourself?" he said.

"She looks pretty to me," Anh said. "She's prettier than the picture, prettier than when you married her, and she's here now, so forget it."

Oh, it was cruel. Anh wanted to run away from their disappointment. She wanted to be seventeen again with no war. She wanted to be someplace where there was no need for American eyes and botched surgeries, no need for all this sorrow.

"I've got a good doctor for you," she whispered in Mrs. Bui's ear. "He can fix you. You'll see."

South China Sea, May 1975

Nguyen Tam had to watch Anh every minute to keep her from throwing herself off the boat. Tam was Auntie Chi's brother, the only one who seemed to care that Anh's heart was broken, that she didn't want to live. He was the one who jumped off the boat while it was still in the harbor and ran to see if he could find the baby. He almost didn't get back on the boat, there were so many people shoving and screaming. The boat motor was running, spitting water into the sky, and the men with the rifles were shouting for him to hurry up and get aboard or they'd leave him behind.

Now he watched Anh every minute. He was as old as Ba and had a wife and two children of his own, but he watched Anh and took care of her as if she were his own daughter. When she tried to drink seawater, tried to poison herself with it, he put his finger down her throat and made it come up again.

The rain never stopped. It filled the boat and sloshed over the sides, and everyone had to bail the water out as fast as possible to keep the boat from sinking. There were a hundred people on the boat, and just a small tarpaulin in one little corner to protect against the rain. The men let their wives and daughters and sisters sit under the tarpaulin, and they sat out in the rain. Me was under the tarpaulin with Khanh and Anh and some of the other women and children. Me seemed unconscious, as though everything that had happened to her in the past five years had finally broken her down.

"Do you want to eat something?" Tam asked Anh. His wife had a small package of dried fish.

"Not now," Anh said. She kept looking at Ba, the way he sat out in the rain, his shoulders hunched over, the rain pelting him. He kept blinking his eyes to see through the drops. Sometimes he tilted his head back and let the rain fall into his open mouth. Oh, she hoped he would choke on that rainwater, drown in it. She wanted to push him off the boat and hold his head down in the water till he was dead. She wanted to beat him on the head, crack open his skull, look inside his brains to see why he had done this to her. She wanted him to suffer the way she was suffering. She hated him. Oh, no ocean in the world was big enough to hold the hate she felt.

21

The real estate office was next to the ferry on Balboa Island. Mitzi Flowers, Realtor, the sign said. Anh had never seen an office in a house before. Not one like this, anyway, with pansies in pots along the walk. And a wooden cow on the roof. The door was open, so she walked in. It smelled good inside, like cinnamon and lemons. And it was bright and clean, not even a speck of dirt on the bare wood floors. A knitted afghan hung over the back of a footed leather couch in the living room. An oak coffee table held a square stack of magazines, a porcelain rooster, and a small plaque that said Thank You for Not Smoking.

"Hello!" Anh called out, and she heard her own voice like a stranger's echoing through the cheery, sweet-smelling rooms.

"In here," a voice called back.

Mitzi Flowers was at her roll-top desk in the dining room. She had bright yellow hair and big round glasses that dug into the bottom of her cheeks. The small dog at her feet sat up and began to growl when Anh entered.

"That thing bite?" Anh said.

"Yorkies don't bite," Mitzi said.

"I let a dog in my house one time. Vietnamese people, they think it good luck you let an old dog come in, and then you feed it—any old dog, it don't matter, it in the neighborhood and want to come in, you let it. It suppose bring you good luck. No way. No way. Don't you believe it. I let that dog in, and he bite me."

Mitzi smiled, but her blue eyes, blue as the bay water a few steps from the door, were wary.

"I want to buy a house," Anh said.

Mitzi's face changed right then. Oh, it wasn't a big change, like boom, I don't want you here, or shit, get out before I call the cops. It was more like how am I going to get rid of you and not get a headache out of it.

"Well, the houses are very expensive," Mitzi said.

Anh's beeper went off in her purse right when Mitzi said that, and Anh said excuse me and reached into her purse for her cellular phone.

"I don't go nowhere I don't take my phone and my beeper. My office never leave me alone, wanting me day and night, day and night." She showed the phone to Mitzi. "Top of the line. Mitsubishi. Japanese. They do the best. Don't cost no arm and leg neither. I got connection in Little Saigon. You need telephone cheap, best there is, little one like this so you can put in your pocket, or like this, right in your purse, no big heavy thing pull your shoulder down, I get it for you."

"You can make your call in the sunroom, then have a cup of coffee before you go," Mitzi said.

Anh put the phone back in her purse. "Cookie—that my cousin—Cookie call me day and night, day and night. See, we got case won't quit." She put her hand to her chin to demonstrate. "Up to here we got case."

"Maybe it's an emergency."

"Cookie always got emergency. I bring her down here so she stay away from some boy. She from Santa Maria. My uncle up there grow tomato, he say she all lovey-doovey with some Mexican boy, some druggie that already got two kid. He say the boy going to kill hisself, he so lovey-doovey over Cookie. What I gonna do, my uncle ask me. So I tell him, never mind the boy, just send Cookie to me, I got job for her. I got couch she sleep on. I feed her. Don't you worry. I don't know what happen to the Mexican boy. Maybe he kill hisself when Cookie leave Santa Maria. Maybe not. But Cookie here now working for me."

"We have a quiet group of residents on the island," Mitzi said. "People who've been here for generations. Some of them are grand-children of the people who built the houses."

Through the door of Mitzi's cozy office Anh could see the sunroom with the coffee urn and the cardboard cups and the sugar and creamer, and then the big window with the bay like a picture right outside, sailboats and windsurfers flitting across it on the breeze. And on the far side, looking small as a baby's toy, the Ferris wheel Boy and Little Boy were going to ride on someday.

"Did you see my car out there?" Anh said. It couldn't be that the woman thought she was poor. Not in that silver Porsche with its wire wheels that gleamed so bright it hurt your eyes.

"Everyone has a car on the island," Mitzi said, not even glancing out the window at the shiny sports car. "But they use bicycles. It's faster that way and keeps the traffic down."

"Oh, I got bicycle. Good one. Thinh—he my brother—he left good bicycle in my house. I got it in my bedroom, so no one steal it."

The look in Mitzi's eyes was turning Anh's stomach.

"See this linen jacket? Little Saigon. Real designer label, but I get it cheap, I don't waste my money."

The woman was so cool. Anh wanted to touch her white skin to see if she really was as cool as she looked.

"And these boots. Ferragamo. How much you think I pay? Go on, guess."

"I'm really busy."

"And look at this." Anh pulled her wallet out. "Real Louis Vuitton. No fake. Where did I buy it? Go on. You tell me where."

"I hear that Vietnamese people are like the Mexicans. One person buys a house, and twenty-five people move in."

Oh, so she said it. Anh knew if she stood here long enough she'd say it. And she did. Well, she knew how to take care of things when someone was shooting right at you. It was when they had the gun hidden that she didn't always know what to do.

"Oh, oh." Anh nodded her head in understanding. "You think I gonna buy this house for myself. Oh, oh, I see what you mean." She gave Mitzi the biggest grin she had. "I ain't gonna live in this house. You think I gonna live here? Oh, oh, that the problem. There it is. This house for my boss. She big lawyer in Little Saigon. No Vietnamese. Jewish. Jewish people. But she don't look like it. Very quiet. One kid. I see what you thinking. You thinking I was coming here with my sister and her four kid and my mother and Cookie and me. No wonder you so scare." She walked over to the window behind Mitzi's desk. The sun was getting stronger and stronger as the days moved toward summer, the morning haze burning off now before eleven. Reflected water gleamed in Mitzi's yellow hair. It made the lacquered strands sparkle and dance. Like clusters of rainbows. Like rain-dipped flowers. Anh patted Mitzi's shoulder gently. "No wonder," she said.

22

he lot's deeper than most," Mitzi said as she pulled her big white Cadillac up to the curb. She leaned across Jana and peered out at the house. A jacaranda tree bloomed in the small front yard, its velvety lavender blossoms arching overhead like a spotted umbrella. The house itself was set back, hidden by shrubs, the roof blanketed in jacaranda blossoms.

"It look pretty small to me," Anh said from the backseat.

"It's really quite large inside," Mitzi said. "What we call a fooler. Island people don't like ostentation."

"That tree sure make a mess," Anh said, eyeing the purple smears on the flagstone walk.

"The tree's as old as the house," Mitzi said. "There's a picture of it in Swenson's Bakery when it was nothing but a sapling. Nineteen twenty, I think it was."

Anh listened to the way she talked. She didn't talk this way last week. Oh, no. She was pretty quiet last week.

"Where did you say you went to school?" Mitzi asked, not making a move to get out of the car.

"Berkeley," Jana said.

"My nephew went there. John Church. Do you know him?"

"What year?"

"Seventy-five."

"I was later than that."

"Oh." Mitzi kept staring at the house. Anh could see her assessing, figuring. "We never did pin down what you were willing to spend. A house like this is more expensive than most."

Jana glanced back at Anh.

"You got plenty in the bank," Anh said.

"It's seven hundred fifty thousand," Mitzi said.

"Hmm," Jana said.

"How long did you say you've been practicing in Westminster?"

"Five year," Anh piped up from the backseat. "Big case. We got the biggest case in Little Saigon. Everyone come to us. They know we honest, gonna give good deal. We just settle case with boy got scar on his face, his uncle die in the wreck, and the boy all mess up in the face, we got him two hundred thousand."

Mitzi took another long look at the house, and then said, "I really thought this place was sold. I just took a chance driving by. But there's the sign, still on the lawn."

"What do you know," Jana said.

"This is one of the oldest houses on the island," Mitzi said. She had the door open and was picking up the mail that had accumulated on the parquet floor inside. And talking. About the island, the ferry, the dance pavilion. About the boat that used to take people to Catalina in four hours, and how the hydroplane now did it in one. About the neighbors, how they had Fourth of July parties and blocked off the island streets. About how you didn't have to lock your doors, because everyone knew everyone else and was watching out for strangers.

Anh rapped the brass knocker against the solid wood and listened to the nice, firm sound it made. A permanent sound. A sound like it wasn't going to change ever in anyone's lifetime.

"Does anyone live here?" Jana said.

"The family's in Europe," Mitzi said. "In France, actually. They have a house there."

Mitzi led the way through the rooms, marching on her high heels, hardly stopping to let Anh look at the carved fireplace mantel or touch the blue-and-white cotton covering on the couches or go up close to the wall to examine the blue plates hanging around the Florentine mirror. She just talked to Jana. Ignored Anh and talked to Jana. Just once when Anh reached for a photograph on an end table, Mitzi turned and said sharply, "Don't touch anything."

The bedrooms were standard, but large and filled with antiques. None of the bathrooms seemed special to Anh until they reached the large one off the library. Opposite one mirrored wall, a big, smooth marble tub sat right in the curve of the windows. Windows so clean and shiny that Anh couldn't tell if the flowers were inside the house or out. She turned her head right and then left, right and then left, and flowers bounced back and forth between the sheer panes of glass and the long wall of mirror so quick, it made her smile.

"The way the island's laid out, with hardly more than a scrap of land per lot, it takes special design to build Jacuzzis so you've got privacy like this," Mitzi said. "They put the Jacuzzi in in 1985 and had a landscape architect do the garden so it looks like there are no other houses around, even though there's only twenty-five feet from the back door to the next house."

"I like an ordinary bathtub," Jana said. "Spigots and a drain is all a person really needs. You take a bath to get clean, then you get out. I'm not too interested in anything fancy."

"Don't do that," Mitzi said, but Anh already had the faucet on and was fiddling with the jets, bending over the tub, kneeling on the imported marble bench. Water shot out, splashed against her fingers, warm and soft. Oh, she felt lost, up in the sky somewhere, looking down from a cloud. This was America. This house. This bathroom. This Jacuzzi tub.

Mitzi bent over and turned off the water faucet.

"Why don't you leave us alone a minute," Jana said to Mitzi. "Do you mind?"

"Of course not. I'll make a few quick phone calls and be right back."

"This is the house I want," Anh said to Jana when Mitzi was gone. "I don't like that tree in front, it make too much shit. But I got people to fix everything. Take it out. Put what I like back in. Maybe a fountain right by the door."

"You can put a zoo in the bedroom, for all I care," Jana said. "Let's go. We can walk back to the real estate office from here and pick up my car. I'll make the offers this afternoon, and we'll get the escrows started. You'll give me power of attorney on this one, but it'll really be for you. I'll word it so she doesn't have a clue. She's not too bright."

Anh stopped. "Wait. Maybe you want this one, I take the other one."

"They're both about the same. It doesn't matter to me one way or the other."

"You take this one. The school close here. Andy won't walk so far when he start to school. It better for you."

"What about Boy, he'll be going to school, too. You like this one. You want to put a fountain in the front. Take this one."

"I want you to have it."

"Look—"

"No. This one for you. The other one for me. You like this one better. I see it when you look at it, you like it a whole lot better than the other one."

Jana smiled at her. "I pay next time."

A sharp scream came from somewhere to the rear of the house. There were some shouts now. A man's voice. Mitzi yelling at someone to get the hell out.

Mitzi, yellow hair flying around her face, was standing in the middle of the sunny kitchen, a stained, torn sleeping bag in her hands.

"What happened?" Jana said.

"I don't know how he got in," Mitzi said. She was out of breath and wheezing. "We're so careful with the lock boxes."

Anh had the side door open, looking out at the cement path alongside the house. The man was running as hard as he could. Oh, she knew about that running, how your legs won't go as fast as you want, how your heart nearly stops with fear. He wanted this house, too. He needed it, too. She wanted to run after him, call him back in, tell him she'd give him a job in Little Saigon, find him a room, feed him, give him pocket money, get him a shave, take him to a doctor. She got such an urge to help him that she felt like crying. But he was gone. She might as well chase a ghost.

"Did you know him?" Jana said. She was looking in the cupboards, opening door after door.

"No," Mitzi said.

"Where are the glasses?"

Mitzi pointed to a cupboard over the stove. She was holding one hand against her chest.

"You got heart?" Anh asked anxiously.

"What?"

"Heart condition," Jana said. She had found the glasses, tall berry-color glasses to match the Italian floor tiles.

"He punched me in the chest," Mitzi said.

Jana filled a glass with water, then stood over Mitzi while she drank it.

"He scared me to death," Mitzi said. "God knows what he'd have done if you hadn't come in when I screamed."

"Well, he gone now," Anh said. "Poor thing."

"Poor thing?" Mitzi exclaimed. "What in the world are you talking about?"

"He scare, too. People get scare, you know. This house got hundred-twenty-volt electric?"

"What?" Mitzi said.

"Everything in the United States is one-twenty," Jana said.

"I just want make sure," Anh said. "In Saigon you get electric shock if you just got wet hair. You go up on the roof, and—pfft—you die when you touch a wire."

"Balboa's always been so safe," Mitzi said.

"You're not safe anywhere," Jana said.

"Jana gonna buy this one," Anh said. "And she want to buy that one we look at near the school. For her mom and dad. Jana real good to her mom and dad. Take care of them like Vietnamese people do."

"I don't know what to say," Mitzi said, looking confused and upset.

"You give Jana cut on commission, because she buy two. Okay?"

"My goodness," Mitzi said.

"I'm sure glad we don't have to look at any more houses," Jana said.

"He could have killed me," Mitzi said.

"It's not impossible," Jana said.

"You sound okay now," Anh said, "not like someone who just almost got kill."

"Selling two houses in one day can fix anything," Jana said.

Anh kneeled down on the marble bench again and turned the jets on. Mitzi didn't say anything this time when the water spurted out.

"It doesn't look like he did any damage," Jana said.

They had gone through all the rooms, checking walls and fixtures and furniture and carpets to make sure nothing had been broken or stolen or mangled.

"I think I'll buy a gun," Mitzi said.

"I can get gun for you cheap," Anh said.

"Studies show you're forty-three times more likely to shoot yourself or someone you know than you are to shoot an intruder," Jana said.

"Numbers don't mean a thing when it's you about to become a statistic," Mitzi said. She was calmer now. She had combed her hair and put on fresh makeup. "And if you want my opinion, I think the homeless like it that way. There's something to be said for living outside and experiencing the change of seasons firsthand."

"Something like camping, you mean?" Jana said.

"You can laugh if you want, but everyone talks about freedom. Isn't that the ultimate freedom? No job? No home? Confidentially—and just keep this information to yourself—I think the seller will go as low as six-fifty."

"I was kidnapped once, and my husband was murdered," Jana said.

"Really?"

"The guy was a student of my husband's at Berkeley. He just burst into our house one evening after dinner and shot him dead and kidnapped me. I remember what we ate that night. Pot roast and string beans, with rainbow sherbet for dessert. In water glasses. Plain ones. Glass glass. No color. Someone gave me sherbet glasses for my wedding, but I never could find them. Isn't it a conflict, you representing both the buyer and the seller?"

"That's the way it's done," Mitzi said. "Did they find your husband's murderer?"

"Oh, yes. He's in prison. The police ambushed him in the parking lot of the motel we were in in Wyoming. Burt—Burt Steele's the one who got him—said he had the clearest shot at him he'd ever had at anyone. Shot him in the neck. Almost got the jugular. Chris—he's the murderer—was going out for hamburgers. With large fries. Real crisp, or he wouldn't eat them. Burt said he left a trail of uneaten french fries behind in every motel we stopped at. You know, if the seller's willing to take back some paper, we might be able to do business."

The water tickled Anh's fingers. All those streams reaching toward the middle of the tub, mixing, swirling, then dropping into the shiny chrome drain.

"I'll pick the escrow company," Jana said.

"That's fine," Mitzi said.

Anh slipped off her shoes and hose and put her feet down flat on the bottom of the smooth marble Jacuzzi. That man must have liked this house. He didn't even dirty the tub. Maybe he didn't know how to work it. Jana was talking business. Without feeling, without emotion. She could hide who she was pretty well. Talk about murderers and houses and escrows all in the same way. It made Anh nervous the way she could do that, made her think she couldn't trust her, made her wonder when she was going to run away. Oh, Sam could say Jana was loyal all day long, but Anh didn't believe it. Maybe she didn't know about Jana, but she knew about Americans. With Vietnamese, it was honor that kept you together. With Americans, it was money.

"How long an escrow will you need?" Mitzi asked.

"Ninety days should do it," Jana replied.

Oh, this was going to be a good place to live, this island, this American town. How could anyone hurt her here? Nep Lai would be afraid to come across on that ferry. He wouldn't put blood on American streets. Not where grandchildren lived in the houses their grandparents built.

"You were pretty lucky, you know, that the guy didn't have a weapon," Jana said.

"I was lucky, wasn't I?"

What was Mitzi Flowers talking about, lucky? No, Anh was lucky. So lucky. Oh, lucky, lucky, lucky. What did anyone else's luck have to do with it?

In the car, after the papers were signed, and Mitzi Flowers was left behind in her office with the cow on its roof, Anh told Jana about how she lost her baby in Vietnam.

"He was almost three," Anh said.

"I don't know how you lived after something like that," Jana said. She was driving, and didn't even turn once to see Anh's face, see if she was crying, see if she was upset. She just kept looking straight ahead. Driving, driving, driving.

"I didn't live," Anh replied.

"Who wants hot dogs?" Jana's brother, Bart, always had charge of the barbecuing. He said he came down to Newport to see their mom and dad, but Jana knew it was because his lover, Ron, liked the ocean. While Bart was standing at the grill in Jana's front yard, Ron would jog on the beach so all the surfers could see how cute he looked in his tank top and cut-off jeans.

"Hot dogs make me sick," Jana's mother said. "Your father likes them, though. Give him one. He hates relish. No relish."

"Dad, do you want a hamburger," Jana asked, "or a hot dog?"

"He isn't listening," Bart said.

"He hears every word," Jana's mother said. "Give him a hot dog."

"He's getting awfully close to the ocean," Jana said. Andy was playing in the sand on the other side of the walk, pouring it from one pail into another one.

"Andy, sweetie, go get Tweetie Bird and tell her Grandpa's going to fall into the ocean."

Andy ran across the walk to the house and came out with Tui, the maid Anh had found for them. She could speak English and drive, and Andy called her Tweetie Bird. Now everyone did.

"He just can't stay away from the water," Jana said. She was standing with her hand shielding her eyes from the sun, watching Tui run across the sand and catch Jana's father just before he began to take his trousers off.

"He belongs in a home," Bart said.

"Never," Jana's mother said.

"We're managing," Jana said. "I'm buying a house, a bigger place, so Tweetie Bird can live with us. Days aren't enough. We need her nights, too."

Bart looked up from the grill. "Business is that good?"

"It's that good."

"Well."

"Anh's buying one, too, a couple blocks away from mine."

"You two are awfully friendly."

"We're in business together. Why not?"

"Nothing. I just said you're awfully friendly."

Ron was back from his jog, his muscled arms glistening with suntan oil and sweat. He had had a face-lift and a hair transplant, and although he was older than Bart, he looked younger.

"Great run," he said, and reached for a diet soda.

"Jana's moving," Bart said.

"Just when I was getting used to this," Ron said. "Where to?"

"Balboa Island," Jana said. "You'll still be able to come and use the beach. There's plenty of beach in Balboa."

"The Vietnamese are very nice," Jana's mother said.

"Hmm," Ron said.

Bart was turning the hamburgers, poking at them with the edge of the spatula to see if they were done. "I don't understand this thing between you and this girl. What do you have in common, anyway? I mean movies, books, you name it. And what about jokes? I bet you can't laugh at the same jokes, either."

"I laugh at the Vietnamese ones, and she laughs at the English ones. It evens itself out."

"Huh?"

"Your sister's pulling your leg, Bart," Ron said.

"Well, it's peculiar," Bart said. "How do you know who she really is, anyway?"

Tweetie Bird was back, holding Jana's father by the hand. She sat him down on the sand and put a napkin on his lap, then went over to the picnic table and fixed a hot dog and put some salad on a plate for him.

"How does anyone know anyone?" Jana replied. "How can you explain what makes you click with another person, why you like them, why they like you?"

"She probably got everything she knows about Americans from watching television," Ron said.

"Give Dad some Jell-O, too, Tweetie Bird," Jana said.

"He doesn't like Jell-O," Tweetie Bird said.

"He doesn't like Jell-O," Jana's mother said.

"Oh."

"Aren't there gangs in Little Saigon?" Bart asked.

"Sure," Jana said. "They don't bother us."

"There's always something in the newspaper," Ron said. "They're worse than the Mexicans. Always killing each other."

"I don't think you can trust them," Bart said. "How do you think they won the war?"

Tweetie Bird looked up.

"We should have nuked them," Ron said.

Jana felt her face turning red. The skin prickled, drew itself up and prickled, as though it were trying to separate from her body. Bart glanced over at her and saw the change. "We're joking, Jana."

"Sure."

It was an effort to control herself. She wanted to hit him. She wanted to kick Ron in the face, tell him to get off her beach.

"Are you all right?" Bart said. He looked genuinely sorry.

She just kind of waved her hand at him and walked down toward the water. Bart and Ron talking about nuking the Vietnamese. She could open her mouth, blister them with her hot words. She knew how to do it. She looked back at Bart. He had the spatula up in front of him, and he was staring at her, looking as if he was going to cry.

She stood at the edge of the water and watched the sand holes bubble when the waves went out. Bart was calling to her now, telling her the food was getting cold. Come on and eat, he said.

She walked back slowly.

"I fixed this hamburger exactly the way you like it," Bart said. "Not too rare, not too well done."

"Well, I think I'll go take a dip in that ocean," Ron said.

"Take one for me, too," Bart said.

Their father was eating quietly, and their mother didn't even notice the sand crab crawling between her toes. Andy was sitting on Tweetie Bird's lap giving her bites of his hot dog. Bart handed Jana the hamburger and smiled at her.

"Feeling better?" he asked.

Oh, she could pulverize him if she wanted to. Make him disintegrate. Make him hysterical.

"Anh lost her son in the war," she said. "Her little boy, Bart. Her own little boy. A little boy like Andy. Like your nephew."

Bart started to cry. Jana put her arm around his shoulder. "Don't," she said. "Please don't."

~

SOUTH CHINA SEA, MAY 1975

On the fourth day, it began to rain. And the boat stopped. The engine wouldn't go anymore. Uncle Kou and Ba and Tam and some of the other men tried to fix it. While they were pounding at the engine with hammers and fists, another boat, the one that had left Vung Tau the same time they did, came alongside.

"You promised to save us," Uncle Kou yelled at the priest, his words nearly lost in the roar of the rain. "Our engine is broken. Take us onto your boat."

"We have too many people now," the priest yelled back. "Our boat will sink if we put any more people on it. Put your trust in God."

Some of the people from Anh's boat jumped overboard and tried to swim to the other one, but it turned and chugged away into the storm.

"Nineteen people are gone," Uncle Kou said as one by one the people in the water dipped their heads and sank. The last one to disappear beneath the waves was a young girl. Anh watched her, not moving from where she sat hunched beneath the tarpaulin.

"The boat will float easier now," Ba said. He had been taking turns with Khanh tending Me, who was sick with fever, each of them trying to coax drops of water down Me's throat. Anh sat thinking about the people who had drowned, wishing she were one of them.

Oh, it didn't matter to her if Me died. She didn't care whether the boat sank. There was no meaning in any of it for her.

They drifted for three weeks. Each day a few more people died. Just lay back, shut their eyes, and died. The boat grew lighter and lighter, but it seemed not to be moving at all, merely staying in one place while the rain pounded it, tried to flood it, tried to tip it over, tried to force it beneath the waves. Then the rain stopped, and the sun came out, a burning sun that left everyone panting for breath.

"Take your turn caring for your mother," Ba said to Anh. "Khanh is tired and wants to rest. You don't do your share."

"She's a selfish, rotten daughter," Khanh said.

Anh got up from where she was lying and took the can of water from Ba's hands.

"I'm sorry, Ba," she said.

There were fewer people beneath the tarpaulin now that so many had died, and Anh held Me against her breast, stroking her forehead and speaking to her in a low voice. "I don't understand how Ba can have two wives. I don't understand why you were the one to bring her to him. Did you ever love me, even for a minute, even at the moment I was born and before you knew I was an unlucky girl? How could Ba have thrown my baby away?"

Me was unconscious, her mind flitting from unintelligible words to no words at all, and she only moaned in reply.

In the fourth week the rain started again, and there was water to fill the cans. But the food was gone, and everyone lay waiting for death.

"I want to die," Anh told Tam. His wife, Hao, was now sick with fever, and Anh moved from Me's side to help him with her. "I want to take the place of the ones who are dying," Anh said. "My heart is broken. My own father has broken my heart."

"He is still your father," Tam said. "And deserving of respect."

They drifted, and people died. They drifted some more. It was as if the boat had a purpose, a direction, as though it were making its own way on tides and swells and ocean breezes, turning when it thought it should turn and anchoring itself to a patch of sea when it tired of the journey. Tam, who had been an engineer in the South Vietnamese army, said that according to the stars, they had hardly moved from the place where the boat's engine died.

The smell on the boat was sickening, the passengers relieving them-

selves in buckets that were overflowing because no one had the en-
ergy to lift them and empty them over the side. Some people couldn't
reach the buckets at all. Me's fever was gone, but she was listless and
sat staring at the water, her lips moving soundlessly, as though she
were counting the swells.

The storm was over, and the boat languished, unwilling even to
drift any longer. On the morning of the forty-fifth day a boat ap-
peared on the horizon. A speck at first. No more than a mosquito on
the edge of the sea.

"It's a fishing boat," Uncle Kou said.

"No, it's not," Tam said.

Anh crawled to where her father was and lay at his feet.

"You're an obedient daughter," he said, and put his hand on her
head, as though she were a child.

The boat came closer.

"It's from Thailand," Uncle Kou said.

"No, it's from Malaysia," Tam replied.

The boat scraped alongside, and one of its men came aboard. He
was in a crisp, clean uniform, and as he walked the littered deck of the
broken boat, he could scarcely hide his disgust. "We will take you to
Malaysia, but you can't stay. We have no provision for refugees."

By the time they reached Malaysia, of the one hundred people who
had set out from Vung Tau, sixty-four had died. Among them Tam's
wife, Hao, and Anh's two older brothers, Vuong and Trung, the
ones who had been away fighting the Vietcong for six years.

23

nh had put on the invitations for everyone to come at four, but she knew Vietnamese always add an hour, sometimes more, so she didn't even bother to get to the restaurant until five. Mr. Bui and his wife were there already, sitting at a table in a rear corner next to the exit door, the gold rails encircling the bandstand right at their backs. Anh felt excited, as if the party were for her. Parties always made her feel like that. You forget everything at a party. The whole world turns pretty at a party.

"You two are here early," Anh said. "Where are the flowers? You seen the flowers?"

"On the tables," Mr. Bui said.

"Corsages, I'm talking about. They promised a carnation for you and an orchid for Mrs. Bui. Oh, they bug me so much, those people on Magnolia. They promise to deliver the flowers on time, and then they don't. Just wait till they see me. Hey, look at you, Mrs. Bui, how good you look."

Mrs. Bui was wearing a red *ao dai* with crystal beads at the collar and across the bodice. She had had another operation on her eyes in August, and it had fixed the roundness so she didn't look like a rabbit anymore. But the fold above the lashes wasn't right. It was too loose. Puffy. Like maybe she had been in a fight.

Mr. Hwong, the restaurant manager, appeared with two little plastic boxes of flowers.

"Where were you hiding those?" Anh said, and snatched them out of his hands.

Anh pinned the carnation to Mr. Bui's lapel. "Hey, you feel like a newlywed, Mr. Bui?" She could see his eyes now. They looked red and cloudy.

"I feel sick."

"You been drinking, Mr. Bui? I never knew you were a drinker. How come I never saw you drink before?"

"He hates me," Mrs. Bui said.

"This is no place to start this stuff," Anh said.

"I don't hate her," Mr. Bui said.

"So why did you leave me in Vietnam?"

"I was in the camp in the north for two years with a broken skull."

"Oh, are we going to go through this now?" Anh said. "Aren't we through with this by now?"

"I was in a camp, too," Mrs. Bui said.

"Hey, where did you get that dress?" Anh said. "Did you put the beads on there yourself?"

"You got out of Vietnam, but you didn't care about me," Mrs. Bui said.

"There was only money to smuggle me out," Mr. Bui said. "When I could, didn't I send money for you?"

"Was I going to go and leave the children behind? Do to them what you did to me?"

"Then it was your fault."

"Hey, look at this orchid," Anh said. "Red. I've never seen a red orchid in my life. It matches your dress, look at that." She pinned the orchid to Mrs. Bui's shoulder. "You better be happy, Mrs. Bui. This party is costing me a lot of dough. All the flowers, renting the whole restaurant, hiring an expensive photographer, ordering special invitations with red-and-gold envelopes. And what about that piece of red silk on the table by the door. Real smooth silk with no bumps in it, so people can write their names on it nice and easy. That costs money, silk with no bumps in it, no rough spots in it. And Kim Pham is going to sing. She made a big hit record this year, and she's going to sing for your party. And booze. No cheap booze, either. Good stuff. Wild Turkey. The best."

"Were you his girlfriend?"

"Are you trying to shock me or insult me, or what are you trying to do to me? I take you to the doctor, get your eyes all fixed up, make you this party—"

"He doesn't want me."

Mrs. Bui was now sobbing quietly into a handkerchief. Mr. Bui had gotten up and was pacing in front of the fish tanks across from the bandstand, stopping every once in a while to stick his hand down into the water and try to pet one of the rock cods. Mr. Hwong watched him from the kitchen door for a few minutes and then came over to Anh. "It's not sanitary, him putting his hand down in the fishes."

"So you go stop him. I've got people coming in already."

The guests were pushing through the double doors of the restaurant, piling up in the little foyer where the carved chairs and temple lions were. Everyone was lining up at the reception table, standing over the red cloth and signing their names on it. Clumps of them at a time, all dressed as though for Tet, the men in dark suits and the women in bright silk gowns and all their jewelry. Anh had never seen so much jewelry in one place at one time. Eight, ten bracelets on each bare arm. Rings with stones so big, knuckles wouldn't bend. It looked to Anh as though her party was going to be one of the best. All of Little Saigon was coming into the Seafood Garden and parading itself around, showing off, letting everyone check it out.

"Where is that damn singer, Cookie?" Anh said. "Did you call her again, like I told you?"

"She's parking her car." Cookie looked like a skinny child wearing a grown-up's black sequined dress. Lovesick Nam was with her. "I saw her just now in the lot. I got so stoked, just seeing her. Christ, Anh, I never knew you knew Kim Pham. Gawd, she's like the most there is."

"And what are you doing here, Nam?" Anh asked. "You're supposed to be guarding the office, not coming to a party with Cookie."

He acted as though he hadn't heard her, although she knew she said it loud enough. He just kept looking around at the carvings and gleaming mirrors, as though he had never been in a fancy restaurant before.

Vy was in line, too, with her boyfriend Ruben. Vy wasn't pregnant yet and looked slim in one of Anh's dresses, a silk one Anh had found hanging in a dressing room at Bullock's with no price tag on it. People do it all the time, the saleslady said. Come in here, try on a dress, leave the one they're wearing behind, and walk out wearing the new one without paying. Anh would never do that. Maybe switch a few price tags once in a while, but always pay something. The saleslady gave her the left-behind dress for nothing.

"That dress sure looks good on you, Cookie," Anh said. "Did I tell you you could wear that dress?"

"You weren't wearing it."

"So?"

"You can only wear one dress at a time, Anh."

The lady from the doughnut shop and her husband were there. The couple from the market with their five kids. Didn't she tell them to leave those kids at home? Oh, and the meat man, the one who always gave her a couple more pounds of pork than she paid for just because she signed the loan paper when he bought his first truck. And the people from the cleaner's on Beach Boulevard, the ones who lost Anh's white Anne Klein dress and had no insurance; so she had told them to forget it, everyone loses things sometimes. And the guy from that big building they just finished on Margo Street who made mortgage loans for fifteen percent for his friends, twenty if he didn't know you. Oh, it made Anh dizzy looking at all the people that were there.

"As soon as we sign the final papers, you get over to those two houses on Balboa and fix what I told you," she told the drywall guy. He owed Anh ten thousand dollars for the equipment in his business and four thousand for the doctor bill for when his kid was sick in the hospital. He was looking pretty good tonight, pretty rich, in a dark suit and his wife wearing fifteen gold bangles on one arm. "When we get the papers all signed up, you go and fix all the picture holes in Jana's house, and paint all those walls," Anh said. "Then you send some guy over to pull the shitty tree out from in front of the place and put in a fountain."

"I don't do fountains. I'll get you someone for the fountain."

The line in front of the red table was getting longer and longer. Anh wasn't sure now she had invited all the people who were coming in and standing in the line and writing their names on the red cloth. She thought she recognized most of their faces. But they were coming in so fast, everyone tugging at her, telling her how pretty she looked, making a little quick joke, saying a few nice things, then letting the next one catch her, so that she couldn't look at anyone long enough to tell if she recognized them or not.

"Why didn't you tell me it was formal?" Jana said. She was wearing a brown skirt and a sweater Anh had seen a thousand times before. Sam Knowlton was with her.

"You look like a bride in that white dress, Anh." Sam had hold of her hand, squeezing her fingers, rolling the flesh.

"White is for funeral. But I don't believe in that stuff."

She yanked her hand away. She didn't want him here. Not in this place where she was spending her money. Where she was giving a party.

People were coming and coming and coming. Mr. Hwong was looking nervous now at all the people who were crowding into his restaurant.

"You said twenty-five tables would be enough," he said.

"You just go get some more tables, Mr. Hwong, and don't bug me. Oh, look over there. Kim Pham, the singer. Maybe you don't know it, Mr. Hwong, but she's the best singer in Little Saigon."

"Mr. Hwong, where's that steamed fish?" Anh said. "Steamed fish is supposed to come after the shark soup and before the rolled beef. I ordered eight courses. That means eight courses."

"They're bringing it in a minute."

Waiters hurried from table to table clearing the empty dishes and putting down full, steaming ones of whole fish, fins and tails and heads intact.

"I can't eat another bite," Jana said. She and Sam were at the special table with Anh and Cookie and Nam and Mr. and Mrs. Bui. That Sam, he just sat there having a good time, smiling and talking a lot. Oh, it made Anh nuts that he could come here and have a good time.

"Vietnamese like to show how much money they have by giving you food," Cookie said.

"You," Anh said, and pulled the glass away from Cookie's fingers and hissed at her, "What did I tell you about drinking booze?"

"It's a Coke, Anh," Cookie protested.

The music was loud, and Kim Pham had the microphone turned up as high as it would go. She was only a few feet behind Anh's chair, behind the gold rails, up on a little platform with the three musicians. She was singing "I'll Be Seeing You."

"Oh, my favorite song," Anh said.

"I never heard that one," Cookie said.

"It's as old as the hills," Jana said.

"Twelve years is a long time not to see your wife," Sam said. He was sitting next to Mr. Bui. He never seemed to shut up, just talking and talking to Mr. Bui, while Mr. Bui drank glass after glass of that good Wild Turkey whiskey. Mrs. Bui had put on her sunglasses, but Anh could see a glint of tear pop up every once in a while behind the dark lenses.

"You going to give me a party like this when Ruben and me get married, Anh?" Vy asked.

"You gonna marry this guy?" Anh said. "Who gonna support you?"

"I will," Ruben said.

"Hah! From your mouth to God's ear."

"I taught her that one," Jana said.

"I was in Vietnam in seventy-one and seventy-two," Sam said to Mr. Bui.

"My wife and I were both professors at the university in Hanoi until we were put in a camp by the Communists," Mr. Bui said.

"If I had a dollar for every intellectual I saw driving a cab in Saigon, I'd be rich," Sam said.

"I escaped and went south, where my mother lived. She paid smugglers to get me out of Vietnam."

"He left me behind," Mrs. Bui said.

"What did you teach?" Sam asked.

"English," Mrs. Bui replied.

"I was a professor of law," Mr. Bui said.

"Four children, and he left me behind," Mrs. Bui said.

"Get that photo guy over here," Anh said. "Why he taking so

many picture on those other table when we got Mr. and Mrs. Bui right here?"

"Why do you let her keep calling you Bui when your name is Le?" Sam said.

"Because he like that name better," Anh said.

"She got used to calling me that, so why stop her?" Mr. Bui said.

"You ever try stopping Anh?" Cookie said.

"Mind your business," Anh said.

"She's his lover, that's why," Mrs. Bui said.

"Give Mrs. Bui another drink of whiskey," Anh said. "She's getting crazy on us."

"Kim Pham wants you to go up and sing a song, Anh," Cookie said.

"I should have stayed in Vietnam," Mrs. Bui said.

"I don't sing," Anh said. The photographer, who worked days for the *Little Saigon News Report,* was blocked by the extra tables the manager had put out. He waved to Anh that he was coming.

"All those expensive picture he taking, and we ain't got none of Mr. and Mrs. Bui," Anh said. "And make her smile, or the picture will be no good."

"I met my wife in Saigon in seventy-three," Sam said to Mr. Bui.

Anh lifted her head. What wife was he talking about?

"I don't need to have a drink to know what I know," Mrs. Bui said.

The photographer had stepped up on the bandstand and then over the gold railings and was now standing beside Anh's chair. He was a plain-faced man with narrow eyes and very large, bad teeth.

"I've been trying to get over here all night," he said.

"No excuse," Anh said. "Just take our picture."

The photographer started lining up his shot. Anh put her hand over the lens. "How many are you taking?"

The photographer looked up at her. "As many as you want."

"I don't mean how many. I mean how many. Mr. and Mrs. Bui and me, that makes three. Three is an unlucky number." She pulled at Jana's arm. "Come on, you in the picture, too."

"I don't belong in this picture," Jana said.

"Three is unlucky," Anh said.

"What if there were three people in your family and you wanted a picture?"

"You call friend or neighbor."

"Then when you look at the picture years later, you don't know who the stranger in the photograph is."

"I always know."

"As soon as I got home from Vietnam I joined the police force and was back to looking at dead bodies again," Sam said to Mr. Bui. "I didn't have any post-traumatic stress syndrome, although I did notice that things didn't bother me as much as they did in Vietnam. Dead bodies or live ones, it was all the same to me. Then I became the hood ornament of a Dodge automobile during an arrest and was disabled. That's when I went to law school."

"Law is an honorable profession," Mr. Bui said.

"I suppose. I used to be a hell of a competitor when I was a kid. Played football in college. That's one thing I don't have anymore, that competitive spirit."

"*Joie de vivre* is what they say in French."

"Yeah. I don't have any of that. I've got enough drive now to practice law, go home, and go to bed."

Kim Pham was singing again, a Beatles song.

"Oh, 'Yesterday,' " Anh said. "I love that one."

Sam was still talking to Mr. Bui, but he was looking over at Anh now and then.

"It's very nice of Anh to give this party for you and your wife," Sam said.

"Anh is very nice," Mr. Bui said. "Bad temper, but very nice."

"Hey, who said I got bad temper?" Anh said, and Mr. Bui blushed.

"In Vietnam it was weird watching the Vietnamese, how they were with people," Sam said. "If they like you, they'll do anything for you. If they don't, they'll watch someone knife you and won't even blink."

"There nothing wrong with that," Anh said.

"In Vietnam they don't steal your husband away from you," Mrs. Bui said.

Mr. Hwong was about to have the waiters bring the dessert in when Anh caught sight of her brother Thinh. He was standing in the front, near the red table. Standing there like he was lost.

"What's Thinh doing here?" Vy said. She spotted him about the same time Anh did.

"Bad news," Anh said. "When Thinh comes, it's always bad news."

He walked slowly through the restaurant. Kim Pham was taking a break, and there was just the sound of people talking. Everyone was drinking, and the talking was real loud. Some people were having such a good time, they were almost screaming.

Anh stood up, and Thinh saw her, too, now. Then he stopped at a table with some of those people Anh didn't recognize. The guy put his hand on Thinh's arm, like he was a friend or something. Thinh pulled it away.

"I think we should get out of here," Sam said. He was standing now, too, his hand reaching out for Anh's.

"You crazy. This my party," she said.

Anh squeezed past tables to get to Thinh. He was shaking as though he had a fever.

"Nep Lai's guys are all over the place, Anh," Thinh said. "They—they—"

Anh looked around her at the crowded tables, at the faces she hadn't recognized.

"So they eat at my party," Anh said. "So what?" She shook him by the shoulders. "What's the matter with you? Are you sick? Do you want to come home? Is that what you want? Tell me what you want."

"I don't want them to hurt you."

"Nam," she shouted. Nam was walking toward them on the tables, hopping across like they were stepping-stones. He jumped down from the last one in front of Anh and Thinh.

"I'm sorry, Anh, so sorry," Nam said.

"You stupid, what are you sorry for?" Anh shouted. "Get Thinh out of here."

"Ask Nam who he really works for," Thinh said. "Go on, ask him."

Nam looked embarrassed. He bowed a few times to Anh. "I'm so sorry, Anh, so sorry." And he looked it, looked really sorry. Then he raised his fist and hit her in the face. As she fell, she saw him punch Thinh, saw the blood spurt out of Thinh's nose and drip down his chin onto his white shirt.

"I'm going to kill you," Thinh said.

"Come on, come on, do it," Nam said.

"You shit!" Thinh swung, and the blow landed with a sharp crack on Nam's jaw.

"Stop it, stop it," Anh cried. Two more guys were punching at Thinh now, and Nam was jabbing at him, too. And then it just grew. Real fast. Wild. Like a wave. Like a disease catching from one table to another. Chairs falling over, people slamming their fists into each other's faces, pushing each other down. All those pretty dresses now full of blood. All those white shirts with big wide red splotches down the front.

Anh got to her feet, grabbed Thinh's waist to keep him, protect him, but he was pulling away, and she was sliding down, down, down till she was clutching his leg, being dragged along the carpet.

"Stop, stop, stop," she screamed. She felt Thinh's body shudder every time someone hit him, and still she clung to his leg, as though she could save him if she didn't let go of his trousers.

The whole room was spinning now. The walls were vibrating with the sounds of war, men butting into each other with heads and fists, women clawing at each other's hair. Sometimes it seemed that the fighting was going to stop, everyone was taking a breath, and then there'd be a little scuffle, a shout, and it would explode again.

Anh hung on to Thinh's leg and waited for bombs to fall, for people to go outside to their cars and get their guns. There was such meanness here, such animal meanness underneath all the fancy clothes. No one looked good now. They looked like animals let loose from the zoo.

Kim Pham was on the microphone, pleading. "Calm down, everyone. Calm down."

Anh saw Vy on top of a table. She was throwing liquor bottles as if she knew who she was aiming at. Cookie was throwing glasses, tossing them the way she must have tossed tomatoes up in Santa Maria, like a baseball pitcher, winding up, spinning her body, and letting go. Mr. and Mrs. Bui were scrambling over the gold rails and heading for the exit. Only Jana was still standing at her place, shaking her head as though she couldn't believe what she was looking at.

"You can't fight these guys," Sam said. He was on the floor, among all the flying shoes, prying Anh's fingers away from Thinh's leg. "I was in Vietnam. I oughtta know."

24

$\mathcal{M}$e hovered near the door, watching Sam carry Anh into the house.

"There was a fight at the restaurant," Sam said.

"Go watch TV, go on," Anh told her. Vy's boys were in their pajamas, looking scared at the sight of Anh's ripped hose and the blood all over her pretty dress.

Sam shut her bedroom door. She was on her own soft bed now, and he was taking off her clothes, checking her skin, looking at the spot under her eye where Nam had hit her.

"Fuck you," Anh said, and she began to cry.

"I don't care what you did in Vietnam," he said. "It's over."

"That Nam, I give him a job, too, and he do this to me. Go away." She stood up and walked into the bathroom. "You always watching me, watching me."

"They won't let up on you now."

"I get even with them. If those police didn't come, maybe Vy could hit one of them with a bottle and kill him. Did you see Vy and Cookie—whoosh, pfft—throwing those bottle like they ain't afraid of nobody? So you got a wife. I heard you tell Mr. Bui you got a wife. So where is she?"

"In Vietnam."

"Too bad."

She ran water in the tub and then sat down in it before it even filled up. He was in the bathroom now, sitting on the edge of the sink.

"We both lost everything in Vietnam," Sam said.

"I didn't lose nothing," Anh said. "Go home. I fuck you some other time."

He didn't move. And when the tub was filled, he got on his knees and washed all her cuts and bruises. Softly, gently, moving the washcloth so carefully, she could hardly feel it.

～

"One time I fuck a guy in the United States," Anh said. Sam had undressed and was lying beside her beneath the sheet, his hand across her bare stomach. "He say he want to marry me. Then his mother know someone in Saigon who know who I am. In 1981 I fuck two more. I don't fuck anyone after that. Twelve years I don't fuck."

"How old are you now?"

"Thirty-five." She turned her head toward him.

"I don't like Americans," she said.

"I don't blame you."

～

Anh remembered those Americans. Some of them could fuck all night and never get tired. Some of them, quick, in and out, and they were done. Some of them only liked to look at her, touch her breasts, maybe suck her nipples. This one is slow and steady, acting as if he cared about her, stroking her hair, calling her sweetheart. He didn't fool her, though. She had been through it all. She knew about men.

She was astride him now, holding his penis, massaging it, pulling gently at its tip, smoothing it, rubbing the round testicles, feeling their firmness. Everything in the room smelled of him, his lotion, maybe even the stuff he put on his hair. She ran her finger along his rectum, up and down, up and down, then bent close to his face and kissed him. He was breathing so fast, like he couldn't get enough air, like he couldn't get enough of her, shoving himself into her with all his might, holding her buttocks so tight, she knew his fingers were going to leave marks.

"Don't move," he said. "Don't move."

They were still now, him hard inside her. She could feel it like a knot, like something hot, something foreign. But good. Oh, it did feel good. She did want him to stay there.

"Go faster now," she said. "Faster."

It was the best. She knew it. She wouldn't tell him that, but she knew it. Him pushing in and out, in and out, talking like he was crazy, muttering all kinds of strange things, calling her strange names. Oh, it felt good when he touched her there. Oh, it was so good. How could she ever think there was no feeling left in her, no sensation, no joy?

Anh could hear Me's TV still going. The boys must all be sleeping with her. Oh, she was going to get a bed big enough for six people, and she and Me and the four boys were going to sleep in it in the new house and never leave each other and never worry about gang boys coming in and doing anything, because she was going to keep a rifle under her big bed and a revolver under her pillow and a grenade in the closet.

"Gai was from Bac Lieu," Sam said. "She was the interpreter for the airborne division I was attached to. When we walked on the street, we'd walk separately, or the GIs would catcall—'whore,' they'd call her. 'Gook whore' most of the time. We got married in seventy-three just before I left to go stateside. When I got home, I tried everything to get her here. Nothing worked. I went back in eighty with money to bribe anyone I had to. But she'd married someone else. Like she didn't even know me, like she hadn't said she'd wait till I could get her out. She married a rice farmer in Bac Lieu. I send her money a couple of times a year for the kids."

"Sad story," Anh said. "I lost my baby in Vietnam. My story sadder than your story."

He wouldn't let go of her. It was four in the morning, and they were still awake, still touching each other, still waiting for it to be over. She was sore inside, they had done it so many times. And still she wanted to do it again.

"I haven't felt right since I left Vietnam," he said. "Not till now."

She rolled away from him, then sat on the edge of the bed. His face was like all the others in the dark. She had to look hard at him to see the difference. "Did you come to Uncle Kou, to the house where I work in Saigon?"

"Probably."

"You see me there?"

"I was doing a lot of hash then. What's the difference?"

She got out of bed and pulled a robe around her. "Where did Thinh go tonight? The police take him to jail, or what?"

"I didn't see him in the police car. I had hold of him once in the parking lot, and then some guy hit me with a stick and grabbed Thinh. I let him go. I was more worried about getting you home."

"Okay. Okay. Nep Lai want a war, I give him war. I not afraid of nobody."

He got up and walked toward her. Oh, she remembered those American bodies, those long arms and wide chests, the hips that barely moved when they walked. He put his arms around her now. She didn't want him to comfort her. Didn't like it. It felt bad. Made her want to cry. Made her head hurt.

"It could even have been my baby you left in Vietnam," he said.

"Oh, God," she said.

❧

MALAYSIA, 1975

The first few months in the camp, Uncle Kou acted like the boss. Always telling everyone what to do. The camp grew crowded as the refugees kept coming, but Uncle Kou had the biggest tent. The Malaysian soldiers brought them food, but it wasn't enough. Uncle Kou bought extra food for the family, and it made the other people jealous, and that worried Uncle Kou. He had put the gold bars in a suitcase, and although Ba and Uncle Kou's son Tuyen took turns guarding it, Uncle Kou checked the suitcase a couple of times a day, counting out the bars to make sure no one was stealing any.

"Your son Tuyen has stolen some of your gold," Ba said.

"My son's not a thief," Uncle Kou replied, and counted out the bars. There were ten missing.

"Maybe you didn't count the bars right," Auntie Chi said.

"I saw Tuyen take it," Anh said. "I saw him dig a hole and put gold bars into the ground." She hadn't seen any such thing, but Uncle Kou had a knife and was looking at Ba like he wanted to kill him.

"I don't believe it," Uncle Kou said.

"My son doesn't steal," Auntie Chi said.

"I saw it," Anh insisted.

That same day Uncle Kou took his wife and her relatives to another part of the camp and wouldn't speak to or look at Ba again. Only Auntie Chi's brother Tam and his two children stayed with Anh's family.

"Kou is unfair," Tam said. "His son is rotten, but Kou is worse. He is unfair."

In July the American soldiers came and took over the camp. It didn't seem to matter to Ba that the Americans were there. He still played cards to get extra money for food and slept with his knife in the sleeve of his jacket in case Uncle Kou came in the dark and tried to kill him. And Me and Khanh acted as if they were back in Nga Tu Bay Hien, taking care of Khanh's baby and cooking the meals and sweeping the dirt floor. Sometimes they were so busy, they didn't pay attention to Ba at all, and would leave it to Anh to give him his tea or his bowl of rice.

"Ba, the Americans are here," Anh told him. "Lots of churches from America sending people over here wanting to take Vietnamese people home with them. You can get rich in America, Ba. Richer than Uncle Kou. You can buy gold bars yourself and sleep on them like a bed, you'll have so many. Twenty-four-carat, Ba. Why don't you go register, tell them you want to go to America. Ba, go tell them you want to go."

"Our family is too big," Ba said. "Fourteen people, counting your mother's sister Vo and her family. I heard they only want families with four or five people in them. What's the use of telling them anything?"

Anh went every day to the big tent where the American soldiers sat at the desk and took names of people wanting to go to the United States. She knew enough English to do a little interpreting for them in exchange for cigarettes for Ba and chocolates for Me. What she couldn't use she bartered away for shoes and clothes. And American magazines. The pictures in the American magazines were better than chocolates. All those pretty houses, taller than the tallest ones in Saigon. With flowers around them that she had never seen before. And women in pretty clothes sitting on soft-looking chairs talking to men, and the men looking at them as if they were listening.

"Who going where today?" Anh asked.

"We've got three families going to South Dakota," Captain Murray said. He was a redhead with a freckled face who let Anh ride around the camp with him in his jeep.

"I like South Dakota," Anh said.

The line was longer today than Anh had ever seen it.

"Too many people in your group, Anh," Captain Murray said. "If you could get rid of a few, there might be a chance."

"I sure like South Dakota," Anh said. "Ba said, 'Anh, you get me to South Dakota, and I make you my favorite daughter.' Better than Vy even. I said, 'Ba, Captain Murray going to do it. One time I go speak to Captain Murray, and he say, "Anh, you want to go to South Dakota?" and I say—' "

"How old are you?" It was a blond woman, standing right there behind Captain Murray's desk.

"Seventeen," Anh said. "How old are you?"

The woman laughed. She was plump and had skin the color of steamed chicken.

"Miss Larson's from Holy Grace Lutheran Church in Sioux Falls, South Dakota," Captain Murray said. "Anh's got fourteen people in her family."

"Some of them are small," Anh said. "Kid. You know how kid eat. Almost nothing. Put them on the airplane and take them to South Dakota. Hey, you want to hear your fortune, I got helluva good fortune-teller over on the other side of the camp. She tell your fortune in two minute flat. She do a number on you, you won't believe."

"Who taught you all that slang?" Miss Larson said.

"Careful, she'll take your shoes off your feet without you knowing it," Captain Murray said.

Anh followed Miss Larson around all that day and the next while Miss Larson was deciding who her church group was going to sponsor.

"I can work hard," Anh said. "Take me to America and see me work."

"But fourteen people, Anh," Miss Larson said. "I promised my church no more than six."

"Eight more. Just eight. And some of them small. You ever see eight Vietnamese eat? Like bird they eat. Don't notice any food gone when they eat. Don't open their mouth more than three time, and they finish, can't eat no more."

Miss Larson was always laughing at her. Talking to the people in the camp, asking how many children, whether they could speak any English, whether they had any other relatives in the United States who could sponsor them, whether they had any skills, any education. And all the time, riding around, talking to the people, Miss Larson would say, "Anh, you crack me up."

On the third day, when Miss Larson was getting ready to leave, when it seemed to Anh that there would never be another chance, that no one would take her away from here, that she would stay here forever and never be able to go back and find her baby, that she decided to tell Miss Larson what had happened to her in Vietnam.

It took all afternoon. It was a long story.

When Anh went back to the tent, Ba was squatting in the dirt outside, eating a bowl of rice. Khanh's baby was playing in a puddle of dirty water, splashing it on herself, sticking her dirty fingers into her mouth.

"You shouldn't let that baby do that," Anh said. "Haven't you ever heard about germs? Captain Murray says that's how babies get sick, from germs."

"You keep your mouth shut," Khanh said.

"Say it again," Ba said, "about South Dakota."

"We're going there, Ba," Anh said.

"Where is that?" Me asked.

"In America. The United States in America. Sioux Fall in South Dakota."

"You can't tell your father to go to America," Khanh said. "He has to say he's going to America. You're a rotten daughter if you tell your father what to do."

"They have big houses in South Dakota, Ba," Anh said. "Like in the pictures in the magazines. Beautiful houses." Oh, did she have to convince them, too, when she had chewed up all her words with Miss Larson, and there were just crumbs left behind?

"Your father is the one to tell us what to do," Me said.

"If we pack our things tonight, we can go tomorrow," Anh said.

"I have to be the one," Ba said. "You can't tell me I'm going to America. I have to be the one to tell you."

"But we can go, Ba," Anh said. "Miss Larson said we could go."

"Who is Miss Larson?" Me said.

"She's from the Lutheran church," Anh replied.

"Not Buddhists?" Khanh said.

"There are no Buddhists in South Dakota," Anh said. "You'll be the first one."

"I don't want to go, then."

"Tomorrow?" Ba said.

"Tomorrow. Miss Larson will make sure we have a house when we get there, and food and money to buy things. She said it was all right that you had two wives, Ba. She said you can bring both your wives. You can only live with one of them. But she likes me, Ba. She says I'm smart. She says—"

Me screamed. Khanh kept raising and lowering her eyebrows as though she had an itch on her forehead. Ba just kept shoveling the rice into his mouth with the chopsticks. Looking at the ground and shoveling the rice.

"They're my wives," Ba said. "I can live with two wives if I want to."

"Not in South Dakota, Ba," Anh said.

Ba took a long time thinking about whether they were going to go or not. All night he sat outside the tent thinking. Anh's stomach was jumping, thinking they would stay in this refugee camp in Malaysia forever. Tam was sleeping nearby on a mat with his son and daughter. Anh woke him up. "If we go to America, will you help me some way to get back to Vietnam and find my baby?"

"I looked for him, Anh," Tam said. "He's gone. Go to sleep. I told you, he's gone."

"Promise me."

"I promise."

In the morning Ba was still sitting outside the tent thinking. Anh brought him his tea, and he looked up at her.

"We'll go to South Dakota," he said.

25

*a*nh had been expecting Nep Lai to do something more to her, something bad. But it still made her stomach twist when she drove into the lot and looked upstairs at the office window and saw their sign all covered over with black paint. Shiny black paint that had dripped down the stairs and left a puddle of still-wet goo at the bottom. Even the doorknob to the office was sticky with black paint. She opened the door, and the smell of paint and wet papers made her choke.

Mr. Bui was standing inside the door, just standing there, helpless in his rumpled clothes, while Mrs. Bui, still in her red dress, flung coffee cups and income tax books at him from across the room.

"Where did you sleep last night?" Mrs. Bui screamed at Mr. Bui. "With her?"

"In my car. I slept in my car," Mr. Bui said, ducking his head back and forth to keep from being hit, and blinking his eyes, as if it hurt to see.

"You lie," Mrs. Bui cried.

It was worse inside than Anh thought it would be. Someone had brought a garden hose and a paint spray gun up here. The walls had Vietnamese gang slogans sprayed across them. Everything was painted black. Desks, good-luck plaques, couches, partitions, chairs. Even Mr. Bui's tree. File cabinets dumped out, and paper everywhere, some of them painted black, some of them hosed down with water into a pulpy grayish mass.

"What happened here? What in hell happened?" Anh said. Oh, she felt desperate. How to fix this. What to do. She started picking up papers. Black paint glued them to her fingers. Like jam. Like pancake syrup. One paper stuck to another one stuck to another one.

"It was like this when I came upstairs," Mr. Bui said.

"I didn't need to come to the United States and have you look at me the way you look at me," Mrs. Bui said. Her voice was hurting Anh's ears. It was almost as loud as the black paint, almost as noisy as the ruined files.

"Jesus Christ!" Jana was at the door, staring at the black paint on her hand where she had touched the knob.

"It only a little dirty," Anh said. She wiped her hands on her skirt. "I can clean up. Don't you worry. Everything is fine. Everything going to be fixed."

Jana ran to the overturned file cabinets. Stared at the heap of stuck-together papers. "Nothing left," she said. "I don't believe it."

Mrs. Bui was at the coffee machine now, taking it apart, throwing it piece by piece at Mr. Bui and screaming at him in Vietnamese, the veins in her throat sticking out like blue roads. A glass coffeepot landed at Mr. Bui's feet, bounced once, and then smashed to pieces against the leg of a desk.

"Take Mrs. Bui downstairs and get her some coffee," Anh said to Mr. Bui. "She'll feel better with a little coffee in her. Give her some sugar, too, make her sweeter."

"The same guys who broke up the party last night did this, didn't they?" Jana said.

"Oh, no," Anh said. "This stuff happen all the time. Kid come in and play around with paint can and have a little fun."

"It's the Nep gang, isn't it?"

"Oh, no, not that one. Nam, that boy that suppose to work here, suppose to keep trouble out, he start the fight with Thinh. He the one who did it. We get rid of Nam already. He won't show his ass around here no more. No way. We get rid of all those other coffee shop guy, too. We get another bunch. I know some good one hang around in Asian Garden Mall, they all looking for job. I get some people in here, clean up this place. No problem."

Jana was looking at her like it was her fault. A razor look, cutting her heart in two. Oh, there was no way to fix this. She could tell in

Jana's face there was no way at all, no lie she could tell, no excuse she could give for this.

Mr. Bui looked sadly at his wife. "Come on, Ha. I'll take you home."

"Good idea," Anh said. "She looks sleepy. Maybe needs a nap."

"What about the computer?" Jana said, looking around. "What happened to the computer? Where is it?"

"Gone," Mr. Bui said. "My computer's gone, too. And my printer. That was a good printer."

"I never like computer, anyway," Anh said.

"It's disgusting," Jana said, "just disgusting."

"That the way kid are," Anh said. "Kid always do disgusting thing."

"Here, the paper you got from immigration for me," Mrs. Bui said to Mr. Bui. "I'm ripping it up, throwing it away. What do I want with it when you don't want me, when you want her?"

"Keep her quiet, Mr. Bui," Anh said. "I've got to think here. I've got to concentrate."

"It took me four years to get these papers," Mr. Bui said. He was on his knees now, picking up pieces of Mrs. Bui's immigration papers.

"I don't care," Mrs. Bui said. Her semiround eyes were bright and fuming, her cheeks wiggling with anger.

Anh walked up close to Mrs. Bui, so close she could see where the surgeon had tried to fix those rabbit eyes. "You see this office? You see this mess? This is my life, this place. This place is for college for Vy's kids. What are you yelling about? You were in Vietnam? You're alive now. You've got your husband. You've got your kids. So shut the fuck up."

Jana was looking at her now. Listening to her yell at Mrs. Bui in Vietnamese. Oh, she was listening all right. Anh could tell. This was the end, the finish. She wouldn't stay around now. Not now.

"Come on, Ha," Mr. Bui said gently. He put his arm around his wife's shoulder, and she let herself be led to the door.

"Hey, you all up early already." Nep Lai was standing in the doorway. Wearing a clean shirt. Looking fresh. Looking happy.

"You do this shit?" Anh said. She couldn't see what was behind him. It was like a big shadow.

"We'd better go now," Mr. Bui said.

Nep Lai moved out of the way to let Mr. and Mrs. Bui pass, and then Anh saw what it was. It was Thinh. Two of Nep Lai's gang boys had hold of his arms and feet, and his eyes were closed, and red stuff was coming out of his ears. They swung him back and forth a few times and then tossed him into the office like a bag of laundry.

"You beat him up good, huh?" Anh said.

Mrs. Bui wasn't making a sound now, just moving ahead of Mr. Bui quickly, quickly out the door and down the stairs. Oh, Anh wished she were Mrs. Bui, all safe with her husband and four kids and no fear.

"I don't know what happened to him," Nep Lai said. "One time he was joking around, and then he just stopped living."

"Ayy!" Anh's breath came out in a rush.

"He was making jokes," Nep Lai said. He smiled like he was remembering one of Thinh's jokes, was savoring the memory of it.

Anh ran to where Thinh lay spread out, face looking up at the blackened good-luck plaques. She pulled at his shirt, felt his neck with her fingers. There was dried blood all over, caked to his trousers, stuck to his hair. Oh, there was a hole where the blood was still oozing from his head. A little hole, as if someone had pounded a nail in there. A smooth, round hole that a hammer and nail would make. Anh pressed her fingers into the cold skin of his neck, looking for a pulse. Oh, where was the beating heart?

Anh looked up at Nep Lai. "You shithead."

"Don't call me names, Anh," he said. "I told you we could do business. But you won't do it. I warned you. You know I don't fool around. What can I do? I got no choice. It's the way things are."

"Do you want me to call an ambulance?" Jana said. Nep Lai and his gang boys were gone. Gone so quick, Anh felt the breeze from their leaving like a dark chill in the morning heat.

"Too late," Anh said. "Too late."

"Call anyone?" Jana's face was impassive. There was no emotion that Anh could see. "Your mother maybe?"

"No, no, no, don't call anyone."

"Then I'm going to leave. I can't stand here. I can't stand any more of this."

"He only seventeen," Anh said.

"I'm going to be sick if I stand here any longer."

"You go ahead. It don't matter, anyway."

～

Anh sat alone in the office, on the floor next to Thinh's body. It was time for the office to open. Nine o'clock. She looked up at the black window, at the faces peering through the clear spots into the office. Some people opened the door and stared inside awhile before they went away. Mostly quiet, like what they were looking at reminded them of their own sorrows. And the phone was ringing and ringing and ringing. The answering machine kept picking up the calls, with Jana's voice saying over and over, voice plain as paper, to leave a message at the beep. Vietnamese messages, disembodied messages, some urgent, some quizzical. All those messages about depositions and court dates. Where do I park? What freeway do I take? Can I bring my sister? Do I have to go?

"Anh, it's me, Sam. Call me at my office."

Oh, that voice. She shuddered at the sound of that voice, thinking of what she had done with him. She picked at the dried blood clinging to the hairs around the hole in Thinh's head.

"You're so smart, you're stupid, Thinh," she said. "I told you I'd put you in medical school. We could have had a doctor. An American doctor. Now look. Look what you did." She smoothed his hair back from his forehead. Something smelled bad. She didn't even want to know what it was that smelled so bad.

"Now everything's gone. No doctor. No house. No Ferris wheel for the kids." She patted his hair gently. "Oh, you should have seen the Ferris wheel, Thinh. It looked so scary. The kids would have screamed their heads off if they went up in that Ferris wheel. I was going to ask you to come back, Thinh, live with us in that new house and go with me and the kids up on that Ferris wheel."

She stared at his eyes, already sinking, sinking, sinking into his skull. "Idiot," she said, and gave his face a sharp slap. Oh, that felt good. She gave him another slap. That felt even better. Then another one and another one. She kept slapping his face till her hands were stinging and the palms were red.

"Oh, what did you do, you stupid boy?" she said, and then she touched his face, oh so carefully. Sorry she had hit it. Sorry, sorry, sorry. But there was no sign of her slaps, just the same bruises, the same crusty blood.

"You fixed it so I've got to get even, you know," she said. "I've got enough trouble, and now I've got to get even for this, have to protect Me and Ba and Vy and the kids, have to do it, Thinh, have to kill Nep Lai, let the others see I don't take crap from anyone, show them what a crazy girl I am. And it's all your fault. All your fault."

She got up and went into the ruined bathroom and wet a paper towel in the sink. They had filled their spray gun here, she could tell. There was no purposeful paint in here, no slogans. Only careless paint. Spilled paint. She wiped at the sink with the paper towel, threw it on the floor, and got another one and wet that one. Then she came back and stripped Thinh's skinny body of its clothes and began to clean him up so Me wouldn't see him looking so bad.

~

SIOUX FALLS, SOUTH DAKOTA, 1975

"And this is your house," Miss Larson said.

"They love this house," Anh said. "We love you, and we love the Lutherans of Sioux Fall, and we love this house, Miss Larson."

"What did the woman say?" Ba asked Anh.

"She said I'll be the one she'll talk to when we need anything," Anh replied.

Me understood enough of what Miss Larson was saying to know that wasn't what she said. But Anh was looking hard at her, and Me just took another sip of the soda the welcoming society at the Lutheran church had brought to the house as part of the delivery of food that Khanh was now looking through. The food was in a big red cooler. Piles of little boxes and bags were jammed in the cooler from bottom to top and side to side. Me's sister Vo and her husband and kids were already upstairs, looking at their room. Anh could hear their feet stamping over her head. And Tam and his two kids were in the kitchen, their voices echoing. It sounded to Anh as though the kids were chasing each other. The house was a big, two-story house, with five bedrooms, empty except for beds. Downstairs there was no furniture in the living room. But here in the dining room, right next to where Khanh was bending over the cooler, there was a long wood table and chairs with a light hanging over it, and the glass-paned cupboards on both sides of the door into the kitchen had dishes and glasses inside them.

"I don't like this food in this thing," Khanh said. "Where's the rice?"

"You're not staying here to eat it, anyway," Anh said. "You and Ba and Cuc are going to another place. I told you the Lutherans won't let you live here. Ba can't live here if you live here. Ba can't have two wives in Sioux Fall. That's their law."

"Ba's the one to decide that," Khanh said.

"What's the matter?" Miss Larson said.

"Khanh's stupid, that's all," Anh said. "She want rice, want to know where the rice is."

"Oh, my Lord, I forgot. There are mashed potatoes in a container in that cooler somewhere. Will that do?"

"Sure. We like potato. Sure. Don't worry. Potato is good. Don't listen to Khanh. She complain so much, give me a headache."

Ba didn't look at Anh when he left. He just gave Vy a little pat on the arm. Me bowed to him and said, "I'll be here whenever you come."

Ba went outside with Khanh and their daughter, Cuc. Miss Larson lingered in the house, walking through the rooms with Anh, telling her again about the jobs the Lutherans had lined up for them. Ba could do some gardening. Tam could drive for the Lutheran minister and clean the church. Me's sister's husband, Phu, could work in a plastics factory.

"You're going to high school," Miss Larson said. "You have enough English to do well."

26

The apartment house was a block off Ocean Avenue in Long Beach. You couldn't see the *Queen Mary* from here, or the Hyatt or the Sheraton. All that dropped off the minute you passed the second block off Ocean. Then it turned to ugly streets, with no ocean in sight. Just paintless buildings, run-down boarding-houses, cheap motels.

Anh had never been inside the building before, but she had passed it every time she took Me to church, and Me always pointed it out. It was dingy and almost as dark as night inside. Lots of little Vietnamese kids were playing beneath the broken skylight, running up and down the stairs, wrapping their bare toes around the slick wood banister, sliding down it, hanging from it feetfirst, making noise. The kids got quiet, hung back against the wall, and watched Anh walk up the stairs and knock on the door at the end of the hall.

Her father opened the door himself. "You come to bring me good luck or bad luck?"

The inside was smoky. Shadowed by heavy curtains. Noisy with the sound of men gambling at a big square table near the window, a plastic lamp hanging on a chain over their heads. Ba didn't wait for Anh to answer, but turned and went back to his seat at the table.

"I brought you tea," Anh said, and put the tin on the edge of the table near Ba's pack of cigarettes. "The good kind. The kind you like. Expensive. From China."

A woman came out of the kitchen. She had a little girl in her arms and two more following at her feet.

"Is that you, Khanh?" Anh said. "I don't recognize you, you're looking so old." She hadn't seen Khanh since Sioux Falls. Khanh had still been Ba's pretty girl then, her skin tight and pale. Now tiny lines had turned her cheeks from smooth pillows to broken teacups.

"I hear no one wants to marry you," Khanh said. She sat down with the kids on the worn green couch. There was no rug, no furniture. Just the green couch, the card table, a small shrine, and the curtains that shut out the sun.

"Have you got any boys back there hiding in that kitchen, or just these no-luck, no-use girls?" Anh said.

"You're too old to get a man. Too mean. Too ugly."

"You don't look too good yourself."

"They suspended my driver's license," Ba said. He didn't even look up from the cards. Anh remembered how he could gamble. Day and night and talk and eat and still know what cards he had left to play. "Now that you've got a law business, maybe you can fix my license."

"I could use some water," Anh said. "My throat's so dry, I can hardly swallow. Have you got water in this place?"

"This is no restaurant," Khanh said.

Ba gave a little shrug, like he didn't want to hear any more of this.

"When you passed twenty-two years old, you turned useless," Khanh said. "And now you're thirty-five. Who wants you now? You'll never find a husband now."

"And if Ba gets another concubine, what will you do, the way you look, so old, and with all these kids?"

"The fortune-teller said when Ba is through with me, I'm going to meet a rich American and marry him."

"Hah!"

Khanh went off to the kitchen, and Anh stood behind her father's chair and watched him play. A pockmarked man next to her father threw some money in and said, "Mr. Truong, maybe you can tell me what I can do about my brother-in-law. I put the down payment and signed the mortgage on his house because my wife felt sorry for him. He rented the house to Cambodians and keeps the rent money, doesn't pay the mortgage, and now the bank is foreclosing. How can I get my money back?"

"Go ask your sister for it," Ba said.

"She died."

"Too bad."

"The Nep family gang boys wrecked my office," Anh said. "I don't have a business left. All the papers are ruined, messed up with water and paint."

"Don't ask me for anything," Ba said. "I bet on football with a Frenchman. Thirty thousand dollars we lost. He ran away, and now the bookie's going to kill me for his share."

"How did you lose your license? Were you drinking?"

"*Pai gow*," Ba said, and paid money to everyone at the table. "Khanh bumped a car in Von's parking lot, and we have no insurance, so they suspended my license. Did your mother send you to find out why I haven't been to see her this week?"

"No."

Khanh was back with a glass of water. She handed it to Anh.

"Maybe I should make you drink it first," Anh said. "Make sure you didn't put poison in there."

"Khanh has had three accidents this year," Ba said. "Maybe you can put the insurance in your name for me, so I can get my license back."

"It'll make me liable, then," Anh said.

"You never do anything good for your father," Khanh said. "You're such a selfish daughter. You never gave him money for a restaurant, like you promised, and now he's got to gamble to feed all these kids."

"I've got a son can do air-conditioning," one of the other men at the table said.

"Have you got a job for a son who can do air-conditioning, Anh?" Ba asked her.

"I'll find out," Anh said. "You give me your name and your son's name, and I'll find out."

The man wrote something on a scrap of paper and handed it to Anh.

"He's got to be paid under the table," the man said. "No tax. He's got people after him for money, so he likes to keep his property in my name."

"I'll find out for you," Anh said.

"You still like bad-luck cats?" Khanh said.

"Sure," Anh said. "I'll bring you one and see if you get sick and die."

"Anh had a cat back in our village," Ba told the father of the air-conditioning son.

"Oh, bad luck," the man said.

"The cat ran outside, and Anh sat in a tree all night trying to get it back in."

"You're brave letting a cat live in the house with you," the man said.

"Our house was bombed because of that cat," Khanh said. "We had to go live with relatives."

"You didn't come to give me money for a restaurant," Ba said, "so why are you here?"

"Your son Thinh is dead," Anh said.

Ba looked up from the cards for the first time.

"How?"

"He got a bad beating, and that was it."

Ba shoved his chair away from the table and stood up. He went to a corner of the room where the shrine was and the pictures of dead relatives. "You get a picture, and I'll put Thinh's picture with the rest of them."

"The funeral's tomorrow. Me wants you to come."

"Funerals make me sick. Just get me a picture. That's enough."

GRANDVIEW NURSING HOME, SIOUX FALLS, SOUTH DAKOTA, 1981

"Payday," the head nurse said. Anh was emptying bedpans when she heard her. They were all supposed to go to the lunchroom to get their checks. Finish what they were doing and run over there before the head nurse left.

Anh wiped the old lady's rear carefully. There were all those wrinkles and folds to clean up, or she'd get a rash. Just like a baby. You had to wash them and powder them just like babies. Anh raised the shriveled legs with one hand, they were so thin.

"Don't want to hurt you now," Anh said. That was what the head nurse told them to say whenever they were hurting one of the patients.

Anh was the last one into the lunchroom.

"Did you wash your hands?" That was Cindy talking. Anh always knew she would get a smart remark from Cindy on payday. It was like the sun. Who didn't expect the sun to come out? That was Cindy. Like the sun.

"Sorry I late," Anh said. She didn't pay attention when they made remarks. She got a paycheck on payday.

The head nurse was handing out the checks.

"I see you got a new car, Anh," Rose said. She was another one who said things. But she wasn't like the sun coming up. She was more like once a week. Like Sundays. She was like Sundays.

"We put our money together," Anh said. "Everyone in the house work and put the money together, and we buy cars. How am I driving an old one in all the snow and wet stuff? If I do that, I never get to work on time." She didn't tell them she delivered newspapers, too, to get money. Got up at four o'clock in the morning to deliver papers. Slept maybe three, four hours a night.

"You people don't pay income tax," Cindy said. "Don't give us that garbage about everybody working. Everyone knows you're all rich. You all came here rich and got richer."

"The Mexicans do that, too," Rose said.

"No, they don't," Cindy said. She had a Mexican mother-in-law. Anh had seen her once sitting in a car at the grocery store watching Cindy's kids while Cindy was inside.

"Well, maybe not like the Vietnamese," Rose said. "They're really awful. The government gives them a house to live in, bigger than mine. They lost the war, so everything's free now for them. Everyone knows that."

The head nurse was finished handing out the checks, but she was listening. So were the other attendants. It was like they were relishing what Rose and Cindy were saying. They had waited eagerly at the Mexican part, hoping that would get Cindy and Rose into a big fight, something they could talk about at lunchtime, but they were still interested now that it was back to the Vietnamese. Anh knew none of the others would have said anything like this to her if Cindy and Rose weren't there. Maybe it was the cold weather. Anh noticed that people said the worst things when the weather got cold.

"We pay rent for that house," Anh said.

"You don't pay income tax," Rose said.

"You think the U.S. letting us off, giving us something for free?"

"I think you're living off the rest of us."

"We work hard, that all we do is work."

"I don't have three cars in my family," Cindy said.

"We got ten people living in that house. We pay income tax."

"Then show us your check," Rose said.

The head nurse was smiling at her. She was a nice lady, had taught Anh all about how to clean people's asses, how to do it so they didn't smell and didn't get a rash.

"Show them your check, Anh," the head nurse said. "That'll settle it once and for all, and then they'll leave you alone."

Easy, easy, easy. Tell them all about your private life. Tell them what happened to you in Vietnam. Make them cry over your lost baby. Make them like you.

"Fuck you," Anh said. "You pay me money to look at it, I show you my check. I don't take crap from no one."

Then Anh went and got her purse and her jacket and left. Right at the beginning of her shift. Went and got in the new car, pulled out of the rest home parking lot, looked at the windows in the brick building one last time, and then drove down to the cafe where Tam was working.

Tam could cook anything you wanted. Bacon and eggs, hotcakes, steaks, liver and onions. He never ate any of it himself, but he could cook it just the way Americans liked it. Billy, the owner of the cafe, paid him a good salary and was always telling him how trustworthy he was for a Vietnamese. But he also watched him, checked the amount of pancake batter that was left at the end of the day, counted the eggs, weighed the bacon.

Anh went in the back door so Billy wouldn't see her go into the kitchen, where Tam was working. "I quit my job," she said.

It was eight-thirty in the morning, and Anh could see into the cafe through the narrow space between the serving counter and the heat lamps. People were sitting at the tables in their heavy jackets, waiting for Tam to make them breakfast.

"I think we'll go to Vietnam," Tam said. "It's time." He was sliding eggs onto a plate, being careful not to break the yolks, slipping those greasy eggs from the frying pan onto the white plate as skillfully as a magician, as though he expected the eggs to float in the air, as though the plate weren't there at all.

"I haven't got the money yet," Anh said. "I'm still saving. I don't have enough. And I've got to worry about Me, she can't sew anymore. Her eyes are only good enough for TV these days, not for working. And Vy needs school clothes. You know how girls are when they're thirteen, always worrying they don't have the right thing to wear. But I've got plans. No one has to worry about me. Maybe I'll open a store, sell dresses, get the money to go to Vietnam that way."

"There's people going over to Vietnam now, carrying money to people from their relatives living here."

"The Vietcong will kill you if you try that."

"There is no more Vietcong. It's a government now."

"That's not the truth. I read the newspapers. That's not the truth. Couriers get killed all the time in Vietnam."

"Like any other place. People get killed everywhere in the world, Anh. Vietnam's no different."

"What about them making you stay there once you get there? What about that? They'll keep you there. Do you want to do that, stay there in Vietnam without your TV and your nice car?"

"Stay there? I'm not staying there. The Communists don't want us. They just want dollars. They like it when dollars come in. They don't care how they come in."

Oh, it was too scary what Tam was talking about. Carrying money to Vietnam. Smuggling money to Vietnam.

"I know a lady who can sew dresses you can't tell them from Diane von Furstenberg," she said. "Fancy dresses. You know the kind I mean, with a top that folds over and then is tight until it hits the waist, and then it flares out?" She had her hands to her waist, showing him. "I'll open a dress shop, sell Diane von Furstenberg knock-offs, and get my money to go back to Vietnam that way. Legal. Not smuggling money. Just looking for my son. They won't try to hold me if I'm just there looking for my son."

"I know some people who've gone and come back already. Every thousand dollars you carry, you get two hundred. You smuggle someone back with you, you get ten thousand. That's better than fancy dresses in a store. And you can make money and look for your son at the same time."

Tam put the plate up on the counter and slammed his palm down on the chrome bell so the waitress would come and get it. Anh had been talking without breathing. Oh, she knew how to do that when she was scared and excited and happy at the same time. Talk and hold her breath. She was sitting on a stool next to the stove where Tam was cooking, and he didn't even know she wasn't breathing.

Tam started another order. Hotcakes.

"I dream about my baby," Anh said. "Did I ever tell you that? Every night. He's right there in front of me. Sometimes he's standing by the window. Sometimes he's at the door. He calls me mother. Mother. Then I wake up. Every night."

"I'm going to marry someone and bring her back. You get ten thousand if you marry someone. I'll marry her in Vietnam and divorce her in South Dakota. I promised to take you back to Vietnam to look for your son, and this is the time to do it."

He spilled the batter onto the griddle. Five perfect rounds with edges that bubbled and curled.

"Who is this girl they've got for you to marry?" Anh said. Tam was old enough to be her father. He was the only one who cared about her, who remembered a promise he had made such a long time ago. It made her jealous thinking he was going to marry a stranger, even if he was going to divorce her in South Dakota.

"I don't know her. Her father came in the cafe and asked me if I'd do it. He said he's afraid for her to try to get out herself. She's only eighteen. I can buy some farm land in California with the money. Grow broccoli. Americans like broccoli."

He took off his apron and left the five perfect rounds on the griddle. Just left them there to burn and walked out the kitchen door with Anh.

"Where are you going?" Billy asked. He was at the cash register reading the newspaper.

Tam didn't even look at the customers waiting at the tables for their breakfast. Didn't even answer Billy. Just took Anh's arm and walked out the door.

27

The main thing Anh had to do was to hold the umbrella steady over Me's head, keep the sun off her so she didn't faint. Vy was on her other side, holding her arm, letting her lean against her, but Anh could see Me's eyes fluttering as if she were going to fall over, anyway.

"To lose a child," the priest was saying. Their Vietnamese priest had a wedding and two burials and couldn't come. He had sent this one instead, an American from Michigan, a slightly bald man with a tanned face who couldn't speak Vietnamese. Anh supposed he had stood at a lot of graves in the hot sun to get that tan.

He was pronouncing Thinh's name wrong. It made Anh sad to hear the strange way he was saying it. And Truong. Why couldn't he just say it. Truong. Truong. And he was trying so hard, oh so hard, Anh could tell, to say the right things about Thinh. Before all the cars started lining up on the Beach Boulevard side of the cemetery and people started walking toward the grave, he had taken Anh aside and asked her what sports Thinh had played, if he was a good student. Oh, yes, yes, she had told him. He was the best.

"He won the fifty-yard dash in his freshman year in high school," the priest was saying. Anh was glad not too many people listening to the priest could understand English, or they'd know what silly stuff he was saying about the brother she loved.

"Lucy over at Magnolia Market knows a good fortune-teller,"

Anh whispered to Vy across Me's fluttering eyes. "Someone who can help me get my luck back."

"Thinh's the one that died, not you," Vy said. Her eyes were all red and swollen. Even now, the tears kept falling down her cheeks. Even when she didn't look like she was crying, she was. Anh didn't cry when people died, the way Vy did. She knew how not to cry.

Me opened her eyes straight, as though she were just waking up. "I want to go home."

"In one minute, Me," Anh said. "The priest's almost through."

Everyone was there, standing in the hot sun, feet baking on the crisp grass. Some had umbrellas. Some were holding newspapers over their heads. The Lutherans from South Dakota had sent a delegation from their church. Anh recognized one of the girls from the youth group, the one who had taken her to Weller's Department Store and bought her her first American clothes. A tall, blond, square-shouldered girl who smiled a lot and hardly said anything to anyone. But she could bowl and play baseball and run faster than the boys. Anh couldn't even remember her name.

"A boy who loved to run," the priest was saying. "And so his life sped by. Too fast."

Mr. and Mrs. Bui were there with their four kids and the new grandbaby. Mr. Bui was holding Mrs. Bui's hand.

"Looks like Mrs. Bui's got him now," Anh whispered to Vy. She didn't want to hear any more things about Thinh. She couldn't stand it if that priest said one more thing about the brother she loved so much, about the brother who was right now lying in a box in front of them, not breathing. Not breathing. Never was going to breathe again.

"What is he saying?" Me said.

"He's saying what a good boy Thinh was," Anh said.

"If I were Mr. Bui, I'd send Mrs. Bui back to Saigon," Vy whispered back.

"He wasn't such a good boy," Me said.

The rest of Anh's cousins from South Dakota had shown up with their kids. Even brought some of their in-laws with them. A whole caravan of cousins and kids and in-laws, driving pickups and vans, and bringing food from South Dakota, like there wasn't any in California. They were all staying at Anh's house, sleeping on the floor, sleeping in the bathroom, sleeping in the kitchen.

"If we knew God's plan for us, who among us would wait to find out what it was?" the priest was saying. "Mystery. Mystery is all."

All of Me's brothers and sisters from up north in Santa Maria, and her cousins on her mother's side, the ones who lived in San Diego, were there. Cookie was standing next to her mother, her arm around her waist, crying as though it were her fault Thinh was dead.

"Life is like bingo," the priest was saying, "and only God knows what numbers you have."

And Khanh and Ba's kids were there, the older ones. They were standing off to the side. Not like family at all. Just curious people come to see the boy the Nep family gang boys murdered.

"There's your American boyfriend, Anh," Vy said.

Sam was coming across the cemetery grounds from the direction of the flower shop, walking briskly. Anh watched him coming. He was beautiful. Oh, God, he was a beautiful man.

"He's not my boyfriend," Anh said.

"I want water," Me said.

"When we get home," Anh said.

"Is Ba here?"

"I told you, he went to Fresno to be with his sick brother."

"He doesn't have a brother in Fresno."

"Maybe it was Stockton," Vy said.

It was nearly over. Anh would be able to breathe once it was over. Me turned her head around to look at the people, and the priest noticed her turning and stopped talking until she was through looking, and then he said, "Who knows a mother's grief?"

Me went into her bedroom to rest, but Anh could hear the video going through the kitchen wall. A Chinese musical, all squeaky tunes and screeching voices. Out in the living room, long picnic tables had replaced the furniture. Everyone who had been at the cemetery was here eating. Those people who couldn't get in the house were standing in the yard, and Anh could hear them talking and laughing through the window while she stirred the food. The phone kept ringing. She didn't have to answer it. There were plenty of people answering it. There were plenty of people in the kitchen, too, washing dishes, frying things, cutting things.

Sam was standing near the door to the kitchen, his arm resting on the top of the refrigerator. It made her sore heart jump just to look at him.

Vy was back in the kitchen now, with a handful of dirty paper plates.

"I'll give you my new jade ring, Vy," Anh said, "the one you like so much, if you help me kill Nep Lai." Oh, what good were funerals, anyway, when they could make you feel this way, make you feel like you still had something that needed burying?

"Come on, Anh," Sam said. "Cut it out."

"How are you going to kill him?" Vy said.

"I'm making a plan now," Anh replied.

Vy thought a moment. "I don't think so."

At midnight people were still eating and drinking, going in and out like it was daytime, sleeping a little bit if they had to. There were people asleep under tables, leaning against a couch or the wall.

Anh filled a plate for Sam and one for herself. They sat down at the table where all the cutting and dicing and preparing was still going on. Most of these women didn't understand English. They were older women, like her mother, who just came out to help at funerals and weddings. Women who left their shoes at the door and walked around the house in their bare feet.

"I've got an offer to go up north," Sam said. "We can go together. Leave all this crap behind us."

He reached his hand across the table and took hold of hers.

"I can't," she said. "I got something to do here."

"She means what she says about killing Nep Lai," Vy said.

"I'll help you, Anh," Cookie said. She was washing dishes, her hands flipping cups out of the soapy water onto the drainboard.

"You can't even rinse those dish right," Anh said. "You know about germ, how people get sick when you don't rinse the dish?"

"You're serious?" Sam said. "You're going to kill this guy?"

"You like *gà hấp muối?*" Anh said. "Salt steam chicken." She loved to feed him, watch him eat, sit close and see his jaw go. Smell him. Oh, she could never get too much of his smell. This whole week, every night after Me had gone to bed, he had come to the house and sat in the living room with the relatives and friends that were arriving for the funeral, and when everyone had settled into their sleeping bags, he and Anh went into her bedroom and closed the door, and he comforted her. Oh, no one could comfort her like he could. He knew all the places to touch to make her feel good. He knew all the sweet words to say to make her forget. And in the morning when he left, his smell, musky sweet, clung to her skin as though he were still there.

He shoved the plate away. "I'm not hungry."

"I heard a story about a boat coming out of Saigon, trying to escape Vietnam," Anh said. "There was pregnant lady, and everyone said don't let her on, pregnant lady is bad luck. So they kick her off, and another boat take her, and that one sink. Everyone gone. Everyone. It was her time. Nobody fault. So if I kill Nep Lai, it not my fault. That his time to die."

"She told you that story because she thinks she's pregnant," Vy said, and poured a beer into a glass and began to sip it.

"Don't speak for me," Anh said to her in Vietnamese.

"How could you be pregnant?" Sam asked, confusion in his eyes. "What's going on?"

"I'm not," Anh said, "so don't worry."

"She dreamed she was pregnant," Vy said. "Anh's dreams are really powerful."

"I'm going to take a trip to Saigon when relations are normalized," Cookie said. She was examining each dish carefully now, holding it up to the light to check for spots. "Anh's going with me. I want to see where the war was. Did you see *Platoon*, Sam?"

He leaned closer to Anh. It looked to her as if he were going to kiss her right here in front of everybody, going to embarrass her by doing something sexy. But all he did was breathe close to her mouth. "Give up this vengeance shit, and come up north with me. We can have a good life. Start over. Forget everything."

"Come back tomorrow," Anh said. "We gonna be at this for a couple day more, and I make you stuff to eat tomorrow will melt your mouth."

"Your mother know what she's up to?" Sam said to Vy. She began to laugh. Cookie was giggling at the sink.

He stood up. "You think this is funny?"

"You want some more tea?" Anh said. "A cracker? I got American-style, with peanut butter in it."

He shook the table when he got up. Tea spilled all over the remains of the salted steamed chicken.

"Cute ass he's got," Vy said, watching him leave.

Anh could hear the front door slam. An angry slam, slapping at the frame of the house and everyone in it.

"Take it, if you like it," Anh said.

"I couldn't find the cemetery," Jana said. It was three in the morning, and nearly everyone in the house was asleep, bodies everywhere you looked. The television was on in the living room, and there was a row of dazed-looking people sitting cross-legged on the floor watching someone spray black paint on a man's bald head.

"Don't look like you try too hard to find the cemetery," Anh said. She had been dozing on the bed with Vy's kids, dreaming about pregnant women jumping out of boats into the South China Sea when Cookie woke her up to tell her Jana was there.

"All I found was the pet cemetery on Newland." Jana was in sweatpants and a pullover sweater and didn't look like someone who had been wandering around all day looking for a funeral to go to.

"The cemetery is right there on Beach Boulevard," Anh said.

"I thought it was on Harbor."

"Right there on Beach."

"So I went home."

"It don't matter, anyway."

"If it doesn't matter, what are you looking at me like that for?"

"We bury Thinh in Westminster Cemetery. Big funeral. Everyone in Little Saigon come to the funeral. You so smart, and you can't find the cemetery."

"I don't like funerals. I never go to funerals."

"You said you couldn't find it."

"I didn't try too hard."

"That always the way it is with American people. You come in, throw some bomb around, shoot some people, toss candy to the kid, and don't come to the funeral. I treat you like relative, you treat me like shit."

"It's just a funeral, for Chrissakes. A dead body is a dead body. What difference does it make if I was there or not?"

"Nothing. You can go home now. You come here and tell me you don't like funeral, and now you can go home."

"I came here to tell you we can still have a business, it's not too late."

"I don't want no business no more."

"I admit I've had to do some thinking about whether I wanted to stay mixed up with Little Saigon, with all that nastiness, or get out. And I thought, Well, if I'm going to get out, this is the time to do it. Anh will understand. She can't expect me to stay after what's happened."

"Sure, I understand. So get out."

"I said to myself, It's too dangerous. Nep Lai's goons are going to make more trouble. Maybe I'll get caught practicing law without a license. Maybe I'll get hurt. Maybe I'll get killed. Maybe I'll go to jail. I was going to tell you that today, that I was through, but I couldn't find the cemetery."

"People from South Dakota, from San Diego, from Santa Maria, everyone come to the funeral, don't get lost. You come from Balboa, and you get lost on Harbor Boulevard."

"Then tonight in bed I couldn't sleep, just kept listening to the damn ocean. I never heard it like I did tonight. So loud, it made my pillow jump. So I finally said what the hell and went outside. There was a lunar tide tonight, and the waves were higher than my house. That's why it was so loud. If those waves could have come on shore, they would have swallowed the beach all the way to Pacific Coast Highway. Would have drowned my house, my kid, my folks. Would have killed me. What's a little beach house to the ocean, anyhow? And I kept watching the waves, and after a while I sat down and put my bare feet in that cold water, and just let it tug at me to see how far it would go."

"I don't swim," Anh said, "so I don't care."

"Oh, you swim, all right. You swim with the best of them. You think I just got in the car and drove over here without thinking about it, without weighing the risks? Well, I didn't. I said to myself, What bad am I doing that I should run away? I'm helping people, giving good advice. I'm not cheating anyone. I'm not that scared kid anymore being dragged around the country by a maniac murderer."

"Look at that guy head, with all that gunky black stuff on it," Anh said. Oh, she couldn't listen to any more of what Jana was saying. It was just mixing her up to listen.

"I can resurrect the files," Jana said. "We don't need a computer. I can pull it all out of my head. I told you I have a photographic memory." She held both hands to the side of her head as though she were trying to squeeze something out of it. "It's all here, right here in my head. Are you listening to me?"

"Sure."

"Cookie can type up everything, redo the pleadings, set up new files. I don't have the contents of letters or stuff like that in my head, but that doesn't matter. The main thing is I can remember clients' names, their addresses and phone numbers, accident dates, file numbers, case numbers."

"You think he fool anyone with that paint on his head? He go out in the rain, it gonna wash off."

"I said to myself, Haven't Anh and I been through it all? Don't we both know you can only die once? If I run away now, I lose, and everyone else wins. I don't like to lose."

"I'm going to kill Nep Lai, so it don't matter what you like."

Jana wasn't listening to her, didn't believe what she said about killing Nep Lai. Oh, she could see in her face she wasn't listening, didn't believe it.

"So I've told you what I can do," Jana said. "You think about it and let me know."

~

HO CHI MINH CITY, 1981

It was easy getting out of the U.S. with the money, easy to fool the American customs people. Tam and Anh between them had collected five hundred thousand dollars in American hundred-dollar bills from Vietnamese in the U.S., all of it going to relatives in Vietnam, except for the commission Tam and Anh got to keep for taking the chance on maybe getting killed for it on some street in Ho Chi Minh City. And when they got to Vietnam, Tam was going to marry a girl he didn't even know so he could bring her back to her family in South Dakota. That was another ten thousand dollars for doing that. Add that ten thousand onto the commission for carrying all that money, and split it down the middle. Half for Tam. Half for Anh.

"They say it's not against the law in America to carry more than ten thousand dollars out of the country," Tam told Anh. "Just fill out a little form, they say, and they'll let you take whatever you want. That's a lie. They'll steal it. Or want a bribe. Maybe they even have a connection to Vietnam and will let them know we're bringing all that money with us, and they'll rob us before they even let us off the plane."

They hid the money on their bodies.

"Tape it to your shoes, inside," Tam said, and showed Anh how to do it. Hundred-dollar bills keeping her feet warm, making her walk like a pigeon. He bought nylon stockings and filled them with money, then taped the stockings to his body. All over his body. Every little crease filled up with money.

"Feels funny," Anh said, patting his back and chest. It felt soft. Not like money. Like fat. It made a noise like money, but it felt like fat.

"My friends told me some people put money in their baby's diaper to hide it," Tam said. "But the money stinks when you get to Vietnam. And people on the street know the stink of money that's been kept in a baby's diaper. They told me couriers are robbed just walking on the streets of Ho Chi Minh City because their money stinks of baby shit."

Tam looked like anyone's relative, going back to see his sick mother. Anh looked like his daughter.

"Are you carrying more than ten thousand dollars with you?" the customs inspector at LAX asked before they got ready to board the plane for Manila.

"We got sick relative," Anh said. "No money. Just sick relative in Manila. Maybe we got some money, but not much. Enough to get there and buy medicine for our sick relative."

Tam wouldn't sleep in the airplane, he was so worried about the money. Just sat awake the whole time while Anh slept. When they got to Manila, they had to wait in the airport for a plane to Ho Chi Minh City.

"Me said I shouldn't try to find my son," Anh said. They were in the coffee bar of the Ninoy Aquino Airport, near the window, out of the way of anyone who might bump or push Tam and hear the money crinkle under his clothes. "She said he's ten years old now and what do I want with him, anyway? She says he won't know me. I don't care if he's ten years old, if he doesn't know me. I'll know him. I want to take him home with me. Send him to school. Make him fat. Make him healthy."

The airplane was full. It seemed to Anh there were a lot of people doing what she and Tam were doing, everyone walking like their shoes were too tight, probably bringing money to relatives for a commission, probably planning to charter boats and smuggle people to Singapore or Malaysia or Thailand.

They landed in Ho Chi Minh City in late afternoon. From the air the city looked cleaner than Anh remembered. The paddies were green, and the jungle had renewed itself, grown out of its scorched leaves and broken limbs.

"They can call it Ho Chi Minh if they want to, but it smells bad, like garbage and shit," Tam said as they got off the plane, and the sticky heat and the odors enveloped them. "Did it smell like this when it was Saigon?"

"I thought it smelled like spices and flowers when it was Saigon," Anh said.

"We've been in the U.S. too long, I think. Do you have the two hundred dollars ready?"

"It's in my shoe."

"Take it out."

The official they were to see had an office not far from the main door of the airport.

"You have come back after the Tet celebration," the official said as Anh handed him the two one-hundred-dollar bills.

"We weren't able to come before this," Tam said. "But we're happy to be back where our ancestors are buried."

"Was it a good celebration?" Anh said. "Did you have enough good things to eat?"

"I eat well all year," the official replied. "I'll escort you to the baggage area and see that no one keeps you from leaving the airport."

He held his office door open for them, then escorted them

to the baggage area. Tam got the bags, while the official waited with Anh.

"You won't have to pay anyone else," the official told her. "But beware. Everyone has his hand in your pocket these days."

"Nothing has changed," Anh said.

Tam hired a cyclo for the short trip to the hotel. The streets. Oh, Anh remembered the streets. They hadn't changed, either. Full of bicycles and buses and cyclos, no one paying attention to traffic signals, everyone crisscrossing from north to east, south to west, beeping, honking, jingling bells.

"America?" the hotel clerk said. "Việt Kiều?"

"How can you tell that?" Anh said.

"Your clothes are too clean, and you smell like Americans."

The elevator didn't work, so they walked up the stairs to the fourth floor. Tam went to his room and slept, and Anh just sat by the grimy window and looked out at the street. She had come back. That terrible trip to escape this place. And here she was.

"You look like a child," Tam said when they met for breakfast the next morning. "As young as when we left."

Anh had left her jewelry in Sioux Falls. The jade bracelet, the jade earrings. She wore no makeup, no American clothes. Just cloth sandals and a cotton blouse and baggy trousers. "I'm trying to look Vietnamese."

"You look like a baby."

"I'm an old woman, Tam. Twenty-three years old, and an old woman. Me says I was born old, born knowing everything, and that's what's wrong with me." She leaned toward him over the table. "This hotel needs a good paint job, and the toilet water doesn't flush, and there isn't any toilet paper and no towels. This is some shitty place we came to. When can I look for my son?"

"First we get rid of this money." Tam had taken the hundred-dollar bills out of the nylon stockings and put some of them in a backpack and some in a money belt inside his trousers and some in his shoes.

"They could use air-conditioning here," Anh said. There were fans overhead, but they moved as though they were waiting for a shove. Spun so slowly, they scarcely rippled the air. "Maybe we should go in the air-conditioning business, bring air-conditioning units over here. We can get people together, put all our money in one pocket, and bring air-conditioning to Vietnam."

"You know how much you'll make on this trip?"

"I don't want to know. I don't care about money, anyway. I'm just hot. That's all."

"Fifty-five thousand dollars each. I don't think you can sell enough air-conditioning to the Communists to make that kind of money."

28

*S*am's name wasn't on the big board in the lobby of the building, but Anh remembered the firm's name. Ketchin, Ketchin, and Throop. Thirtieth floor, the board said. Take the elevator around the corner if you're going higher than the twenty-second floor, the black guy in the uniform sitting at the circular desk in the lobby said.

The elevator around the corner zipped up to the twenty-third floor without stopping. A girl with a yellow notepad in the crook of her arm got on at the twenty-fourth and got off at the twenty-eighth, and now the elevator light was steady for the thirtieth.

Oh, what an office this was. The elevator opened right into it, like a door opening into someone's living room.

"I got dizzy in that elevator," Anh told the girl at the French provincial desk, "this office so high up."

"Ketchin, Ketchin, and Throop," the girl said into the mouthpiece dangling in front of her mouth. "Ketchin, Ketchin, and Throop," she said again. She had a pleasant voice, a machine-made voice, saying that name—Ketchin, Ketchin, and Throop—so smooth, with no rough spots in it no matter how many times she said it.

Switchboard lights were blinking in front of the girl, and she was pushing buttons and pressing levers and smiling at Anh and waving at someone in an office that Anh could see had a big brass figure of a crane, as big as a man, standing in a corner of it.

"Can I help you?" the girl finally said.

"No one can help me," Anh replied.

Sam was standing by the window looking out, his back to Anh. He was listening. Anh could tell he was listening. His shoulders didn't move, but once in a while his body seemed to shake, as though what she was saying were too hard to listen to.

"It wasn't bad in the brothel," she said. "Everyone took care of me. Outside was terrible. Outside was the war. But I forgive you. It wasn't all your fault. It was everyone's fault. So don't think I blame you, because I don't. Even if the baby was your baby, how was it your fault? We all were there. Caught. You were caught. I was caught."

Sam's office was plain. He had no giant cranes standing in the corners, just a messy bookshelf and coffee cups everywhere. Anh wanted to clean the place, scrub those cups, fix the place for him, make him comfortable. Oh, she wished she had time to make him comfortable.

He turned around. Came toward her. Put his arms around her. "You're not going to do this crazy thing, are you?"

"I'm cleaning my house, leaving instruction," Anh said. "I don't want to die with my house dirty. Somebody liable to say, 'What the fuck the matter with her, she didn't clean before she go?'"

"Oh, Jesus," he said. He sat down on the couch and leaned his head against the back of it and closed his eyes. Smooth eyelids he had, like a baby's, little blue veins almost the color of his eyes underneath.

"If you were in Vietnam, how come you don't understand why I have to kill Nep Lai? Thinh die because of me. Because I think I'm so smart, I know everything, know how to do everything, handle people. Figure it out. Figure it out. Everything I do is with my head. I only do it that way because my heart is so sore."

His eyes were open now. "When are you going to kill him?"

She put her hand on the inside of his thigh. "We have time," she said. "We can make love one more time."

Sam was kneeling beside the couch, his mouth sweet and warm down there, when the girl with the machine-made voice came in.

"Mr. Ketchin would like—"

Anh caught her eye, but it didn't matter. People had watched her before. Sometimes men in Uncle Kou's brothel would come from the other rooms to watch the thirteen-year-old prostitute do her tricks.

Sam raised his head for a moment. "Go away," he said. But he didn't get up, didn't move from where he was, didn't stop what he was doing.

"My God," the girl said.

"That feels good," Anh said. The door was shutting now, the girl's face was gone.

~

Ho Chi Minh City, 1981

"Look at all those children on the street with American eyes and noses," Anh said. One side of the dining room was open to the street, with just a rusted metal railing separating them from the bicycles and the noise. The vendors had already set up their cauldrons and stools and were selling fried noodles and sweetened pearl barley. "Maybe Manh is one of them."

"Just pick one," Tam said. "Any one of them will be happy to be chosen."

"He comes to me in dreams and yells at me in Vietnamese for leaving him here and not even writing him a letter or caring when he's sick."

"He was a baby. How do you know his voice?"

"A mother knows her child's voice. I heard him speaking to me last night in the hotel room. It was very clear, like you're speaking to me right now."

"That was from the street. Kids sleeping on the street. I heard it, too."

They caught a bus in front of the hotel. It swayed to a stop, suitcases and boxes on the roof sliding from side to side. People clung to the steps and hung out the windows. The bus looked like a fat insect, the packages on the roof its antennae, the arms dangling out the windows its legs.

They went from village to village giving away the American money they had carried to Vietnam. All those relatives in the U.S. giving away money to Vietnamese brothers and sisters, mothers and fathers, cousins, nephews, nieces. In some places the bus let them off to walk because the road was gone or the bridge was out or the holes in the road were so full of water that a bus could sink out of sight in fifteen minutes.

Walking along the rutted road, with the steam hovering over the rice paddies, Anh remembered her brother and the corpses he loved to draw. "My brother Manh was an artist before they blew him up," she said.

The houses in every village looked the same. The people in them looked the same. Poor, without possessions, without color or comfort or beauty around them. Like this house. A sprawling house with a dirt floor and a thatched porch. A house full of people. Old ones, young ones, children, babies. Most houses had mats to sleep on, though, and this house had none. It had no chairs. No table to put your food on. Each person in his own corner, squatting on his favorite spot of dirt, shoveling rice from bowl to mouth, holding the bowl close, guarding every grain.

"Maybe we'll be back with an air-conditioning business," Anh said, "and you can all get rich. And I know people in the sewing business, they need operators to run sewing machines. We can open a factory here, and all of you get so rich you'll think you won the war."

But all anyone in any of the houses in any of the villages wanted to know was what was it like in America. Were the people nice? Generous? Had they forgotten the war? Was the food good? Did families stay together and help each other? Or was America, like the Communists said, a bad place, full of murderers and thieves?

The last village was Nga Tu Bay Hien, and while Tam waited in the shade of a rubber tree, Anh walked down the road to Uncle Kou's house. She remembered where every bomb hole in the road was. They were still here. Like a roadmap. This hole led to that one, and that one to the other one, and this smaller one fell into the pit of this *bigger one, and there was the house, at the edge of the field, looking dilapidated, but still standing. Oh, she knew the way to this house. There was the rice paddy and the jungle, and the road running along into the stand of rubber trees. Oh, she'd never forget how to find this house. Never.*

Loc was living in the house with his wife and four children, and his mother-in-law and father-in-law and his mother-in-law's sister and her husband, and the husband's niece and her three children. One of Loc's wife's relatives was outside the house washing dishes in a bucket, not so much washing them as wiping them off with a dirty rag. Loc was inside the house lying on the dirt floor, the side of him that was missing the arm and leg propped up by pillows. He was confused as to who Anh was.

"My sister Anh lives in the U.S.," he said. "She never comes here. Did she send you?"

"Your sister Anh is here," Anh said, and tried to embrace him, but he pushed her away with his one good arm.

"He's been very sick," his wife said. She looked Amerasian, with brown hair and round eyes. Oh, Ba would yell if he saw Loc married to an Amerasian. "Sometimes he acts this way because he's in pain. He needs to be bathed, but the only water we have is what collects in the ditch outside. We boil it to drink it. But it's too dirty to bathe in it."

"Have you taken him to a doctor, to a hospital? What's the matter with you that you let him lie there on the ground in this filthy place? Pick him up. Do something to help him, or I will."

Loc's wife laughed. Then she turned to her mother and father, and they laughed, too. Loc's oldest daughter got a bottle from the table and poured a green herb-smelling liquid into a spoon and fed it to her father.

"Dog medicine," Loc's wife said. "When the pain is too bad, we give him dog medicine to calm him down."

"Here's five hundred dollars," Anh said, and everyone in the house gasped. "Take him to a doctor. If you don't, I'll come back and kill you all."

Tam was fanning himself with a newspaper when Anh got back to where he was waiting. The air was heavy with moisture, and lizards darted across his feet, some of them stopping on the top of his shoes as though the dirt were too hot for them.

"My brother is an addict," Anh said. "I left money for a doctor, but they'll feed him opium with it instead."

"He chose his life."

"Ba chose it for him."

The next day Tam went to see the family of the girl he was supposed to marry. Anh went looking for Manh.

She could have gone to the orphanages, done it that way, put her name down. But she knew Manh wasn't in an orphanage. Her son would try to take care of himself. He would be on the street, selling something. He would be bright-eyed and have lots of quick, smart remarks to make to anyone who came by. He would be handsome, with a high-bridged nose and hair that grew back from his forehead in a soft wave. He would recognize Anh. She would recognize him.

She looked all day for such a boy. Scanned the faces of the mixed-blood children that lived on the street. They ran in packs, never fewer than four together, sometimes as many as ten.

"Sacramento," one boy said to her. "Are you from Sacramento?" And he showed her a picture of an American soldier grinning into the camera.

She gave money away to every child she spoke to.

That night Anh went into Tam's room.

"Did you find him?" He was in bed, the dingy sheets drawn across his knees.

"No."

"Maybe tomorrow."

"Maybe tomorrow."

"Will you sleep with me?"

"Was the girl ugly?"

"Older than they said, but not too ugly."

Tam was a squat, plain-faced man. But he had been kind to her. There were very few people who had been as kind to Anh as he had been.

"I'll sleep with you," she said. "We'll do whatever you want. We'll make it a good time, something you won't forget. But we won't talk about it afterward, and we won't do it again. I don't want to hear about it next year coming out of someone else's mouth, talking about me. I don't want you to tell your kids or the ugly girl you're going to marry or anyone else about what we did or how we did it."

"I wouldn't tell anyone about you, Anh."

She could tell that he had been to prostitutes. He did things that Anh remembered the men doing in Uncle Kou's brothel. He came in her mouth. He ejaculated in her rectum. He sucked her breasts. She didn't mind. She felt nothing. He lay his heavy body across her, and he felt no heavier than an eyelash. There were things she could do to take herself away, things she had learned. Tricks. Her mind was full of tricks.

When he was through, he fell asleep, and she went back to her own room. In the morning, when they met for breakfast, Anh looked for something in his eyes, but there wasn't even a shadow.

"I married the girl yesterday," Tam said. "We'll leave tonight."

"I haven't found Manh yet."

"You'll never find him."

"You go home. I'll stay here."

"You're more American now than Vietnamese. You want to live in this filth?"

"Fifty thousand dollars is a lot of money. I can live here a long time."

"You take it home and loan it out for interest and forget about your son. It would have been better if you hadn't come at all. I told you you would never find him. He's lost. Dead, probably. Or too ruined, too sick, too bad for you to want him, anyway. You're lucky you didn't find him. I'm picking the girl up this afternoon. She's from a good family. Educated. Don't tell her you were a prostitute."

Anh met the girl—her name was Minh—at the airport. She wasn't old or ugly. She looked like the girls Anh remembered when she was in the Catholic school. Clean-faced girls with innocent eyes. But she wasn't eighteen.

"You're going to like it in the States," Anh said. "We'll get your hair fixed and buy you some clothes. Do your relatives have enough money to buy you some pretty things, or are they stingy? I know how to find things cheap. If your relatives are stingy, I'll loan you the money. Vietnamese girls have to look good if they want husbands in America. Tam's going to divorce you, and if you don't look good, you'll be an old maid like me. I can show you everything you need to know to get a husband."

All Minh did was nod and smile, and it disgusted Anh to see the way she walked behind Tam, carrying a little black suitcase in each hand, like an old lady. Wouldn't even look at him when he spoke to her, just bowed and bobbed her head and made little sniggering sounds instead of words.

"She makes me sick," Anh said to Tam when the girl left them in the airport waiting room and went to the bathroom.

"I'm divorcing her when we get to California."

"You're not going to Sioux Fall?"

"I don't think so."

When it was time to board the plane, Minh spoke to Anh for the first time. "I won't have room for two suitcases in the airplane. Will you please put this one under your seat for me? It has gifts for my cousins in America."

When they changed planes in Manila, a policeman at the customs gate stopped Anh. She was still carrying one of Minh's little black suitcases.

"Miss, this way, please, miss," he said.

"We'll meet you on the plane," Tam said, and he took Minh's arm, and this time she walked alongside him, little suitcase in her hand, hurrying, hurrying, hurrying. Not like a schoolgirl now. Like someone who was afraid she'd get left behind.

"Yes, you, miss," the policeman said. "And bring your suitcase with you, please, miss."

"I'll see you on the airplane," Anh shouted to Tam as the policeman led her away.

They put her in a little room that had windows looking out into other little rooms.

"Any watches? Jewelry?"

"No, no. You think I'm going to wear jewelry in Vietnam with all those poor people who'll kill you for a carton of cigarettes?"

"No rings?"

"I told you. No jewelry." She was getting angry. "I'll miss my plane. I'm an American citizen. You better not be fooling around with an American citizen. They'll bring the army over here and bomb you if you try anything with one of their citizens."

He left her alone then. Went out to one of the other little rooms where people were sitting on chairs like she was. Missing their planes, too, probably. She wished she did have a watch. She'd have given it to him. Bribery. That's how they do it here. Like in Vietnam. Pay the guy, he lets you go. Give him your watch, he lets you go.

"Look what I found," she heard one of the policemen say. She stood up and looked over the partition. There was Minh's bag on a table. Open. That little black suitcase that schoolgirls carry their books and papers in. Open. The one that had gifts in it for Minh's cousins in America. Open.

"Heroin," the policeman said. "A suitcase full of heroin."

29

Oh, if there was one thing Anh knew, it was that you had to take charge of your life. You had to plan how you wanted it to go. And that plan had to be easy, like waking up in the morning and brushing your teeth. And it had to be neat. And you had to do it with heart. And so when she decided to kill Nep Lai, she made her plan and went about it the way she did everything. With neatness and with heart.

The last one on Anh's list of people who owed her money was the Family Pham Liquor Store on Bushard. She had already been to the cleaner on Magnolia. He gave her six thousand, although he owed her seven. The insurance guy, the one who had the boy in a wheelchair, gave her the whole five thousand he owed her. The flower shop lady, the doughnut shop couple, the lady who made silk flowers so real you had to smell them to tell the difference, they all gave her back the money she had given them. Maybe not all of it, but most of it. They didn't even ask why she wanted it, but put the dollars in her hands. Went to their safes, their boxes, their old purses, and gave her everything they had. Oh, it sure made her dizzy thinking how many people owed her money. It seemed that sometime or other she had given everyone in Little Saigon money for something. Business lease.

Inventory. Sickness. Sometimes she had had to borrow the money from someone else to give it.

"I feel bad asking you for the money back," Anh said to Mr. Pham. He was a flat-faced, suspicious man, always looking at people as if they were going to steal crackers off the shelves. Sometimes following them out into the parking lot, asking if they paid for the sodas. Once he got punched in the face by a Laotian he accused of slipping a bag of potato chips into his pants. It made his nose flatter than it had been before.

"It made me crazy all the way here," she said, "driving in the car, thinking I've got to ask you for the money, Mr. Pham. I kept saying to myself, When have I ever asked Mr. Pham to give me the money back? Never. When people are ready to give money back that they borrowed, they do it. I know that. You don't ask for it, or it makes you look greedy and selfish. But what am I going to do if I need it so bad and I don't have any other way to get it?"

Mr. Pham owed her the most. Fifteen thousand dollars. She had met him on a bus coming back from Las Vegas. He was sitting on the seat next to her, and when they stopped in Barstow, he stood off by himself near the telephone pole looking hot and thirsty while everyone else went inside to buy a cold drink. Oh, Anh knew when someone was broke. She knew when someone had lost all his money playing *pai gow*. So she bought a Coke for him, and when they were back on the bus, she gave it to him. He didn't even thank her, but drank it down in one gulp.

"I gambled pretty big in Las Vegas," he said.

"Me, too," Anh said. "I won big this time, too. Twenty-five thousand."

"Why don't you take an airplane, then, if you won so big?"

"It scares me to fly. All the time I want to go in and poke the guy steering the thing, see if he's doing it right. I feel better on a bus. How did you do in Las Vegas? Did you gamble a lot?"

"Day and night for five days. No sleep. Just gambled. I can taste the cards in my mouth, all that paste and plastic stuff, I gambled so much. I never lost as much as this time. I don't have money left to pay the lease on my store. I have five kids and a wife. I'm going to kill myself when I get to Los Angeles."

He was looking at Anh now with his flat, suspicious face. What was he thinking of her asking him for the money back? Oh, she felt so ashamed to have to ask.

"See, I've got a plan, Mr. Pham, and I need to have the money."

"No, no, no, no, no, don't tell me anything," he said, and left Anh standing at the checkstand while he disappeared somewhere to the rear of the refrigerator cases. He was back in a few minutes carrying a rusty metal box.

"You only owe me fifteen thousand, Mr. Pham," Anh said as he began counting out the money. He was counting way past fifteen thousand. Three hundred past. Five hundred past.

"Keep quiet," he said.

"I'll keep quiet if I'm able to keep my teeth quiet," she said. "It sure is cold here by this 'frigerator."

Mr. Pham was still counting. Licking his fingers and snapping the bills off one by one. Anh sat down on an upended milk crate and shook her leg and stared at the eggs in the big steel refrigerator. She could see Mr. Pham's reflection in the frosted glass. Counting, counting, counting.

"It's so hot outside," she said. "I was fainting it's so hot. But it's nice in here. It feels like winter in here, you've got so much ice in this 'frigerator. My car is hot, though. In winter all I get is air-conditioning in that car. But in the summer, no air-conditioning. It's like that car knows the time of year. Those Porsches are no good, screwing up winter and summer, summer and winter."

At three thousand past he stopped.

"See, this gang boy killed my brother Thinh," Anh said, "and so I've got to take care of it."

"Don't tell me," Mr. Pham said. "I don't want to hear."

Anh had been to Sheree Morgan's gallery maybe three times since the day she and Jana made their deal with her. She always sent Sheree's fourteen percent with Cookie, cash in an envelope. She didn't like Sheree much. Made her itch when she was around her, made her skin turn red and itch like when she ate too much dried radish soup.

"Wow! What happen to this place?" Anh said. Someone had emptied it out. No more fruit clusters on the walls. No twisted neon tubes. Just a few leftover hemp hangings near the front door. Looked to Anh as though someone had robbed the place. Maybe it was too dark to see how ugly all that stuff was when he did it.

Sheree was in the back office, wrapping things up in brown paper. Huge paintings, metal sculptures, neon tubing. The neon was in all shapes and sizes. Looked like broken noodles.

"I've got a new address where you can send the money," Sheree said.

It looked tough to Anh, how Sheree was tussling all that brown paper. Every time she got one end of something hooked in, the other end popped out. Anh went over and held the roll steady while Sheree cut it with a pair of tiny scissors, the kind that came with a nail file and a cuticle clipper.

"Where you going?" Anh asked.

"Costa Rica."

"You gonna sell this stuff in Costa Rica?"

Sheree straightened up. She had a cotton duster over her silk suit, and hairs were falling down out of the big twist she had on top of her head.

"Auction. I'm auctioning it off in New York. There's no market for avant garde in Laguna Beach. Do you know I was mugged last week right out in front of the store. In daylight. In Laguna Beach."

"That kid stuff. You know what new stuff they doing in Little Saigon? They go to doctor office, two guy, and one guy hold a gun to the doctor head and the other guy make the doctor write a check. That gun stay at the doctor head till that other guy get back from cashing the check in the bank. They think of all good kind of trick in Little Saigon. Pretty soon they be doing it here in Laguna Beach, too. Good trick like that travel fast."

"Well, I'm not waiting. Costa Rica has no army, did you know that? The last peaceful place on earth, and I'm going there."

"How Dennis feeling?"

"He died."

"I didn't see no notice of no funeral. When did he die?"

Sheree looked like she had to think. "A month ago."

"Why you don't tell me? I would come to the funeral." She put the envelope with the thirty thousand dollars in it on the desk. "Did you give him a big party?"

"I sent his body to his mother in New Jersey for burial." Sheree opened the envelope and counted out the money. "You must have had a good month."

"A present from me to you."

"Well, I don't know what to say." She was smiling at Anh now, patting the green currency and smiling.

"My brother Thinh got killed by Nep Lai and his gang boy. They come in the office and wreck it, too, so there no business now, no more money for me. No more money for Jana. No more money for you."

"What are you talking about? I was counting on that money. I'll need it in Costa Rica."

"Didn't Dennis have no insurance? Smart man like Dennis, he must have insurance."

"A little."

"You don't look too sad to me. How come you moving so fast? You ever been to Costa Rica?"

Sheree set her lips in a tight line. "If you're implying that I've done anything fishy, anything—"

Anh shrugged. "Don't matter to me what you do."

The ad ran for a whole week in the *Little Saigon Newsletter*, in the *Little Saigon Report*, in the *Little Saigon News*. Anh even put a small ad in the personals in the *Orange County Register*, just in case a few clients couldn't read Vietnamese.

"If you have a case with the law office of Dennis Morgan on Bolsa Avenue in Little Saigon, come to the office on September 4. We will be open from 9:00 A.M. until 10:00 P.M. We give you money."

Jana was the first one to show up. Eight-thirty in the morning, and there she was in the office. The landlord of the building had cleaned out the trash and ripped up the carpet and painted the walls so the new tenant could move in, and now it was just a big square empty space.

"What do you think you're doing?" Jana said. She was wearing jeans and a T-shirt and looked as though she had read the ad in the

Register while she was eating breakfast. She still had doughnut crumbs clinging to one sleeve.

"Taking care of business," Anh said.

"You can't just give money to people who have lawsuits pending. Did you take it out of the trust account?"

"You insulting me or what? I don't take no money out of no trust account. This is my money, money I borrowed to people and asked for it back."

A few people were at the door now, lining up the way they would at a bus stop. Lining up to get their money, all eager-faced, as though it were a television show and they had won the prize.

"You can't come in," Jana said. "The ad was a mistake." She was pushing the door shut, leaning against the glass.

"You making me pretty mad, you know that," Anh said.

"Where's Cookie?" Jana said.

Someone was pounding on the door now, kicking at it with his feet.

"We through. No more business. I don't need you here. Cookie going back up to Santa Maria. I going to give money to client so they don't lose because we took their case."

"I can do the legal work on the cases, get money for them. For God's sake, Anh, stop giving money away."

"Miss Anh!" The man kicking the door had his mouth at the hinges. "I've got a case for you. A big one. Lots of injuries, lots of medical bills. Open the door."

"What's that guy saying?" Jana asked.

Anh glanced at the door. The man was still babbling in Vietnamese. "He got a case."

"What kind of case?

"You said it was disgusting here, right here you said it, in this office. You said you can't stand it anymore. And you didn't come to Thinh funeral."

"What kind of case is it?"

Anh went over to the door and said in Vietnamese, "What kind of case have you got? Hurry up and talk. I'm not going to stand here all day while you yell at me through the door."

"A boy sixteen driving a car." It was just a pink mouth and white teeth moving against the door hinges. "His kid brother was in the car with him. The sixteen-year-old wrecked the car and was killed. The kid brother was really messed up. Scars and everything, Anh. It's a big case. Open the door."

"Any insurance?"

"Lots of insurance. A cement truck hit him."

"Well?" Jana said. "What did he say?"

"He said he got million-dollar case."

"Well, let him in, for Chrissakes."

"The only thing I sorry for is not getting that house in Balboa."

"You can still get it. We'll start the business up again."

"I was going to give Vy kid such a good life in Balboa, in that house."

The pounding on the door had stopped. The silhouettes were thinning. Anh could hear footsteps going down the stairs.

"Stop him," Jana said. She ran to the door and opened it. "Hey, come back."

"He don't speak English."

"Go get him. Are you crazy, Anh? Go get him."

Anh sat down on the floor and folded her arms over her knees. She rocked back and forth, back and forth. "You got nerve, you know that, coming here and bossing me around. Coming here and telling me what to do like you know everything."

"When I tell you before I'm going to kill Nep Lai, you don't believe me," Anh said.

She and Jana were downstairs in the noodle shop. An overweight man in a security guard uniform, a gun on his hip, was standing at the door, watching the people come in.

"See how bad it is," Anh said, "they even hire police in a noodle shop. Like they selling diamond here. Plain old noodle, and they need a gun to protect it."

"People say all kinds of things when they're angry and upset," Jana said. "Talking about killing someone and not really meaning it comes naturally to some people. I didn't think you were serious."

"I'm serious."

"Did you settle up with Sheree?"

"Sheree going to Costa Rica. I settle up what we owe her. She said

Dennis die and she bury him in New Jersey. I think he didn't die. I think he leave the hospital and went and start to gamble again. I think he lose so much in the casino that he pretend to be dead so he can get insurance. Sheree know how to play trick on people. Dennis, too. Good pair."

"Isn't there something else you can do about Nep Lai? Pay him off or something?"

"Not now. Too late now."

"Have you figured out how you're going to do it?"

"I got the plan nearly set. Just a few more thing I have to do to it."

"I'll help you."

Jana ate her noodles like a Vietnamese now. Oh, she was an expert noodle eater, using the chopsticks to hold the slippery things against the edge of the spoon, and then just sliding them into her mouth.

"You crazy," Anh said. "What do you want to kill Nep Lai for? I'm the one he want. He won't go after you, won't do nothing to you. The police don't care if some gang boy kill a Vietnamese girl. You stay out of it."

"I want to do it."

Oh, she was eating those noodles, and her eyes weren't even quivering, her hand wasn't even shaking.

"You know where I go on Thursdays? To the prison where Chris, my husband's murderer, is kept. I go to make sure that he's still there, that he can't get out and come after me again. I know a thing or two about wanting to murder someone. Every time I see his face, I get this tremendous urge to erase it, make a blank spot where his face is. I didn't sleep for months trying to figure out how I'd do it. At first I thought I'd shoot him, so I could see his brains splatter like my husband's did. But there was no way to smuggle a gun in there. They'd make me undress, make me empty my purse every time. Every single time. So I thought, Okay, poison, that's almost as good. I won't be able to see him suffer, but at least he'll be dead. But they put me on a list of visitors who couldn't bring him anything to eat.

"Then I had a brainstorm. A hypodermic needle. I'd put it inside me, sneak it past the guard, and then when Chris and I were talking, I'd just bend forward and jab him with it. I was ready to do it. Just thinking about doing it made me happy. But I couldn't find anyone who'd tell me what you have to put in it to kill someone." Jana took a last spoonful of soup and pushed the bowl away. "Killing someone isn't so easy."

Anh was quiet for a long time. Oh, this was a strange girl all right. Why hadn't she noticed before how really strange she was?

"I was going to have an abortion," Jana said, "but the doctor said it might be Tim's—my husband's—child, and not his murderer's. I wasn't sure till later, much later, after the blood tests and the DNA and everything else scientific had been done, and then it was too late for an abortion. It gives me the chills to know how close I came to not having Andy—not having my little boy." She put her napkin to her mouth and rubbed her lips with it. Stared at the guy at the door with the gun and rubbed her lips with the napkin again. "You want to kill Nep Lai, fine. I'll help you. You figure out your plan, tell me what I have to do, and I'll do it."

MANILA, 1981

They put Anh in a prison for political prisoners. She was twenty-three years old. Every day a different man came to ask her questions. All of them spoke perfect Vietnamese.

"Where did you get the heroin?"

"I didn't know I had any heroin."

"Where did you get the suitcase?"

"It's not my suitcase."

"Whose suitcase is it?"

"I don't know."

"Where did you find it?"

"I don't remember."

"Why were you carrying it?"

"Someone handed it to me."

"Who handed it to you?"

"I don't know."

"What did they look like?"

"I don't remember."

"Was it a man or a woman?"

"I don't remember."

"What did you do in Vietnam?"

"Went sightseeing."

"Alone?"

"Yes."

"No one was traveling with you? No other Vietnamese? A man maybe?"

"No one."

"You didn't meet anyone?"

"No one."

"Where did you go sightseeing?"

"I don't remember."

"The ocean?"

"I don't remember."

"How did you pay for your airplane ticket from the States?"

"I don't remember."

"No one gave you the suitcase?"

"I found it."

"You said someone handed it to you."

"I forgot. Maybe it was you."

The questions went on for months. She couldn't see daylight, because there were no windows in her cell. The food was terrible. Peanuts and rice. Rice and peanuts. Once in a while a dried-up banana.

Finally in the fourth month, a man who said he was from New Zealand came to talk to her. He was, he said, an Anglican minister. He had a beard and brought her a box of chocolates that had melted together in the box.

"Do you have anyone I can call?" he said.

"My mother."

Within a week Uncle Kou flew from California to get her out.

Oh, it was so simple, he said.

"I know a Philippine actress, she used to work for me in Saigon. Emeline. Do you remember Emeline?"

"Sure."

"She's very famous here. She knows the right people to bribe."

Uncle Kou took Anh to Hong Kong. He was very sweet to her,

took her to buy new clothes. Took her to eat in good restaurants. There was nothing she could give him in return. So she slept with him. In the Hong Kong Hilton. In a beautiful room. Overlooking the harbor. And then he put her on a plane and sent her home to Sioux Falls.

30

This was the day. Either Nep Lai was going to die or Anh was. The certainty of it gave her comfort as she watched the sky turn from dark purple to grayish blue. She tried to remember how many times she had lain in bed, wakeful, watching the sky lighten outside a bedroom window.

She sat up, felt the blood rush. Little Boy was rolled up in the sheet next to her, his feet up against Boy's shoulder. Oh, that sweet smell of two little boys, sweating through their dreams, their faces all peaceful and quiet. She could hear an airplane way, way high overhead, whining away to someplace new and fresh. Then Vy's bedroom door squeaking open and the sound of her feet going down the hall. Vy had a heavy way of walking in the morning, as if she were angry at the world for having to get up at all. Twenty steps, and Vy was in the kitchen, turning on the water for the tea, the pipes groaning, as angry as Vy was to have to wake up and pour their water into the sink.

Anh crossed to the bathroom door and opened it, sat down on the toilet and let the pressure, so strong lately, especially when she first got up, fall away in a gush of pale yellow. She wiped, then washed her hands and brushed her teeth. She listened for sounds from the next room. Ba was in Me's bedroom. Anh had heard his voice sometime during the night, the actual words lost to her in a stream of dreaming. There, she heard it now. The walls were so thin in this house. Paper walls. Cardboard walls. Not strong, sturdy walls like the house in Balboa. Everything everyone said or did in this house came hazily through its walls.

She scrubbed at her face. Scrubbed it so she could feel the skin move. Oh, it made her sad to think she might never wake up to another morning like this. Sweet morning. Safe morning. Vy making the house jump with her angry feet and talking water. And now the rocking of the bed in the next room as her father, despite war and concubine and fourteen children, showed her mother his passion.

$\sim$

CALIFORNIA, 1985

Anh took the bus from Sioux Falls to Los Angeles. Then she rented a car and started north. She had never been to California before and didn't know anyone in Santa Barbara, so she didn't stop there. She didn't stop at all, not even in Goleta, where one of Me's sisters lived, just kept driving up the highway. She didn't care when the guy in the gas station in Buellton said she ought to take the scenic route up the coast, that the ocean and the beach were something special to see, that people came from all over the world just to take that road up the California coast. She wasn't here as a tourist.

When she reached the town of Guadalupe, she stopped for gas again. The town looked Mexican. The signs were Mexican. Even the ones telling you to drink Carta Blanca beer. Tome Carta Blanca, lo Mejor Cerveza en el Mundo. She didn't have to know Spanish to know what that meant. A girl and a boy drinking Carta Blanca beer with teeth-baring grins on their faces.

Guadalupe was only a few blocks long and four or five blocks deep, surrounded by miles of fields, their flat, even rows of summer vegetables stretching all the way to the scenic coast.

"How far do I got to go to Halcyon?"

"No hablo Inglés," the station attendant said.

"You American, or what? Speak English for Chrissakes."

"It's not too far," an elderly man in a battered felt hat who was putting water in his car's radiator said. "Just keep your eye peeled, or you'll miss it. It's straight on down that road. Smallest town in California. No more than a dip in the road, as they say."

The fields were hypnotic passing by the side window of the rental car Anh was driving. She wanted to get out and sit down in the middle of one of them, smell the dirt, see if it smelled different from the dirt in Sioux Falls, different from the dirt in Vietnam.

Tam's ranch was half a mile from the Halcyon general store. The old man had been right. She almost missed it, didn't see the Halcyon sign at the side of the road. Just that store was all there was, and a few shacks here and there. And all those fields stretching up to a mesa on the east and dropping like steps toward that scenic coast.

There were guards with guns at the gates. Vietnamese guards. It made Anh laugh to see them standing in front of that sign that said Paradise Ranch, Where Broccoli Is King.

"I'm a friend of Nguyen Tam's," she said, and they let her drive the rental car through and up the road. She drove for a couple miles before she reached the house. Oh, it was beautiful all right. He sure had gotten himself something beautiful for the heroin that was in Minh's other black bag.

Tam acted as though she were his sister, acted as though he had missed her these four years since they had been in Ho Chi Minh City together.

"You know how to spend your money," Anh said. "And look at these little kids you've got running around here. How many have you got?"

"Three."

Tam brought her into a room Anh knew no one lived in. It had department store furniture in it. The couches were brand new, with no stains on the arms. A Vietnamese woman brought tea, and Tam asked about Anh's family.

"Everyone's fine. We're doing fine."

Anh could hear children playing in another room, and then a woman came in and sat down on the couch next to Tam. She looked about six months pregnant and was wearing lipstick and eyeliner, and her nails were manicured, but Anh could still tell it was that girl in the airport. Minh.

"You didn't divorce her," Anh said, smiling.

"It was too much trouble," Tam said.

"Well, it looks okay to me. Isn't that wonderful, starting all over

again? I never found a husband myself. Me tried to find one for me,
but his family didn't want me."

They sat for over an hour talking about things that didn't matter.
Then Anh told him why she had come all this way. Four years later.
Driving straight from the car rental place in Los Angeles. Without
taking the scenic coast. Just to see him.

"There was this Vietnamese guy, Thai Quoc Em, in Sioux Fall,"
Anh said. "He opened a big TV place. Pretty young guy. Everyone
knew him. I bought Me's video from him. Pretty soon he says he's
going to open more stores. All over the country."

Two little kids had come into the room and were trying to climb
up onto Minh's swollen lap.

"Do you give your kids candy? I've got candy in my purse. I
always carry it around with me in case I run into a kid that doesn't
have any."

Minh murmured something about teeth, but Tam said, "Sure, you
can give them candy if you want to."

All the kids lined up at Anh's knee, and she spoke to each one of
them and patted their heads and then gave them a piece of candy.
Little green candies wrapped in paper.

"I can't think straight when kids are pestering me. Kids have to
know where they belong. I don't mean spank them. I never touch
Vy's kids. But there's a way to do it. Do they have someplace to play
so we can talk and they won't bug us?"

Minh got up from the couch and herded the children out. She
didn't come back.

"She's not too ugly," Anh said. "If you had divorced her, you
probably couldn't have found anyone better, anyway."

"Did you give the TV guy money?"

"Sure. Everyone did. He was giving forty percent interest, for
Chrissakes. If you were there in Sioux Fall, you would have given
him money, too."

"So he ran away with the money and didn't open the stores. Is that
right?"

"To Vietnam. I went to Ho Chi Minh City to talk to him, spent
money for airplane tickets. No deal, either. Straight fare, I was in
such a hurry. He was easy to find. Everyone knew where he was. He

took me to a restaurant and bought me dinner. We laughed a lot together when I told him how everyone in Sioux Fall was trying to find a way to kill him. I told him it wasn't a good idea his taking that money. He told me to go chase myself."

"I'm not in the killing business. I raise broccoli."

"I heard you do anything."

"For myself. I sent the money you made in Vietnam to your mother. Didn't you get it?"

"Sure, I got it."

Anh got up from the chair and went to the window to look out at the fields. "You got pretty rich on that heroin. I never told anyone about the two of us going to Vietnam together, not even Me or Ba. Never told anyone your name. Never said what we did there. Never said anything about Minh. I told Me I was there alone, just looking for my son. I didn't even tell Uncle Kou about you and Minh when he came to get me. He thought I was the one trying to smuggle heroin back into the States."

"I didn't know what was in the bags, Anh. It was Minh's brother. He put the stuff in the bags. Tricked all of us."

Anh turned around and looked at him. "He didn't trick you. Look at how you live. So beautiful. This Thai guy took Ba's money he was saving for a restaurant, he took my money. I worked two jobs for that money he took from me."

"Minh didn't know anything about it."

"I didn't say she knew anything about it. Did I say that? I was in jail four months. Maybe I'd still be there if Uncle Kou hadn't come and paid for me to get out."

"I'd have paid for you to get out. No one told me."

"This Thai guy has bodyguards. Everywhere he goes, they go with him."

"If I do it, it's because we're friends, not because Minh knew anything about the heroin."

"We don't care about the money anymore. We have to take care of him, though, teach people they can't cheat. I've got money for you. Everyone in Sioux Fall who invested in him chipped in money to kill him."

"I don't need any money. I'll take care of it."

"I'll have to go with you. I know where he is."

~

"You won't get away with it," Vy said. "You know how plans are. They break. Someone always breaks them."

Vy was in an old T-shirt and jeans, buttering toast for Little Boy, sitting on the edge of her chair and buttering away. Slapping that butter on like it was going to save Anh's life. Baby Boy was in the high chair, chewing on a piece of dry toast. Little Little Boy was crawling around on the floor, smearing butter up and down the table legs. Boy was in the living room, eating his breakfast on the coffee table in front of the television.

"You can have all the jewelry in that carved box by my bed," Anh said. "Take it. Me doesn't like my jewelry. She says I don't pick the jade right, don't know green from blue. It's yours. Wear the jade ring with your hoop earrings, the ones with the diamonds in them. I like jade and diamonds together. Some people think you have to wear jade with jade, but I like diamonds. Sparkly ones. The good ones, none of that dull stuff the Thanhs sell down on Brookhurst. Remember, don't buy jewelry from the Thanhs, they'll trick you." Anh was still in her nightgown, sipping a glass of cold milk at the table and eating a bean cake. "This bean cake is stale. You have to remember to go to the store. I won't be here to tell you when you run out of things."

"You're sounding like you're dead already," Vy said, "giving me all these instructions, disposing of your things."

"You're a slob, Vy, you know that," Anh said. She pulled Little Little Boy onto her lap. "Why are you always letting this kid eat off this dirty floor?"

"It's not dirty. I washed it myself last week."

"Once a week isn't enough. How do you know what people bring in on their shoes and drop off on the floor? It could be dog shit this baby's putting in his mouth, for all you know."

"Oh, Anh."

Anh glanced over at Little Boy. "And what about him? His teeth are coming in screwy. Take him to that American dentist in Westminster I told you about, and ask him what to do to fix them. That Vietnamese guy you're taking him to doesn't know anything about kids' teeth."

"He's cheap. Twenty dollars a visit."

"And that's what you get, twenty dollars' worth. Are you going to let that Indian guy move in here?"

"We've been talking about it."

"He can't move in unless he promises to pay the rent. If I'm not here to pay, I don't want Ba to have to."

"Jesus Christ, Anh."

"This is just in case." Butter was in Little Little Boy's hair. His face was shining with butter. He slid nicely into Anh's arms, fit there like he belonged. "Just in case," she said.

"You have to study hard," Anh said, "do your homework, get A's. B's aren't good enough. A's will get you into college. Mathematics is the most important thing. Not everyone can work numbers. You can be anything if you learn how to work numbers. Make computers. Design airplanes. Be a doctor." Boy was listening to her all right. Not the way a child listens, halfway, eyes wandering, but with his ears wide open and his tongue rolling in his jaw, as though he were actually chewing the words he heard so he could digest them better.

Little Boy wasn't listening, though. He was walking around the store, putting his fingers on the shelves and pointing to the things he wanted. Cookies. Plastic toys. Beach balls.

"Can I have chewing gum, the bubble kind, Auntie Anh?" Little Boy said. Boy tapped him on the back, and he turned quiet. It bothered Anh to see how meek Little Boy was. Why were some Vietnamese boys so timid when they were little? How did some of those same boys get so violent when they grew up?

"I told you, you can each have three things in the store today," Anh said.

"Buddy always picks out the wrong thing," Boy said. "And he chews his gum up fast, sometimes a whole pack in his mouth at one time, and then he wants mine."

"That's all right. You both have to share. You're brothers, aren't you? Who's going to share with you if your own brother doesn't do it? So you'll remember what I said about learning to do mathematics?"

"I'll remember."

"And about getting A's?"

"I'll remember."

He was so serious, so grown-up, not like a child at all. He must have been a child in some other life.

"And you'll take care of your brothers and your mother? You won't turn into an American and forget your duty to your family, will you?"

"No, Auntie Anh."

They walked up and down the aisles.

"I changed my mind," Anh said. "You can have four things today instead of three."

She wanted to spoil them today, make them feel good. Just in case it was her last day, she wanted them always to remember how generous she was.

Anh lingered in the shower, letting the water run over her skin. Thinking, thinking, thinking. Vy pounded on the door, then came inside. She could see her through the glass just standing there inside the bathroom, steam circling her head, her eyes and nose blurry, not saying a word.

"I'll do it if you want me to," Vy said finally. "I'll help you kill Nep Lai."

"No," Anh said. The water was turning cold, she had stood here so long thinking. "Jana's going to help me."

"But I'm your sister."

"You told me you don't want to. That means you might lose your nerve."

Anh slid the shower door open and stepped out.

"Give me a towel."

Vy handed her a towel, but she didn't leave. She just stood there as though she had something on her mind.

"You know what I think? I think Jana's the one who brought bad luck to this house. Ever since you started up in that business, I could see our luck changing. Everything bad that's happened has happened since you met her, since you started letting Americans into our house, since Sam's been coming here. All bad luck, Anh. Do you hear me? It's been all bad."

"I hear you."

"What'll I do, Anh, if you get killed? What will happen to me?"

"You'll be happy. You won't have to listen to the terrible way I speak English. You'll slop up the house all you want and feed the kids hot dogs every night. You'll sleep with a different guy every week. You'll get pregnant every year. That's what you'll do if I'm not here."

"That's not what I mean. You know that's not what I mean."

"You don't think, that's your problem. If you thought, you'd know how lucky you are. You have your kids. Do you know how lucky you are to have your kids? I would die ten times if I could have one day with my little boy. Just one day."

"I'm going to call Sam, tell him what you're doing." Vy was crying now, her words breaking into raspy pieces. "He'll stop you. You're such a crazy bitch, Anh. Such a crazy, crazy bitch."

Anh couldn't remember which photograph of herself she liked the best, the one where she was in the backyard sitting on the grass in shorts and a halter top or the one Vy's last boyfriend, Baby Boy's dad, took the day they went to the Tet carnival down on Brookhurst and Bolsa, where the police had to come later because people were throwing rocks and someone got hit in the head. That was a good picture of Anh. She was wearing an *ao dai* that day, green silk, looking like a real Vietnamese girl. Anh remembered how strange the weather was that day, like summer in Saigon instead of winter in California.

"You look pretty," Vy said when Anh came out of her bedroom, the photographs in her hand. She had put on a suit. Red, for good luck. And pinned a jade frog to the lapel, for double luck.

"Which one do you like?" Anh said, and showed Vy the photographs. "This one or this one?"

"This one," Vy said, and picked the one with the green silk *ao dai*.

Anh stood outside the door to Me's room. It was quiet in there. No bed rocking. No talking. She opened the door, pushed it inward, let it swing on its hinges until it hit the wall.

Me was sitting in a chair. Her kimono, the one with the dragon and peonies embroidered on it, was open to the waist, her breasts poking up like a young girl's, all high and firm. No baby had ever suckled those breasts. She had always had someone else's tits for her babies. She turned slowly now to look at Anh. She had let her hair down from its knot, all that long, gray-flecked hair hanging down her back, and Ba, standing behind her in nothing but his socks, brushing it. So gently. Running the brush down the silk strands as though they were made of gold threads and he were shining them, looking at that hair through half-open eyes as though he didn't want all that shine and gleam to make him blind.

"I've got a picture of me, Ba," Anh said. "Vy says she likes it better than the one I've got in my album."

Me reached over to the bed and picked up Ba's trousers and handed them to him. He gave her hair one last brush and then, with hardly a glance at Anh, pulled his trousers on over his naked buttocks.

"You're too skinny, Ba," Anh said, and placed the photograph on Me's lap. "You're going to blow away, you're so skinny."

"What's this for?" Me said, looking at the photograph.

"For Ba's shrine, to put next to Thinh's picture in case Nep Lai kills me tonight."

Me stared at the picture. Ba didn't say anything. He just picked up the brush and started shining Me's hair again.

"Say something to me, Ba," Anh said.

"Leave Ba alone," Me said.

"What do you want?" Ba said.

"I want you to tell me about Saigon, about that last day, about what you did. I want to understand why you did it, how you could do such a thing."

"Leave me alone," Ba said.

∼

HO CHI MINH CITY, 1985

Thai Quoc Em had a coffee every afternoon in the same cafe near the Tan Binh Market. His bodyguards accompanied him, sitting at the three other seats at the table, eyes looking around, heads moving all the time, while Thai drank his strong black coffee and read the newspaper.

"How many days are we going to watch him drink coffee?" Anh said.

Tam was methodical. She hadn't remembered him being that way before.

"I can't kill him in his house," Tam said. "He's too smart. He was in the electronics business, so he's got electric eyes and motion sensors hooked up in every room."

"Put a bomb in his car, then."

"His wife sometimes drives the car and takes the children in it with her. I never know what day she'll do it. I don't want to kill children."

"Then shoot him now. Look at him, spending my money, drinking his coffee. Being happy while he's doing it, too."

"If I shoot him here, his bodyguards will shoot me back. Maybe shoot you, too."

"Then what are you going to do? We came all this way to sit in the sun and bake, and you can't think of how you're going to kill that thief?"

"Maybe I won't kill him at all."

"You promised me. He took millions out of Sioux Fall. He even took the money from people who had bought things on layaway. He never paid his bills. He owed everyone for everything. His rent on his buildings, the electric, the telephone. Who's going to kill him if you don't?"

"He'll be dead all right. I told you I'd get it done. I know a guy here, Dong Thanh, who has a big reputation for knowing everyone, knowing what they need. He was a Vietcong soldier and knows how to do things in Ho Chi Minh City."

It was so fast and simple and brilliant.

They met Dong Thanh on the Song Be Bridge, north of Ho Chi Minh City. "Thai's bodyguards only make twenty dollars a month," Dong Thanh said.

"Ah," Anh said. And she gave Dong Thanh two thousand American dollars for his advice. Then she gave him one thousand American dollars for each one of Thai's bodyguards, and they killed him themselves.

31

*L*ai's narrow face was in shadow, his right cheek hidden by the plastic sign that said New York Cheesecake Flown in Daily. But Anh could tell he was plenty worried—she could tell by the way he looked around the coffee shop, then behind him to the casino, then at Nguyen Tam, who was already sitting in the middle of the booth with his water and napkin in front of him.

"The gambling's good tonight, Lai," Anh said. She was standing next to the booth, waiting to see what Nep Lai was going to do. "I can always tell when the gambling's good by all the happy faces at the tables."

Nep Lai had brought a kid with him. Danny. Anh remembered him from when he was with the Cheap Boys and two of his brothers got killed in a fight with some guys from the Santa Ana Boys at a girl's birthday party in Garden Grove. Danny was a tough kid. A brutal kid. Probably the one who hammered the nail into Thinh's head. Oh, Lai was sure scared all right, bringing this wild kid with him to a public place, a gambling casino, where there were police guards at the doors and more guns hanging in holsters inside security men's suits than you could count in an hour. It made Anh smile inside to see how worried Lai was that he brought this stupid kid with him.

"How do you like my suit?" Anh said. "Pretty, huh? I paid full price for it, too. I'm making so much money now, I don't need to even look for bargains anymore. I've got the money to pay the price

265

now. Look at Lai laughing, like I'm not serious. You tell him, Tam, tell him how much money I'm making with you."

"Danny's got to check you both," Lai said. "He's got to make sure you're not going to try and kill me."

"You think that's what this meeting is all about?" Anh said. "You think I'm going to kill you? Are you insulting me on purpose or by accident? How can you think I'm going to kill you when I told you I'm not angry at you anymore, I don't even blame you for killing Thinh. I thought about killing him myself a few times. Rotten kid. He never listened to anybody. It proves it. He didn't listen to me. And he certainly didn't listen to you."

"What kind of business?"

"And I certainly don't kill people when I want to do business with them. Why would I do that? You think I'm some kind of crazy nut?"

"I think I'm the one who's being insulted," Tam said. "I don't carry guns. They're dangerous. People get hurt if you carry guns around with you."

"Stand up," Lai said.

"Go ahead, Tam, stand up," Anh said. "Show him your pockets are empty. Go ahead and show him."

"Danny will take care of it," Lai said.

"I'm just trying to make it go faster, smoother, so we can talk," Anh said. "This shit about who's got a gun and who doesn't have a gun and whether I'm still mad at you and can't be trusted—all that shit just takes up time and goes nowhere."

Danny looked inside Anh's purse first, and then Tam slid across the leatherette and stood up and let Danny pat his trousers and check his pockets.

"Okay," Lai said when Danny was through checking. They all sat down, except for Danny, who went over and leaned against the big metal stanchion near the steps leading down to the floor of the casino. The gaming tables were packed, and people were waiting to play, standing two deep some places waiting for a seat so they could lose their money. The smoke coming up from all those mouths was so thick, it made it look like the place was on fire.

"I heard from people you were still mad about what happened to your brother," Lai said. "People who are mad like that don't forget so easy."

"You know what I say about those people? They don't know what they're talking about. Can they see inside my brain, know what's going on? No."

"It just doesn't make sense, your calling me, telling me you want to do business with me. It doesn't make sense."

"Why do you keep saying that? I'm sincere. I'm doing what the fortune-teller told me to do. Forgive my enemies, and I will have success."

"I came to do business," Tam said. "If we're not going to do business, I'm leaving. I came a long way by car to talk about this, and if you waste my time, you won't get another chance."

"It just seems too strange to me, that's all," Lai said.

"No tricks," Anh said. "I promise you."

"I don't know."

"Well, I know. I told you no tricks, and there won't be any."

"What kind of business?"

"The best kind. Drugs."

"You told me he was a courier."

"Sure. He was a courier. He was everything. How do you think he got the money to start the drug business? Do you know how much Tam used to charge people to get their relatives out of Vietnam? Ten thousand dollars each. Sometimes he had twenty people to get out. He'd charter a boat to carry them all. Do you know how to multiply? Ten thousand times twenty is a lot of money. He did that for ten years. When it was dangerous. When if he got caught, the Vietcong would have shot him. Stolen the money first, and then shot him. Some kind of bravery, isn't it, risking your life for people?"

"I don't think it was for people," Lai said, and Tam laughed. A good, natural laugh that made Anh grin.

They had all ordered hot tea, and the waitress brought the cups and the hot water and a bowl full of little bags that looked to Anh like dust rolled up into dumplings and tied with string. She took one of the bags and was dunking it into her cup of hot water as though she intended to drink it when she saw Dennis Morgan standing at one of the *pai gow* poker tables, looking big and healthy, not as though he had almost died from all that coke.

"Are you sick?" Lai asked, staring at the way Anh's fingers were shaking, holding that dry little tea bag.

"Healthy as a horse," Anh replied. It was Dennis, no question about that. She knew the way his hair went toward the back of his head, how he combed it, the kind of clothes he wore, all dark brown pants and jackets, as if he didn't know there was any other color.

"It's a dangerous business you're in, drugs," Lai said, turning his eyes back to Tam.

"I'm a very careful man," Tam said.

"He needs more people helping him," Anh said. This was the important part, like a piece of music, where everything had to fit, or it all sounded like shit. If Dennis saw her, he could ruin it. He could ruin everything.

"How do you two know each other?" Lai said.

"He's my uncle. We left Saigon on the same boat."

"How come Thinh never talked about him?"

"I live up north," Tam said.

"He has a ranch," Anh said. "A big one. And he's getting tired. You know, people get old, they get tired, don't want to work as hard as they did when they were young. So Tam asked me if I know anyone who's not afraid of anything, someone who can help him with the drug business, take a share."

"What's in it for you?"

"A cut. What do you think I'm doing this for? I'll get a cut, too. I've got big expenses. My mom and dad and my sister and her kids. Big expenses. So when Tam told me he's getting tired, I told him, I said, I know this guy, Nep Lai, he's got gang boys who'll do anything for money. Travel anywhere, go anywhere, carry drugs in their bowels if you want them to. I said, Why do you want to kill yourself for half million a year when you can get people to work with you and give you a cut of what they do? You'll make maybe two million a year. With a little bit for Anh, of course. Can't forget Anh putting the deal together, introducing everyone."

"I think it's a trick," Lai said.

"What?" Tam looked angry.

"Lai's just a little suspicious, Tam," Anh said. "He needs a little something for himself to take the suspicion away."

Lai had his hands against the edge of the table, pushing against that sharp plastic edge as though he were getting ready to boost himself up out of there. He was even raising his rear end up in the air a little, getting ready, when Nguyen Tam slid the envelope with the money in it across the table at him.

"What's this?" Lai said.

"Confidence," Tam said. "A hundred thousand in confidence."

"That's so you'll know Tam is straight with you," Anh said, "so you'll know I'm not trying to screw you for killing my brother."

Lai picked up the envelope and pressed the flap in so he could see the green wad inside. Then he slipped the whole thing into his inside jacket pocket. "What part do you get?"

"Ten percent," Anh said. "Tam takes the biggest chance. Everyone knows him. He's in charge of the whole thing. He gets sixty percent. The rest you get, and you pay your gang boys any way you want."

"Ten percent for you is too much," Lai said. "Way too much."

"I can cut it a little bit. Eight."

"I think we can do business then." Lai looked relaxed now. He stood up, nodded once at Nguyen Tam and once at Anh, and then started down the steps into the casino. Dennis was walking, too, moving away from the table where he had been placing bets over some guy's shoulder, walking toward the door to the parking lot. Oh, God, he was going to ruin everything.

Jana was at the top of the steps outside the casino, just where she was supposed to be, with her face toward the glass doors. The idea was to concentrate on the faces of the people coming out. Never mind all the other stuff going on around her. Doors slamming, parking attendants taking the little white stubs from people's hands, asking what car they were driving. Nep Lai would be coming out soon, walking past her. Stanley, Cookie's brother from Santa Maria, was ready, too, standing down at the bottom of the stairs, looking like a burglar with that gray overcoat on his skinny frame. And on a hot night like this. She was to gesture to him when she spotted Nep Lai. Gesture, point, shout. Stanley was supposed to shoot Nep Lai, shoot him before anyone knew what was happening, then run away. He hardly looked brave enough to do it, seemed kind of shy, as a matter of fact. The parking attendants kept bumping into him as they ran up and down the steps. Where do you get cousins who'll kill for you?

No problem, Anh said. You got a reason for them to kill for you, they do it, and are happy about it, too. He's a smart kid, she said, and a fast runner.

Deep breaths. Deep breaths. That'll get her through it. Anh said wear something comfortable. But how do you dress for a murder? Do you wear jeans and a blouse, or is it a dress-up affair, maybe a silk dress? Anh knew things like that. Anh knew a lot of things. Where the hell was she? Stanley looked as if he wanted to run away before, not after, he shot Nep Lai.

It was unbelievable that she was standing here doing this thing, helping Anh murder a Vietnamese hoodlum. Had she thought about changing her mind? Never. Not for a single moment.

Jana was sure she'd remember Nep Lai's face and be able to point him out to Stanley. She had assured Anh that she'd remember it. But it was dark that night in the nightclub, Anh said. Maybe you need a picture or something. No, no, no, I told you my memory is photographic. Nep Lai's face is in the computer. He won't get past me. I'll trip him, pounce on him, beat his head in with my shoe, but he won't get past me.

It seemed a long time they were inside talking. Jana looked at her watch. Ten-thirty. The gamblers were really coming in now, and the parking attendants were running faster and faster to keep up with the traffic of cars in and out of the lot. Jana moved a little to the right of the glass doors to stay out of the way, get a better view of people going out.

"Jana?"

She had her computer set on an Oriental face, a thin, tall man with a Vietnamese face. Not on this broad American one.

"Dennis?"

He looked embarrassed, but healthy.

"Sheree said you were dead," Jana said. She backed up, tried to look over Dennis's big shoulder.

"Sheree exaggerates."

He was blocking her view, moving from side to side as if he didn't really want to stay and talk, but didn't know how to get away. This wasn't good. She could feel it. This definitely wasn't good.

"I was a little sick, that's all. I don't know what all the fuss was about."

Was that the guy walking toward the door now, with the kid walking a few steps behind him? She couldn't tell. Dennis kept getting in the way. She couldn't see Stanley, either, now. Oh, Jesus, this wasn't going to work.

"Costa Rica," Jana said. "They buried you in New Jersey, and Sheree was going to Costa Rica."

"Well, they dug me up again, and here I am."

"You really have to get out of my way, Dennis."

"Have I stopped you? Jesus, we let you run that business, use my name. Did I stop you?"

"I don't mean that. I mean now."

He had that flush on his face, the one he always got when he was about to lose his temper.

"Look here, Jana." He had hold of her arm.

"Not now, Dennis. I'm waiting for someone." There. Nep Lai and some kid. Anh was following them, stopping a moment to talk to the policeman at the booth inside. Nguyen Tam was behind her. It was going fine. Everything was fine, except Dennis had her arm and was starting to argue. Stanley was beside her now.

"Hey, get away from her," Stanley said.

"Who the hell are you?" Dennis said. He looked at Jana. "What are you up to, Jana?"

"Oh, Dennis, you're going to fuck it all up."

"Who is this guy?" Stanley said.

"Whoa," Dennis said, and tried to grab Jana's arm again, but she was poised for it, and she let her arm swing. It got him below the neck and knocked him against the metal rail. He staggered, then got up and started toward Stanley.

"Get out of the way, Stanley," Jana shouted. "I can't see the door."

Stanley was punching Dennis in the face. Had him on the ground, covering him with blows.

The door swung open as Dennis rolled away and stood up and grabbed Jana around the waist.

"Let me go, Dennis. For Chrissakes, you're such an asshole, let me go."

Nep Lai was coming out the door, with the kid beside him. Now. It was now. There it was, Anh shouting, "Thief! Stop that man, he steal my money! He got my money!"

Jana tried to slip out of Dennis's grasp, but he had a hand like a wrestler's, all meat and muscle. There were policemen running out the door now, men in suits, jackets flapping open, their guns in their hands. Nep Lai was running across the lot with Danny sprinting along beside him. Stanley had his hand to his head, looking dazed.

"That guy took this woman's money," Jana screamed, just as she was supposed to do, just as she had rehearsed on the sand in front of her house. But this wasn't like yelling at the waves. There was no spray spitting back in her face. Just Dennis's bulk blocking her so no one could hear her, no one could see her. Stanley was no use at all, standing there with his hand on the gun in his pocket. No use at all.

"What the hell's going on?" Dennis said, and he let go of her arm so suddenly, she almost fell over.

"Oh, shit, Dennis, you ruined it," Jana said. "You fucked it up real good this time."

The policemen weren't running after Lai, weren't shooting at him or doing anything to him. They had stopped Anh instead, were questioning her, had her in a little ring and were sticking their faces into hers like she was the one running through the lot with a hundred thousand dollars in a small white envelope.

"There's a dead guy laying out next to a white Mercedes," the attendant said, bounding up the stairs.

"He stole one hundred thousand three dollars," Anh said. "That the guy. You check it. You count it. It all mine."

"He took her money," Tam said. "I was there and saw him take her money."

Suddenly Anh could breathe. The policemen were moving away from her, interested in what the attendant was saying.

"In that envelope in his jacket pocket," Anh said. "He got it, and it belong to me. Did you see a kid with him, one of his gang kid?"

"I saw someone hop the fence," the attendant said. He was excited—the boring job was finally turning into a good time. "And then the guy with the gun shot the other guy. Sounded like a car backfiring. A little pop. Didn't you hear it?"

Stanley had shot him. Good boy, Stanley. He had taken care of his family obligation. He would forever be on the list of people she owed special favors to. Oh, Stanley. Good, good Stanley. The air turned crisp and clean around her, no more of those tobacco mouths asking her questions, treating her like some kind of criminal. And Nep Lai hadn't turned around and shot her, either. She was still alive, still standing. Oh, sweet air, she was still breathing.

Then she saw Dennis standing next to Jana and looking as if he'd walked into the ladies' restroom by mistake. And Stanley next to him. Oh, God. Stanley was shrugging his shoulders, and Jana was shaking her head. Sweet, sweet Jesus, Stanley didn't shoot Nep Lai. So who was dead out in the parking lot?

Everyone was running now, policemen and attendants, Anh and Tam and everyone else, down the stairs, across the flower-covered strip, down the rows and rows of big fancy black cars, to a dark spot near the fence where the white Mercedes stuck out against all those dark cars like a moonbeam or a small sun, to where Nep Lai was spread out on the ground, blood all around his crushed head. He had his eyes open, like he couldn't believe what had just happened. Sam was kneeling beside him. Oh, why did he want to get mixed up with this?

"He's dead," Sam said.

"Did you kill him?" one of the policemen asked.

"Me? Hell no. I didn't kill him."

"He's not the one who did it," the attendant said.

"Is this yours?" Another policeman was holding an envelope up for Anh to see. But it was all blurry. Two men in suits were bringing someone across the lot to where the body was, holding him by the arms, shoving him along.

"Is this the guy?" one of them asked.

"Yep," the attendant said. "He's the one I saw shoot him."

"He kill my son," Ba said.

Everyone was looking now. People coming out of the casino to see the murder. Like a movie. They were watching it like a movie, pointing fingers. Pointing fingers at Ba. At her father, standing there in his old army uniform, looking so pleased, looking so happy.

32

*H*e doesn't have to stay here," Sam said. "Tell him that. If we find the bail money, he can go home and won't have to come back till the arraignment."

They were in the visiting room of the jail, and Ba wouldn't speak English. Oh, he knew how all right, sitting there like an emperor, in his jail jumpsuit, flicking ashes on the floor.

"Did you hear what Sam said?" Anh asked her father in Vietnamese.

"You don't have the money for bail," Ba said.

"I can get the money. You know I can always get money when I need it."

"Seven-hundred-fifty-thousand-dollar bail? Where will you get the money for that?"

"I can find it."

"Your Uncle Kou is the only one who can give you that kind of money, and for what he did to you and your mother, I don't want his dirty money."

"Ba said he won't come out," Anh said in English.

"But why?" Jana said.

"I don't know. You never know what Ba going to do."

"Tell him I think he fits the insanity plea."

"No, he doesn't," Sam said.

"Didn't you see those cases I pulled for you?"

"I saw them, and they don't fit."

"He won't let you say he crazy," Anh said. And then to Ba in Vietnamese, "Are these the cigarettes I left for you?"

"Those were too weak. Khanh bought me these. I don't like the kind you brought. I like the ones that make you cough. When will these Americans be through and let Khanh and your mother come in? I'm tired of listening to this foolish American talk."

"They're just trying to help you, Ba."

Khanh and Me were waiting outside, sitting on a bench together. Holding hands. Acting the way they had in Saigon. Like eighteen years of silence between them had never happened.

"Anyway, even if we try for insanity, we'd never pull it off," Sam said. "We'll need Vietnamese psychiatrists to examine him and testify, and the state will get American ones, and the American ones will turn what the Vietnamese guys say inside out. It'll never work. It's all cultural, Jana, you know that."

Oh, they were picking Ba apart, like an engine that wasn't running, like a car that needed a little wheel or some grease to make it go again.

"Little Boy and Boy are writing you a letter, Ba."

"Which ones are those?"

"Vy's kids. The two older ones, Ba. You know which ones they are."

"Oh."

"Ba want to know can I bring bring him some tea in a thermos next time," Anh said in English.

"I'll find out," Jana said.

"They might be afraid he'll try to scald himself," Sam said. "There are so many fucking regulations in this place. I've been trying to get them to give him his heart medicine, and I'm getting nowhere fast. They need affidavits. They need doctor certificates. Put that on the list, Jana. Medical affidavits. I'll sue the bastards if he dies."

"If your American friends want to help me," Ba said, "they can bribe the people here in the jail. Everyone can be bribed. There's no one who doesn't want money. And tell them I won't go out of here if they say I'm insane. I won't go out of here if I have to explain myself to anyone. I'll stay here and die first. You tell them that."

"What did he say just now?" Sam said. Oh, his eyes were so intense. His and Jana's. Probing Ba's insides. Thinking they knew everything, but knowing nothing. All these words they wanted her to say to Ba, when he understood perfectly what they were doing. Working at him the way Americans work at everything.

"Ba said don't work too hard. Ba said he appreciate everything you doing for him."

Oh, she loved the look on Sam's face now. She knew how to ease him with American words, knew the things to tell him to make him happy. He thought he knew the Vietnamese because he bombed Vietnam. But he didn't know. How could he know when she didn't?

"Ba worry you gonna work too hard," Anh said. "Ba all the time is thinking of people before himself. That the way Ba is."

Goodbye, Saigon

*L*abor Day weekend, and all down along the bay the cars were coming, full of kids and moms and dads, jamming the highway, driving down the narrow streets hoping for a parking space, envying the people who found one, sitting at the corners in their cars eating chocolate-and-peanut-covered bananas and listening to the horns honk behind them while they watched limber kids do spins and jumps and wheelies on their bikes. And the sun didn't disappoint, shining like it was showing off, bright as neon up in the sky.

Anh had driven up the coast and over to Balboa on the little finger of highway going out into the peninsula. Driven through the pretty streets of the island past the house she had almost bought, then waited an hour for the ferry, just so Boy and Little Boy could feel the breeze on their faces, know what it was like to be out on the bay sitting in a car, feeling it glide across the water without its motor on, seeing how the pier on the other side got bigger and bigger and finally was as big as the one they had just left.

Anh gave Boy a five-dollar bill and watched him cross through the crowds of people on the boardwalk toward the cotton candy wagon. Oh, there were no locked gates here now in these last few days of summer, no sign yet of the weather changing, just an even warmth that lay snug as a baby's blanket across the bay. There were people here now all right, waiting in line like Anh to take their little kids on the Ferris wheel.

"I want to go up there," Little Boy said, pointing to the Ferris wheel. It was slowing down now, jerking unevenly each time it came to a stop and a seat emptied out.

Oh, he was heavy, getting too big almost for Anh to hold in her arms, but still too small to stand by himself with all these people around. Someone could steal him. Oh, she'd die if someone stole him.

"Are you going to cry when you go up on that thing?"

"No," Little Boy said, and Anh squeezed him real tight because she could tell he was scared.

Boy was back with two tall pink webs of cotton candy. He handed one to Little Boy and then pulled the change from the five-dollar bill out of his pocket.

"You can keep the change if you tell me how much it is without looking at it," Anh said.

Boy tilted his head and shut one eye, grinning a little, the way he always did when he was figuring. Figuring in Vietnamese or English, it was all the same to him.

"Two dollars and eighty cents," he said.

She wanted to pull another five from her purse, maybe even a ten, and give it to him, he was so smart. But she just shifted Little Boy from her left arm to her right so he wouldn't get sticky pink stuff on her blouse.

"You going up with them?" the kid said as he held the gate to the Ferris wheel open.

"What you think, I let them sit in the chair by theirself and slip through and fall in the water?"

The kid wasn't even listening. He just pulled the bar open on the chair and helped Anh in, and then Boy and Little Boy.

"Wow, there's the ocean," Boy said.

"Where?" Little Boy asked, stretching his neck as far as he could.

"There."

Little Boy shrieked and Boy yelled as the Ferris wheel swooped upward. Anh tried to spot the house that she had almost bought, but all she saw were roofs. It didn't matter about that house, anyway. All the work that needed to be done on it. A gym set for Vy's kids. A soundproof room for Me to watch television in. Special closets with locks that no one could break into. Too much money to spend just to live in a house on an island where there wasn't even a Vietnamese market for Me to walk to.

Little Boy was crying now.

"It's all right," Anh said, and held on to the waist of his overalls to keep him from climbing over the back of the seat. "Look how smooth we're going. See, no one's even falling out."

He was clutching the shoulder of her blouse now, hiding his face under her arm.

"Buddy got cotton candy on your blouse," Boy said. "He's such a baby."

She didn't like Orange County, either, anymore. Too many bad things happened here. Las Vegas, that was the place. There was this guy, a bookie she met when she was at the jail visiting Ba, said open a Vietnamese restaurant in Las Vegas, and you'll make a fortune. All those Vietnamese gambling in Vegas and nowhere to eat.

"What's the name of that ocean, Boy?" Anh asked.

"The Pacific," Boy answered without hesitating.

Sam said it was crazy. What did she know about the restaurant business? Everything, she told him.

"Tell me the name of another ocean, and I'll give you another dollar," Anh said. She didn't want to spoil him, let him think just because he was smart, she'd give him five dollars for every right answer.

"The Atlantic," Boy shouted.

People lose their shirts in the restaurant business every day, Jana said. Sure, Jana could say whatever she wanted. No to this and no to that. She was almost a lawyer. Working as a clerk in Sam's office during the day and going to school at night. Could speak English. Had round eyes and light skin. She didn't have Me and Vy and Vy's kids to worry about. She wasn't pregnant and feeling lousy. Oh, Jana's life was easy compared with hers.

"And there's Upper Newport Bay," Boy said. He was pointing to the cliffs that fell so steep and straight down to the ocean. Near the highway the cliffs turned into a watery lake, a bowl of tea, dark and strong. Tea that the ocean didn't want.

"How do you know what it's called?" Anh said.

"I read it in a book," Boy said.

Or she could go into the mortgage business. With what, Sam said. With money people give me, she told him. There's lots of people want to give me money. People are getting rich loaning money on mortgages, she said.

"I don't see our house," Boy said.

Little Boy had unglued himself from Anh's shoulder and was waving at the people down below.

It was crazy, this thing with Sam. What was she going to do about him and this baby of his? Marry him? Oh, no. No way. No way. She knew how Americans were, loving you, loving you, loving you, and the next minute, pfft, they're gone. Then what do you do? Ruining her life was all he was good for. And bugging Ba. Always trying to make Ba say he was crazy so they'd let him out of jail. Ba would never tell anyone he was crazy. Ba would die before he'd say a thing like that.

"Our house is the green one," Little Boy said.

"I don't see any green houses," Boy said. "Auntie Anh, wipe Buddy's nose. It's making me sick. Yuck."

"There are some green houses over there," Anh said, and she wiped Little Boy's nose with the paper from the cotton candy. Little Boy's nose was always running. That Vy, she didn't give him the right food, the right vitamins. She didn't know anything about taking care of kids.

"I don't see ours," Boy said. "I can't see the bushes in front."

And there was that guy in Oakland whose wife ran a nail shop, he said his brother's an attorney, a real one, American license. He wants to move back to Vietnam. You can use his license, he said, he just wants a cut. I know a lot of people, he said. Maybe you want to start another law business up here, we'll be partners.

Boy was looking at her. Sometimes she thought he could read her mind the way he looked at her.

"Are you having a good time?" she said, and he nodded.

She leaned back now and let the Ferris wheel take her. She had never been on a Ferris wheel before. It made her feel like a bird, flying and floating, hardly noticing the grind of the motor, just listening to the sound of the wind.

Oh, she hoped Vy's boys didn't end up like Thinh, cold in the ground before they had a chance to grow. Or like Ba. Ba was always at the edges of her mind. Even up here, flying like a bird, there was a little picture of him in her head, sitting in his plain cell, smoking one cigarette after another, refusing to let Sam tell the judge he was crazy, refusing to let anyone bail him out, all stubborn and satisfied with himself. I'm waiting for Tet, he told Anh, as though he had a plan in his head, as though when Tet came, he would tell everyone what that plan was. Maybe Ba was happy in that jail cell. Maybe he liked it there. Wanted to stay. Never wanted to come out.

She tried to remember. She didn't think Thinh had ever been on a Ferris wheel, either. And that boy she had never found. Her American child. What would he think if he were here right now, sitting beside her, riding this thing and looking over Newport Bay, with all those boats with their flags and colored streamers and funny names? And eating pink fuzz that disappeared before you could even taste it? Oh, what would he think?

"If we can't see our house," Boy said, "how do we know it's there?"

"I just know, that's all," Anh replied.

Acknowledgments

In this book I have tried to portray life in Little Saigon as fairly as I could, the rough spots as well as the smooth. Many of the incidents in the book are based on things I have seen, places I have been, conversations I have had, stories I have heard, but the characters are fictional and do not represent actual people, living or dead.

I want to thank my friends in Little Saigon for taking me into their lives and hearts. Of special importance to me are Hanh and Tuan Pham, their sons Michael and Andrew, Ngoc Tran, Anthony and Lisa Hoang, Kieu Chinh, Cong Ba Nguyen—survivors, all.

And my gratitude to my editor, Ann Patty, for her valuable editorial suggestions and for buying this book her first week on the job at Crown.

Early in the game, when I thought *Goodbye, Saigon*'s home was elsewhere, editor Nancy Nicholas edited the book with diligence and care, for which she has my deepest appreciation.

Lois Wallace, my agent, who lets nothing get by her, read this book in its infancy and said, "Tell me more." That one small sentence expanded the book's scope, and, I hope, made it sing. Thank you, Lois.

To Alby and Myra Rosen, dear friends who watch out for me in every way they can, and whose counsel is invaluable, my love and gratitude.

And, of course, without my husband, Marvin Vida, who practices law in Little Saigon, there would never have been a book at all. He was the first to enter the Vietnamese immigrants' world, and then he held the door open for me. His Vietnamese clients and associates loved him in the beginning for his expertise at the law, and only later for his gentleness and compassion. And in loving him, by extension they were determined to love his wife.

Nina Vida
Huntington Beach, California
September 1994